Praise for *USA Today* bestseller Pamela Crane's psychological thrillers:

"You are not prepared for the twists...Pamela Crane has in store for you. The schemes...are sure to have you at the edge of your seat." – *POPSUGAR*

"Crane succeeds at painting families and friendships in vivid detail; women will see their tussles and triumphs in these pages, and will relish the twists and moments of brave camaraderie and bold revenge... A satisfying read that has echoes of Liane Moriarty and of Emily Giffin's *All We Ever Wanted*." – *Booklist*

"Pamela Crane's anthem to female friendship and the empowerment of women proves one thing. Friends will do anything for each other...including lie, cheat in bed, and kill. This novel is a read for our tumultuous times." – Jenny Milchman, Mary Higgins Clark award-winning author of *Cover of Snow* and *The Second Mother*

"One of the most chilling opening scenes I've ever read, and the tension keeps right on building. My advice: don't read this book...unless you're prepared not to put it down until you're finished!" – *New York Times* bestselling author Wendy Corsi Staub

"I loved it! It's so well written, with sharply observed characters and the kind of fast-paced, twisty plot that keeps you turning the pages..." –*Sunday Times* and international bestselling author Debbie Howells

"There is always great depth to Pamela's writing and this is no exception." – Bestselling author Patricia Dixon

"A captivating mystery with prose that fans will devour." – Literary Lover Reviews

D0840138

A
SLOW
RUIN

A SLOW RUIN

PAMELA CRANE

Tabella House
Raleigh, North Carolina

Thank you for supporting authors and literacy by purchasing this book. Want to add more gripping reads to your library? As the author of more than a dozen award-winning and bestselling books, you can find all of Pamela Crane's works on her website at www.pamelacrane.com.

To Talia, for letting Mommy take a million pictures of you for my cover. I know you love the attention.

To Mary Kaja, my budding creative genius niece. You gave Vera flesh when I only had bones. At age fifteen your talents already far surpass most. Never stop using them...or else give them to me!

To Linda Milito Martin, the muse behind Barkalicious Boutique. It wouldn't be the coolest fictional dog shop without you.

To Noelle Nuzzi, Melissa Borsey, Emily Cheang Wai Kuen, and Vicky Brunner for participating in my Choose Your Own Adventure game to give Marin and Felicity jobs I would never have come up with on my own. I love how you guys think!

To the real-life Alveras who sacrifice so much for a greater cause. Family, freedom, time, money...all in the pursuit of a better future for others. Your passion is not in vain.

To all the mothers. It's the most beautiful burden that we carry. May your shoulders remain strong, your heart soft, and your love wide.

Author's Note

The story you are about to read isn't just mine. In fact, it's unlike anything else I've written, steeped in personal connections and mystery. While all of my books are rooted in real-life experience and people, this one especially so.

Depicted on the cover is my daughter, Talia, a child passionate for art and literature (a writer mom's dream kid!). And my creatively brilliant niece Mary scripted many of the journal entries to offer teenage authenticity to Vera.

Woven into the newspaper articles are true facts recounted from an actual 1910 missing heiress case that to this day remains unsolved. You may notice the news reporting style is a bit different—and completely authentic of the era.

Yet the most exciting and intimate part of this book revolves around suffragette Alvera Fields, loosely based on a heroic ancestor of mine who fought passionately for the rights of women. Not only was she the inspiration for this story, but for generations of women who reaped the benefits of her sacrifice.

Digging into the cold cases of the past, and the lives steeped in mystery, added a layer to this story that makes it one of my favorite books I've written.

And now this labor of love belongs not just to us who poured ourselves into its words, but also to you as you pour yourself into our story.

The Pittsburg Press

Pittsburg, PA
Sunday, April 17, 1910

WOMAN'S SUFFRAGE VOLUNTEER AND MOTHER OF NEWBORN STRANGELY MISSING

No Limit to Reward, Husband States

Mrs. Alvera Fields, wife to millionaire Robert Fields and mother of three-month-old daughter Olivia Fields, disappeared from her home on the evening of April 16, and although a nationwide search has been made for the young woman, no trace of her has been found. She is thirty-two years old.

Through an announcement by her distracted husband, having hired private detectives and Pinkertons to aid in the search in vain, it was made known that Alvera disappeared mysteriously in the late hours after taking leave from the Fields Estate, heading into town. The private search exhausted every possible clue that the family could advance, and her husband has nearly given up hope in his wife's return. Her disappearance was casual and apparently unpremeditated that the army of detectives working on the case decided that violence or enforced detention of some kind must be responsible for her absence.

On Saturday morning Mrs. Fields remarked to her husband

that she would be going out that day to purchase a dress for an upcoming debutante party. When he offered to go with her, she said, "It will be a bore for you. I'll telephone you when I find the right dress."

Alvera left her house that evening at five o'clock wearing a tailor-made blue serge suit and black velvet hat, she wore low black shoes, black silk stockings, and a dark blue silk waist with a white jabot and tan walking gloves. She has not been seen since by her family or friends. She carried between $20 and $50 in her handbag and wore her usual jewelry, a diamond ring and plain gold earrings. In her hair she wore a shell comb, a carved barrette, and a dark blue hatpin with the head of a lapis-lazuli. Her hair was worn in a full pompadour.

Mrs. Fields was last seen stopping at the Women's Equal Franchise Federation, a women's suffrage group she volunteered at until her daughter's birth three months prior. Her last known whereabouts were at eight o'clock that evening, where Mrs. Fields spoke with a friend, Miss Cecile Cianfarra, who attested that Alvera showed no signs of distress.

Every known relative of the family was called upon, branches of the detective agencies were set to work upon the case, hospitals were searched, and trains and even steamships were watched, but to no avail. She had received from her husband a monthly allowance of $100 and had a small bank account. She withdrew $40 on April 14, but as the investigation showed similar withdrawals frequently, no significance was attached to that.

Her description was given to the police as follows: Thirty-two years old, 5 feet 6 inches in height, light brown hair, blue eyes, well developed, striking appearance, weighed about 150 pounds.

A handsome reward has been mentioned by her husband, a silk importer, who stated, "Money is no object, and any information leading to my wife's safe recovery will be greatly rewarded. I beg of my fellow Pittsburgers to help bring home my wife and my daughter's mother."

Due to the family's wealth, social status, and Mrs. Fields' involvement in the women's suffrage movement, detectives are considering the possibility of harm having befallen the missing woman for financial gain, or as a political statement.

Prologue

Certain moments cleave a life in two, killing off one life in order to birth a new one. This labor and delivery sometimes creates a phoenix. Other times it creates a monster.

These pieces of myself I sorted into *before* and *after*. *Before* marriage I was an untethered version of myself. *After* the "I do," I slipped on new flesh that resembled my husband, every decision captained by compromise. "*Leave and cleave,*" my mother once told me. She never mentioned how painful the rip could be.

Then my firstborn child arrived. The most vicious tear, separating me from my husband, my sleep, my friends, my dreams, my life as I recognized it. *Before* the baby, my time was mine. My body was mine. My life was mine. *After* the baby, everything was hers, as this tiny suckling infant wrapped in perfect creamy skin owned my entire world. And I willingly let her take it.

These were the thoughts that had followed me across the backyard of a house that wasn't mine. Then in through a creaky door that should have been locked but wasn't. I stepped into an unfamiliar kitchen, with only the purr of the fridge and the dim light from the oven hood orienting me. I shouldn't have been in that kitchen. I shouldn't have brought that letter. It was that single ill-fated choice that cleaved my life for the last time:

Before, when my daughter was alive.

6

After I killed her.

All it took was one ruinous secret, one deadly mistake to cut my life into pieces. The transgression was a scythe, and one swing of the sickle took everything away from me. The worst part? It was All. My. Fault.

The envelope holding my confession was still in my pocket when I flicked on the light, then slipped my way across the bloody floor to my daughter's fallen body, her legs and arms splayed out between the sink and oven. Red smeared across the linoleum like a child's fingerpainting. I dropped to my knees next to my daughter, coating my kneecaps with two crimson blossoms. She slumped in my arms, eyes fluttering closed like morning glories bidding farewell. Gently lifting her neck and head, I rested the weight of her on my lap, trying to figure out where the bleeding was coming from.

A stickiness seeped into my pants, staining my skin. Slowly working my hands across the back of her skull, my palm sank into a matted mess of wet hair. My fingers traced a gash where her skull should be, but instead gaped open. Trying to pull her upright against me, her body slid across the floor. So much blood. Too much. I hefted her up to my chest, cradling her as best I could, as our groans joined in unison. I felt my back pocket for my phone, feeling instead the thin crumple of the envelope. My reason for being here. The same reason my daughter was bleeding out.

Pain swept across my temples as the stress intensified. I needed to call 9-1-1 now. Where was my cell phone? Had I brought it with me? No, I couldn't remember where I'd left it. The car I'd hidden down the street, maybe? I didn't have time to run that far.

Slowly lowering her head to the cool floor, I rose high on my knees, my gaze darting across the room. Where was her phone? Nothing but a mess of dishes and countertops strewn with mail.

My body thrummed with the pulse of terror.

It frightened me that I didn't know what to do. It frightened me more that my own child might die in my arms.

Her eyes flicked open, not registering me. Thank God she was conscious.

"Where's your cell phone? I need to call 9-1-1." I didn't want to scare her, but the calm wouldn't stay put in my voice.

She didn't move. Didn't blink. Then recognition dawned in her eyes. Her mouth cracked open.

"Do you know what happened?" I asked her.

She didn't speak at first, then her mouth parted just enough to let a word escape. "No."

"Don't close your eyes. Stay awake until an ambulance arrives. I need your phone!"

Her body shivered with a weak breath, her face seemed to empty its color onto the floor, mixing with the blood that leached out more each second.

"Not…until I get answers." Her jaw clenched. I recognized the stubborn teen in her.

I clucked in irritation. Of course she was going to make me barter for her life. Didn't she realize she was dying?

"What do you want to know?"

Her chest rose with a breath. "I want to know why. Why you lied. Why you did what you did."

The eternal question, one I asked myself daily for the past fifteen years. The question I couldn't answer.

"Tell me where your phone is first. You're not looking good, honey. I need to call for help. Now, please!"

"No!" A grunt slipped out with the effort of speaking. "First tell me the truth."

"Will an answer take it all back? Will it make everything better?"

"No…" Her words were slowing, slurring. "But maybe I'll understand."

I reached into my back pocket and slid the envelope out, letting it hang between us.

"Here," was all I could muster. "This explains everything."

She weakly accepted my offering, then her arm dropped to the floor. A trickle of red ran down her nose, sliding over her top lip. She was drifting on the fringes of consciousness. I was running out of time. I searched her pockets, feeling for the hard case of a cell phone. Nothing.

I stood and scanned the kitchen, finding a 1970s-avocado green landline phone hanging on the wall near where the kitchen poured into the dining room. I picked up the receiver and listened for a dial tone. Dead.

"Your cell phone—where is it?" I screamed, begging her to answer me, to save her own life.

"Living room…table," she breathed.

I rushed through the dining room, blindly circling into the living room where the kitchen light couldn't reach. The faint glow drifting from the hallway upstairs was enough to identify the shape of a lamp. I fumbled for the knob, fingers slipping until I heard a click. I found the cell phone, in a pink plastic case, next to the sofa and swiped up. It demanded a passcode.

I ran back into the kitchen, adrenalin-fueled panic pushing me. "I need your passcode."

"0509."

I gasped. The significance of that number didn't escape me. Only I knew what it meant, only I knew how it bound us together in chains.

I dropped to her side, punched the passcode on the screen, swiped until I found the green call icon, and dialed 9-1-1. Pressing my fingers to her wrist, the radial artery barely thrummed with a weak heartbeat. I hadn't prayed in so long, but the entreaty poured out to whoever was listening as my child bled out, that for once in my pathetic life full of regrets, help me save her. With the phone to my ear, I glanced down at her ashen face. Peaceful. Sleepy. Dead?

No, she couldn't die. I wouldn't let her die. I felt her neck for a pulse and found nothing, not even a faint throb against my fingertips.

"Don't leave me!" I cried as the phone line connected.

The operator calmly asked, "What's your emergency?"

My fingers lost all feeling. The phone cracked against the floor. The screen went black. I saw my tear-stained reflection mouthing the word *goodbye*.

My daughter was dead.

We had loved each other through everything, through all the mistakes and broken promises. Through laughter and tears. Through fights, hugs, joyrides, and late-night movie marathons. Why couldn't she have held on for me? We had even loved each other through murder.

After all, I'd already done it once before.

Chapter 1
Felicity Portman

A good mother knows when she's needed and starts running. But I was not a good mother. When a daughter needs you, when she's in pain or struggling, a mother hears her cry and goes to her. Saves her. So why hadn't I heard Vera's cry for help the night she disappeared? Why couldn't I save her?

This thought nudged me awake every morning from fitful sleep. It taunted me throughout each day when I passed Vera's bedroom, or found strands of her blonde hair embedded in the sofa cushions. Every little thing reminded me of Vera. And it suffocated me every night when I lay restless in bed beside a snoring husband oblivious to my suffering. I shouldn't have resented Oliver for that; it was to his credit that he was able to move on, where I couldn't, over the past six months since Vera first vanished. But I hated him nonetheless. It wasn't fair that I alone carried this burden of guilt. I alone hefted the what-ifs on my fragile shoulders. What if we hadn't gone out that night? What if I had checked in more with Vera? What if…what if…what if.

That same thought pushed me into Vera's bedroom when I was supposed to be getting Sydney a Band-Aid for her paper cut. While my three-year-old daughter wailed in the background,

11

clutching a bloody tissue to her fingertip, I told Eliot to keep an eye on his little sister and continue cutting colorful construction paper ghosts and pumpkins to make Pappy Joe and Nana a Halloween card. Maybe I expected too much of an eight-year-old boy as I headed upstairs to the bathroom to grab a Paw Patrol Band-Aid. But I needed my fix.

I should have known better than to pause outside Vera's room. The detours taken throughout the day to search her things for clues I blamed on my obsessive-compulsive brain. To smell her on the sheets. To sit in her space. Even now, six months gone, I knew there was something I hadn't found. A secret I hadn't unearthed. *Secrets.* I had them too.

My scattered thoughts weren't anything new. Every morning I misplaced my half-drunk coffee cup, or forgot to finish my half-eaten breakfast. And this year I had neglected to buy Halloween costumes for the kids. With trick-or-treat quickly approaching, even Amazon two-day shipping couldn't save me. So I handed the kids a bin full of costume oddments and told them to take their pick. This was probably why Sydney was dressed from the waist down as Snow White and the waist up as a ninja. Eliot always chose Iron Man. Vera would have posed with the little ones for a selfie and called them *drippy,* which was a compliment in Vera-speak. To me it sounded like an STD.

My stomach rumbled, my brain seized. What was I supposed to be doing?

Oh yes, the Band-Aid, then eat something. Had I even eaten yet today?

The forgetfulness predated Vera's disappearance, first becoming noticeable when Vera was a baby. Back then it was new-mom sleep deprivation. But lately it had gotten worse, because I didn't want to drink my coffee or eat my breakfast. The perpetual grip on my stomach made all food intolerable, as if my body wanted to die along with Vera's.

No. Nix the word *die.*

I didn't believe that Vera was dead, no matter what the Pittsburgh Police Special Victims Unit or Detective Courtney Montgomery said.

Idling in the doorway, I noted how Vera's bedroom looked exactly like it had the day she disappeared, minus a few items after the police had rifled through it with tornado intensity, looking for clues. With the expectation that Vera would come home and accuse her siblings of destroying her bedroom, I had straightened her London-themed comforter splashed with turquoise and gray images of Big Ben and the London Bridge, closed dresser drawers, tidied the closet. Things I'd done for the past fifteen years of her life. Inspired by her love of all things British, we had planned a trip to the United Kingdom as her graduation gift. I even baked two dozen scones—cranberry and chocolate chip, her favorites, using Brit gourmand Mary Berry's recipes—and stored them in the freezer, waiting for her return. Back then I had *expected.* Now I *wondered.* Would we ever see Big Ben or the bridge together? I could only cling to pale hope these days.

I stepped inside. The bedroom suffocated me with its emptiness. No dirty laundry overflowing from her basket. No stained Vans scattered across the floor. No scent of beachy coconut lotion. Outside her window hung clouds pregnant with rain, reminders of the gray, eerie April day she had disappeared. Any minute now the sky would crack open and weep with me.

I felt a strange sensation, like something under the bed trying to grab my ankle, and stepping backwards I gave a little cry. Looking down, I saw Meowzebub's orange and white paw clawing at the carpet, and then she poked her pumpkin head out triumphantly as if to say *gotcha!* The long-haired calico cat had been Vera's boon companion ever since the spring night she showed up on our doorstep after a torrential downpour, drenched and shivering. Usually I was the softie that couldn't resist a stray critter, no matter how woebegone, but this time it was Vera who pleaded with Oliver to let her keep the kitty. Oliver was putty in her hands.

Under Vera's care Meowzebub—so christened because of her bone-chilling yowl, akin to some netherworld denizen—was restored to robust health, and became a member of the family. Meowzebub possessed in spades the calico's infamously temperamental nature. Vera preferred to say that Meowzebub simply had *cattitude*, which she regarded as a virtue. The mischievous cat was likely to turn up anywhere in the house, at any time, and loved to ambush unsuspecting victims. Oliver tolerated her, the dogs were terrified of her, the kids loved her, as did I; she was a living link to Vera.

Suddenly Meowzebub gave her trademark yowl from hell and darted out from under the bed, careening down the stairs at breakneck speed. The crazy cat often got the zoomies in the middle of the night, racing around the house until she was exhausted, but not before waking the entire family. Syd and Eliot found these antics hilarious. Oliver wanted to turn Meowzebub into an outdoor cat. Over my dead body!

Ambling to Vera's desk, my gaze settled on a framed 1910 tintype of her great-great-grandmother Alvera Fields. We had found this photo when digging into the family archives for Vera's school project on the women's suffrage movement, in which Alvera had been a prominent and outspoken figure. In the yellowed photo, Alvera and her millionaire husband Robert were resplendent examples of Edwardian-era haute couture. Alvera looked smart in a dark twill suit with a hip-length jacket, lace gloves, and a whimsical hat bedecked with white roses and ostrich plumes, her arms wrapped around her newborn daughter, precious in a white lace gown and bonnet.

Robert was dapper in a cutaway morning coat with paisley vest and puff tie, walking cane in one hand, the other holding his top hat in the crook of his arm. Following the fashion of the day, the couple wore dour expressions, which had prompted Vera to joke that they looked like they had a hellacious case of hemorrhoids. But that was just teenage irreverence talking. Vera had in fact been named in honor of the pioneering suffragette, and the school project had sparked in Vera an obsession with her ancestor's life…and eventual disappearance.

Alvera had vanished one fateful day without a trace, a baffling event chronicled in newspapers from coast to coast, and sparking countless theories from professionals and detectives alike as clues came to light. As a cause cèlebré, and to some a controversial and polarizing figure, it was widely believed Alvera died in service to the cause of establishing women's right to vote, but no one knew the truth. Now, a hundred and eleven years later, my Vera had followed in the footsteps of the woman she revered—in the most tragically distressing way imaginable. A terrible coincidence, a family curse.

I traced my finger across the antique desk, smiling at her scribbles that marred the wood. A DIY project she had worked on with Oliver back when she was ten...back when she still craved her father's attention. We had found the writing desk on a visit to the Fields Estate, a forlorn ancestral mansion whose designation by the state of Pennsylvania as an historical landmark had saved it from demolition. The home had belonged to Oliver's great-grandfather Robert Fields, a silk importer tycoon, and Alvera, his wife. The couple's only daughter, Olivia, had inherited the home, and while she had maintained its magnificence for many decades, in recent years it had fallen into disrepair after her death. Oliver and his brother Cody were hopeful of restoring the structure to its Edwardian era splendor—a mammoth physical and financial undertaking—and had secured an Historic Preservation Tax Credit for that purpose to honor Alvera Fields' legacy.

The desk had been covered in dust, yet the bones solid. An intriguing piece, Vera had discovered a secret hollow leg that contained old letters, a fun find when they were restoring it. Together Vera and Oliver sanded and painted it in a rich white chalk paint. The project kindled a creative spark in her. Since then she'd collected and restored a four-poster bedframe, a dresser to match, and a stool that fit snugly under her desk. That winter I watched Vera and her father sweat and work their fingers raw in the freezing cold detached garage, warmed only by a single space heater while they created this bedroom, bonding over paint swatches and knob hardware. Vera had seemed so happy back then. What changed in my daughter that made her run away?

I cried this question daily.

I could never hear an answer through the sobs.

Up to 2.8 million teens in the United States run away from home each year. Ninety-nine percent of them return home safely. The stats were supposed to comfort me as Detective Montgomery delivered them by rote the first time we met on April 16, the blackest black-letter date of my life. Where was my 99 percent assuredness of my daughter's safe return home? Because it had been six months and still no Vera.

We had scoured every inch of the Steel City, from the projects where crumbling brick townhomes decayed along with the desolate steel mills, to the money-soaked upper-middle-class neighborhoods like ours. But in a city of three hundred thousand faces, I couldn't find my daughter's.

I admit the staggering number of missing children shocked me, but not as much as the possibility that Vera would willingly choose to leave her beautiful home, her parents who loved her, her siblings who adored her. She had everything. But believing Vera had chosen to leave was better than the alternative: that she'd been kidnapped or murdered, which the police told me was unlikely.

No body had been found. No evidence of an abduction.

She was a straight-A student. Book nerd. No drugs. No shady friends. No deviant behavior—that I knew of. Private school. Affluent town with a keen neighborhood watch. No one saw a thing. Kidnapping didn't fit the profile. I wanted to be glad for that…but my daughter was still missing. It had been too long. A mother can't help but slip into worst-case scenarios as the minutes, hours, days, weeks, months tick by.

It didn't make sense for a girl from a loving home to just up and leave. But it often happened, Detective Montgomery gently reminded me. So here we were, 184 days post-disappearance, with no clues as to where she had gone, or with whom, or why. The detective had searched every angle, interviewed every close friend, but sometimes there simply was no explanation for why an ambitious honor roll student from a good family decides to disappear. But as the detective told me again and again as the months dragged on, everyone is hiding something. Even my perfect fifteen-year-old daughter.

Pulling open the desk drawer, I didn't expect to find anything new. The police had been through it at least once, and me a dozen times. With eight bedrooms and over 9,000 square feet in our home—dubbed the *Execution Estate*, after the horror that marred this house forever—endless hiding places and secrets lurked behind these walls and haunted every room. But every day I hoped, prayed that maybe, just maybe, we had missed something that would lead me to Vera. Something I hadn't noticed before. Something with hidden meaning.

Beneath pages of scribbled notes, Vera's women's suffrage report remained unfinished. I picked up the same art notebook I had leafed through countless times. The pages were jammed front and back with original drawings displaying real talent and growing artistic maturity. Mostly manga-inspired cartoons, elves, with the occasional self-portrait or sketch of our imposing Victorian home, which always seemed to be just one coat of paint away from being declared Oakmont's unofficial haunted house.

In one hilarious cartoon representing Vera at her irreverent best, she depicted the house as a popular retreat for a motley crew of horror icons. *Psycho*'s Norman Bates, in drag as his dead mother, sat in a rocking chair in an upstairs window. Edward Scissorhands was busy sculpting a topiary shaped like Cerberus, the monstrous three-headed dog that guarded Hades—and their heads looked suspiciously like our own three dogs. Demented author Jack Torrance from *The Shining* was busting down the front door with an axe. Vera had sprinkled our family into the drawing too, as the Addams Family. Eliot and Sydney as Pugsley and Wednesday were setting dynamite charges under the mansion's foundation. Oliver, rakish in a pencil mustache and double-breasted striped suit, was Gomez, canoodling the arm of pasty-faced Morticia—representing none other than me—in a sprayed-on mourning dress with octopus tentacle hem. And in the foreground stood Vera clapping her hands to her ears like the spectral figure in Edvard Munch's *The Scream*, with a word balloon over her head saying *It's a madhouse! A maaaaadhouse!* Luckily the detectives read no deeper meanings into the macabre masterpiece.

Flipping through the pages, I paused on a sketch of some sort of symbol. Celtic, maybe? I traced the image with my eyes, searching for something. But what?

A crash split the silence somewhere in the house, followed by

Eliot's screams, but I couldn't shift my attention. There was something significant about this drawing. A moment later the dogs erupted in a cacophony of barking; a loud wail echoed.

"Mommy, help!" Yelling reached my ears, but my focus was hooked on the image.

Yes, I knew this image. It was important; I could feel it in my bones.

While the noise intensified, the questions in my head shouted over it. Where had I seen it? On my phone, perhaps? Had Vera sent me a picture of this before? It felt urgently meaningful.

I pulled my cell phone out of my back pocket—it was always on me in case Vera called or, more likely, texted. I scrolled through my ancient texts from her, the most recent one six months ago. April 16. The cursed day. She had texted me shortly before she vanished. I should have seen the warning behind the green bubble of letters and abbreviated words. But I saw the hidden message now, tucked in between the text slang and the emojis:

Mom pls don't be mad at me when u get home. but i need 2 clean up the mess.

Heat radiated up my neck, cooked my forehead. Her text hadn't been about the dirty dishes cluttering the counter that she was supposed to put in the dishwasher. Or the toys scattered across the area rug that she was supposed to put in the toy box. The mess was our *family*. Vera had found out something she shouldn't have. And if I didn't find her soon, it could get her killed.

Panic stole my breath as I found myself slipping back in time, back to the day Vera disappeared…

Chapter 2
Felicity

"I think it's time to tell the kids the truth." *The truth.* What a subjective word. These days, truth was a fog I wandered through. Impossible to grasp and as fleeting as a thought.

But the truth had been weighing on me a lot lately. Along with the half-truths that attached themselves to it.

"What truth, Felicity? About Sydney?" Evening sunlight darted across Oliver's face, brightening the blue of his eyes. Other than fine lines that raked the edges, he hadn't changed much since college. While time hit pause for him, for me it marched cruelly on.

"Yes, about Sydney. What else would I be talking about?" Lately Sydney's diagnosis was all we talked about. We never spoke about the *other* thing.

His lips tightened in a crooked slash. "Are you sure that's a good idea? It will only upset them. It seems a bit premature to be discussing it with Vera before we talk to the doctors first."

I inhaled the moist air as seagulls squawked over the Allegheny River that flowed past the dock where we enjoyed dessert at one of our favorite taprooms in downtown Pittsburgh's North Shore. Speedboats sped across the water, trailed by jets of spray and party music in a strange cacophony. The Allegheny

River teemed with water lovers eager to let go of the long winter and embrace a warm spring. It had been a perfect night for outdoor riverside dining, a rare treat during April in Pennsylvania, but the scent of rain and a brooding sky portended a coming storm. The weather had held off long enough for us to get through dinner and half of my tiramisu, but now a chilly wind made me pull my sweater tight around my shoulders.

I reread the text that Marin had sent me after our Sisters Day Out earlier that afternoon, encouraging me to be strong after I told her the secret Oliver and I had been keeping from the whole family for months:

Thank you for entrusting me with your secret about Syd Squid. I know you're scared, but I think you need to come clean to Vera. She'll understand. I'm here for anything you need. You're closer than blood to me, sis.

Although we were family by marriage, Marin was the closest thing to a sister I had, and loyal to a fault. Her husband, my brother-in-law Cody, often jokingly—or not so jokingly—reminded me of this when Marin put me before him.

Marin was my rock when motherhood tried to sink me. When Vera entered her tween rebellious stage, Marin stepped in to support me against Vera's demand for an eyebrow piercing. When I needed extra help after opening Barkalicious Boutique, Marin groomed a dog or five when I was understaffed and overbooked. When Oliver's promotion at his marketing firm enslaved him at the office, Marin delivered meals to him for me. And when my green-grass world turned bleak and brown, Marin comforted me with the vow that Sydney would be okay and we'd get through her sickness together. Marin convinced me I wasn't a monster for what I wanted to ask Vera to do. Marin reminded me I was doing the right thing.

I trusted Marin. Oliver, on the other hand, I didn't trust.

I had noticed the shift between my husband and sister-from-another-mister, the way his gaze lingered a little too long on her. The way his attention zeroed in on her every word. I couldn't blame *her* that my husband was a flirt. It came with the package when I married him—take the good with the bad—and it had helped him charm his way to the top of a billion-dollar company. I accepted it, but I didn't have to like it.

"Marin thinks Vera can handle the news," I said. "She's fifteen years old. Old enough to know what's going on, Ollie." A droplet spattered on the glass mosaic bistro table, another pelted my silk blouse.

"It's not the news about Sydney that I think will upset Vera. It's what we're asking her to do that's the issue," Oliver replied.

"I have a feeling she might already know after all the bloodwork she's gone through."

Our waitress, her curves shrink-wrapped in black Lycra, rushed by. Oliver's gaze trailed behind her, then darted back to me when he realized I'd caught him.

"Like what you see?" I asked.

"She's hideous compared to you, honey." There was that charming grin again. Irresistible, even after twenty years.

"She *does* kind of resemble a pug." Her upturned nose, expressive face. Who was I kidding? Pugs were adorable.

Another raindrop made waves in my drink. I was ready for the check, but Oliver seemed unfazed by the weather.

"You think Vera realized it's not normal to do a full blood panel in order to go to lacrosse camp?" Oliver's eyebrow bowed upward.

I huffed. "I'm pretty sure she knows something's up."

"What about Eliot? He's only eight. I'm not sure he'll understand that his little sister is sick. And I don't want him to be freaked out."

"We don't need to go into great detail, Ollie. Just the basics." The *basics*. Another subjective word. How basic could we get when trying to explain to the kids that their three-year-old sister was dying? All she knew from her trusting perspective was that several times a week she got to play games with her new nurse friends at the hospital while hooked up to the dialysis machine. "I don't want them being angry at us for not telling them sooner. It feels like we're lying to them."

"Since when have you felt bad about lying to the kids, Felicity? We've been doing it since they were born."

I shrugged the implication away. It was date night; we weren't supposed to be fighting.

"Speaking of the kids, do you think I should check on them?" The clouds darkened with a final warning. I was as ready to change the subject as I was to avoid the rain. "Maybe I should call Vera to make sure they're okay."

My phone was already out of my purse, my fingers swiping to dial. Oliver rested his hand on mine, stopping me.

"Hey, stop worrying. The kids are fine. We're on a date. Let's enjoy it while we can." He grinned, creasing the face that wasn't quite movie-star handsome, but close enough. A face I still loved waking up to even after two decades together.

"You're right, Ollie. I can't help it. I'm petrified something will happen to Sydney while we're out and Vera won't know what to do."

"You worry too much, Felicity," Oliver replied. "They're probably just watching a movie and eating junk food. Besides, Vera's a capable girl. She knows what she's doing."

"Yeah, I know. But have you noticed something…different

about her lately?"

I couldn't quite pin down what it was. Not the typical teen sullenness or mood swings or rebellion. It was something else. Something darker.

Oliver scraped his fork across his plate, scooping up the last morsel of his cheesecake. I pushed what remained of my tiramisu toward him to finish off. "No. What do you mean?"

"I don't know. She just seems...quieter than usual."

"Isn't that a good thing? You're always telling the kids to keep the noise down. When they do, you think something's wrong. There's no pleasing you, Felicity."

"Not true. I'm easy to please, if you'd take a minute to bother trying." In a mutter I added, "You have no problem pleasing everyone else." I shouldn't have said it. The jab was unnecessary when we were having such a good time on our first date night in months. Well, good up until now.

"Seriously? You're bringing her up again?" He stabbed his fork into the tiramisu. Tossed the last bite into his mouth. Shoved the empty plate to the other side of the table. The fork skidded off and jangled on the deck floor. Heads turned.

"Well, as your wife, it bothers me that you flirt with Marin. She's your brother's wife and my best friend."

Oliver slammed his fist down, upsetting his water glass. "How do I flirt with her?"

I should have stopped right there. Instead, I plummeted right off the edge. "You two are constantly whispering and laughing and touching each other. It's inappropriate. I'm not the only one who notices it; your brother and parents do too. And I'm sure Vera does, which may be why she's acting so strange, seeing her father blatantly flirting with her aunt."

"So the whole family is talking about me behind my back?"

"I didn't say that."

"Yes, you did." Oliver raised his hand, motioning to the shrink-wrapped waitress. "Check please."

With a dip of her chin, the waitress stooped to pick up the fork and was off.

"This is supposed to be a fun night out, and I really don't want to fight about this. Whatever flirting you think I'm doing, it's all in your dirty little mind. If it bothers you how I act around Marin, then let's cancel family dinners with them, okay? You know I love you, but this jealousy has got to stop, or it's going to start affecting our marriage."

It was already affecting—and infecting—our marriage; Oliver was simply oblivious to it. I could give them a pass at being naïve, but the line between flirting and falling was growing thin. Letting his hand linger on her forearm for too long. The way he laughed too loudly at her jokes, while ignoring everyone else. And they always picked seats next to each other at family dinners. Anyone with eyes could see it, but Oliver remained blind. Or pretended to be.

A mist thickened the air as we paid our check and sprinted to the car. Oliver opened my door—since our first date as freshmen in college he remained ever the proper gentleman, even in the middle of a fight—and I stepped in, flipping down the mirror to check my mascara while he slid into the driver's seat. The thirty-minute drive home to Oakmont was tensely silent, me brooding over Oliver, Oliver brooding over traffic, both of us stuck in the middle of a fight that neither of us would end. Sometimes it lasted through days of silent treatment or one-word exchanges.

My phone chirped with an incoming text:

Mom pls don't be mad at me when u get home. but i need 2 clean up the mess.

Vera. The reliable distraction. "It looks like we'll be coming home to a messy house. I hope that Vera at least puts Eliot and Syd to bed before we get home."

Oliver grunted, his passive-aggressive way of moving on without actually moving on. He was still angry at me, though I doubted he remembered why. That's what grudge-holders do. It was the Portman Family Plague; we were gifted grudges.

The downpour hit just as we turned onto our street. Rain smeared across the windshield as we pulled into our winding orange brick driveway that matched the orange brick of our three-story Second Empire Victorian home. My stomach churned from looking at my phone. The perils of carsickness were unavoidable when multitasking on my phone while in motion, which mainly consisted of scrolling through my Facebook and Instagram feed. I'd never actually hurled, but the tiramisu was knocking at the door.

I liked several posts of my friends' book club picks, kids, pets, inspirational memes, and spring flower gardens, then clicked over to Vera's profile. Sure, I was being *sus,* a Vera-ism for "suspicious," but I always checked her Instagram just to make sure everything she posted was parent-approved. It had been a big battle when she first wanted a phone, then a war when she wanted to join social media, so I obliged only after her assurance that if I ever found anything *sus,* I'd take away her phone and disable her social media accounts. Our mutually-agreed definition of *sus* was yet to be determined.

Vera mostly posted drawings. The artist within her was emerging, a blooming talent she inherited from her father, not me. I first noticed it when she turned ten. It was sweet how she avidly watched her dad design my new business logo for a dog grooming venture, Barkalicious Boutique. Her eyes had traced his graphite sketch pencil swirling confidently across the paper. That's when her spark ignited. The calligraphy and acrylic paint sets we bought her that year for Christmas fanned the flame.

Thunder shook the car as Oliver rolled to a stop. I was flicking through the last post before putting my phone away when an image held me captive. A photo that tagged a @blythesampson4ever in a tribal design image. A pretty, swirly triangular design. Inked on pale *flesh.*

That looked way too much like Vera's skin. And way too much like a tattoo. A tattoo that Vera knew better than to desecrate her underage body with.

"You ready to run?" Oliver asked me.

"Huh?" Momentarily confused, I glanced up at him, his hand cradling the door handle.

"To the porch. I'll hold my jacket over you while we run."

"Oh, yeah." I'd table the conversation about the ink in question until we got inside.

Oliver held his coat over my head as we dashed across the brick walkway, rain sluicing off our backs. Once up the stone steps leading to the tiled wraparound porch, we shook off like two drenched dogs before I noticed that the oak door that led into the foyer was cracked open. It wasn't exactly unimaginable seeing a door left open, with three kids constantly running in and out. The strangeness of it only struck me when I walked inside.

A chill followed me in, crawled up my legs, hung in the foyer. Water pounded the roof like a drum, but the heart of the house was eerily quiet and black as a scorched wick. I had expected to find Vera awake with Eliot and Sydney watching a Disney movie marathon, popcorn scattered across the floor, but only the squeak of our shoes disturbed the hush.

It was far too dark and far too quiet for this early hour with a night-owl teen among us.

I ran my hand along the wall until I felt the switch and flicked it on. Light from the chandelier bounced off the glossy woodwork.

"It looks like Vera actually put the younger ones to bed on time." Oliver stepped out of his wet shoes and hung up his coat.

"I'm going to go check on the kids really quick," I said as I headed up the staircase. At the top of the first floor, the stained-glass reflections of the original owners—an 1880s glass-manufacturing power couple—stared dully at me.

I rounded the corner, aiming straight for Eliot's room first. He'd likely still be awake, because he couldn't sleep until my lips touched his forehead, my arms squeezed him close, and my prayer over him reached God's ears. I was surprised—and admittedly a tad wounded—that he was already asleep in bed, his Marvel comforter twisted around his feet and pillow fallen to the floor. For his eighth birthday he had wanted a whole new room décor. Marvel everything, from the Thor nightlight, to the Spider-Man lamp, to the Iron Man chair. I hoped some other little boy was now enjoying the Tigger-themed bedroom set that we had donated to Goodwill. I tiptoed to his bed, lightly pressed my lips to his sweat-dampened head—both he and his father got as hot as furnaces when they slept—and pulled his blanket up to his chin.

Next was Sydney's princess pink room, where I found her with two fingers tucked upside down in her mouth. An involuntary tremor shot through my carpal-tunneled wrists. It looked painfully uncomfortable, but she preferred it to her thumb and we hadn't made the effort to break her of it yet. By kid number three, we had given up on the child-molding we had applied to Vera and Eliot. I figured we could tackle the upside-down finger sucking once she reached her fourth birthday.

Both Sydney and Eliot were asleep in their bedrooms. Great—but where was Vera?

I scanned her bedroom. Dark and empty.

Then the bathrooms. Dark and empty.

I checked the spare bedrooms we never used. Dark and empty.

I skipped the library because we seldom entered it, especially not at night.

Trotting downstairs, I found a freshly pajamaed Oliver lying on the sofa, socked feet propped on the coffee table, channel-hopping for something worth watching at this late hour. The rain was growing heavier, heaving sheets of water on the mansard roof.

"Have you seen Vera?" I asked.

"Isn't she in her room?" He continued to stare at the television.

"No, Ollie. Syd and Eliot are sleeping, but I can't find Vera."

"Did you try calling or texting her?"

"Why would I need to call or text her when she's supposed to be *here* watching her siblings?"

I was growing worried. Where the hell was my daughter? I called her cell phone, expecting to hear its familiar ring echo somewhere in the house. It chirped in my ear once, then slipped into voicemail.

"Her phone's off," I said. By now the worry escalated to panic, yet Oliver remained transfixed by an episode of *Doctor Who*. "Oliver, shut the TV off and help me find Vera!"

"You really need help with that? This house isn't *that* big."

Wrong. It was too big. Sometimes I wondered why we'd poured all our money into such a monstrosity. The upkeep was impossible.

I tripped up the stairs to her bedroom and turned on the light. Her space was a crumpled mess of bedding and clothes, schoolbooks and art supplies tossed everywhere. Nothing unusual for my teen daughter. What was unusual was her purse on her desk. She never left the house without it. I pulled the mouth of the leather bag open, rummaged through the contents. Lip gloss. Hair brush. Wallet. But no cell phone. At least she had her phone with her, though it was useless off.

Something hard sat on the bottom of her purse. A book. I pulled it out and recognized the beautiful personalized journal I ordered for her birthday last year. I fingered the filled pages. Held the leather binding to my chest. A memory gave me pause. Of the day my own mother read my own journal. The betrayal I felt then resonated with me now. There's an unspoken pact between a mother and daughter that you never—*never*—read your child's journal. And yet here I was, flipping through the pages, searching for anything in my daughter's secret words that would help me figure out where she had gone.

I knew I shouldn't, but right now my daughter was missing. I had no choice. Slowly at first, I turned page by page, lured in by her bubbly handwriting, noting several torn edges where entries had been ripped out. Giving those missing pages only a single thought, I started reading her most recent musings. The carefree letters turned jagged. The words were dashed across the page in an angry flurry. I could tell by the harsh lines and deep ink.

Then I read an entry. A message intended for me.

"Ollie," I tried to yell, but my voice tiptoed out in a whisper. The television blared on. "Ollie!" His name exploded from my mouth. Oliver's footsteps blended with the electronic pulse of the *Doctor Who* theme song. When he stampeded into the room, I held out the open journal in front of his pissed-off face.

"What?"

"Just *read.*"

Oliver's face blanched with dread as our daughter's message sank in. "Oh my God. Do you think she knows? This is bad, Felicity. Really bad."

Yet Oliver didn't even know the half of what I had done. If Vera had somehow found out the whole truth of it…I couldn't let my worry go there.

"What do we do?" My voice cracked open as the questions tumbled out. "Do you think she ran away because of…this? Because of me?" I thrust the journal up, as if that made my point any clearer than the terror in my voice.

Oliver's arms reached around me, pulled me in. "I don't know, honey."

From the very beginning of our relationship Oliver always knew how to temper my flareups. It was one of the many things I loved about him. But this time there was no tempering. Only scorching fire.

"Do you think she went to the police? Could that be where she went?" I searched my husband's face for answers, but he said nothing. There was nothing to say. Everything would come out soon enough.

Or maybe not everything. There was still so much hidden.

Then somewhere buried in the ocean of my thoughts, a fear rose to the surface. This was only the first journal entry I had read. There were hundreds more. What if I discovered something worse in here? As I reread that last entry, I realized Vera's journal was an omen…

Every buried secret was about to be disinterred.

Chapter 3
Felicity

I found out something horrible about Mom. I don't know if I should tell the police or not. For the first time in my life I'm scared of her. She's a monster, but she's my mom. I hate that I love her. The worst part is that I think my whole family is protecting her, which makes them just as guilty.

"Felicity!" Oliver's voice dragged me out of the awful memory of the night Vera disappeared, back into the even more awful present.

The scribbled words of Vera's journal dissolved into her bedroom comforter. It took a moment for me to realize I'd been standing in her room, holding my phone…doing what? Looking up something on the Internet? Oh yeah, the tribal design. I recognized it from somewhere, the memory sticky like taffy. But from where?

"Mommy!" Now Eliot's voice joined the commotion of Oliver yelling for me, the dogs barking somewhere in the house, and Sydney screaming. All I wanted was a minute to try to remember where I had seen the drawing before.

I didn't know if it was a clue, or if it was some small insignificant detail of Vera's life that I wasn't a part of. But nothing about her life felt insignificant anymore. Every little piece of her was now evidence essential to finding her.

Downstairs the crying and yelling grew louder, so loud that the sound followed me into Vera's bedroom, smashing against my eardrums. When I turned around, Oliver stood directly behind me, handing me a bloody child, a cordless phone perched between his shoulder and ear.

"*Please*, sweetheart," he said in a wheedling tone I knew all too well, "take care of Sydney. I'm on a work call and the kids need their mother."

Blood gushed from Sydney's lip, dripping down her chin onto my shoulder where she rested her head. One chubby arm clutched the velveteen rabbit that had been Vera's as a baby, Sydney's self-soother in her sister's absence. Another bloody dribble fell on the rabbit's ear. How the heck had a paper cut turned into a bloody lip?

"Oh, sweetie, what happened?"

"Idiot"—her name for *Eliot*, which Oliver and I had found hilarious the first time she said it; the poor kid's nickname had stuck—"pushed me and I owied my lip." She thrust her swollen bottom lip out in a crimson and purple pout.

It was always something with these two. One pushing the other. The other biting back. Someone always ended up in tears…and it was usually me.

My lips brushed against her salty cheek. "My poor babycakes. Let's get that owie feeling better, okay, Syd Squid?"

She nodded meekly. Taking her into the bathroom across the hall, I dabbed at the cut while she squeezed the life out of the rabbit, until the bleeding stopped, then I dotted kisses on her cheeks and nose and neck until she collapsed into a giggle fit. She held out her finger, where the paper cut had turned an angry red, and I kissed that too before wrapping it in a *Paw Patrol* Band-

Aid. When I had discovered that the kids show supported the American Society for the Prevention of Cruelty to Animals, I happily purchased the cartoony Dalmatian- and German-shepherd-themed bandages. Sydney smiled and hugged her tiny arms around my neck, squeezing her thanks. Owie cured.

"You're the best mommy ever." Her standards were pretty low.

I hefted her into my arms and tossed the Band-Aid wrapper in the trashcan. Downstairs the dogs continued barking as Eliot yelled at them, his voice growing more frantic by the moment.

The disciplinary part of my job always escalated the drama, but I couldn't let it go.

"Eliot!" I yelled over the dogs' baying as I descended the stairs. "Syd told me you pushed her." My voice lowered an accusatory decibel. "You know better than to hurt your sister." I reached the first floor when a piercing cry nudged me into a sprint.

"Moooooommmm! Help!" Eliot sobbed.

I whipped around the doorway, finding Eliot in the kitchen trying to pick up shards of glass with his little bare fingers.

"Whoa, what happened here, bud?" I shifted Sydney to my hip and rushed to where Eliot knelt on the glass-besieged floor, his face apple red.

Tears streamed down his cheeks as he looked up at me, grabbing Brutus by the collar to keep him from cutting his paws.

"It was an accident! I was getting a cup and it dropped and broke, and when Syd came over I tried to push her away so she wouldn't get cut, but then she fell and hurt her lip. And I can't clean it up without the dogs trying to run through the glass..."

When he finished his breathless defense, I realized—once again—how I failed as a mom. Here my eight-year-old son had been scrambling to keep everyone safe while I obliviously

34

wallowed in my sorrow upstairs. It was a recurring theme lately: my negligence, my absentmindedness, my disconnect. My despair.

I couldn't seem to find my way out of the darkness. Not when my only light—my daughter—was missing.

"I'm so sorry, honey." I said that a lot these days. "It's okay, Eliot." I pulled him aside, drying his tears on my shirt. "Let me clean this up while you put on *Captain Underpants* for you and Syd."

Patting his flat little bum, I sent them to the living room while I dragged all three dogs by their collars out through the back door and into the yard. While sweeping up the shards, a macabre thought slivered into my brain. What would it feel like to just jab one of these glossy spikes through my heart and end it all? Wouldn't work. There was already a gaping black hole there…in the place where my love for Vera had been.

Stop.

Enough.

I couldn't let go when so many people needed me to hang on. But it was so damn hard to hold on to so much at once.

When the glass had been cleaned up, I wanted to make it up to the kids with a treat. If I was being honest, I *needed* to more than I *wanted* to. I owed them so much more than a sugary bribe, but I found it harder and harder each day to be who they deserved me to be.

"Who wants brownies?" I called out from the kitchen with a fake cheer that the kids believed.

"Me!" both kids replied in unison. When do we outgrow childlike simplicity? I wondered now if I'd ever had it.

"No nuts in the brownies, Mom!" Eliot added over the sound of the show.

I pulled out my mother's recipe for homemade double-chocolate-chip brownies, mentally adjusted the ingredients for Sydney's kidney-friendly diet, and slipped into the pantry. Within ten minutes I mixed the batter, poured it into a glass baking dish, and slid it into the oven. While it cooked, I swept clean the espresso-stained butcher block island—a rich contrast to the white quartz countertops throughout the rest of the kitchen—then shifted my brain to what to make for dinner tonight. I dreaded meal planning almost as much as I dreaded grocery shopping. Eliot hardly ate anything but tacos these days, and Sydney wouldn't touch a vegetable unless I smothered it in cheese.

As I piled the dirty bakeware into the sink, my phone beeped with a notification. Opening up my Facebook app, I checked to see if it had anything to do with my latest post about our ongoing search for Vera. The Crimestoppers post featuring last year's school picture and her physical details had been shared over 5k times and had 1.4k comments:

MISSING: Vera Portman
Missing since: 4/16/2021
Age: 15
Race: White
Sex: Female
Height: Approx. 5'2" tall
Weight: Approx. 105 pounds
Hair: Blonde
Eyes: Green

Six months of shared posts. Six months of friends' crying emojis and sympathetic comments. Six months of nothing helpful.

Captain Underpants' *tra-la-lahhh* battle cry faded in the background, along with everything around me. My heart sank; it was just someone commenting with yet another prayer emoji that the police would find her soon. Except I had already given up hundreds, maybe even thousands of prayers for God to bring her back to me, and He had yet to deliver. What was the point of faith if God wasn't listening?

As my finger continued clicking, scrolling, clicking, scrolling, my eyes scanned for anything new. Anything relevant to Vera. Day after day I found nothing but #momlife memes and book club recommendations and kittens and political noise. It killed me, like tiny paper cuts slowly bleeding me to death, when I watched the world continue to live while I died. Each day slicing deeper. Each morning bringing fresh pain. Each breath a weep.

Everyone else got to live their lives, while my daughter stayed missing, lost somewhere in the world, unable to make her way home. The pettiness of everyone else's "problems" infuriated me, not so much that I wished their own kids would go missing, but better theirs than mine. Because a missing child was a real problem, not some make-believe offense over supporting the wrong sports team, the latest celebrity victim of cancel culture, or whether or not you're properly wearing your face mask in public.

I clicked over to a Facebook support group for mothers whose children had gone missing. The consolation it offered was mostly symbolic, but it helped, a little. As my fingertip touched the screen, my phone was ripped from my hand.

"Hey!" I looked up to find Oliver holding my phone out of reach. "What the hell?"

"What the hell is right. I've been trying to get your attention for five minutes, Felicity. You spend more time on Facebook than taking care of the kids."

Touché. Maybe I *had* been wrapped up in my phone…and my emptiness again. But didn't a missing child warrant it? "I'm trying to find our daughter, Ollie. That's more than you're doing."

"Right now I'm more concerned about whatever's burning in the oven," he said, gesturing toward the smoke billowing against the oven window.

The brownies! Had it been fifteen minutes already? I turned off the oven and whipped the door open, releasing a fog of charred chocolate smoke into the kitchen and fanning it away with my mitted hand before the smoke alarm started screaming. First the broken glass, now the burned brownies. And none of it mattered because Vera was missing and I had no idea if she was dead or alive.

"You're constantly on your phone or in your own head," Oliver continued ranting, "and it's like the rest of us don't exist anymore. There's a point where we have to move on...accept this as the new normal. Without Vera—"

"Don't you dare say that!" I needed him to stop. Stop talking. Stop guilting me. Stop. Stop. Stop! "Do you even miss her?" My voice dropped to a low growl.

Oliver showed me his scolded puppy look.

"I'm sorry." I was on the verge of tears. "I didn't mean to say that. I'm sorry I'm a terrible wife and neglectful mother and horrible housekeeper. I'm sorry, I'm sorry, I'm sorry! But I just don't know what to be anymore, because I will never be who I used to be—Vera's mother."

I felt it before it arrived, the tide pushing against my eyes, my throat, my stomach. A mother's heart shatters daily, but nothing like this. It should never hurt like this. Unable to stop the tears, I sobbed as the pain swelled. So many tears over so many days. It had been six months, but it felt like six years.

"Of course I miss her," he consoled. "And I don't expect you to just move on like she never existed. But there's nothing else we can do. We've done everything we can to find her. But we have to stay strong for Eliot...and especially Sydney." Oliver pulled me into his arms. "And for each other. I know you're hurting—I am too. But we still have two little kids who need you...here...now. You can't get so caught up in the life you lost that you forget the life you still have. With us."

Still holding me, Oliver turned us toward the living room where Eliot and Sydney laughed at some loud, goofy antic escalating in the cartoon.

"You're right. But I don't know how to move on. I can't stop worrying about her. Wondering if she's...okay." I couldn't say *alive*. I could never let that doubt creep in.

Oliver handed me back my phone, releasing me with a kiss on my cheek. "All I ask is that you try to be present. For us and for them."

Oh my heart. Two pieces of it sitting on the sofa snuggled together. I tried every day for them, but trying didn't seem to be enough. Not enough to cover the guilt that haunted me for what I had done. And for what I continued to do.

Maybe I deserved the hell I was in. Payment for my sins. I had never been punished for that terrible act, or all the lies following it. Maybe I was overdue.

On the counter behind me Oliver's phone chirped, and I reached to pick it up and hand it to him when he grabbed it. I thought I caught the name *Vera* in the text message that blinked off the screen.

"Geez, you're awfully protective of that thing. Are you hiding something from me?" I lifted an eyebrow, and he nervously grinned. I had been joking, but maybe it wasn't a joke. What *was* he hiding? "Oliver, who are you texting about Vera to?"

"Vera? I wasn't texting about Vera."

"Yes you were. I just saw her name in that text."

"Oh." He glanced at the floor, as if he'd find a more convincing lie in the grout between the tiles. "Cody was asking if we heard anything new on Vera's case, that's all."

It seemed an awful strange thing for Oliver's brother to ask via text, considering we saw him every week for family dinner where we always kept him well-informed. Which, now that I realized the time, was quickly approaching. Oliver's family usually arrived around six o'clock for dinner, and it was already four thirty. That didn't leave much time to figure out a meal, prepare it, and serve it.

"You're just as bad as I am," I grumbled as I tossed a cookbook on the counter.

"What are you talking about?"

"Your phone—you're just as possessive with yours as I am with mine."

"No I'm not." He laughed it off, but something inside me wilted with the awareness that my husband had a secret too, and it had to do with Vera.

Once upon a time we shared everything, with no space between us. Until lies and secrets broke us apart, made us strangers, and nothing could fill the breach.

Chapter 4
Marin Portman

The blue flame on the gas stove licked my fingertip. Something inside me wanted to touch it, feel it sear me, cook my skin. I wanted to see my flesh bubble and pop. I held my hand there for just a moment, soaking in the heat as it blistered red. It should have hurt, but I didn't feel anything. Maybe my body had become so used to the ache that it was numb. I used to get burned by fire, but now I was forged by it. Into something inhuman. Something dark and evil.

"Marin!" Hearing my name jarred me back to my body, standing in the kitchen, while the kettle shrieked, and a flare of pain shot up my arm.

Maybe I wasn't immune to pain after all.

Turning off the burner, the kettle died down but I couldn't remember what I was supposed to be doing. Oh right, taking the sweet potato casserole out of the oven, the side dish that I had committed to bringing to family dinner tonight at my sister-in-law Felicity's house. I doubted anyone would eat a bite, as most of my cooking turned out to be inedible experiments, but *the family*—it sounded so *Sopranos*-ish in my head—insisted we all be there to support Felicity through "this difficult time." *Difficult time.* That's how my mother-in-law Debra had worded it, as if Felicity losing a daughter was just a minor obstacle to hurdle.

I was devastated for Felicity. Angry at myself. These hot

emotions coated me like melted wax, hardening the place where my heart should be. It felt dishonest being the shoulder for Felicity to cry on when I was the reason for her tears.

Opening the oven door, I stepped aside to allow light from the mismatched hood into the oven to see if the marshmallows on top of the sweet potatoes had melted into goo yet. The oven that came with the house predated the time when they installed lights inside the guts. It was an O'Keefe and Merritt model, circa 1940s, old enough that I had to manually light the burner with a match when I turned on the gas. Somehow the porcelain was still in great shape, and I loved the look of it—a vintage mint green. It was the only thing I liked about my home.

Home felt too intimate a word for the house that Cody had purchased before me, furnished with cheap Walmart décor that screamed broke bachelor. From the goldenrod linoleum floor that looked perpetually dirty, to the original single-pane windows that did nothing to keep the Pennsylvania chill out, to the money-pit furnace that couldn't keep up with the extreme lows. You'd think we could have afforded a little modernization—like trading up from wall units to central air-conditioning and replacing the leaky galvanized plumbing with PVC—but the attribute I loved most about my husband was the thing that kept us perpetually broke: his love for me above all else.

While other men slaved at their jobs, dedicating endless nights climbing whatever ladder brought them bigger pay, Cody was satisfied with just getting by. Sometimes his single-minded adoration was a huge pain in the ass. He clocked out at work at exactly five o'clock just so he could bounce through the front door and smother me with kisses. He could work an hour or two overtime every now and then to earn extra money, or take a job further away that paid more, but no, not *my* Cody. I was the center of his universe, and he was a pesky satellite, revolving around me. Sometimes I wished he'd get swallowed up in a black hole.

As Cody gorged himself on our love, I starved for something more.

The white plastic timer dinged just as I carried the casserole dish from the oven to the orange Formica counter with metal trim. It was a mystery why an owner from the past picked this permanent color palette, as it didn't match a single detail in the kitchen. Heat seeped through the cheap oven mitts, burning my palms. As I rushed to set it down, I felt my feet slipping…then my body falling backward.

The *crack!* impacted my tailbone first, shooting a jolt of pain up my spine.

After my butt hit the floor, scorching magma spilled across my lap. I screamed and pushed myself upright, feeling sticky orange sweet potatoes covering my legs, chunks of it falling to the floor. I cried out for Cody, partly in pain, partly in fury. In a mental instant replay, I imagined my fall looked something like Joe Pesci tripping on Macauley Culkin's Micro Machines booby trap in *Home Alone*. I had never empathized for the sawed-off tough guy until now.

By the time I had scooped most of the food off of me, Cody showed up, laughing hysterically as he grabbed a wet wash cloth to help wipe off my pants. Cody had also laughed like this through *Home Alone*. God love him, but the man had the attention span and the sense of humor of a ten-year-old boy.

"Are you okay?" he managed to ask.

"It's not funny!" I wanted to yell at him, but my throbbing tailbone dialed my voice down to a whimper. "I think it burned my legs."

I glanced at the space on the floor where my feet had given way and saw a puddle of water seeping into the sweet potato juice. Pulling open the cabinet under the sink, I watched a *drip, drip, drip* trickle down the elbow pipe, splattering on the cabinet base before streaming onto the floor.

"I thought you fixed the leak in the pipe already," I groaned as I hooked my hands on the metal edge of the counter and pried myself back up. I let Cody lift me, even though I was pissed at him for a reason I couldn't explain. My rear hurt so bad I could hardly stand.

"I did. I replaced the whole thing." *No he didn't.* "I guess the leak is coming from somewhere else." *Wrong again.*

It was the same leak I offered to fix countless times, and countless times Cody told me it was a *man's job.* He called it chivalry; I called it chauvinism. When it came to home repairs, or anything do-it-yourself, Cody had no clue what he was doing. That's what growing up privileged afforded him, the luxury of relying on others for basic survival. My life hadn't afforded me the same blissful ignorance. By age ten I knew how to change a tire; by age thirteen I could replace a water heater.

Let me fix the damn plumbing, Cody.

Cody tossed the hand towel on the growing puddle and knelt down on it as he reached under the sink to shut off the water. Glancing up at me, he asked, "Are you able to still go to family dinner, or do you want to stay home? Everyone would understand if you'd rather not go, Marin, considering everything going on with Vera…"

I shrugged, partly wanting to stay home to nurse my aching ass, but I needed to be there tonight. I could never tell Cody why. I could barely admit it to myself.

"I'll be fine. I just need to get changed really quick. Could you text Ollie and tell him we're running late? And obviously I won't be bringing sweet potatoes like I planned."

"Don't worry about it. I'm sure Mom whipped up a ten-course meal, which I doubt any of us will have the stomach for anyway." Cody rubbed my back comfortingly, as if I was the one whose daughter had run away.

"Mind cleaning up while I change?"

"Sure, I got it, hon." He came off self-congratulatory, as if he was doing me a favor cleaning up the mess that his incompetence caused.

I exhaled my irritation, inhaled patience. "Thanks."

Cody grabbed a wad of paper towels and scooped up a handful of mush. "Go do what you do best and look beautiful."

Most women, I guess, would be flattered by daily affirmations of how beautiful and sexy you were. It wasn't that I didn't appreciate my husband's attraction to me, but more often his endearments smacked of the kind of sexist compliments that went out of style with fifties swing dresses and bouffant hairdos, when the Man of the House went to the office, and the Adoring Housewife stayed home cleaning and baking.

I stood in front of my closet, half of my clothing stuffed into four square feet of space dimly lit by a single dangling lightbulb. The other half overflowed into the spare bedroom. Several hangers hung empty where Vera had raided my wardrobe when a growth spurt boosted her up to my size. I didn't have the heart to take the clothes back, and now I clung to a desperate hope that she'd be wearing them all again soon.

I tried to match together an outfit that showed proper respect for a grieving, stressed-out mother on the verge of losing her mind. No black, because black meant death and that was the last message I wanted my outfit to put in Felicity's head.

Picking out ripped jeans that showed a dash of thigh here, a sliver of leg there, and a cream turtleneck, I stepped into the only expensive shoes I owned—a pair of $400 genuine leather Freebird boots that I bought myself as a Christmas gift courtesy of my uber-rich boss (I never did tell him just how big a bonus I gave myself) and checked the full-length mirror hanging on the closet door. My father's Caribbean-soaked skin glistened with coconut butter, while my mother's hazel eyes popped beneath green eye shadow. It wasn't too much—I'd managed to channel my inner hoochie mama while retaining the veneer of the supportive sister.

Not that how I looked should have mattered. I wasn't trying to impress anyone.

Liar.

I slipped into the bathroom, wondering what Cody meant by *do what you do best.* Did he really think that was all I was good for, looking pretty? I admit I didn't contribute much financially to our neglected life in our neglected house, but not all of us had the same opportunities for advancement and wealth. There wasn't much earning power or promotion above "personal assistant."

At least working for a high-powered attorney was a step up from my last job, because waitressing when my passion was acting was too much of a cliché, even for me. I had settled for community theatre during my early twenties, then pursued the whole Hollywood thing, only to return home weighed down by the baggage of rejection and humiliation. Now that I was pushing thirty, acting seemed like a childish dream. One that I still longed for, but one that I simply couldn't dedicate every waking moment to anymore. I still auditioned for local theatre gigs, but wiped away the vision of my name in giant letters on the silver screen. After years of *almost*s, I finally gave up and faced reality—a boring and predictable *Groundhog Day* existence where the white picket fence was riddled with termites, the plumbing leaked, and the kitchen looked like a Waffle House. Much like my regrettable past, I finally let my future die.

I added a swipe of lip gloss and smacked my lips together.

Touched up my mascara, though my lashes didn't need it. One time I had been offered an acting gig because I reminded the casting director of Rihanna. I possessed that "wow factor," he explained. I could only assume it was the hazel green eyes that you rarely saw on a Black person. Well, *mixed*, in every sense of the word. My whole life I hung on the outskirts. Too poor for the cool cliques. Too white for the girls in the hood. Too black for the white-bread suburbanites. I felt like a puzzle piece that never quite fit.

I still did. Until I met the Portman family.

The family that I singlehandedly targeted and unintentionally destroyed.

Slowly making my way down the stairs, I winced with each step as my tailbone pulsed in pain. At the foot of the stairs Cody waited for me.

"You look hot, babe." He paired it with a devilish grin.

If only all of this was for him.

"You too." I turned around as my adoring husband held out my cognac vegan leather jacket—fake crap peeling at the elbows. I'd trade every one of Cody's syrupy compliments for an Armani lambskin coat.

We headed out the door, squinting into the low evening sun. Although I pasted on a smile, wickedness lurked beneath it. Fine clothes couldn't disguise my darkness; money couldn't repair what I had done. The evil had already emerged, and there was no stuffing it back inside.

Chapter 5
Marin

The short but scenic drive from Wilkinsburg to Oakmont followed the Allegheny River past trees set ablaze by the sinking sun. Although Wilkinsburg was a decaying town, it was home to me and one of the most architecturally unique train stations on the East Coast—a 1916 masterpiece boasting a massive skylight that floodlit the terrazzo and mosaic floors, and whose clock tower reminded me of the one in *Back to the Future*. Like most Gen Y'ers, I tended to see real-life things through the prism of pop culture.

Foliage in the hills of Pennsylvania was breathtaking, every turn on the winding roads a brand-new shock of color and beauty. A marbling of pink and burnt orange set the sky afire, in blinding contrast to the gray river with its whitecaps churning against the wind.

As we pulled into the driveway of Oliver and Felicity's house, I felt the familiar jab of nervous energy and jealousy. Intimidation came with the property. Their driveway wasn't paved, it was *brick*. Their landscaping wasn't nice, it was *manicured*. Their house wasn't big, it was a freakin' Victorian mansion. As in ten-foot-tall double solid oak doors that opened into an *atrium*. There was a mural of a baby angel on the parlor ceiling, for crying out loud. But the heartbreaking side of it all was that in their huge, safe house, they couldn't protect their family. We all saw the writing on the wall as their lives figuratively crumbled away. Still, envy held a stranglehold on me.

I didn't want to feel this way, bitter that I picked the wrong brother to marry. I loved Cody, despite his cloying affection, but sometimes love wasn't enough. While my house literally crumbled, I scrimped and saved every penny, worked for Scrooge's evil twin, and watched YouTube DIY videos on how to fix busted plumbing, while Felicity threw money hand over fist at gardeners to turn her bushes into whimsical topiaries. Well, la-di-da. To me, they were just tacky animals.

Cody parked in our usual spot by the rabbit bush, next to the llama bush where my father-in-law parked, and my boots *tap-tap-tapped* across the brick walkway, past myriad flowers in full bloom. Hell, even their soil was "rich."

We let ourselves in and found Felicity and Oliver in the living room talking in low tearful tones with my in-laws, Joe and Debra, while Sydney stuffed her mouth full of hors d'oeuvres and Eliot scrutinized each one warily. Several boxes of games were spread out on the carpet. Connect 4. Candyland. Twister—a personal favorite of mine. The children were oblivious to the angst living rent-free inside us all; Debra made sure of that as she spoke in cheery tones with them, filling their fat cheeks with food and their ears with chipper words.

Felicity, on the other hand, looked as war-torn as she must have felt. Her weary blue eyes were streaked with midnight-flight red since the day Vera went missing. Pacing the room with arms tightly folded across her chest, I was pretty sure she was wearing the same clothes she had worn yesterday. In happier days she been the talk of the town, admired for her glamor and elegance. Now her name was on everyone's lips for an entirely different reason. Tragedy always brings out the crazies with an axe to grind, from the neighborhood gossips to the social media vultures with the whole world at their malicious fingertips. From social butterfly to "terrible mom"—quite a fall from grace.

My eyes drifted to the smorgasbord of food artistically arranged on a period marble-topped coffee table. On a white platter were caprese bites arranged in a smiley face pattern. Eliot bravely tried one but found the medley of mozzarella cheese, basil, and tomatoes not to his liking—I saw him spitting out the half-chewed mush into his napkin and tucking it into his pocket. On another plate were tiny hot dogs wrapped in equally tiny croissants, which were Sydney's favorite. Another dish contained meatballs stabbed with toothpicks, a recipe I had given Debra back when Cody first introduced me to his parents. Though I'm sure she didn't make her sauce with grape jelly and chili sauce like my dad had taught me. Debra was way too classy to use jelly in any recipe. Maybe *preserves,* but never *jelly.*

Only now did Sydney take a break from her food coma to notice me. "Auntie Marin!" she squealed, rushing me with open arms. Swooping her up in the air, I planted kisses all over her sticky face. We had been explicitly told by Debra to keep the mood light for the sake of the kids.

"You taste delicious! How's my little Syd Squid?" I exclaimed, setting her down.

"Nana made teeny tiny hotdogs. O-M-G, try one!" Sydney had recently started talking in text. *OMG* this. *BTdubbs* that. I imagined she had picked it up from Vera.

"I bet they taste almost as yummy as your face."

A moment later Eliot slammed into my legs, wrapping his arms around me like a mini left tackle.

"Hey, bud!" I knelt down to speak to him at eye level. "You practicing your football moves, huh?"

His cheeks were inflated like a chipmunk's. He flashed a picket fence smile flecked with chunks of meatball.

"Don't answer until you swallow, okay?" I grinned.

"Okay, Auntie Marin," he said, spraying bits of beef all over my face.

After the kids wandered back to the sofa closest to the food, I felt the heat of tension rising up my neck and face. I didn't know how to act, what to say. Every word could be a bomb; every gesture a grenade. Felicity shuffled in front of the long line of windows, checking her phone every couple minutes as if it might ring at any moment with the news that Vera had been found safe and sound. Oliver seemed to have lost the energy to follow her as he hung back, standing awkwardly in the middle of the room. Debra distracted the kids with a game of Connect 4, while Cody approached Joe, who grabbed him in a greedy hug.

Joe's shoe-polish black hair always had a soft gloss to it, and while Cody had inherited the rich dark color, the thickness gene had skipped over him and went straight to Oliver. Cody's receding hairline took a hard *whack* at his self-esteem, but I actually liked it. It kept him humble.

"Hey, Dad. Everything okay?" Cody said.

"Nothing new, slugger. Where's that pretty wife of yours?" Then Joe turned to me. "There you are, Mare!"

Joe opened his arms for a hug, and I let his six-foot-three frame envelop me. He smelled like what a good dad was supposed to smell like—cedar chips (in retirement he'd become a master gardener) and aftershave, not cigarettes and hard liquor. His glasses sat crookedly on his nose, but he didn't seem to notice until Debra pointed it out. Joe was a wheat stalk of a man, easily swayed by his wife's breezy opinions.

Since day one my father-in-law had been an over-greeter. Always ready with a hearty hello and a hug. Cody and I had been dating for about a month when he asked if he could introduce me to his parents. I was a mixed girl from the inner city dating their good old boy. The thought petrified me, especially if they were anything like my own parents. I could only imagine what my parents would have thought about Cody, had they ever had the chance to meet him. Probably that he was an entitled man-child with something to prove. Dad said that about every guy I dated.

When Dad wasn't insulting my boyfriends, he was telling my friends enough terrible dad jokes to embarrass me for a lifetime. And my mother—God rest her soul—wanted so badly to be friends with my friends that she forgot to be my mom. But that first dinner with Joe and Debra sealed the deal for me as Joe recounted stories of run-ins with the police back in the early 1960s during his drag racing days along The Ardmore, a miles-long stretch of road with endless stoplights, perfect for attracting hot-rodders, along with the Steel City's most hard-ass cops—or the fuzz, as Joe called them. Joe was proud that his black '57 Chevy Bel Air had routinely blown the competition off the road, and he wore his jail time like a badge of honor.

I desperately wanted their approval ever since that day. It didn't take much. They liked me for me—the version of me that I showed them, at least.

"You look beautiful, Marin," Debra whispered in my ear, taking her turn for a hug. It was one of my favorite things about my in-laws, their natural paternal charm that I missed so much. When you're parentless, you notice such things and appreciate them. Cody, on the other hand, stiffened as his mother hugged him against his will. Cody was clearly spoiled on affection. He didn't know how lucky he was.

"Thanks. You too, Mom." I kept my voice low in respect of the strain tightening the air.

Even amid crisis Debra looked put together. Hair coiffed to perfection. Crispy ironed pantsuit matching the rosy shade she wore on her cheeks. She was one of the classiest women I'd ever met, though I'd been told she didn't come from money. She only looked it. I didn't know much about my in-laws' past, only that Debra worked for every penny she had. Her work ethic was what Joe first noticed about her…and the reason he fell so hard for her. He knew with Debra at his side, they could accomplish anything together.

"How's Felicity hanging in there?" I asked, afraid to ask Felicity myself. There was something terrifying about approaching a mother consumed by anticipatory grief.

Debra shook her head sadly. "She's going through a difficult time." There was that phrase again. I loved Debra, but sometimes she resorted to useless clichés. She rested her hand on my arm, adding, "Go talk to her—sister to sister. She needs support right now."

If only Felicity viewed me as a sister and not the villain. Suspicion darkened her blue eyes as I inched my way over to her and silently hugged her. An embrace of solidarity. And a total sham. Glancing away, I felt like my lies flashed across my forehead in neon:

Liar! Traitor! Killer!

"It's going to be okay." My words were empty and I knew it. "Vera will come home. I just know it." But I knew nothing, really, other than I was the reason she disappeared.

"That's what the police tell me, that it's common for teens to run away. And most return home…" Felicity's voice trailed off hopelessly.

"It's true," Oliver added matter-of-factly. "We have to trust the statistics."

"Trust the *statistics*? Our daughter is not a number, Oliver."

"I'm not saying she is, but in today's day and age, kids run off all the time. She could be holing up at a friend's house for all we know."

"What friend? We've spoken to all her friends. The police have too. I can't imagine that she had friends we didn't know about."

"It's possible. Teens keep all kinds of stuff a secret." All eyes pivoted to me. I should have kept my mouth shut.

"Then tell me, what was Vera running from?" Felicity's sharp glare cut into me, and suddenly I wondered if she knew what I had done. Sweat trickled down my armpit, soaking into the fabric of my sweater.

"How about a nice, calming glass of wine?" Debra offered, placing one in Felicity's hand for her, nudging her to sip.

A gulp later, Felicity resumed. "Answer me, Marin. What was so awful that Vera was running from?"

"Maybe it's not what she was running *from* but what she was running *to*," Debra suggested. "Maybe a boy?"

"You think she had a secret boyfriend?" Felicity asked. Another gulp. "Why wouldn't she tell us?"

"Maybe she knew you wouldn't approve. Look, Vera is a smart, sweet girl, but every girl is hiding something. And for good reason. I would hate to know the details of what Ollie and Cody were doing as teenagers." Debra glanced at her boys. "Secrets are part of life."

"Not for a fifteen-year-old *child*, Debra," Felicity snapped. *Mom* had become *Debra*, which meant Debra had crossed a line.

"*Especially* a fifteen-year-old child. Teenagers are the biggest secret-keepers of all."

I couldn't correct Debra that it wasn't necessarily true. Nothing compared to the depth of my secrets.

Felicity ran her hand over her walnut brown hair, noticeably grayer than when I last saw her, and tightened her drooping ponytail. A sole gray strand here and there had become sprinklings of silver. Stress was taking its toll. As her bony wrist dropped back to her side, it flashed against the lamplight. I couldn't help but be awestruck by the diamond bracelet with a striking inset turquoise stone that matched the one she had given Vera for her fifteenth birthday. Turquoise—Vera's favorite color. Vera had paraded around the house showing it off for days afterward. At the time I had wondered how many cars they could have bought for the same price. Now I only wondered if Vera would ever wear hers again.

I glanced at Cody standing alone in the corner of the room, watching me. He looked sad. I ambled over to him.

"I saw you eyeing Felicity's bracelet," he said. He noticed everything and yet nothing. He caught me ogling a shiny bracelet but was clueless to the deep guilt that kept me up at night.

"So what?"

He didn't say anything for a long moment.

"I know you wish I could afford to buy you stuff like that. I'm sorry I'm not a better provider for you, Mare."

I shook my head. "Are you for real with that? You're everything I want, Cody." Almost.

"So you're saying you would never want a gift so extravagant?"

"Nah, it's way too expensive for my taste." I winked at him. It was an easy lie after all of the other bigger lies.

"Riiiight, who needs diamonds when you've got love like ours?" Cody forced a weak grin, his cheeks flushing an embarrassed pink. We both knew love was fleeting, but like the old ad slogan said, a diamond is forever. "One day I'll show them all. I'll be making bank soon, babe."

I hated when he called me *babe*.

Debra announced that dinner would be served soon, begging Felicity to eat a bite—*wine isn't dinner,* she added. "Just a bite to keep up your strength," Debra pleaded, to which Felicity raised her wineglass for a refill.

As we headed into the dining room, Oliver walked in step with us, making the differences between the brothers more noticeable. Where Oliver was six-foot-two and hard-bodied, Cody was five-foot-ten and soft. Where Oliver inherited his mother's thick blonde hair, Cody hid his receding hairline under a baseball cap. Both possessed the same intense blue eyes that burrowed into your soul, but where Oliver's were broody, Cody's were guileless.

Unfortunately I had always been attracted to broody.

"You okay?" I asked Oliver quietly, not wanting to invite the whole family into this conversation.

"To be honest, I'm a mess inside but trying to keep it together for the kids. I don't know how to act when my wife is falling apart, but someone has to be strong and..." He glanced at Cody. "Never mind." His lips curled into a halfhearted smile, then drooped.

"I get it. I never know what to say...or not say. I can't imagine how hard this is for you and Felicity." Except I could imagine it. I imagined it every hour.

"I just wish we had answers."

I brushed my hand against his. "Me too."

The doorbell rang, broadcasting an elegant, eight-note Westminster sequence throughout the house. All our house had was a plain old *ding-dong*.

"I'll get it!" Eliot yelled, racing Sydney to the front door.

Only one person showed up unannounced at the Execution Estate these days, and never brought good news. Eliot hefted open the heavy door and stood in awkward silence. The whole family wandered to the foyer with Oliver at the fore.

"Detective Montgomery." Oliver reached out to shake the plainclothes detective's hand while Felicity tensed up behind him.

I couldn't imagine the thoughts tumble-drying in Felicity's head, but I had an idea just how dreadful they were.

"I'm sorry to bring bad news tonight, but I wanted you to hear it from me first," the detective said. "We've found a body."

A *crash* of stemware, then all heads pivoted as Felicity collapsed to the floor.

Chapter 6
Felicity

Three things occurred every time Detective Courtney Montgomery showed up at my doorstep. First my heart went wild, like an animal clawing its way out of my chest. Then an overpowering nausea erupted in my belly. Lastly my vision blurred, and my world became a Monet painting viewed too closely, sucking me down, down into a whirlpool of gauzy colors. By the time I resurfaced, the panic had drained away but always left a ring of fear.

"You okay, Felicity?" Oliver's arms steadied me, but the room still wobbled.

"I…um, I'm fine." I shrugged his hands off of me and turned to Detective Montgomery. "What were you saying?"

Oliver led the detective through the door like this was a welcome visit with an old friend. I suppose we kind of were, weren't we? We'd spent more time with the detective than with our actual friends, who had slowly disappeared over the months. I suppose there's only so many cancelled play dates and unanswered calls a friendship can suffer before it dissolves. Depression is a lonely beast.

"Oliver." The detective nodded to him, then me. "Felicity." Her eyes skimmed the circle of anxious faces. "I hope I'm not interrupting anything."

I hated that it had come to a first name basis, because it

meant that we still needed the detective's help, and that Vera was still missing. Yet it was a small comfort as well. Because a final goodbye to the detective would mean one of two things: Vera was found alive and was home safe, or Vera was found dead.

"No, not at all, Detective," Oliver said.

"Mind if we have a quick chat?"

"Of course. Come in." Oliver waved the detective further into the foyer.

With crisp footsteps, the detective approached me, the honey-gold glow of the setting sun framing her. Oliver tensed. Debra clutched Joe's hand and whispered for the kids to run along. Cody shuffled awkwardly. All of us waiting, worrying, wondering.

My whole body had rejected seeing her on my porch, now in my home, parting the sea of people standing in the hallway. The perpetual state of alarm had become my default setting. Every phone call a jolt through me; every doorbell a wave of panic. Tonight, especially. For it was the anniversary I didn't want to remember. Six months from the day Vera disappeared.

"How you hanging in there, Felicity?" the detective asked.

"Just trying to get through each day," I said.

"That's all you can do." She patted my arm.

Packed into a gray button-down blouse, Detective Montgomery wore black jeans and flat shoes too manly for her pretty, fresh face. Her golden retriever-blonde hair was tucked into a neat bun. While she had been working with us since day one, I had been less than enthusiastic back then to meet this young rookie. It was a detail I bemoaned often enough, only wanting the best and brightest investigating Vera's disappearance. A seasoned professional. I wasn't going to speak delicately when my daughter's life was at stake. So far I had been right in my harsh judgment, because Vera had yet to be found.

Detective Montgomery swept the room with a glance. "I wish

I had some good news for you, God knows you deserve it, but unfortunately I'm here to speak with you about a possible development. Before you see it on the evening news." Her voice was low and husky, a perfect fit for the man shoes.

My heartbeat instantly stopped or spiked—I couldn't tell which. All I knew was that my body felt cold. "What news?"

"The kids," Oliver interjected. "Can we speak in the kitchen? I don't want the kids to hear something they shouldn't."

"Of course," Detective Montgomery said.

The walk toward the kitchen was a countdown to some unimaginable fate. As we collected around the island where I prepped brownies earlier that day, the detective's eyes settled first on Oliver, then swerved toward me.

"I'm just going to lay it all out. We found a teen girl's body in the Allegheny River, and her description matches Vera's."

My hand involuntarily flew to cover my mouth. A scream sat deep in my throat, coming out as a gasp.

"This doesn't mean it's Vera." Detective Montgomery rested her hand on my shoulder and squeezed.

A couple days into the initial investigation, the first time they found a body that matched Vera's description, I broke down in the detective's arms, breaking all personal space boundaries with it. Since then, I'd come to realize Detective Courtney Montgomery was a toucher. A hugger. An arm-squeezer.

The detective continued, "Remember, we've been through this before in April and it wasn't Vera. Plus, this time the remains are pretty decomposed, so we don't know anything for certain yet. We don't have an ID, but I wanted you to be prepared in case you saw the news tonight. There's a good chance it's not Vera, but in case it is, I wanted you to hear it from me first."

"What makes you say that the description matches Vera's…if it's…decomposed?" Oliver's question stumbled awkwardly from his mouth.

"Based on the height and gender, and hair color. But that's about all we have right now. So like I said, it might not be her."

I felt my heart crack in half. I parted my lips to speak, but the words dropped. I tried to scoop them up, but instead my voice poured out a sob. It physically hurt to imagine my daughter's body rotting at the bottom of a dirty brown river.

The butcher block tilted; the room trembled. I tried to seize the walls, the floor, but they slip, slip, slipped from my grip. I fell downward, barely caught by Oliver's strong arms. They had held me more in the past six months than in twenty years of marriage. It was a shame that our closeness deepened at the cost of our daughter.

I had been so certain Vera was still alive; I could *feel* her lifeblood pulsing through me. She couldn't possibly be gone. Forever. Dead. Hope that she was hiding out somewhere was the only thing keeping me sane, breathing, waking up each morning. Without that hope…what else did I have?

"Mommy," a tiny voice reached me through my weeping, "are you crying because of sissy?" I turned toward Eliot's voice. His hand touched mine. I felt his yearning for me, warm in his palm. His face was at my hip, distorted through my tears.

Oliver knelt down to speak to his son. "Hey, buddy. Mommy's just having a hard day. But you don't need to worry about any of this stuff, okay?"

Eliot wrapped his pudgy arms around his daddy's neck, then recited the same words Oliver spoke to him too many times to count: "It will be okay."

"You know, you're exactly right," Oliver agreed, squeezing Eliot until he popped out a laugh. "Why don't we let Pappy Joe and Nana give you a treat and let Mommy rest a bit."

While Oliver led Eliot back into the living room to taste test cookies—one of the rare things Eliot *would* eat—that Debra had brought for dessert, I found a breath. Found my voice. Found a million questions I needed answered. I speared Detective Montgomery with the first one that came out. "Be honest with me. Do you think it's Vera?"

She shook her head. "I don't know. I wish I could answer that, but until the coroner comes back with a DNA workup and the autopsy report, we have nothing concrete."

"How long will that take?"

"Since the body was found outside of our jurisdiction, it's in the hands of the city police department. But we're offering our resources to help speed things up, and they're keeping me in the loop with their investigation. At this point, let's not assume the worst. We have nothing that shows it's Vera. Nothing."

"What about the clothes? Were there any on the..." I couldn't say *body.* The word refused to drop from my tongue.

"No, nothing identifiable. But—" Her tone resonated with something bad.

"But what?"

Her eyes grazed Oliver as he returned to the kitchen. "We think the body has been in the water for a while. Around six months or so, based on the level of decomposition."

"So it *could* be Vera." There it was. I said it. The worst-case scenario, out in the open.

"Let's not go there just yet. There's still a lot of information that's missing. I'll be back with an update as soon as I have one, but it could be a while before I hear anything. I'll keep in touch. Stay strong for your family, okay?"

"Okay." I hesitated a moment, then blurted out something I instantly regretted. "Are you sure you're doing everything you can? I mean, you are awfully young. Maybe there should be someone a little more...seasoned on the case."

"Felicity...Mrs. Portman...I understand your concern," she said in an even, practiced tone. "It might ease your mind to know that I have a degree in criminal justice, and after completing training at the police academy, I spent four years on the beat as a patrol officer. I had a perfect score on my promotional exam to become a detective. I've cracked numerous high-profile cases. I've paid my dues. Now if you would like me to turn this case over to a certain disheveled, cigar-chomping detective in a rumpled raincoat, I'll see what I can do."

"I'm sorry. I didn't mean—"

"Don't worry, Felicity, I get it all the time." She smiled and gave my arm a squeeze, then turned to leave. *Oh, just one more thing...* " She spun around, brow furrowed, scratching her head.

"Yes?"

She winked. "Just a little *Columbo* humor for you."

After shooting me a reproachful look, Oliver escorted Detective Montgomery to the door. I couldn't face my family waiting in the living room as the full impact of her report belatedly sucker-punched me in the gut. I crashed to the floor, back propped up by the cabinet. When Oliver found me slumped over, sobbing, he knelt beside me.

"Hey, you okay, honey?"

I shook my head. I would never be okay. Not until Vera was home safe. "I can't, Ollie. I just can't."

"Can't what?"

"Can't go through this again. Last time it was unbearable...the wait...to find out if it was her. And what if it is? I can't accept that she's gone."

"You heard what Detective Montgomery said. It's probably not her."

"But what if it is?"

"If it is...then we take it one day at a time."

63

I whipped my head back and forth. "No, it can't be her. I know she's still out there alive. I feel her, Ollie. A mother knows these things."

"I believe you. And I believe Vera will come home." He held me against him, pressed my face against his chest until I could hardly breathe. For a moment I wished he would suffocate me, put me out of this revolving door of misery. Then the moment passed. Vera needed me to hang on. For her.

"Do you want to lie down?" Oliver asked.

I blinked slowly, my eyelids begging to close. "No. I just need a minute." I couldn't rest. Not until Vera was found. Not until I knew for sure. I pushed myself up, with Oliver lifting me, and followed him into the living room. The muted conversation paused as I entered, all heads turning toward me.

"I know you all think I'm delusional," I said to the room. "Clinging to a false hope that Vera will come home soon. But I can't give up faith in that. I need to believe it, even if it's just a lie to myself."

No one knew what to say. But I read them well, because I knew them well. Debra, an empathetic gloss on her eyes. Joe, a concerned dent between his brows. But the look Cody aimed at Oliver, a sharp glass-cutting stare, told me they knew something I didn't. Perhaps I wasn't the only one lying.

Chapter 7
Marin

A girl's body was found yesterday. While the family comforted Felicity like an emotional wagon circle blocking out villainous theories of kidnapping or murder, all I could do was try to hide my guilt. Apparently my acting skills only went so far, because even after she got sloshed, Felicity saw right through my sympathy. And she made sure to voice it, too.

"I know you're hiding something." Drunk Felicity had pulled me aside, whispering these words in my ear last night. *"And when I find out what it is, family or not, I will destroy you if you're the reason my child is missing."*

In that moment I had wanted to reply that I knew about her secrets too, but her tightening grip on my arm silenced me. My flesh still wore the half-moon bruises her fingernails had inflicted on my skin.

Cody and I had returned home well after midnight, the open windows gawking, the front yard yawning sleepily. Trapped in a bedroom dripping with secrets, I shut my eyes to the shadows crawling up the walls. The waxing crescent moon was as bright as a spotlight, and I couldn't sleep, not when Cody's niece could be dead because of me. I flipped through a Rolodex of thoughts, anything to distract me. Lines from various beloved scripts. My boss's ridiculous to-do list. The stack of overdue bills on the dining room table.

My thoughts were once mine. Now they belonged to Cody's family.

A tornado of regret ripped through me. So many shouldn't-haves I lost count. Only busy hands and a caffeinated brain could save me now. I got out of bed, the mattress squealing almost as loud as Cody's snoring, and shuffled downstairs to the kitchen to brew coffee. When you're plagued with OCD, the most relaxing thing in the world is dismantling your entire spare-bedroom-turned-storage-room, followed by putting it all back together in tidy color coordination. Thank you, *The Home Edit*, for the inspiration. Books in rainbow order—not genre, as Cody would have preferred—were neatly lined on the bookshelf against one wall. On the opposite wall I had installed gray wooden cubbies with cream linen baskets, where I borrowed Marie Kondo's *Tidy Up* wisdom to fold and store clothes in colorized harmony. Cody had no dispute left in him about that.

All that was left were a couple shoeboxes full of God knows what. You'd think shoes, but they were mostly filled with scraps of memorabilia. The script from my high school role as Shelby (the first Black lead our director cast, I proudly add) in *Steel Magnolias*. Prom photos. Actress headshots. More headshots. A callback letter for a television series out in Los Angeles that I didn't end up getting. A starred review for one of my performances printed in *The Wilkinsburg Sun*. All the good parts of my life tucked into a couple of dusty shoeboxes.

Picking up the largest shoebox in the stack, a heaviness shifted inside the cardboard, tipping the weight too far to one side. Out fell a pile of old pictures, musty with time and captivity. I picked them up, leafing through them as I dropped each one back into the box. I paused halfway through, catching the sepia hue of a photo taken before my time.

My father and mother, younger than I was now, foreheads

touching, faces beaming, arms entwined. The contrast between Dad's umber skin and Mom's latte white had melted into my pecan flesh. Her eyes, his lips, her smile, his oddly long middle toe. Pieces of them created pieces of me. I saw a blend of my parents in the mirror every day, and missed them every day. I flipped it over and read Mom's handwriting:

Devin and Josie forever (1989)

Setting the photo aside, I continued my trek into the past as I found another picture, newer, this one 1990s bright. There I was, mini-me, baby me, small enough to fit in the nook of my father's arms, my mother beside a picnic basket, the three of us in the backyard of the house I grew up in. I recognized the yellow shed with green trim in the background. My mom leaned back on her elbows, her thin, strict lips turned up in a smile aimed at the sunshine while my father's gaze met the camera.

I traced my father's handsome face with my fingertip. A face made for the big screen. Cheekbones like a tiny mountain ridge. A Denzel Washington smile of perfectly aligned chiclets. My father had shoved most traces of my mother's sun-hating genetics aside, giving me all of the best parts of him.

A surge of emotion tugged on my heart as I stared into the past, back when my family was whole. Like so many young men in the months after 9-11, my father had joined the service in a patriotic fervor and had been killed in action in Operation Enduring Freedom on his first tour of duty. I was nine at the time. We met the military aircraft bearing his remains at Dover Air Force Base in Delaware for the dignified transfer, as the solemn ritual is called, and wept openly. Mom had received a personal letter of condolence from then President George W. Bush; the respectful gesture did absolutely nothing to assuage her grief.

A SLOW RUIN

My father's homecoming, taking place upon the sprawling sylvan grounds of Allegheny Cemetery with its magnificent gatehouses, statuary, and mausoleums, had seemed like a scene out of a storybook to my young and innocent eyes. After a lone bugler played "Taps," the American flag was carefully removed from Dad's casket and two soldiers, in full dress uniform, folded it with mesmerizing precision into the symbolic tri-cornered shape, and reverently presented it to my tearful mother. My gaze strayed to a starling singing in the dense tree canopy. I thought that was my daddy, saying goodbye.

Which reminded me, it had been too long since I visited his grave.

I flipped through several more pictures, each one chronicling a different part of my life. Me sitting on Dad's shoulders with a Kennywood Amusement Park sign above me, hair braided in neat rows and decorated with a rainbow of beads. Me snuggled on Mom's lap as she read from a stolen copy of *A Wrinkle in Time*, the borrower's card tucked inside the front endpaper pocket inscribed with the names of children who had checked it out over the years, the last one being *Josie (smiley face)*. Mom had chuckled over the astronomical library fees she had probably accrued over the years while I was sure the Library Police would show up at any moment and haul her off to jail. Pictures of birthdays, Christmases, Fourth of Julys. Most were of just me, the only child, with Mom presumably behind the lens. But on occasion there was Dad, home on leave, or Mom, on the few occasions she found a third party to hold the camera.

As the years slid by in each image, my mother's pink-cheeked beauty slowly faded. She wore the toll of life as a military wife in the lines of her face. Later, after Dad died in battle, she wore military widowhood on her spirit and mind. She was never the same after my father died. But I liked to think that she was reunited up in heaven with him now, spending endless days in perfect contentment and fellowship, free from all earthly care, with her first love, her best friend. *Devin and Josie forever.*

In the bottom of the box was a picture frame, empty. Holding it in my hand, I couldn't quite remember what picture had been behind the glass. The one of Dad holding me as a newborn? I remembered a baby picture had been here, but which one? And why had I taken it out? It felt important for some reason.

I closed my eyes, pushed my memory into a jog. Flashes of moments flew by. I recalled the day I moved in with Cody, unpacking boxes. This specific box. Opening it and seeing this picture frame. Then I remembered. I knew what had been in the frame. A picture worth a thousand words, blackmail if ever I needed it, a life insurance policy. There was no way I would have removed the picture without knowing where I put it. Somewhere safe. Somewhere hidden. Somewhere Cody would never find it. Because if he ever saw it…I didn't want to think what would happen then.

But if I hadn't removed it, who had? And why?

Footsteps in the hallway yanked me out of the questions fizzing in my brain. Scooping up the pictures, I dropped them haphazardly in the box. Cody peeked around the doorframe just as I shoved the box into a cubby.

"What'cha doing awake, babe?" he asked.

I still hated *babe* just as much as yesterday. I rose to my feet a little too quickly. "Nothing. Just cleaning. I couldn't sleep after everything that happened at family dinner."

"It's pretty awful, isn't it? A body found. Honestly, I don't know how Felicity is still standing."

I met him at the doorframe and slipped under his arm. "I'm done in here. I made coffee, if you want some."

"As long as it's not that flavored crap." He kissed my

forehead.

I shut the door behind me and followed him downstairs to the kitchen. "You didn't happen to go through my stuff in there, did you?" I asked.

"I've learned the hard way never to go near your things, Mare."

It wasn't exactly an answer.

"What's that supposed to mean?"

He chuckled lightly. "You know how protective you are about your possessions. Remember that one time I used your face moisturizer? I got a two-hour lecture about it afterwards. Besides, God knows what you're hiding in there."

I knew exactly what I had been hiding. And it was now missing.

"So no one was in that room?"

"Why are you so worried about it?"

Another non-answer.

"Because I'm missing something that's pretty important to me."

"What—a pair of shoes?"

I closed my eyes and inhaled, summoning patience. A wheeze of air slipped through the window, chilly with night barely hanging on.

"Does it matter what I'm missing? I just need to know if someone was going through my stuff, Cody."

"Hey, calm down." Cody filled my mug with coffee and handed it to me. "Nothing is irreplaceable, Marin. Whatever it was that got misplaced, I'll get you a new one. Unless it's those expensive boots you own. Unfortunately we can't afford to replace those." He poured himself a cup of coffee and sipped. Slurped. I cringed at the sound.

"Not this—this I can't replace. It was something my mother

70

gave me."

"Oh, I'm sorry. I didn't know. What are we looking for? I'll help you find it."

I couldn't involve him. He could never find out. Unless he already knew but wasn't telling me.

"Don't worry about it. It's gone."

"I'm sure whatever it is will turn up."

"I hope so."

"Even if you don't find it, nothing meaningful is ever really gone because it stays right here." He patted my heart, lifted my hand, pressed his lips to my knuckles.

But some things could be torn out of there too. My mother made sure of that before she died.

My pocket beeped, and I pulled out my phone. I recognized the fake name that dropped down from the edge of my screen, then pressed the phone against my thigh.

"Everything okay?" Cody asked. "You don't look so good."

I hadn't realized I'd been holding my breath until the room swayed. I could only imagine what kind of shock passed over my face right now.

"Um, yeah. Just the boss texting me about something I forgot to do."

Cody huffed. "That man has too much time on his hands."

"That's how rich people are, so bored they need to make up stuff to do." I leaned toward the dining room, looking for an escape. "I've got to make a quick call, then I'll make breakfast. Western omelet okay with you?"

"Sounds great." Cody slid a scrutinizing glance over me. "You sure you're okay?"

I grinned, but I didn't know if he was buying it. As he walked out of the kitchen, I swiped to read the text message, and my heart stalled:

A SLOW RUIN

Vera isn't coming back.

Chapter 8
Felicity

The moon and stars were hiding tonight, sweeping the porch in a cosmic blackness. I could barely make out the figure of Brutus lying at my feet, his beefy black body absorbed into the shadow. The night felt bitter, circling my legs, nipping at my lips and ears. I wrapped my blanket tighter around my shoulders, but the air snuck through the folds, drugged with cold.

Tonight would have been book club, I realized as I shifted against the hard seat of the rocking chair. It squeaked against dead silence as I leaned forward, back, forward, back, listening to the nothingness in the yard and beyond, wondering what book the girls had picked to read and discuss for October. A thriller, *Little Does She Know,* I remembered seeing on our Facebook group page. The title resonated a little too much with my own life. Although I read each month's selections, I had stopped attending book club the week Vera disappeared. I cancelled meetups with friends two weeks after that. Church went out the window a couple weeks later.

My faith didn't die quickly. The first few weeks after Vera went missing I attended church and support groups as if her life depended on it. Maybe if I proved to God I was good enough, believed in Him enough, He'd give me my daughter back. But eventually I had lost all hope. I didn't know how other mothers did it, clung to God when they lost a child or faced a life-threatening illness that would leave their motherless children behind. I wanted that kind of relentless trust in a higher power, but I didn't know where to find it or how to cling to it.

After last night's visit from Detective Montgomery, my family was afraid to leave me alone. Unsupervised. Like I was a reckless child running with scissors. One trip and *oops, she cut herself.* Yet even I didn't trust myself alone with such hopeless thoughts. Every night they darkened my bedroom door. Every morning they rose from shallow graves. There were lots of guns in the house, World War I relics Oliver collected over the years. Oliver kept them under lock and key, lest they fall into the children's hands. Or so he said. He was probably more afraid I would take one and *bang*! Instant widower. But I'd never shoot myself; the old gun would probably misfire and instead leave me disfigured for life. Whatever way out I took, it would need to be quick, painless, and guaranteed.

Not that I was plotting my own death or anything. I tried my best to shoo away such impulses.

My neck ached with a shooting pain that jumped from the base of my skull up to my temples. Oliver had given me a relaxing neck and shoulder massage, but despite his best efforts, I didn't sleep. Couldn't rest. So Oliver had sent me upstairs to bed—where I spent a few short hours soaking my pillow with tears while soaking up Vera's journal—while I'm sure my family whispered late into the night assurances that it wasn't Vera's body they found, that everything would be okay.

This morning Debra and Joe showed up before the sun did, ready to prepare a full breakfast that I didn't dare eat. My stomach clenched in painful knots, resisting anything that would sustain me. It was as if my body had already surrendered. By early afternoon a shift change as Cody arrived bringing alcohol and sympathy. No one wanted to speak the words that would surely break me—the police had found a body—or ask me the question I couldn't bear to answer—did I think it was Vera? Only the dogs seemed to respect my self-indulgent torment as they hung back just enough to give me space, but close enough to offer fur-between-my-fingers comfort. Though Brutus, being an American Bully that we saved from a dog-fighting ring, had less fur and more slobber than the average breed and a tail shaped like a lightning bolt. He groaned as he rested his jowls and a string of saliva on my lap, like he understood my sadness. Dogs have a sixth sense, I've always believed.

I sipped my dinner of Kahlua and cream, wondering if Sydney and Eliot were keeping my in-laws awake. Oliver had sent the kids home with his parents to give me—meaning *the kids*—a reprieve. I was difficult to be around; I knew this. What mother wouldn't be while waiting for autopsy results that determined if her daughter was dead? I had come out here on the porch to brood alone, until Cody joined me, sitting in the chair to my left and matching the rhythm of my back-and-forth rocking. A little later Oliver joined us, taking the rocker on my right. Apparently I needed constant supervision.

"Comfy, boys?" I huffed. The brothers made caveman-like grunts of contentment.

The sickly sweet scent of gutted pumpkins and decaying leaves hung in the air, chilly with the promise of winter. A couple of weeks after Vera had gone missing, Oliver had taken it upon himself to start a pumpkin patch for Eliot and Sydney—to distract them, he said, from all the crap. He threw himself into the project, renting a rototiller to break up a garden in the side yard and planting seedlings in mounds according to YouTube instructional videos. He enlisted the kids in the watering and fertilizing, and they took to the task with eagerness and pride.

Sydney was hopeful of growing a humongous pumpkin—as

big as Cinderella's coach, she said—and was no less pleased when the garden yielded nine gorgeous, plump pumpkins. The kids picked their two favorite specimens and, with Oliver's help, carved a pair of jack-o'-lanterns—Syd's with traditional triangular features, Eliot's a rather grotesque attempt at the orange-skinned Thing from the Fantastic Four. The kids' pumpkins, along with several more that hadn't been massacred, graced the front porch. The rest had been left to rot in the patch, becoming midnight snacks for the abundant foxes, opossums, and raccoons. That pumpkin patch had done wonders for lifting everyone's spirits, if only for a while.

While some trees surrounding our yard clung to their fiery oranges and buttery yellows and bloody burgundy, others had already dropped their leaves. Oliver swore he was going to get around to raking them up; our on-call gardener could take care of it, but Oliver claimed it was good therapy. Our property was an island among the suburbs, our house shrouded by six acres of forest, no other dwelling in sight. There was something both eerily serene and terrifying about it. The isolation. The mysteries. The secrets we could bury with no one watching.

We had privacy to spare, but every now and then a curiosity-seeker would defy the wry "Trespassers Will Be Shot, Survivors Will Be Shot Again" sign Cody had erected on our property line at the end of the road, hell-bent on seeing the Execution Estate up close.

Today happened to be one of those days.

A beam of headlights swung across the driveway, and a minute later a rattletrap Corolla with two suicide tires and no hubcaps pulled in front of the porch. Two unkempt slackers in their early twenties got out and stood brazenly gawking at the house in all its grandiose glory.

"Oh no, not again," Oliver grumbled. He stood and walked to

the edge of the porch. "Can I help you…gentlemen?"

"Is this the Execution Estate?" said one of the boys.

"What if it is?" said Oliver with more restraint than I gave him credit for.

"Dude, we just drove up from Perryopolis—"

"And saw Buffalo Bill's house from *Silence of the Lambs*," the other finished. "It was frickin' awesome. But not half as awesome as this joint."

"Yeah, we're on a tour of cool murder manses, and the Execution Estate was next on our list. This place is the *shit*!"

Oliver took a sip of his drink. "Gee, thanks."

"Some couple's gonna turn Buffalo Bill's house into a hotel," the first boy said. "You guys gonna turn this place into a hotel? That would be—"

"Frickin' awesome?" Oliver supplied. "No, no plans like that. Guess you boys didn't see the sign about trespassing."

"Yeah, we saw it. Figured it was a joke."

"No joke," said Oliver. "I've got a loaded shotgun just inside the door. I'm going to walk back to my chair now, and if you two douchenozzles aren't back in your heap by the time I sit down, you'll find out the hard way the real reason this house is called the Execution Estate."

The slackers tripped all over each other clambering back into their clunker and hauling ass down the driveway. Once they were a safe distance away, the driver flipped Oliver the bird.

"You handled that remarkably well," I said.

"Sometimes I wish I did have a shotgun." Oliver sighed, easing into his rocker. "And a trophy room."

"What you really need is a gate, bro," said Cody.

"Yeah. You're probably right."

The evening wore on. On one side of me, Cody attempted tipsy conversation. On the other, Oliver downed glass after glass of vodka, rum and Coke, whiskey. Pretty soon he began to give off a vinegary reek, and I scooted my chair away from him. Bitterness burrowed inside me that he could so easily numb himself on alcohol while I felt every damn emotion.

When Oliver cracked a joke about his newest hire—predictably a bumbleheaded blonde whose breasts got her the job—and Cody laughed, I had had enough. Only yesterday the police had found a body. There would be no laughing today.

"I think it's time to cut you off," I said, standing up and grabbing Oliver's half-full tumbler from his hand.

He grabbed it back, glaring at me. "Who made you in charge? I'm allowed to drink if I want to." His voice was high-pitched with a nasally twang, a sure sign he was drunk.

"Not if you're going to be partying the day after we found out our daughter might be dead."

"Partying? You think I'm partying? We don't all want to steep in the pain like you do, Felicity. I think about our daughter every damn moment of every damn day! For once I'm trying not to think about it. I just want to feel...nothing." He saluted with his glass, sloshing the contents on his shirt.

My mouth dropped open, and the creak of Cody's chair stopped. Not even a cricket dared chirp. Oliver shoved himself up from the rocking chair, dizzily circled to the front door, and slammed it shut behind him. Curse words wafted outside.

Cody placed a hand on my arm. "Felicity, I get what you're going through, you know I do, but you need to relax. Let Oliver process this the way he needs to. Besides, you don't know that it's Vera. It could be anyone."

I yanked my arm away. His touch burned me. "And you don't know that it's *not* her! Don't talk to me like you know what I'm going through—it's not the same. You're not a parent."

Cody shrank away from me, face etched in hurt.

"I'm going to ignore what you just said, because it comes from a place of pain. And for the record, I want to be a father, but unlike you, not all of us can get what we want when we want it."

"You—a father?" I scoffed. "You couldn't even be a loyal husband and brother."

I had no idea if Cody had ever wanted children, or thought about having kids with Marin, but I struck a nerve...and instantly regretted it.

"You're one to talk. It wasn't all me that night. You are just as responsible for what happened as I am."

"I think it's time we called it a night." Rather than letting it all pour out—accusations I knew I'd regret later, a defense that couldn't hold water—I pointed to the porch steps leading out into the night. An owl screeched in agreement.

Cody slid out of his chair, pulling keys from his pocket. "You know—" He paused, one foot on the top step, and turned to look at me. The edges of his face hid in the gloom. "I could have gotten you if I wanted you. Just like I could have destroyed your entire life but chose not to. Remember who you're talking down to."

Then he was gone.

And shame took his place.

I ran inside, bolting the door shut, locking Cody and his words out where they couldn't reach me. Heading upstairs, somewhere in the recesses of the house Oliver's voice echoed, but I couldn't hear him through the blood pounding in my eardrums. As I rounded the corner to my bedroom, I slowed at the doorway to Vera's room, my eyes skimming the black innards.

No, not today, daughter.

Gripping the banister for support, I turned down the hallway, past the stained-glass power couple hidden in gray, into my bedroom, straight to my bedside table. Twisting the lamp on, the room burst into light. I pulled open the drawer, revealing a stack of books—mostly book club to-be-reads—and slid out a small wooden box tucked beneath them. Home to Vera's journal. The vault to her secrets.

From the moment I found it Oliver warned that I should give the journal to the police, and I fervently agreed. In word, but not in deed. What he didn't know was that her possible salvation was my damnation. Within the pages not only was I a monster, but I had committed a heinous crime that would put me behind bars. No one could ever know the truth about my past, about what I had done for the sake of love. Not even Oliver. Especially not Oliver. But Vera had somehow found out.

I had memorized most of the words in my redundant search for a clue that would help me find her. The scribble was full of typical teen grievances, heartbreaks, friend woes, and first loves…except for one. One entry that shook me to my core. One confession that meant she was running for her life, or had died trying. I took the journal out of the box and reread one of the early entries that lingered long after I heard Oliver put the house to bed for the night, doors shutting and deadbolts clicking:

Today Nana told me the story of my great-great-grandmother Alvera Fields, the woman I was named after. It's pretty crazy, actually. She was basically forced into marriage to some rich guy, even though she wanted to be a women's rights activist. But then she had a baby, and a couple months later on April 16, 1910, she disappeared. Her family and the cops thought she was kidnapped and murdered by a group of men who used violence to try to stop the suffrage movement, but it makes me wonder what really happened to her…and it makes me worry about what might happen to me because of what Mom did.

Oliver's family history took a dark turn back then, and all these years later the darkness returned for Vera. It was a haunting, chilling thought—first Alvera disappeared, then her namesake Vera. Both on April 16.

Holy hell. I had never noticed the date until now. Both disappeared on the same exact date, one hundred and eleven years apart. Certainly that couldn't be coincidence. But there was no possible way they could be connected...could they? Whoever had been alive back then was long dead now.

Several entries later Vera mentioned someone named BS. The writing was furious, angry slashes across the page. Though the initials didn't ring a bell, I needed to know who this BS person was that deeply affected Vera. Maybe a friend turned foe who had threatened her.

"No, please tell me you didn't."

I snapped the book shut and hid it behind my leg as if Oliver, standing in the doorway with arms folded judgmentally, hadn't already caught me red-handed.

"I had to hide it from the police," I replied. "You know I did."

"Why, Felicity? You're only going to make things worse by keeping secrets from the people who are trying to find her."

"How can it get any worse, Ollie?"

There was nothing worse than what I had already done before our daughter disappeared.

The Pittsburg Press

Pittsburg, PA
Monday, October 17, 1910

HUSBAND OF MISSING WOMAN THINKS WIFE WAS SLAIN

As a result of the visit that Robert Fields, husband of Alvera Fields, paid to District Attorney Whitman late Sunday night, the district attorney dropped all of his regular duties and confined himself to running down a clue that Fields gave him.

When Mr. Fields was asked about his talk with Mr. Whitman, he said:

"I feared from the first that my wife is dead. Since I publicly expressed this belief, I have received letters convincing me that my theory is correct, which I have communicated to Mr. Whitman. I have given him my word that I will not divulge these letters, but I will say that I have every reason to believe that Alvera was kidnapped on April 16, and afterward murdered. Her body, I am convinced, has been disposed of."

He continued to say:

"The stories that my family has been concealing information are absolutely without foundation. We are in perfect harmony with the police and working with one objective—to find Alvera if she is alive or dead. No one is more anxious than I am to clear up the mystery."

A number of personal advertisements, which have appeared over the signature of "Suffragette C," have been generally credited to one of Mrs. Fields' chums. One of these advertisements appeared in a Pittsburg newspaper this morning. It was as follows:

"Expect you here this week. Affairs will be arranged to your satisfaction. SUFFRAGETTE C."

Chapter 9
Marin

Cody had two tells when something was wrong.

The first was when he came home from his brother's house drunk. *Check.*

The second was when he dredged up past grievances. *Check.*

When the front door slammed shut, shaking the bones of the house, and Cody muttered his way throughout the first floor about being the only family member with any sense, I had a feeling he'd crossed out both on the list. *Checkmate.*

"They underestimate me, but I'll show them," he grumbled somewhere in the...kitchen? "They think they're better than me? They're nothing. Nothing!" His argument with himself had reached the foot of the stairs and grew louder as his footsteps rumbled closer. Closer. Until they were stomping into the bedroom where I was lying on the bed reading by lamplight. He moved with a lumbering gait.

"I hope you got an Uber," I said.

"I'm not drunk, Marin. I only had one beer."

"Just one?"

"Fine, two. But I swear I'm not drunk. I'm just pissed."

More like piss drunk. But whatever. He was home. "Another fun family get-together?" I smirked.

Cody scowled.

"I'm so sick of being treated like garbage by them. You

know, I was always the smart one. Oliver just got handed everything to him while I worked my ass off. Fuckin' assholes—all of them!"

I had forgotten about his third tell: swearing like a sailor.

I set the book down and turned on my side, propping my head up on my hand.

"Want to talk about it?" I offered.

I had no desire to put my meager relaxation time on hold to hear all about the competition that constantly brewed between the Portman brothers. Oliver had clearly won before the race even began. He was gorgeous, a brilliant businessman, rich…Mommy's favorite. It was obvious how Debra doted on him like he was a prince, with Cody the lowly serf. But what did it matter as long as Cody was happy? The whole sibling rivalry was so three decades ago.

"No…you don't want to hear about it. You look…busy." He gestured to the paperback beside me, a tattered pink dahlia splashed across the cover.

"I'm never too busy for you." I patted the mattress. "Come. Vent. I'm all yours."

He sat, turned to me. "It feels wrong bitching about my family when your family was crazier than mine."

Crazy. An awful, empty word that reduced people to objects, good or bad, normal or deviant. Was that all I was? An insulting, outdated label pegging me mentally ill and therefore damaged goods? Worthless? Capable of any number of horrors? I felt like the attention-seeking wannabe actress who would do just about anything to catch the spotlight.

A memory with my mother flitted into my mind, then hit me with a closed fist. Our last words before she died. How she pleaded for my forgiveness. How I had called her a *crazy*, selfish, horrible person. My mother had morphed from the hero in my life into the villain, but I couldn't pinpoint exactly when the transition started. Sure, I had been angry with her for letting the darkness win and take over after Dad died, the lurid sadness that held her captive. All that time I thought she was crazy, but maybe I was the crazy one. Crazy for not understanding her, or loving her through the struggle. Crazy for ever judging another person's crazy.

I wanted to say all of this to my husband, but I didn't.

"Well, if you change your mind, I'm here to listen," I said instead.

"I'm going to jump in the shower. I'm too mad to talk about it right now. You wouldn't understand anyway. You never had asshole siblings or asshole parents who always think the worst of you."

Not ones that I cared to talk about, at least. Cody knew the basic details, like my dad's unexpected passing when I was nine and losing my mother when I turned thirteen. While their deaths weren't directly connected, they sort of were. From the moment Dad's remains returned stateside from Afghanistan in a flag-draped transfer case, Mom had become a different person. Cue her self-medication, and it wasn't hard to link the cause and effect. Some wounds simply didn't heal, no matter how much time you gave them.

While Cody had probed me for more backstory throughout the years, I had blotted out most of my troubled past—especially the dark spots. There were too many of those stains, and they would have scared him away. I couldn't risk losing the one good thing I had found, not after all I'd already lost.

Except for one tiny confession, one single slip of the tongue. By that fateful summer night we'd been dating for two months. His arm slung around me, my side pressed up against his in the backseat of his car as we watched Spike Lee's *Jungle Fever* at one of the last drive-ins still standing in Western Pennsylvania. My dad had been a huge admirer of the trailblazing Black auteur's work, and when I'd turned old enough to appreciate the nuances of Spike's movies, I'd become a student of them too. The Starlight Drive-In was hosting a week-long retrospective of Spike's joints (as he waggishly called his films), and that fateful Wednesday *Jungle Fever*, a provocative romantic drama about an interracial affair between a Black man and an Italian-American woman, was on the bill. Although the racial roles were reversed, it paralleled to Cody's and my relationship, which I thought made the film a must-see together.

Despite the movie's deadly serious tone, we'd both gotten a little silly from too much wine. When stars Wesley Snipes and Annabella Sciorra started having hot sex on a desk, Cody joked, "I got jungle fever, baby, and there ain't no cure." I turned to him, smirking, and he'd stolen a kiss. Realizing I was turned on as much as he was, I coaxed his tongue into my mouth.

For the first time it just felt so *right* being with Cody. He felt like *the one*. Wrapped in each other's arms, kissing softly, Cody had taken his finger and written *I love you Mare* on the steamed-up back windshield.

I felt like I could tell him anything. *Everything.*

So I did.

I had said too much, though at first I didn't think Cody heard me. He remained silent. I had expected a reaction, a dismissal, anything but nothing. Yet he acted like what I confessed was the most normal thing in the world.

So I had said it again, making sure he heard me. Dumb, I know. But I had never told anyone my terrible secret, and it felt freeing to release it out into the wild.

"Did you hear what I said? I killed my mother, Cody."

Our conversation came to a standstill for a long minute, and then he kissed me. "I heard you, Marin. And it's okay. Whatever you did in your past, it's not who you are now."

And that was that. No explanation needed. Or so I thought back then.

It was that one too-comfortable moment that brought my entire house of cards tumbling down. A peek into my shadows that would become my demise. Because it remained a part of me.

In retrospect, telling Cody was a mistake, a huge one. I was pretty sure he in turn told his brother and Felicity. I didn't have concrete evidence of this, but when Vera disappeared I suddenly saw judgment in their eyes—that I was the "crazy one" in the family. Capable of anything…like kidnapping their daughter. Or murder. It wasn't a far stretch after what I'd already done.

While Cody stripped out of his clothes and bumbled into the shower, I glanced at my phone on my bedside table, as if the text I had received earlier burned a green thought bubble on the screen and in my head:

Vera isn't coming back.

It wasn't supposed to happen this way. It was never supposed to come to this. Vera was never supposed to disappear. Now I knew for sure that I was the reason she was missing. What I couldn't figure out was why.

I needed answers, and there was only one person who could give them to me. Sliding off the bed, I grabbed my phone and shuffled to the window. An endless row of brick houses depressingly identical to mine stared back at me. My finger trembled as I found the number and pressed the call button. This was my last chance, the only person who could help me bring back Vera. After a single ring it went to voicemail. Of course it wouldn't be so easy. I decided to leave a message.

"Hey, we need to talk," I whispered. "Please. Call me as soon as you get this. It's urgent."

As I ended the call, Cody's voice seized my last bit of nerves. "What's so urgent at"—his gaze slid to the alarm clock—"two in the morning?"

The phone slipped from my hand, clattering on the floor. There was no way out of this now.

Chapter 10
Marin

The hum of the lawnmower outside my bedroom window pulled me awake. I turned over and saw the clock blink a new minute: 8:06 a.m. My first thought was last night's fight with Cody after I lied my way through an explanation about the "mysterious phone call" I had made. Eventually I convinced him it had to do with an errand my boss had asked me to run that I had forgotten about. He didn't press for details after that, but I felt the lie widen between us as we climbed into bed, his body nearly hanging off the mattress to avoid even the slightest waft of heat from mine.

This morphed into my second thought, the truth about my phone call. And the text about Vera. I was as empty of answers as I had been last night, but not for long. I knew where to find them.

I got out of bed and peeked between the blinds. Two stories below, Cody tramped back and forth across the yard, shirtless and glistening, earbuds pumping old-school Eminem into his brain. I could tell by the lyrics he rapped. Or at least tried to rap.

Neatly cut rows trailed him as he pushed the mower through the tall grass. If I hurried, I could make it there and back before he finished the backyard and still have time to serve breakfast and an apology.

With heavy Pittsburgh traffic, it took over half an hour winding through the rolling, twisty hills that made driving in this city a nightmare when I finally pulled into the driveway of the

Grandview Avenue house atop Mount Washington. I barely appreciated the view that lured tourists to this spot, paying five bucks a head to ride the oldest and steepest incline in the United States up the sharp mountain for a sweeping panorama of the Steel City.

Across the street from the house, and miles below, mid-morning sun warmed the city alive. The sparkling landmark skyscrapers of the Golden Triangle sat nestled at the point where the Allegheny and Monongahela rivers met to create the mighty Ohio, where fifteen bridges crisscrossed the scene like yellow spokes.

Although the beauty of the sights escaped my accustomed eyes, the history had always fascinated me. From childhood *Mr. Rogers' Neighborhood* was a hometown favorite, and the 1983 flick *Flashdance*, following the trials and tribulations of aspiring ballerina Jennifer Beals, was a guilty pleasure. Steelworker by day, exotic dancer by night—really? The movie was so corny it was cool, but the music was electrifying, and who could forget that iconic scene where Beals' underdog character, Alex, gets doused with a bucket of water and beats the living daylights out of an innocent chair? Too funny. (Knowing that Beals had an African-American father and an Irish-American mother always stoked me too.)

Pop culture touchstones aside, the firetruck red incline making its ascent before me was a rightful bragging point. Once upon a time these machines carried passengers and freight between the coal mines, local neighborhoods, and rail yard. Even in our high-tech world of drones and 3D printers and augmented reality, it knocked me out that 1870s ingenuity had created this mechanical marvel.

I parked and walked up the mildew-gray brick walkway that had at one point matched the yellow brick house. I gripped the railing as I mounted the porch steps, feeling a dusting of orange rust clinging to my palm. The porch was swept clean, with only a rectangle of discolored concrete where the welcome mat should have been.

Knocking on the door, I heard nothing but an echo of empty rooms. No sound within. No television blaring against hard-of-hearing ears. No *clack* of a walker across the floor. Where was he?

I jiggled the doorknob. Locked. Glancing around me, the place looked abandoned. While well-kept, the grass was yellow and dead, the earth dusty dry. The handmade Adirondack chair that had sat in the same corner of the porch for over a decade was gone. From the state of things, it looked like no one had been home in ages.

Lawn debris crunched underfoot as I headed to the living room window and pressed my hand against the glass, peering inside. The hardwood floors were bare. The outdated furniture gone.

I had been worried before. I was petrified now.

Never had he disappeared like this. And certainly not without telling me. I needed answers, and I wouldn't find them here. My brain buzzed with questions. The only thing I could do now was head home.

Unless...there was one thing I could try.

I rounded the corner of the house heading straight for the back door. I stretched on tiptoes, feeling my way across the alligatored doorframe, through grime, bits of leaves, and dead insects—at least I hoped they were dead—until my fingertip touched cold metal.

The house key he had forgotten about. I slid the key into the lock, twisted, heard the welcoming *click*. The door swung open on a warm breeze. I pushed the light switch up with the heel of my hand, but nothing happened. Had his electricity been turned off? That's when I noticed the utter absence of sound. No purring appliances. No hissing vents.

"Hello?"

My voice helloed back at me. There wasn't a scrap of paper or a ball of dust anywhere, only a tiny cosmos of particles dancing in patches of sunlight pouring in through the bare windows. None of this made sense. My thoughts hit trench bottom as confusion and fear mixed and mingled. This house had always been Fourth of July with colorful banter and explosive laughter. Now it was funeral silent. Where had it all gone?

As mid-morning sun striped across my face, I knew it was time to go. Cody was probably already wondering…worrying…panicking over where I was. By the time I got home, Cody had passed all three stages straight into anger.

"Care to explain where you've been all morning?" he yelled as I thought I had slipped through the door undetected.

"I'm sorry, honey. I wanted to run out to visit my dad's grave, but you were mowing the lawn so I didn't want to bother you." *So sorry, Dad, to use you like that*. It was the only excuse I could think of.

Cody pulled me into a hug. "Oh, Mare. Now I feel like a jerk for getting mad at you. It's just…you've been gone for hours and your phone was shut off, so I had no idea where you went. And with Vera missing…I don't know. Guess my thinking's a little morbid these days. I thought you were dead on the side of the road or something."

"Well, as you can see, I'm alive and well." I grinned up at him.

"Please don't scare me like that again."

"Okay, I promise." I pressed my ear to his chest, listened to his heart thump back at me.

He ran his hand over my hair. "I can't shake this feeling like you're hiding something from me, Mare. I wish you'd tell me what it is. Because whatever it is, we can figure it out together."

I wrapped my arms around him, held him tight.

"What if some things can't be figured out, Cody?"

What if some things were just too horrible that if they ever came to surface, they'd destroy everything?

Chapter 11
Felicity

I'm freaking out and don't know what to do. BS warned me. Told me something bad would happen if I wasn't careful. Guess who wasn't careful? Me. I should have known not to trust anyone. Not my friends, not my family. They only hurt me. BS told me there's no way out of this but one. One that will kill me. And I have a bad feeling it's only gonna get worse. Way worse.

Things couldn't get much worse than they were right now. Every breed of worry attacked my mind. Cody wasn't speaking to me, which was probably for the best after what he did. What *we* did, if I was being honest with myself. Oliver was angry at me for lying to him about keeping Vera's journal instead of turning it over to the police. But turning it over meant turning myself in. It wasn't an option…was it?

I had weighed that choice on every scale. If turning myself in could guarantee Vera's safe return, I would have done it. But there were no guarantees, and I wasn't much use to anyone behind bars. Who would ensure Sydney was properly cared for? Her health was worsening by the day. I could see it in the pallor of her skin, the sluggishness that overtook her by late morning, the whole-body swelling. And Vera, the only one who could save us all, remained gone.

All of our lives hung on Vera. The worst part about it? I

wanted to heft that cross on my own shoulders but couldn't.

The first time I came across the letters *BS* in Vera's journal, I thought it stood for *bullshit*. I'd never heard her swear, but by age fifteen I imagined the arsenal of swear words at her disposal. But only after I pored over the entries and dissected them did I realize BS was a person, a friend in the beginning, an enemy by the end. Was BS capable of hurting Vera? At first glance it seemed unlikely. The more I rearranged and analyzed the parts, the more likely it became.

Top priority: find out who BS is.

Based on the sheer number of mentions of this elusive BS, clearly it was someone important in Vera's life. BS showed up on almost every page toward the end. I thought I had known all of Vera's school friends, but apparently not. Someone not from school? And if not, where had they met?

It couldn't be someone online. She knew better. I had jackhammered the perils of catfishing into her skull from the day we handed Vera her cell phone: be alert, be wary, trust no one. That fifteen-year-old girl you met on Snapchat who plays the clarinet, loves biology, and attends private school? In reality she's a fifty-year-old orthodontist who lives in his mother's basement and collects used retainers from his victims. Don't trust anyone to be who they say they are, I repeated again and again.

Ironically, in all the times I flashed this *Warning: Danger Ahead* at her, I never once considered myself the danger. But I was not the good person I thought I was. And Vera had found that out.

For weeks I scoured social media, wondering where my caring daughter was within the apathetic online persona she had created, and how BS fit into her life. I had lost track of the various apps that Vera used, and without her phone, I'd never be able to find out. Instagram. Snapchat. TikTok. The ones I *did* know about weren't helpful. There were just too many variables to narrow my search down to two initials. That wasn't including the apps I didn't know about. With new ones hitting the market every day, I had no idea what was *in* with the cool kids. The fact that I used that old-lady phrasing—*what's in with the cool kids*—showed just how little I knew about the modern teen or their social media hideouts.

School was the first logical place I could imagine Vera befriending someone, so I'd start by digging into her latest yearbook. I shivered at the thought of going into the room where we kept them. The creepy library, with its original built-in floor-to-ceiling bookcase that wrapped the entire way around the room. It could have been magical, if not for the past entombed in that room.

Daunting as the room was, Vera, the bookworm, couldn't stay away from it, lured by the impressive collection of rare volumes that had belonged to the previous owner, a bibliophile by avocation, a wealthy and powerful literary agent—representing some of the top authors in horror, fantasy, and science fiction—by vocation. The books had come with the house, because the library had remained untouched since the murders; no heirs of the family had wanted them, considering them cursed.

It happened in the early 1980s. According to the estate manager, it was the custom every Friday evening for the family to convene in the library, where the father would read by firelight a classic fantasy tale to his children, gathered round the hearth, while his wife crocheted. On this particular Friday, a bitterly cold November night, the live-in estate manager bid the family goodnight before taking the weekend off to visit relatives downstate. As he later noted to the police, tonight's classic was an Unwin & Allen first edition of *The Hobbit.*

When the estate manager returned the following Monday

morning and found the front door unlocked and the bedrooms unslept in, he immediately began a search of the house, starting, naturally, with the library. The door was closed, which was not unusual, as the library was climate controlled and humidified for the protection of the rare books. When he opened it, he reeled at the ghastly scene before him, and clutched the jamb to break his fall.

The entire family was dead, shot execution-style in the torso. Their bodies were arranged on the floor with their arms and legs spread, feet touching, to form a crude star shape. Upon each of their faces an open book, seemingly randomly chosen, had been laid. Despite his revulsion, the estate manager's curiosity got the better of him, and he peeked under the book resting on the father's face. The murderer had taken a trophy—the right eye; he had done the same with the other victims, the investigation later revealed.

The estate manager had picked up the library telephone to summon the police when he heard a plaintive wail, and looked up to see the family cat, perched upon a shelf beside a bust of Edgar Allan Poe, tail puffed up, pupils gigantic with fright. It was later determined the cat had been shut up in the charnel house all weekend, and had likely been the only witness to the murders. And when it had gotten hungry it had…

Suffice it to say, the tabloids went into gory detail about this grisly aspect of the case, which remained unsolved. Nothing had been stolen, not even a single priceless book. The bizarre clues became the subject of countless sensational articles, books, and documentaries. But the killer remained at large and had not struck again, to anyone's knowledge—at least not in the same confounding and gruesome manner.

The parallels to my family were inescapable…mother, father, three kids…a cat that acted possessed. I tried not to think about it.

The horror that lived in the library was how we afforded this renovated monstrosity of a home in excellent condition on six private acres. When no one else would touch it, we stole it. *You folks got the deal of a lifetime,* our agent congratulated us. Under Pennsylvania law, he was under no obligation to divulge that a death had occurred in the house, much less a mass murder. But he didn't need to; just about everyone in Pennsylvania—Pittsburgh especially—of a certain age was aware, at least to some degree, of the horror that had transpired. Oliver and I certainly knew from the umpteen stories we'd heard since our youth, and we weren't about to pass up this opportunity of a lifetime. We should have known that living in the Execution Estate would have its downside. Like the ever-present sense of watchful eyes beyond the grave. Or the rooms we gave extra distance to. Rooms like the library.

The two flights of stairs moaned as I mounted each step slowly, stealthily, on high alert for any ghosts wandering the hall. Inching down the hallway with Vera's journal tucked under my arm, I thought I saw a stooped, wizened figure in a drab olive-green wrap creeping toward me. I gasped and took a cautious step backward before I realized it was only my reflection in the full-length mirror on the far wall. I didn't like the woman I saw, old and worn—resembling more a slovenly maid than the grand lady of the house. A woman with arms thickened from carrying three babies, hands chapped from endless chores. My brown flap of hair, striped with gray, desperately needed a trim as it limply framed my face, curled around my ears. Not that I had ever been a beauty queen, but the lines spoking my eyes hid any vestige of my youth.

Wasting no more time than necessary, I speed-walked to the bookshelf where we kept the yearbooks dating back from kindergarten onward, organized by year. While Vera hadn't officially finished tenth grade, the school mailed me the yearbook, with a kind note that the whole school was praying for her safe return home. The administration had even passed the yearbook along to Vera's classmates for her friends to sign. I appreciated the kind words and thoughts and prayers back then, back when I still had faith that God answered prayers.

I wasn't sure the yearbooks would offer much help, since the kids had been learning remotely for half the year and few pictures had been submitted. But I hoped to at least find a name and face that possibly matched BS's identity. The books were at knee height, so I leaned down to read the years printed on the spine, running my finger across each once. At the end of the row, I immediately noticed a telltale gap where the newest yearbook should have been. Had I misplaced it, like I did my food and coffee? As spooky as the library was, it just hadn't jumped off the shelf on its own (I hoped).

Moving on, I pulled out the yearbook from two years ago, pre-COVID, back when life and school still resembled normalcy. With legs folded, I sat on the hard floor, set Vera's journal aside, and flipped through the yearbook pages, my own high school memories loitering in the background. Starting with Vera's ninth-grade class, I searched every BS name in her entire grade and came up with no hits. Perhaps she'd known the person before starting high school and he or she was in the grade below her. I doubted my shy little Vera would have befriended someone in a grade above her, but I'd search the entire school if I had to. By the second page of tenth graders, I found a Brittney Sawyer, a Brandy Shoemaker, and a Blythe Sampson. No boys had the initials, which was both a curiosity and a relief.

With three top choices to narrow down, I had no idea which girl it could be. Brittney, wearing glasses and a modest turtleneck, appeared the most likely match—the kind of wholesome, bookish girl Vera would gravitate toward. Brandy, with tidy rings of blonde and flawless makeup, proudly thrust her perky breasts toward the camera, plastered-on smile exuding mindless enthusiasm. She had to be a cheerleader. Definitely not Vera's crowd. Next up was the incongruously named Blythe, who looked anything but cheerful and pleasant. Purplish-black hair styled in bat wing bangs. Extravagant vampiress eyelashes framing lime green eyes. Matte black lips curled in a seductive smirk. Pentagram hoop earrings and spiked choker. Matching leather and lace top. Clearly this girl was making A Statement—though I wasn't sure what it was. One glare from Goth Girl would have sent Vera running. Brittney, it was.

What now? I had a teenager's name, but not her parents'. Or her address. Or any other information about her. How did I find out who her parents were since teenagers' names weren't listed online? I knew this because I had searched; kids' information was locked up tight. And even if I was able to locate Brittney's parents, could I show up unannounced at her house and ask her what happened to Vera? I had no idea what I was supposed to do with this tiny morsel of information…if it was even that.

I could present this information to the cops, but they'd want to know how I came up with Brittney as a potential lead. It wasn't like I could say her name suddenly came to mind after six months. And turning over the journal to the cops, well, I already decided that wasn't an option. Maybe Vera could advise me. I opened her journal back to the place where she first mentioned BS, back when BS was a friend while Mommie Dearest was becoming the enemy. Her words were so angry at me. Unforgiving. Vengeful.

BS is the only friend I have. The only person I trust. I used to think my mom was that person, but all she does is lie and hurt people. One day it'll catch up to her. I hope it hurts when it happens. She deserves it. At least I have my art and BS now.

Her *art* and *BS*. I wondered if they had met in art class. My gaze skipped between yearbook and journal and back again, page after page, leaping between pictures and words. Then I stalled on a yearbook page. There was my beautiful daughter, easel in one hand, brush in the other, surrounded by smiling faces. All but one. The girl standing beside her. Goth Girl.

Below the picture was a caption listing their names:

...Vera Portman, Blythe Sampson...

So BS was Goth Girl. I hadn't seen that alliance coming. It was a hard friendship to make sense of. Vera was a band nerd, a bookworm, a goody-goody. Blythe looked like a rebel, a reject, a troublemaker. But maybe that's what attracted Vera to her polar opposite in the first place—someone different. Someone who made her feel alive. Once upon a time I could understand that. Once upon a time I lived it, I was that Good Girl Turned Rebel. But I was more reasonable now. Perhaps Vera had found her rebellious streak after all. I just wished it wouldn't have cost everyone so dearly.

In the upper corner of the page was Goth Girl's doctorly scribble:

Thx for being my biotch. U always got my back, and I always got urs. If u ever need help with u-know-what, I'm here for u. Ur gonna survive, and I'll be the biotch standing with u. – BS

Seeing the words sent a wave of sadness through me. A tear trickled down my cheek, falling onto the page, turning Blythe's note into a swirl of ink. It broke my heart that Vera felt the need to hide this from me. What else had she been hiding? And what was *you-know-what* referring to? What was Vera trying to "survive"? I couldn't stomach the thought that my daughter kept secrets—monstrous ones she needed to *survive*—from me. Sure, every kid keeps certain things from their parents. Like a phone call snuck in after bed on a school night. Or the money missing from Mom's wallet to buy that cropped top she forbid you from wearing. Or a secret belly button piercing. But this sounded so much more ominous than smoking a joint at a party she snuck out to attend.

I had the prickly sensation that something was watching me. Eliot would say it was my Spider-Sense tingling, warning me of danger. Go! Leave! Never come back! Slowly I got to my feet and turned around, scanning the room until my eyes lit on the rolling ladder. My gaze traveled up the steps to the top rung, bathed in shadow at the bookcase's summit. All at once the ladder zipped along the shelves with a terrible racket, just as a vague shape, yowling like a demon, leapt down and skidded across a reading table, scattering books on the floor.

"Meowzebub!" I yelled. "You scared the life out of me!" *Which is probably what you intended, you hell-spawn,* I thought.

The cat regarded me with contempt for a second, then took off, bunching up the floor rug before sailing through the door with another blood-curdling wail.

I was done with the murder room. Taking the yearbook with me, I scuttled downstairs as fast as my feet would take me without tripping and breaking my fool neck, as if hands were about to reach up through the floorboards and grab my ankles. I headed for Oliver's office and fell into his leather desk chair, letting the tension dissolve into the lambskin. His laptop was open, and a touch of my fingertip brought it back to pixelated life.

Opening up Google, I searched for *Blythe Sampson.* Nothing. Of course an underage girl wouldn't be listed on Google, unless it was for making the news for a major athletic or academic accomplishment—or for murder. Blythe looked more capable of the latter, but I was relieved to see her name wasn't coming up for dismembering and eating her mother. Here I was, stuck at an informational impasse.

Searching the public records for county property taxes under her last name was easy enough, but there were at least a dozen families with the Sampson surname. There was no way to tell which was Blythe's family. I'd need to find another way. But how?

I was screwed.

Unless…

I pulled out my phone and opened my Instagram account, typed in Vera's profile, then searched for Blythe under Vera's followers. Hello, @blythesampson4ever. But I needed more. Another flick of the finger and I popped over to Blythe's profile and checked her followers, searching for anyone with the last name Sampson. Most of her followers only used a first name—which I had in fact insisted Vera do to protect her identity—a security measure that was now biting me in the ass. Without a last name, I had no idea if any of Blythe's followers was a mother or aunt or distant relative.

I considered going through every single post to see who liked each one, then searching each name, cross-checking the profiles for pictures of Blythe and any information I could gather. But there were hundreds of posts, hundreds of likes, hundreds of possibilities. And it still wouldn't guarantee that I'd find her parents. Scrolling through her feed feeling defeated before I'd even begun, I searched under the date for Mother's Day. Score! I found a post of Blythe as a young girl hugging what appeared to be her mother. A name was tagged in the post: @mamabeartoblythe

Well then. Not so defeated after all.

I clicked on the profile and instantly saw an older version of Blythe. Raven-black hair. Bright blue eyes. Beautiful but dark. Tattoos covered every inch of skin beneath her black tank top, dragons climbing up one arm, skulls glaring from the other. A weeping rose circled her neck like it wanted to choke her. Two teardrops were inked beneath the corner of her eye. Did this mean she had murdered two people? What the heck kind of family had Vera gotten herself involved in? I could see where Blythe found her moody fashion inspiration. The name associated with the account was simply Chandra.

I returned to my county search records and typed in *Chandra Sampson*. In a few minutes I retrieved a name and address for the not-so-elusive-after-all BS—Blythe Sampson. Best friend turned worst enemy. It was time to find out what happened that led to their rift and exhume the secrets the girls had buried.

Chapter 12
Felicity

I did some digging into my great-great-grandmother's life today. I wish I had half the courage Alvera had. Once she was mugged while transporting fundraising money raised for women's suffrage and was left for dead on the street. You'd think that would scare her to stop her activism, right? Not her. Instead she posted on every newspaper in the area a reward for whoever brought in her attacker so that she could face him in person. Guess who ended up getting caught and put in jail? Alvera Fields is my hero.

I tucked Vera's journal back into my bedside table, then hustled from the living room, to the kitchen, to the foyer searching for my keys as I heard the grandfather clock *tick tick tick* down the precious minutes I had left. My body prickled. My fingers twisted. My foot tapped. My nerves sizzled. I could feel the pent-up excitement begging for a release. Now I knew how Meowzebub felt when she got a bad case of the zoomies. I'd been counting down all afternoon for the chance to sneak out and visit Blythe Sampson, watching the clock until the magic hour: time to drop off Eliot and Sydney for their martial arts class.

Neither child had ever once shown interest in karate until Oliver featured *The Karate Kid* for Friday Family Fun Movie Night. Friday turned into a Saturday *The Karate Kid* marathon, including the *Cobra Kai* spinoff series on Netflix. *"Syd needs some semblance of normalcy,"* Oliver had insisted. Which was true. When the instructor happily agreed to ensuring Sydney would have plenty of water and breaks, we ordered her uniform— or *gis,* as Eliot reminded me every time I "said it wrong"—and we signed them up. By *we* I mean me, because while Oliver was the dreamer, I was the doer. Those always seemed to be our repeat roles: Dad introduces the fun idea, and Mom gets stuck driving the kids all over God's creation.

After chauffeuring the kids to karate, and reminding Sensei Lee about Sydney's water break and rest schedule, I stopped by the house to grab a knife from the kitchen drawer. I had no idea what kind of person Blythe was, if she was *packing heat*—did anybody say that these days besides uncool moms like me?—but I wasn't taking any chances. If she was responsible for Vera's disappearance, I wanted to be prepared to defend myself. I had exactly one hour to kill, no pun intended. Enough time to drive over to Blythe's house and make it back in time to pick up the kids from karate.

As long as nothing went wrong.

I slid the knife in my purse and found my keys splayed on a French provincial-style mid-century table I had found at a local antique shop. The Italian marble top felt cool against my touch. I carefully shut the front door behind me with a soft *click.* Oliver would never have approved. Certainly not if I told him I was interrogating a teenage kid and bringing a weapon with me. While he preferred to leave everything up to the cops to deal with, I had done that for six long months, forced to wait through body recoveries and autopsy reports while Vera could still be out there. No more waiting. I was getting my own answers this time.

Besides, Blythe was a teenager. How dangerous could she be?

As I unlocked my car door, the crunch of gravel stopped me. I glanced at the pebbled parking area, watching Cody's red truck pull to a stop. I didn't feel like dealing with him right now, not after last night's fight. When he pulled up, blocking my car in, he gave me no other choice. He rolled down his window and leaned out.

"Got a minute?" he asked.

"Not really. Mind moving your truck?"

"In a minute. First I wanted to apologize for last night."

"Apology accepted. Now can you move…please?" I was down to fifty-six minutes.

"Where are you heading off to in such a hurry?" Cody asked.

"If you must know, I need to run a quick errand." I opened the car door and sat, leaving it hanging open. "When you go inside, can you let Oliver know that I'll be back in a bit? He should be wrapping up his work call shortly."

"Actually, I was hoping we could talk, Felicity. Mind if I join you?"

I really did mind. "I'd rather not, Cody."

"Please? I don't like how we left things."

I didn't like how any of my life left things, but I didn't get a say in it. But the least I could do was repair things with my brother-in-law. I was well aware of how much Cody was going through, and I couldn't deprive him of the one thing he needed right now—a friend.

If only it was that simple between us.

"I could really use the distraction today. It's been…one of those days," Cody added.

I understood what he meant.

"Fine. But you're not allowed to say anything about where we're going. And you definitely can't tell Ollie."

"I promise." He parked his truck and jumped into the

passenger seat while I set my navigation for Blythe's address.

"So where are we headed? Some top-secret government compound?" Cody smiled, but it looked weak, his face sallow.

"No, we're going to visit one of Vera's friends."

"Felicity." That one word held a heap of disapproval. "Are you sure this is a good idea?"

"I don't care. It's the only lead I have, so I'm going to follow it. The police have pretty much given up doing anything to help bring her home, so I'm doing it myself."

He knew me long enough to understand there was no convincing me otherwise.

I glanced over at him, his cheekbones more distinct than usual and the pockets beneath his eyes moody gray. "Are you okay?"

He shrugged. "Hanging in there like everyone else. And hoping this doesn't blow up in your face."

"How can it get any worse than it already is, Cody?"

"I guess it can't."

Of course it could, but I couldn't admit that out loud.

I spent the drive anticipating what I would say when we got there, while Cody spent it scanning radio channels, unable to settle on one. I was glad for the company. I couldn't have done this alone.

When we pulled up to the house, I double-checked the address against my navigation. This couldn't be right. Based on what I had seen online of Blythe and her mother, hardcore and tattooed with their dark makeup and dark hair and dark moods, I expected something...different. Not this flower-bedecked garden, pots brimming with mums, aster, and marigolds. Two beautifully carved pumpkins sat like sentries at the top of the porch steps. An autumn-themed flag waved in the breeze, attached to this homey cookie-cutter house in a cookie-cutter subdivision full of cookie-cutter families.

"We're here." I turned to Cody and sucked in a heart-steadying breath.

The image of Blythe's mother's teardrop face tattoos flashed in my mind, something I'd read somewhere was a badge of honor for murder. Or was it for jail time? Did I read that or see it on *Orange Is the New Black*? I couldn't remember, only that it was a bad thing.

I dipped my hand in my purse, feeling for the knife's hilt as I stepped out of the car.

I gripped it tightly as I walked up the walkway lined with purple violas.

I lifted it slightly from my purse as I knocked on the door. Red, like blood. I prayed it wasn't a premonition.

Cody shuffled beside me as we waited. Knocked again. Then a teenage girl answered the door. Her eyes were bloodshot, like she'd been high for days. Her nose was red, like she'd snorted a line of coke. Her face was pale, gaunt, almost skeletal. She looked stoned out of her mind.

Cody must have thought so too. I felt his fingers tighten around my arm, trying to pull me away, but I stood my ground, taking in every detail about the girl who threatened Vera, hurt Vera, and thus hurt me.

Chapter 13
Felicity

Blythe Sampson looked worse than the surly, broody teenage girl I had imagined. I wondered what cocktail of drugs she was on. Her hair was a greasy mess, and her cropped T-shirt was ripped on one shoulder, matching the holes in both knees of her black leggings. When her lips parted to speak, I expected the voice of Satan. Instead, her voice was polite and sweet:

"Can I help you?"

I swallowed an anchor weighing my words down. I could barely breathe, let alone speak. Just uttering Vera's name hurt like hell, but having to explain why I was here, that I needed her help finding Vera, took every bit of strength left in me after six months of hoping she'd miraculously walk through the front door. Six months of asking for help, six months of searching for answers, six months of closed doors…

"You may be the only one who can. I'm Vera Portman's mother. I believe you two were…" friends? enemies? "…acquaintances?"

"Oh, wow. Yeah, Vera was…is…my best friend." She relaxed her grip on the door. "Do you want to, like, come in? I'm not sure if there's anything I can do to help, but I'll try."

I glanced at Cody. His eyes widened, lips discreetly mouthed a *no,* but what choice did I have?

"Uh, sure, thank you. This is Cody, by the way. My brother-in-law. He's here for, uh…"

"Moral support," Cody spoke up.

"You look like a narc," said Blythe.

Cody chuckled nervously. "Do I? Actually, I'm a used car salesman."

Blythe's wry expression suggested that was even worse. "I'm just yankin' your chain," she said. "Come on in."

Blythe swung the door wide and stepped aside, letting me, then a very rigid Cody, step into the entryway. She looked every bit the awkward and uncertain teen, now that we were face to face. I wondered if Vera, too, would have let a total stranger into our home. It didn't matter. I was inside, and that's all that mattered.

My phone buzzed in my back pocket. Without looking at the screen, I reached around and silenced it. Nothing was more important right now than this girl. Nothing more pressing than getting answers.

"Blythe, I'm just going to come right out and explain why I'm here. Vera wrote quite a bit about you in her journal."

Blythe wiped her nose with her wrist. "She did? I didn't know she kept one."

"Yeah, and some of what she wrote suggested that you two had a fight of some kind? Maybe a falling out?"

"Really? No, we never fought. Like, ever. Why—what did she write?"

"That doesn't matter. What matters is if you have any idea what happened to her, or where she would have gone?"

A long-haired calico slinked up to Blythe's legs, circled around her ankles in figure eights. Animal lovers? I suppose even serial killers had pets too.

"I mean, Vera told me she was dealing with some stuff at home, but she never said what. When she disappeared, everyone was shocked. Vera wouldn't even, like, play hooky, let alone run away." Blythe's voice turned earnest. "Mrs. Portman, if I had an idea of where she went, I would have called the police and told them."

I highly doubted that. Considering Blythe was a drug user, I couldn't imagine her willingly approaching the cops for anything.

"So you have no idea what prompted her to run away from home?"

Blythe tapped a skull-bedecked black fingernail against her maroon lips. "The only thing I can think of was that it had to do with her ex-boyfriend, Austin. But she was the one who ended things, not him, and after a while he seemed okay with it, like he had accepted it."

"Wait, wait, wait. Back up. Vera had a boyfriend?"

"Yeah, they were pretty serious."

A shock ripped through my heart. My own daughter didn't tell me she was dating someone. Why would she hide this from me? She didn't give me the chance to disapprove; we never even had a conversation about it.

"How serious?" I managed to ask, though it hurt to speak.

"I mean, not marriage serious, but in love and stuff."

I didn't want to know what exactly *in love and stuff* meant. Or if Vera had acted on that supposed love. And yet I did want to know. I wanted to know everything, every single heartbreaking and terrifying piece of her life.

"What did you say his name was?" I asked.

"Austin Miller. He's a grade below Vera. Got held back in fourth grade. Not really a good guy, but not bad either."

Austin Miller. The name didn't sound familiar.

"What do you mean, he wasn't a good guy?"

"Austin…tended to attract trouble. I warned her about him and told her he'd mess up her life. He was pressuring her to have sex, acting like he cared about her feelings then ghosting her when she wouldn't do whatever he said. I told her the only way out was to break up with him. There's no fixing someone like him, y'know? But she was devastated. I was pretty worried about her mental state after they split. But eventually she got over him. At least she seemed to."

Everything made so much more sense now.

"How long were they dating?"

"I forget. Maybe a year or so?"

"A year!" It came out a scream, startling Blythe back a step. "I'm sorry...I just didn't expect her to keep a boyfriend a secret for that long. When did the breakup happen?"

A furrow creased her forehead. "I think Vera ended it maybe a month or so before she..." She wouldn't say *disappeared*. I often found myself unable to speak it too.

Blythe turned her head into the crook of her elbow and coughed. As she covered her mouth with her wrist, I noticed a tattoo. I had seen it recently, but I couldn't remember where. Rummaging through my memories, it was right there...so close I could see it...

Again my phone buzzed in my pocket. Again I silenced it.

"One sec. I'll be right back." As Blythe's coughing subsided, she left us standing in the entry while she headed into the belly of the house.

"She looks like she's on something," Cody whispered. "I wouldn't count her as totally credible, Felicity."

When Blythe returned a moment later, she unwrapped something and popped it in her mouth. "Sorry, I have a bad cold. Don't worry—it's not COVID." She sucked on what I now realized was a throat lozenge.

Annnnd I had officially dropped to a new low. She wasn't on drugs; the poor girl was sick.

"Is there anything else? 'Cause I need to get back to bed. I have a gymnastics competition coming up and I'm trying to get better before then."

"*You* do gymnastics?"

Blythe couldn't help but detect my judgmental tone but was too polite to embarrass me.

"I'm no Simone Biles, though that girl is everything to me. What she can do with her body...I can only dream. Sucks that she got the twisties at the Olympics. Been there, done that." She grinned self-effacingly. "But yeah, I've loved gymnastics ever since I was two. Won nationals with my floor routine, and was runner-up on the balance beam. I used to want to try out for the Olympics, but...well...it's expensive. My mom works, like, three jobs just to pay for my training now. Though I've been offered a college scholarship already, so it'll be worth it."

Wow. A true athlete. And college-bound. I couldn't believe how wrong I had been about her. I had been so quick to judge her outside I hadn't even bothered to see who she was.

"Thank you for your time, Blythe. And good luck with your competition. I appreciate you being a good friend to Vera."

"She was a good friend to me too. Every day I worry about her and pray she comes home. Can I give you my cell phone number in case you hear something?"

"Of course, Blythe."

Blythe held her palm out. It took a moment for me to realize she wanted my phone. I pulled it out of my pocket and handed it to her, then she boldly navigated her way to my contacts and typed in her info. "Text me anytime. And when Vera comes home...I want to do something special to celebrate. Because she's coming home, Mrs. Portman. I still believe that."

"Me too, sweetie." As she passed me back my phone, I remembered what I wanted to ask her. "Real quick. That tattoo—

what does it mean?"

She glanced down at her wrist.

"Oh, Vera designed this for our matching tattoos. It's the Celtic symbol for courage. I know it's, like, cliché, but we thought it was pretty."

"I'm sorry, did you say that you and Vera *both* got a tattoo?"

"Yeah, Vera begged me to do it with her. My mom agreed to let me get one as long as Vera got your permission too."

I absolutely did not.

"Did Vera tell you I was okay with it?"

"Well, you signed the parental consent form, didn't you?"

I glared at Cody, searching for an explanation. Secret boyfriend. Tattoo. Forgery. What else had Vera hidden from me? And when had she gotten so clever to get away with it? Cody's gaze darted away and he shook his head to deflect my anger anywhere but on him.

Now was not the time to suspect how Vera had deceived me. The bigger issue was what had become of my obedient daughter. Who was she when she walked out our door for the last time, and who had helped create her? Because someone was behind this. And I had a feeling I knew who.

"No, I didn't sign anything. Who took you girls?"

"Some lady friend of Vera's."

"Do you remember her name or where Vera met her?"

"Sorry, I don't remember. It was, like, a while ago."

I couldn't believe this. Vera had friends of legal age, old enough to drive them to get a tattoo and then sign legal consent. This was more than I could bear. There was too much I didn't know about my sweet girl, revealing just how severely I had failed as her mother.

Again my phone buzzed, and I glanced at the screen, wondering what could possibly be so important that they needed to call three times in as many minutes.

Oliver.

He could wait.

I just needed one more thing.

"Do you happen to have Austin's address? Or his parents' names?"

"Uhhh…well, last I heard he was living in a group home. Something about him getting in a fight with his stepdad."

So he was violent too. *Great choice of boyfriend, Vera.*

"I'd still like to swing by to see if I can track him down."

"Sure. I don't remember his street address, but I can give you directions for how to get there. He only lives a few minutes from here."

I pulled out my phone and typed the directions as Blythe rattled them off, then thanked her on my way out the door.

"Mrs. Portman?" Blythe's voice stopped me as I stepped off the front porch. I turned around to see not Goth Girl, but a teary-eyed child missing her best friend. She sniffled, swiped at a tear rolling down her cheek. "I know you believe Vera's out there, alive. Like I do. But why do you think she hasn't come back yet?"

"I don't know. That's what I'm trying to figure out. Hopefully what you've told me can help me find her. I hope you feel better, Blythe."

Blythe watched as Cody and I walked to the car. As we were pulling out of the driveway I waved. She waved back.

A little ways down the road I felt Cody's gaze locked on me.

"What?" I said, stealing a glance.

"You okay, Felicity? I'm sure that felt like a bomb dropping."

A humph escaped through my strained grin. "More like a nuclear missile. But at least this is something. I just wish Vera would have told me who she hung out with, and that she had a boyfriend. Why did she feel the need to hide so much from me?"

"You act like you were never a kid yourself, Felicity. Didn't her call log or texting log show their phone numbers?"

"You would think, but no. The police checked all her cell phone records and listed all the numbers for us. Most were to me, Oliver, Marin, Nana, and the friends I knew about. I don't know how she was contacting these other people."

"It's pretty easy to do through all the social media apps now. Almost all of them have direct messaging."

"You know we can go directly to the source, right?"

Cody groaned. "You're going to drag me to see what the boyfriend knows, aren't you?"

"Of course I am. I'm sure as hell not going alone. You heard what Blythe said about him."

I skimmed the directions Blythe had given me, trying to hold the phone while figuring out which turn I was supposed to make next. On the dashboard Cody's phone lit up.

"It's Oliver. I'm guessing he figured out I'm with you."

"Why's he calling you, Cody? He's acting like a maniac calling me a dozen times. Just answer and tell him I dragged you with me to pick up...I don't know. Something big and heavy. A dog crate that got delivered to my store."

When Cody answered, I could hear Oliver's angry voice from three feet away. Cody held out the phone for me to take. I exhaled and accepted it.

"He—"

"Where the hell are you?" he yelled before I got my *hello* in.

"I'm running errands. Why?"

"You forgot to pick up the kids from karate class! Their sensei left me three messages during my Zoom meeting asking where you were because you weren't there yet and Sydney wasn't feeling well."

"What!" I yelled. "Oh my gosh, I'm so sorry. I must have lost track of time. I'm on my way there now. I'll be there in less than ten minutes."

My babies. I had completely forgotten about my babies. I was about to hang up and freak out when Oliver kept going, anger powering every word.

"You know we have to talk about this later. It's becoming a problem, Felicity. And I don't know if I can keep picking up your broken pieces anymore."

He hung up, leaving the threat growing between us. He was right. I was losing my mind over this. Forgetting my children. Risking Sydney's life. Saving Vera wasn't just about her anymore. It was about saving my marriage, saving my family, saving myself.

Chapter 14
Marin

Cody noticed everything. He grumbled when I moved his shaving supplies over half an inch to make room for my facial cleanser. He commented when the salad forks were mixed with the dinner forks in the silverware drawer. He could tell when I used a teaspoon of his protein powder. And he most certainly noticed every time my phone beeped with a new text.

Cody was also quite verbal about the things he noticed.

"Mare, your stuff is starting to take over the whole sink," he'd tease. Or "Mare, just a reminder to separate the different types of forks." Or "Mare, if you want your own protein powder, I'll buy you some." The absolute worst was "Mare, did you change your text notification sound? It doesn't sound like your usual beep."

I don't know when my husband became so observant of the intricacies of conjugal living, but it terrified me what he noticed but hadn't mentioned. Because someone as observant as Cody couldn't have missed the glaring signs that I was hiding something. Or when my lies didn't match up. I had a feeling he knew more than he was letting on when he asked too many questions or came home early from work unexpectedly.

Like he was doing right now.

"I'll be home late tonight since I'm closing," he had told me this morning on his way out the door to the car dealership. A kiss and the slam of the front door later, I didn't know if he was telling the truth or not, since if I was lying to him, the logical conclusion was that he could be lying to me too. I couldn't track his cell phone, since we had both turned off our location tracking without explanation. Well, my explanation had been that it was draining my battery, but that was just another lie.

It was storming when I ran to my car, dashing through sheets of rain. A bolt of lightning ripped a seam through the freakishly green sky (not a portent of a tornado, I hoped), as I slipped, dripping wet, onto the ripped fabric seat. A peal of thunder shook the air as I swung the door shut. My hand trembled as I inserted the keys—or was that another grumble of thunder shaking the car? Under normal circumstances I would not have driven in this weather. Under normal circumstances I would not have snuck out to avoid Cody finding out. Under normal circumstances I would not have risked everything for this. But this was not normal circumstances. This was murder.

I started the car, pushed the gear into reverse, and slowly backed up. Another streak of white, then the car shuddered and lurched. Not thunder this time, but an impact. Harsh high beams reflected off the rearview mirror, blinding me. I hit the brakes, though the car was already pinned in place, then turned around in my seat and put the car in park.

I couldn't see who I had hit, who was now blocking me in. Until the red of Cody's truck cut through the rain. I barely made out his figure approaching, pause to check the fender damage, then head toward my driver's-side window.

My mind fumbled for an explanation for why I was heading out, in the middle of a raging storm, late at night. I didn't have time to come up with anything as Cody showed up at my window, raindrops swirling around him like glitter in the headlights.

"Are you crazy? Where are you going in this weather?" he

demanded.

"I thought you were working late." Deflection, my father had always taught me. A useful tool.

"My general manager offered to close tonight." Of course Cody would accept the offer rather than take the overtime pay. "So? Where you going?"

"Out." My brain remained blank.

"Okay. Why are you acting so secretive?"

"I'm not acting secretive."

"Fine, then let me park and I'll join you."

I couldn't exactly say no as he was already sprinting back to his truck. A minute later it was parked beside me and he hefted himself through my passenger side door and fidgeted with his seat belt.

"So where are we going?"

I had two choices. Lie and figure out a random place to go, wasting more precious time. Or tell the truth and just take Cody with me. I knew the truth could destroy me. It could rip my marriage apart, turn my family against me, cost me everything I loved. But I had no other choice, if it could save Vera. Truth, it was.

"Cody"—I turned my shamed gaze on him, pleading silently for his understanding—"I haven't been honest with you about something. A lot of somethings, actually."

I couldn't push the confession out. It hurt so bad, ripping my throat.

"Okay…" Worry spread across his face. "Whatever it is, I'm here to help."

His assurance fed me courage.

"Before I tell you this, I need you to know I would never do anything to hurt your family. You all mean everything to me. It was a stupid one-time mistake…and now I'm terrified I'm the reason everything happened with Vera."

"Oh my God. You're having an affair." Cody stared at me, lips parted in a stunned O. "Is it with Oliver?"

"Wha—? No, Cody! I'm not having an affair. Why would you think that?"

"I don't know. You've got some big confession going on here. That's the first thing that came to mind."

"No, that's not it at all. Cody, I was the last person to see Vera alive…and I know this because I dropped her off at her boyfriend's house the night she went missing."

Cody gaped at me. I couldn't read what he was thinking or feeling. Confusion? Disgust? Hatred? Blame?

"Are you saying you know where Vera is and haven't told anyone?" All I heard was anger.

"I couldn't, Cody. Your family would have blamed me if they ever found out! I was terrified of losing you all. You know how Felicity is—she would have never forgiven me." Felicity held grudges like she held her secrets—with a tight fist.

"But we could have already brought Vera home." Cody didn't understand the bigger picture. There was so much more to the story, things I could never tell him. "I don't understand why you would keep this from the family. Or from the police."

"Vera begged me not to tell anyone about Austin, Cody. She swore me to secrecy. I wanted to go speak to him myself before I told anyone else. He's been in some trouble in the past, from what I understand, which is why Vera hid him from everyone. This boy has enough problems without tying him to a missing person's case. No dad. A drunkard mom. But he's finally getting his life together. And he really is a sweet kid and adored Vera. If he got dragged into Vera's disappearance, his life would be over. You know Felicity—you know what she's capable of."

"Why do you care so much about this kid when your niece is

missing?"

"Because putting him at risk isn't going to save Vera. I'm not going to throw an innocent kid under the bus until I have a reason to."

Cody's hands flipped up in the air. "Come on, Marin. Having the police look into him isn't throwing him under the bus. Let them weed out the details. It's not your job to assume his innocence in all this."

My husband was blind to reality—the raw, unprivileged version of it. How could he understand any differently, though? He'd never been racially profiled and pulled over while driving to the grocery store. People didn't fearfully skirt around him when crossing paths on the sidewalk. He never suffered discrimination a day in his life over the color of his skin or where he grew up, nor had a minor brush with the law. His father never had *the talk* with him about how to react to the blatant racism Black kids were constantly exposed to from authority figures, and how to react in such situations, if you wanted to stay alive. My father had *the talk* with me right before he went off to war, because as a soldier he knew he would be living on borrowed time.

A kid with a tainted past would be doomed if he ever came under the radar. I wasn't about to put him there. "*Better to keep your mouth shut and seem a fool than to open it and remove all doubt,*" as Mom would have said.

"Listen, Cody, if I mention Austin's name to the police, he'll end up being a suspect, and with his track record, this could ruin his life if they try to pin it on him. Tons of kids' lives get ruined for wrongful conviction. Look at the Central Park Jogger case and all the kids who lost their freedom for decades over a crime they didn't commit." I had made Cody watch the Netflix series *When They See Us* to show him how corrupt the justice system could be when left unchecked. Hadn't he been paying attention? I was only getting started as I felt the rage build.

"And just a few years ago a boy named Davontae Sanford was fourteen—a kid!—when he was convicted and spent nine years in jail for a crime that a hitman confessed to shortly after the crime happened! These innocent Black kids were victims of bias, corruption, and incompetence. They were convenient fall guys for a broken justice system. I can't risk putting Austin through that without talking to him myself first."

Cody shook his head. His silence was all the disappointment I could handle. He was clueless, but I refused to be. I didn't have that luxury.

"Do you want to come with me to talk to him or not? I don't think he has anything to do with Vera going missing, but I'm going there to find out what he knows."

Now I could read my husband: defeat.

"I'm trusting you big-time with this, Mare. I'm obviously going with you, but if there is anything shady about him, I'm turning him over to the cops to deal with."

"He's a teenage boy, but whatever. That's fine if you want to come. Just don't say anything or threaten him or do anything, got it? Be on your best behavior."

He crossed his heart, like we were in third grade. "I promise I'll be good."

Why did I doubt that promise?

Based on my memory of Vera's directions, Austin—I never got his last name—only lived about eight minutes from us, in a rundown neighborhood on Marigold Street. It was the kind of place where you heard gunshots in nearby alleys and didn't flinch. He should have been in a foster home under the protection of people who could take care of him, assuming he landed with a family that cared. But from what Vera had told me, his mother was functioning just well enough to keep custody. If I could have taken him in, I would have. Countless times I had considered kidnapping him…if only to save him, because he reminded me so much of, well, me. He had a good heart, but life kept trying to beat the good out of him. I hoped Austin would cling to whatever goodness remained and make something of himself. If anyone deserved extra chances, it was kids like Austin.

Eleven minutes later—the rain had slowed me down—his one-story ranch house appeared around the corner, windows as dark as the sky. Nothing sinister. Nothing that screamed "Delinquent Lives Here!" Austin did all the yard work up to the tree line where a coppice of white oaks and sycamores broke up the monotony of houses. Vera had mentioned that on a few occasions she helped him tame the thicket's brambly undergrowth, having learned from her family's gardener how to manicure the peskiest of briars. That thought reminded me just how great the divide was between the haves and have-nots. Felicity's family wanted for nothing and never had to lift a finger for themselves. And here was Austin, who didn't have a pot to piss in, but he knew the dignity and value of plain old hard work. At least Vera was raised thoughtful in that way, always wanting to help those who needed it. That savior complex was probably what had attracted her to a boy from the proverbial wrong side of the tracks in the first place. It was also probably what had led to her downfall.

When Vera first confessed to me that she had been sneaking over to Austin's house after school before her parents came home from work, I remember the angst of being stuck in the Great Crux. Wanting to tell Felicity about Vera's secret boyfriend versus being the cool, trustworthy aunt who kept her niece's secrets. I desperately wanted to be that person Vera turned to, the person she could entrust with anything. Now I regretted wanting that relationship, because it wasn't mine to take. Now Vera was missing, and if I had just told Felicity, maybe Vera would never have disappeared. Maybe…maybe…maybe…

But it was too late for maybes. And it was too late to tell Felicity what I knew. The domino effect of damage would be too great, especially if she found out about Austin and told the cops. I knew what Felicity thought about people like him. Anyone outside her elite social circle was either a criminal or a predator. She never thought to include herself in that class, but I knew. I knew everything she had done.

I parked as close to the house as the driveway would allow, the headlights swiping across the garage door. On the count of three, Cody and I dashed through the rain, crowding under a scrap of awning when we reached the front stoop. Pushing the doorbell, a weak chime rang through the other side, blended with the sound of television gunfire. I knocked just in case. Cody cupped my hand protectively. When Austin answered the door, a smile cracked his pale face and he swung the screen door open, his arms wide with a hug.

Cody tossed me a skeptical look. I saw what he saw. A boy who probably didn't know where his next meal was coming from. Bony shoulders and xylophone ribs screaming out under a throwback Sublime T-shirt, full of holes and two sizes too small. Brown emo hair falling defiantly over one eye. A thousand-yard stare expressing fear, threatening trouble. Yet his smile was pure. His smile was hope.

"Miss Marin!" Austin clung to me like I was his mother. The poor kid barely had one; I didn't mind stepping in when I could.

"Hey, Austin. How are you?" I squeezed him before releasing him, feeling every rib like they'd crack under my pressure.

"Okay, I guess." He shot Cody a critical look, sizing up this clean-cut straight arrow.

"This is my husband, Cody," I said, sensing his discomfort.

"Don't worry, he's cool."

"Hi, Austin. How's it hangin'?"

Austin shook the hand Cody extended without warmth and turned back to me. "Have you heard from Vera yet, Miss Marin?"

I shook my head somberly. "Unfortunately not. That's why I'm here. I wanted to ask you a couple questions."

"Sure, sure. Anything you need."

Stepping into the shadow of his living room, Austin led me inside where a video game on pause glowed from one end of the house, light clawing its way into the adjacent dining room and kitchen, lit by a cracked light fixture that hung over the sink. The crunch of what looked like cereal under my shoes left footprints of powdery cockroach bait across the carpet. Somewhere in the pit of the house I heard a closed-door fight between a man and woman. Cody tugged on my hand, trying to draw me back outside to safety, until I pulled my hand free.

"Is everything okay at home, Austin?" I asked. My gaze shifted toward the intensifying screaming match.

"Oh, that. Yeah, just my mom and stepdad. Nothing new. I'm just trying to stay out of his way. I'm good, though."

Was he *good,* really? I couldn't tell if he was being truthful or not. I had never learned how to read kids.

"Marin," Cody's wary voice broke in, "you wanted to ask him about Vera?" I could tell he was growing impatient to leave.

"Thanks, Cody," I said, silencing him with a glare. My voice softened as I returned to Austin. "The night Vera disappeared, I dropped her off here at your house. What exactly happened after I left?"

Austin's face scrunched. "What do you mean? She never came here."

Liar. Clearly he didn't trust me.

"You can tell me the truth, Austin. I promise I will protect you, and I'm not going to tell the cops anything. I just need to know what happened after I dropped her off."

"I'm telling you the truth, Miss Marin. I never saw her that night. I wasn't even home."

More with the lies. I knew what I had seen that night. But I couldn't blame him for taking the silent defense.

"Then why did she ask me to bring her to your house?"

His bony shoulders lifted, then dropped. "I don't know. After she broke up with me we stopped talking. I wasn't allowed to contact her, and she'd been ignoring me at school."

"Did she text you that night?"

"Hell no. We never texted, only used messaging. She was terrified her parents would find out about me if they saw her phone. It figures. I wouldn't want my daughter with someone like me either. I should have known she'd break up with me eventually."

His cheeks reddened, eyes watered. I wondered how long he'd been wearing his self-shame. I knew from experience that it was a hard beast to tame.

"Oh, honey. It wasn't about you. Never think you're not good enough, okay?"

He nodded wordlessly.

"I'm just trying to make sense of this, Austin. I dropped her off right there." I pointed out the screen door into the night, finger aimed at the patch of concrete where I had parked and let her out. "And watched her walk through your yard. If she didn't go to your house, where would she have gone?"

"I don't know, I swear." He shook his head with an almost believable conviction. "I would have told the police if I knew anything. I loved Vera...I still do. You know I would never hurt her, right?"

"Of course I know that." I grinned, but I felt like weeping.

Why wouldn't Austin just tell me the truth?

A door slammed, followed by a baby's wail. Then a gale of footsteps, and more yelling uncomfortably close as a woman emerged from a hallway wearing nothing but an oversized T-shirt that came down her to knees. She was short and stout, a sturdy fireplug of a woman with a florid face and mean little piggish eyes. I knew the wary, hateful look she shot me all too well. It was clear she wasn't happy about having a Black woman in her house.

"Who the hell are you, and what you doin' talkin' to my boy?" she demanded, spittle flecking my face.

"Mom," Austin said, stepping between me and his mother, "this is Vera's aunt. We were just talking about Vera."

"Vera's *aunt*?" She eyed me with a chilling skepticism.

"By marriage," I explained. "Nice to meet you, ma'am. I'm Marin." I held out my hand, but I might as well have held a gun in it. I let it drop to my side as she stared me down. I felt a strange sensation like this was improvisational theatre and I was winging my lines with a stingy actor who refused to give me something to work with.

"And who's this guy?" she asked, jerking her head at Cody.

"He's my husband."

She raised one pierced eyebrow in disapproval while Cody squirmed under her *got a taste for the dark meat, huh, white boy?* glare.

"So you're Vera's kin, huh? She was a good girl. Sorry for your loss."

It was an odd thing to say when Vera was missing, not dead.

"I appreciate that. We're hopeful that we'll find her soon."

She crossed her arms tight against her stomach. "The baby needs fed, Austin." She stepped toward me, an aggressive get-the-hell-out-of-my-house gesture that didn't match her formal

130

goodbye. "It was nice meetin' you. Give your family my condolences."

With a protective arm around my waist, Cody led me outside straight to the car. The rain had softened to a mist, but the urgency to run felt just as strong as before.

Once inside the car, Cody finally exhaled. "What was up with the mom? She was a bit…much, wasn't she? And I think that kid is lying, by the way. I could tell."

"I don't think he's lying. I know he is."

"You *know*? How?"

A breath caught in my throat, momentarily wedged there, then released. "Cody, I saw Austin in his bedroom window when I dropped Vera off. He watched her get out of my car. I don't know what to think anymore."

My brain felt numb.

"You know what that means, don't you, Marin?"

I couldn't find the strength to nod. I had used it up hoping that Austin had a believable narrative to explain what happened. Anything that would prove his innocence.

"I've got to tell Felicity and turn Austin into the cops. Felicity is never going to forgive me. You know things won't be the same between us after this, don't you?"

Felicity was my family, despite our differences. I loved her like blood. Losing her was a poison I didn't want to swallow.

"Maybe there's a way to avoid Felicity finding out?" Cody looked at me—intense, determined.

"I don't see how. Vera's life is at stake. I've got to come clean to everyone."

I didn't realize in the moment that it wasn't just Vera's life at stake, but my own with it.

Chapter 15
Felicity

"I need a break."

The four most dreaded words in the English language between two spouses. Especially between spouses still in love with each other.

It was the last thing Oliver said to me before I blustered out of the house into nightfall, clutching Vera's journal, not knowing what I was doing or where I was going. Anywhere but home.

It had only taken a stop for ice cream to earn forgiveness from Sydney and Eliot after showing up late to pick them up from karate. Birthday cake flavor topped with sprinkles and gummy bears for Syd, plain old chocolate for Eliot. Their sensei was equally sympathetic after I explained how I was dealing with personal stuff. Forgiveness from strangers came easily when you had a missing child. But not from my own husband. Oliver lost all emotion months ago. All that was left were pragmaticism and survival.

I couldn't handle his judgment any longer. It was torture, the way his words were laced with *bad mother, neglectful wife, miserable woman.* What else was I to feel? How else was I to act? It was a human frailty to just let the despair eat me alive some days. Oliver expected me to don a comedy mask like he did, but I only felt tragedy. Aside from the dogs, only one person truly understood me, supported my need to grieve, and that was Cody.

And it shredded my heart even more that my brother-in-law seemed to care more than Oliver about my missing daughter.

Maybe I was acting *basic,* a Vera-ism I understood a little too well. I needed affirmation, approval. And one person always gave that to me.

I didn't remember driving to Cody's house, parking on the street, staring at the rain puddles glistening on the asphalt like pools of hot tar. The house was dark and lifeless, a sleeping mass of red brick settling in for the night. I didn't know what brought me here, other than the need for someone, anyone, to talk me through the complicated emotions swirling inside me. And yet I couldn't push myself to walk up to his door. So I sat in the car and watched. Waited. For what, I wasn't sure.

Pulling Vera's journal from my purse and turning on my cell phone flashlight, I skimmed through dozens of entries I had read dozens of times. As the tiny moon of light passed over the initials BS, they jumped out at me, now that I knew what it stood for. *BS* was Blythe. *A* was Austin. And *lying*…well, I still needed to find out what Vera had lied about. A flurry of questions cascaded in my mind after rereading the same entry with a new understanding:

I hate lying to my best friend. I've never lied to BS before, but I couldn't tell her the truth about why things ended with A. She would have tried to talk me out of what I had to do. She wouldn't have understood.

Back then I had thought it was a silly friendship battle. Now it held something much more sinister. A second-story light illuminated a window. A silhouette passed. A curtain moved, and I ducked down in my seat out of some unknown instinct—fear maybe? Odd, considering I had nothing to hide.

My phone buzzed with a text:

Felicity, are you outside my house right now?

My heart drummed a wild beat. I hesitated before typing:

Yes. I'm sorry. I don't know why I'm here.

But I couldn't hit *send*. Instead I deleted it, placed my phone in the center console, and started the car. As I shifted into drive and slowly pulled away from the curb, a shadow dashed through the beam of my headlights, and I slammed on the brake. A second later, a distorted face surfaced on the other side of my rain-streaked window. I yelped and lurched sideways, clutching my chest. When recognition dawned, I hit the power window switch.

"Geez, Cody, are you trying to give me a heart attack?" I wheezed.

"Are you trying to hit me with your car? Because I know I deserve it."

I smiled instant relief. "Yeah, you really do."

"I'm sorry, you know. For all the problems I'm causing you."

"It's not just you. I'm so…sorry and angry and sad. I'm screwing up my marriage, letting my kids down, my business is falling apart… I don't know how to pick up the pieces and put them back together. Is there even enough glue to fix it all?"

Cody crossed his arms and leaned on the ledge of the door, our noses nearly touching. "With family there's always enough glue, Felicity."

"Yeah, I don't know about that." I felt his beer-scented breath pass over my skin. "Now I have to live with the weight of another secret for the rest of my life…and I can't even make things right, because making things right means telling the truth, and telling the truth means losing Ollie. I just don't know what to do anymore."

"There's nothing you can do. Just focus on one problem at a time. Like why you're here. In front of my house. In the dark."

I had been asking myself the same question, and came up with only one answer. "I guess I just needed to talk to someone I could trust. But I shouldn't have come. In fact, I was just leaving."

"You don't have to leave, you know. You can come inside. I'm always up for company."

It was an awful idea. I couldn't, not after the fight Oliver and I just had. Especially since Cody smelled like he'd been drinking. And yet it tugged on me like a loose string…a string that if I pulled it would unravel my whole marriage.

"No, I really can't. Besides, I was thinking about stopping by Austin Miller's house."

"Are you serious? Felicity, please just let the cops deal with him."

"I will…after I speak with him first. I deserve to meet the guy my daughter had been dating. I just want to meet him. He's a teenage boy. How nefarious could he be?"

Cody shook his head and straightened upright. "Are you sure you should do that?" His voice hardened. "I mean, it's getting late and he doesn't live in a safe neighborhood."

"Then come with me for protection…or moral support."

"Uh, I don't know…" Cody wavered, gaze hopscotching from my face, to the roof of my car, to the street.

"Never mind. Forget I asked. I'll go alone."

"What is with you women wanting to do dangerous things by yourselves?" Cody grumbled, as he circled around the front of the car and slipped into the other side. "Obviously I'm not letting you go alone. I don't have anything better to do."

"You know it's a bit sexist and narcissistic of you to think women are too weak to handle *dangerous* stuff while you big, tough, powerful men can save us from ourselves, right?" I said as I pulled away from the curb.

"Oh, come on. If it was a woman offering to go with you, you'd appreciate it. If it's a man, you call him sexist? That's a double standard, Felicity. I'm trying to look out for you. Why demonize that?"

"It's the belief systems beneath the words. I don't want to get into a debate about this, but you have a tendency to need to prove yourself. It's like you're in some kind of competition with yourself, with your brother, always needing to be the best, be the savior. But sometimes you focus so much on trying to save others that you don't notice you're drowning."

"I'm not drowning."

"Cody..." He knew the truth. We'd both been floundering for months.

We didn't speak as I tried to read Blythe's directions while squinting against the dark in search of my turns. As I was turning right, Cody blurted out, "This isn't the right turn. It's the next one—on Marigold Street."

"Huh?" I slowed the car to a roll and checked the directions. Cody was right. "How did you know that?"

He was quick to answer, "I remember the directions that Blythe gave you."

"Yeah, but those were directions from *her* house. How do you know how to get there from *your* house?"

"I know the area, Felicity. I know all these streets." He turned toward the window. Avoidance, his biggest tell.

"You're going with that, huh? Not even going to try a better lie than that? Because you knew right away it was the wrong turn…like you'd been to his house before, Cody."

I swerved to the side of the road. I wasn't moving until I had answers.

"If I tell you the truth, I don't want you to be angry with me."

"Spit it out!" I yelled. "This is my daughter we're talking about!"

"Okay, okay. Marin and I talked to Austin already."

"What?" I put the car in park. I was shaking too hard to trust my limbs. A red-hot fury overcame me, and before I could control the impulse, I reached out and slapped him across the face.

"You and Marin spoke to my daughter's boyfriend and didn't tell me? How long have you known about Austin?"

Cody held up his hands apologetically. "I swear, Felicity, I wasn't trying to hide anything from you. Apparently Vera had told Marin about him in confidence, and when we talked to him, he didn't know anything anyway. He and Vera had broken up and he hadn't even seen her the night she disappeared. So there was nothing to tell. I promise if there was something to tell, I would have told you."

"Whether it's something worth telling or not isn't up to you to decide when it's *my* daughter missing, Cody. You should have told me."

Even in the dark my handprint lingered on his cheek. But I wasn't sorry about it. He deserved so much worse than a slap on the face after keeping this from me.

"I know. Marin was worried you'd turn him over to the cops for no reason and he'd end up getting in trouble for something he didn't do."

"I don't want to hear your excuses." My stomach churned. This secret was too big, it threatened to detonate my heart. "You know what hurts worse than your deception? The fact that Vera told Marin about having a boyfriend, but not me, her own mother."

Then...*boom!* I felt it explode. Tears and snot and sobs all at once, a tsunami of motherhood failure.

"But that's what daughters do, Felicity. They keep secrets from their parents and confide in their friends."

"Why was Marin her friend but not me? Why couldn't I have been both to Vera—parent *and* friend? I always tried to be that person she could tell anything to."

"I know you did, but it doesn't always work that way. Kids are complicated. We all need something that is just ours. Even teenage girls who love their mothers."

In a way I understood this, a little too well. I had kept my own secret all this time, and I couldn't tell a single soul, not even with Vera's life on the line. But that time of secrecy was coming to an end. It was jail or finding Vera. As a mother, the choice was being made for me, because I would always come in last. And I was okay with that, if only I could know with certainty that the kids would be okay—if Sydney could survive—without me.

"I guess you're right," I conceded.

"I'm so sorry, Felicity," Cody pleaded. "I didn't think."

"I know, but I can't forgive you for not telling me. Not yet."

Wiping my face with my sleeve, I pulled out from the curb and drove the rest of the way in angry silence, my thoughts restless with questions about what Blythe knew, what Oliver knew, what Cody knew. And what else they weren't telling me.

By the time we arrived at Austin's house, my brain turned numb from overthinking. My body slipped into autopilot as I walked to the front door, Cody trailing in the dark behind me. Questions rattled around in my skull as I knocked. When the door swung open, I gasped. One look at his face and everything crashed down around me.

Chapter 16
Felicity

"You!" I jabbed a finger at the boy secure behind a screen door, a dazed veil over his eyes like I had wakened him. I hoped I had.

I would have recognized that deviant face anywhere. That smug curl of his lips. Those cruel, piercing eyes. That wiry mutt-brown hair. The boy called Austin Miller. But back in fourth grade he went by Lee.

"You're Lee Miller, the psychopath who bullied Vera so badly she had to switch elementary schools!"

"What? Who are you?" He looked wounded, but I was only just getting started.

"I'm Vera's mother. And I want to know why you preyed on her after the damage you already caused her back in elementary school."

"No, ma'am, I never—"

But it wasn't his turn to speak. It was mine. "I'm guessing word got around about you so much that you had to change your name?"

"Ma'am, Lee is my middle name. I go by Austin now, and I adored Vera."

"Bull. Don't lie to me and pretend you have feelings for her after what you did. You scarred her for life."

"I apologized years ago, and I would never hurt her again. I was just a stupid kid back then, but we moved on from that."

"*Moved on*?" This kid was unbelievable! "You think an apology and a new identity make it all better? Her year was a living hell after you got the whole class chanting, '*Vera, Vera, don't go near ya.*' A *sorry* doesn't fix that. She cried *daily* because of you. For months!"

"I know, and I—"

"Spare me your excuses. I just want to know if you tricked her into dating you so that you could finish the job. Was that the plan—pretend to like her then take advantage of her kind spirit and break her heart?"

Austin reached for the screen, ready to step outside.

"Stop right there," I demanded. I searched behind me for Cody, who hung back near the edge of the stoop in the dark. "Don't you come near me. I know what you're capable of."

Austin released the door handle and dropped his hand to his side. "Look, Mrs. Portman, I am not the same kid I was back then. My dad had just gotten thrown in jail, and my mom was in a bad state. I hated myself, and I took it out on Vera, and I'm sorry for that. If it makes you feel better, I got kicked out of school and held back. But I always felt terrible for what I did to her. It's why I went to her personally to apologize. That's actually when we first started being friends."

Empathy wormed its way through me. A tiny little burrow.

"I thought you were boyfriend and girlfriend."

"Eventually, yes. But we started off as friends in middle school…and it kind of grew from there."

"So what happened? I understand you broke up."

"Yeah, we realized we were better off as friends."

I knew what *that* meant. "That's not what I heard. I heard you were pressuring Vera to have sex and treating her poorly."

Austin scoffed. "Who told you that? Blythe? That's not what happened at all. It was a mutually agreeable breakup. We both wanted to end the relationship."

I doubted that. No hormone-amped teens approached a breakup with such amicability. "Who first had this revelation—you or Vera?"

"Why does it matter? Do you think I'd hurt Vera for breaking up with me?"

"I don't know. Would you?"

"No! Never. I loved her, but she was also my best friend. I only wanted what was best for her, and I know I wasn't it. She's brilliant and beautiful and funny and has money and a future...while I'm just...well, nothing like her. But we were still friends after the breakup. Sure, I was still in love with her, but I had no reason to hurt her."

All this talk about this tormentor's love for my daughter made my skin crawl.

"Did Vera ever talk about anything that might give you an idea of where she went?"

"No, I don't think so. Look, like I told Miss Marin, I wasn't home the night she dropped Vera off here, so I didn't see anything. I don't know why Vera came here, or where she really went."

My brain was buzzing with too many facts all at once. "Wait. I don't understand. What do you mean? Did Marin bring Vera here the night she disappeared?"

"Yeah, Miss Marin dropped her off out front, but like I told her, I wasn't home. I have no idea where Vera went after that."

"As you've said several times," Cody interjected.

Austin's attention flashed to Cody, eyes narrowing in on him. "Because it's the truth."

One fact kept blinking in front of me, demanding my attention: Marin was the last person to see Vera alive. How could she not tell me? Not tell the police? Vera's last known location was in this very spot, Austin's house, and my sister-in-law brought her here and said nothing while we frantically searched for clues, for anything that could help us find her.

A million thoughts crisscrossed my mind, but only one surfaced to my lips. "Vera was supposed to be babysitting that night." I turned to Cody, as if he could answer for his wife. "How could Marin have allowed Vera to leave her little brother and sister home alone and take her to her ex-boyfriend's house? And why wouldn't Marin have made sure Vera got safely inside the house before leaving? You always make sure a person gets inside before leaving! Vera would still be here if Marin hadn't left her on the street alone!"

Cody looked at me helplessly. "I don't know, Felicity. Vera's a teenager, and clearly she didn't want Marin to know where she was sneaking off to. You can't blame Marin for what Vera did."

"Why are you defending Marin? My daughter is missing because of her! Vera could be *dead* because of her!"

It was my worst fear. The one thing I couldn't accept, the one ending to this awful, tragic story that I couldn't face had slipped out on my tongue: *dead.*

"Mrs. Portman, it's not Miss Marin's fault." Austin's soft voice just barely cut through my raging thoughts.

I turned on him. "How would you know?"

He shifted nervously. "Because Vera told me a few days before that her family had been lying to her about her sister, and she needed time to process it. I don't know what exactly that meant, because she wouldn't go into detail, but whatever it was, it had been bothering her for a while."

Vera must have found out about Sydney. Overheard a conversation. Saw a medical bill. Pieced together all the appointments and suspected what we were going to ask her to do: save her sister's life.

"What exactly did she say to you? It's important I know everything, Austin." I needed him to understand this was life-or-death, not just for Vera, but for Sydney too.

Austin thought for a moment. "She told me she found out something about her sister and she was really upset about it, like crying and feeling deceived. She called it a big family secret that you kept from her. It was one of her reasons for breaking up, that she needed time to figure stuff out. But then she didn't bring it up again until right before she went missing."

"Figure what out? And where would she have gone for 'answers'?"

"I don't know, ma'am. Vera was pretty closed off about it all. I don't know what was going on, but she felt like her family life was more messed up than mine, and that's saying a lot."

This couldn't be true. Vera was a happy girl. Had she really said such awful things about her family who would do anything for her? And I mean *anything*.

I heard her before I saw her, a woman's voice gravelly from chain-smoking and slurred from alcohol. "What the hell's goin' on here? Austin, who you talkin' to? Better not be someone come to take you back to that group home."

The woman wore obscenely tight leopard-print leggings and a black sweatshirt with the slogan *If the South Woulda Won, We'd Have It Made*, which told me everything I needed to know about her. A toddler followed at her heels. I took a couple of cautionary steps backwards as the woman brought the soggy butt of a Virginia Slims to her mouth, took a long drag, and pooched out her bottom lip to expel a jet of smoke over her frowzy head. My nostrils flared, smelling the noxious medley of menthol and Wild Turkey.

"No, Mom, it's Vera's mother," Austin answered.

Her eyes darted to Cody. "And you—I know you! I don't

know why you're back here, but you need to get the hell off my property."

"I'm talking to your son about my daughter Vera," I tried to explain.

But she wasn't having it. The screen door swung open, banging against the vinyl siding. She poked her nicotine-stained finger against my chest. "I said Get. The. Hell. Off. My. Property."

Cody stepped between us, pushing her back with his puffed-out chest. "Ma'am, we're not doing anything but talking."

The stubby gorgon stood on her tiptoes, her chin nearly resting on Cody's pecs. "Enough talk! Unless you want to do it with the barrel of my gun pointed at your head."

"Is that a threat?" Cody spouted. "How about I involve the cops in this conversation?" He pulled out his cell phone, finger ready to dial.

I grabbed his arm, dragging him away before this got out of hand.

"Cody, just stop. Let's go." He resisted me as a duel rose between them. "Please, there's no need to involve the police. We're leaving."

"Damn right!" the woman yelled as I fumbled down the last step of the porch. "Your kid is better off dead than having you as family."

"I'll kill you, you old cow!" I lunged at her, but she was surprisingly quick on her feet and jumped back as I fell forward, smacking my jaw hard against the porch floor. Cody scooped me up like a pile of wet rags. As I brushed myself off, the woman leered at me triumphantly, tapping the ash off the cancer stick she held against her chunky hip.

"You sick woman! How could you say that to another mother? Expect a visit from the police!"

"Bring it on, bitch!" the woman cackled. "Come on, boy." She flicked the smoldering butt into the bushes and headed inside. Austin stood gawking, his lips mouthing an apology. "I said come on!" She cuffed his ear with the flat of her hand. Austin followed her, dragging his spindly legs like a wounded spider, while Cody hauled me toward the car.

"The nerve of that lowlife white trash," I seethed. "Somebody like *her* talking that way to somebody like *me*!"

"Enough, Felicity! Calm down!"

"You expect me to calm down after what she said? They're probably behind Vera's disappearance!"

Cody nodded with a calmness that annoyed me while he nudged me in through the passenger-side door and took over the wheel.

"Don't listen to them. You can't put much stock in anything they say. Clearly she's got her own issues to deal with. Are you okay?"

"I'm fine." I was anything but fine, but I didn't want to be coddled right now. I'd had enough coddling to last a lifetime. I was stronger than they knew; they just wouldn't let me flex my muscles.

I laid my head back against the headrest as Cody drove, allowing the silence to overtake me.

"What big family secret about Sydney was Austin talking about?" he asked after several turns.

Marin hadn't told Cody. She had kept my secret for me. There was that loyalty again.

When I didn't answer, Cody persisted, "Is Syd Squid okay?"

I didn't want to think about it, let alone talk about it. But I couldn't hide it any longer. Not after all the other secrets that seemed to haunt every person in our family. I was so sick and tired of the secrets, the betrayal, the lies. Everyone was hiding something. I had no idea who to trust or where to go anymore. Too many vaults to open, too many mazes to get lost in.

"Sydney is sick, Cody." I couldn't find the words to explain it, the strength to speak it aloud. Tucked into the words was a reality I wasn't ready to face, one I could never face. I inhaled, then tried again, holding back the tears that threatened to spill. "Dying, actually. And I don't know how to deal with it. We found out that she has nephrotic syndrome. It's basically kidney failure. We've tried treating her, but she's not getting better. The doctors think she'd be better off with a kidney transplant than lifelong dialysis, but it's practically impossible to find a match...until Vera tested positive as one."

Cody said nothing, but his expression said everything.

"I'm supposed to ask one daughter to donate an organ to save her sister. How can I ask her to risk her life like that? It's an impossible situation. But apparently she already found out and made her decision...and now Sydney pays the price."

Finally he spoke, "Oh, Felicity, I'm so sorry. And on top of everything else..."

"I'm cursed, Cody. Some days I feel like maybe if I just died the curse would lift, Vera would come home, Sydney would be healed, and Oliver could finally have the good life he deserved."

Cody rested one hand on my shoulder, the other adjusted on the steering wheel. "Hey, listen to me. You're not cursed. I know it's been an awful year for all of us, but we'll do everything we can for Sydney. Hang in there, because your family needs you."

"What if I'm tired of being needed? That's all I'm good for—fulfilling needs. I'm exhausted from it."

"I know. We're all hurting alongside you, Felicity. But I know you, and you're strong, even when you don't want to be."

I turned toward the window, the contours of my sunken cheeks reflected in the glass as the inky river passed behind it.

"You don't understand, no one knows what it's like to lose one child while another one slowly dies. And the only salvation for the one lies solely on the other. What am I supposed to do with that? How am I supposed to pick who is more important?"

"So you think Vera figured out she's a donor match and doesn't want to save her sister's life? And that's why she disappeared?" Cody asked.

It was exactly what I thought, but I never imagined she'd go to such lengths to avoid helping her family. Or saving her sister's life.

"I'd do anything to take this cup from her—"

As I watched my thin lips move in my reflection, a sudden impact thrust the car forward. The earth swung around, trees spinning, water slipping out of sight, as my body was tossed forward with a loud crunching sound. The car spun off the road, crashing through the metal guardrail that divided the asphalt from a rocky cliff overlooking the river. The front end dipped precariously over the precipice, nodding toward the water.

Headlights played for a nanosecond upon Cody's terror-stricken face, then a dark vehicle sped away with tires squalling, leaving us tip-tip-tipping as the weight of the engine slowly shifted us forward to a certain icy death.

The Pittsburg Press

Pittsburg, PA
Tuesday, October 18, 1910

SIX MONTHS WITHOUT A TRACE OF MISSING MOTHER AND SUSPICIONS GROW

[Special Telegram to Pittsburg Press.]

A veiled woman who called upon Cecile Cianfarra, secretary for the Women's Equal Franchise Federation and Woman Suffrage Red Cross Auxiliary, is believed to be Mrs. Alvera Fields. Wife to the millionaire importer Robert Fields, and mother to daughter Olivia, Alvera disappeared from her home on the evening of April 16 and has not been seen since.

Mrs. Fields is believed to have been seen at the Hacke building sometime after April 16, as nearly as the clerks can recall. For some time there was an earnest talk between Miss Cianfarra and Mrs. Fields. What was the nature of the talk the clerks do not know. From what they observed, however, they were of the opinion that the veiled woman was greatly agitated and that it was she who was particularly concerned about the visit.

The call upon Miss Cianfarra appeared to be a stormy one. Robert Fields, assuming the veiled woman was his missing wife, took the lead and demanded that Miss Cianfarra give up all the correspondence she had with Mrs. Fields and all the telegrams that might have passed between them.

GIVEN UP AS DEAD

Despite sightings of Mrs. Fields circulating, relatives and the attorneys who have been assisting in the worldwide search for her cast aside all theories of her disappearance and came out flatly with the announcement that they believe the woman is dead.

Chapter 17
Felicity

I was afraid to breathe. I was afraid to move. I was afraid even the slightest shift in the environment would send the car plummeting down the cliff face into the river below. One fallen leaf, one rain droplet, could snuff out our lives Just. Like. That. I imagined clambering over the seats trying to redistribute the weight toward the back of the car where the tires still clung to the road. But in every scenario, the car succumbed to gravity and tumbled over the precipice, flipping end over end, tossing us like rag dolls, knocking us cold. The car would smack the water nose first, bobbing like a fishing float for a minute, then righting itself. Then the water would seep into the wheel wells and cracks and crannies, and down the car would go with a slow rocking horse motion, gurgling and bubbling, while Cody and I pounded the windows and kicked the doors until the air gave out and we lost consciousness. Once fully submerged, in ten minutes tops we'd be goners. Tomorrow a search-and-rescue would pull the car from the river, and when the doors were pried open and the muddy water and muck had finally drained, they'd extract our sodden bodies, entwined in a farewell embrace.

That creative writing course I took in high school finally paid off, I thought sardonically after composing the scene in my mind.

Upon impact the engine had stalled and the dashboard lights were extinguished. Dangling over the ledge, the front wheels had spun crazily with a *whucka-whucka-whucka* sound for a good minute until they slowed and finally stopped. Underneath the chassis a small avalanche of rocks tumbled over the embankment with a dry rattling sound. The car shifted with a groan, then settled. The rain-swollen river churned below. In the far distance a buoy light winked. A fingernail moon, peeking out now and then behind the clouds, provided the only light. I heard Cody's disembodied voice next to me in the gloom.

"Are you okay?" he asked with eerie calmness.

"I think so," I whispered, as if the sound waves could lurch the car forward. I couldn't feel anything but terror, but I assumed any bodily pain would come soon enough. All I wanted to do was call for help. But it was too dark to see my cell phone, probably somewhere at my feet; I dared not lean forward to search.

"Don't move."

"No joke."

"Can you see what's outside of your door? Is your side on stable footing, or…?"

I barely turned my head to check. It looked like I could make it to safe ground if I jumped far enough.

"I think so. Are you suggesting we make a jump for it?"

"I don't see any other way to get out of this thing before it falls."

"Okay." It sounded like a ridiculous plan that would definitely kill us, but all I had to offer was *okay*.

Cody reached his hand slowly to his waist and unbuckled his seat belt. "Here's the plan. We're going to carefully open our doors, then jump as far as you can. Be ready to grab onto anything you can to haul yourself up to the road. Got it?"

My "yes" was barely audible as it floated from my mouth.

I unbuckled my seat belt, unlocked the door, then together we counted down:

Three. The age of my youngest child.

Two. The number of children waiting at home for me to get out of this alive.

One. The number of breaths I took before I leapt as far as adrenalin would carry me, until my body slammed against rock and broken asphalt. The impact shot a grunt from my throat. Dirt stung my eyes. Sticks jabbed my legs. Sharp pebbles cut my hands. But never had dirt and sticks and pebbles felt so good. I clawed my way up the hill, nails digging into the earth, the keratin ripping as I hauled 134 pounds of bone, fat, and muscle to the safety of the flat road. My cheek scraped against the ground, and my forehead throbbed like it had split open. But I was alive!

The car wobbled beside me, blocking my view of the driver's side.

"Cody?" I screamed. "Did you make it?"

Only the long call of a whippoorwill answered. I waited for a reply. Any sign that he had survived.

"Cody?" I called again.

The car's rear shocks squeaked ominously as the nose tipped a little further, then leveled out again. My arms had moved past pain as I pushed myself up, rose to my feet, and stumbled my way around the trunk of the car.

Cody was nowhere to be found. I ran to the car, but it was too dark to see inside it. A rustle of leaves somewhere along the ground joined my heavy breaths.

Then a voice, just below my feet as Cody yelled, "I'm okay!"

I dropped to my knees and grabbed at his wrists, anchoring my feet and legs to drag his body weight up the cliff. One last tug propelled him to my side.

We were safe...for now. Or else we were in very real danger.

Chapter 18
Marin

I hadn't seen Felicity for two days. While the bruises she had left on my arms were fading, her vitriol toward me was fully charged. She refused to speak to me, and I couldn't blame her. I only heard bits and pieces from Cody about the investigation into the dead body the police had found. No one else would utter a word. Too many suspicions were growing, too many secrets unearthed, too many harsh words exchanged. Pain feasted on the family like a flesh-eating bacteria.

I couldn't let this go on any longer, the growing chasm between us. My dad always said, if there was one thing that could heal just about anything, it was food. His go-to remedy: Grandma's homemade lasagna. Oliver had requested it when I asked what I could bring over, since even picky Eliot would eat my lasagna if it had enough melted mozzarella on top. It took over an hour to find my grandmother's pasta-maker in the basement among the musty boxes and rat droppings, then another hour to deep-clean the metal contraption of the spiderwebs clinging to the gears. By then I had Grandma's recipe book opened to the right page and all my ingredients ready for the all-day process of mixing and kneading the pasta dough, feeding the dough through the slits, and cranking it down into thin slices that would be layered between sauce and meat and cheese. Let me tell you, this exhausting effort was the fullest extent of my love.

A SLOW RUIN

After knocking on Felicity's front door and waiting for several minutes, I checked the handle. Unlocked. I let myself in and headed straight to the kitchen. Not a soul in sight. The generations-old Corning Ware cornflower blue casserole dish I set on the counter looked tacky amid her classy modern kitchen décor.

The first floor was empty as I checked each room for the kids. A full-body hug from Eliot and wet kiss from Sydney soothed all manner of ailments, and I was ailing today. Especially after a sleepless night replaying Felicity's wrath and my interaction with Austin and his psycho mother. I paused at the foot of the steps, staring up at the creepy stained-glass couple, leering snootily at everyone passing by. Upstairs the chatter of small voices drifted down the stairwell as I overheard Sydney's Barbie doll reprimanding Eliot's Doctor Strange action figure about how to properly treat a lady.

"No, Doctor Strange. You're supposed to hold the door *open*!" Sydney squeaked in her best grownup lady impression.

With a careful stride, I avoided the creakiest steps as I headed up, hoping to surprise them. On my way to the kids' playroom, I peeked into Vera's bedroom, feeling the ache of regret all over again as my eyes grazed over where she had slept, studied, dressed. If only I could get her home safely, maybe Felicity would forgive me. Maybe the family could be whole again. I yearned to reach out and touch pieces of Vera, as if they connected me to her wherever she was.

Slipping inside, I wandered over to her desk, still cluttered with notes she had written, homework she had never finished. Above the desk pictures were tucked into a black and hot pink French memo board. Christmases. Birthday parties. Nature hikes. A shot of me in a Mary Poppins costume, hugging her during an after-party for the closing night of the show, a community playhouse version of the enduringly popular Broadway musical. Lord knows I didn't have Ashley Brown's pipes, but I gave it my best shot. It was that night Vera confessed she wanted to study theatre like me, and it was that night I felt a connection to her unlike ever before.

I missed her smile tremendously. I missed the way she imitated Alexis Rose's "Ew" from *Schitt's Creek* any time someone did something *cringey*—another Vera-ism, as the family called it, when she resorted to teen-speak, which was often. I missed her random texts asking for advice. I missed her laugh. We had gotten so close the past couple years as she turned to me for advice on womanhood, romance, friendship…and somehow that intimacy was the trigger that pushed her away. I had shared too much. She had discovered too much. I could never forgive myself, and soon, neither would Felicity once she found out what I had done.

I meandered to Vera's bookshelf, running my fingertip across the countless spines of thrillers, classics, and romance novels. She devoured pages and plots and characters like they were candy. A thin, gold-embossed book sparkled as dying sunbeams crossed the room. I pulled it out, noting it was this past year's yearbook, which the police had leafed through as we all pointed out Vera's friends. Sitting at Vera's desk, I flipped it open, scrolling through the pages until I found her tenth grade class. I touched her face. Across the top was a note in the spidery handwriting that I recognized as Blythe's, and I smiled as I read it:

To the best friend I could ever ask for, even though we had our battles. Get ur butt home, biotch. We all miss u. The whole school. And u better not have gone on a multi-state adventure without me like Tom Sawyer—or was that Huck Finn? U would know the answer, book nerd. Luv u like a sister. Pls come home soon. – BS

They had been such good friends, especially when Vera needed one back when she started high school. Sheltered, innocent little Vera had been terrified to leap from the nurturing bosom of middle school into the jagged terrain of high school bullies, peer pressure, and raging hormones. *Besties,* Vera had referred to her and Blythe. Until the fallout. A single fight that would launch a missile at their friendship.

I didn't know all the details, because despite my hunger for more, Vera had only grazed the bare bones of what happened between them, but I knew it had something to do with Vera breaking up with Austin and Blythe siding with him. Before the falling-out, the girls had been uber-close—hell, they'd even gotten matching Celtic tattoos—and I wondered if Blythe knew more about Vera's whereabouts than she let on. No matter how much I played up my cool aunt persona, there were some secrets even I couldn't tap into.

After Vera's disappearance, Felicity thought she had cornered the market on grief. She would never understand why, but it broke me just as much. Glancing around the room, I thought of all those secrets that had been dumped here, just waiting to be found. The tears that stained Vera's pillow. The whispers into her cell phone. The fervent scrawls in her journal. I returned the yearbook to her bookshelf, where it caught a gap in the wood and fell between the shelves.

"Shoot!" I mumbled.

Unable to reach it, I decided I'd leave it for now, then I turned to her desk. I slid open the top drawer. My fingers rummaged, my eyes searched, my heart thrummed. I would unearth nothing new today, so I slid the drawer shut. Almost. It wouldn't quite close all the way, as if a tissue or something soft was stuck in the gap. Opening it back up, I felt along the back of the drawer, sliding my fingertips across the smooth wood. Nothing there. I closed it again, but again it left a gap.

I knelt down and crawled under the desk. Peeking up, I noted a long sliver of space where the leg met the base of the desk and a loose piece of wood normally created the seal. I jiggled the piece of wood free, exposing a hollow leg. No kidding.

Sticking out from the gap in the leg was a clear plastic something or other. I grabbed it and ripped it out, replaced the wooden seal, and shuffled out from under the desk. Once back on my feet, I recognized the baggie of pot I'd given to Vera, turning it over in my palms. I opened the baggie and inhaled the floral tang of Pineapple Express. Good stuff. I'd gotten it from Brad, a friend since my early theatre days. Clever girl, Vera, hiding it behind her desk like that.

Footsteps startled me into dropping the baggie on the floor. Shit! I wasn't supposed to be here.

I picked it up just as Felicity blocked the doorway.

"What are you doing in Vera's room?" Her question was terse, her anger palpable.

"I was just dropping off a lasagna and wanted to say hi to Eliot and Syd Squid before I left." I tried to tuck the baggie behind my back, but her senses were honed to razor sharpness from fifteen years of raising kids.

"What's that you're hiding behind your back?" When I shrugged stupidly she slid toward me, grabbing my shoulder to physically pivot me. She yanked the bag from my grip, stared at it. "What is this? Drugs?"

"Why are you getting your panties in a wad? It's just pot, Felicity. Recreational marijuana's legal now in a bunch of states."

"But not Pennsylvania. Where'd you find it?"

"Hidden in her desk."

"I'm not going to ask why you were looking in her desk, but we need to turn this over to the cops. Whoever sold this to her may have been involved in her disappearance."

I absolutely could *not* let that happen. Involving the cops in something as trivial as a dime bag was just plain silly. "Felicity, stop. No pot dealer abducted Vera."

"How do you know, Marin? Maybe she owed them money or something."

"I'm telling you, this tiny amount is only worth $10. No drug dealer would abduct a kid over ten bucks."

"Well, I'm still turning this over to the police." Felicity stepped toward the door, paused, and glared back at me. "And you—you need to leave."

She turned to leave. I faced a choice: watch the oncoming bus hit the stranger, or run into the traffic and sacrifice my own life. I ran into the traffic.

"Wait! Felicity, I'm the one who gave it to her."

Felicity stopped, her back facing me. Then she slowly twisted around, ire in her eyes as she stormed up to me. "*You* gave drugs to my daughter?"

"It wasn't like that. I swear. She had asked me if I knew how to get some for a friend. I told her no, but when she said she'd find her own source, I got scared. If you don't know the dealer, you have no idea what the marijuana could be laced with. So I offered to get it for her since I didn't want her getting something dangerous."

"So you thought it was a better idea to give drugs to my child than talking to me—her mother—about it?"

"I didn't think—"

"Exactly, Marin. You didn't think! Instead you endangered my child."

"I'm sorry. You know how teens are—they're going to do

what they want, regardless of what a parent says. I figured at least if she was determined to try it, it was better off coming from someone I know and trust."

Felicity's eyes circled in her sockets. "Wow, Marin, you've really crossed a whole new line. You were my best friend, my *sister,* but I don't even know you. I don't know why you have drug contacts, or how you think what you did was remotely okay, but I am about to turn *you* over to the cops for giving drugs to a child. I'm sure it's illegal."

"Are you serious? You'd turn your own sister in to the police?"

"Maybe then you'd think twice before handing out an illegal substance to your own niece."

"Felicity, I said I'm sorry! I was trying to avoid a big issue about it. You realize marijuana is less addictive than cigarettes, right?"

"You may think I'm a prude, but you're not a mother, so you don't understand. It's one thing if you were a child who didn't know better, but you're a grown woman who made a stupid decision for someone else's child without asking. You should have told me! And what's worse is that you don't know that this doesn't have something to do with her disappearance. If she was keeping this secret from me, what else was she hiding?"

This was rapidly getting blown out of proportion. Turning me over to the police for an eighth of pot? I was family! For the past four years we'd been shopping buddies, made coffee runs, shared inside jokes, were *soul sisters*—and had matching T-shirts to prove it. How did it degrade to this? It would have been laughable if it didn't shine a dangerous spotlight on me.

"Felicity, you act like every single thing is a clue, and every single person is a suspect."

I felt like I was stuck in a real-life version of *Clue* or *Knives*

Out. Every character a villain, every backstory a motive. Felicity daggered me with a cold stare.

"Until Vera is home safely, everyone *is* a suspect, including *you.*"

Chapter 19
Felicity

The Barkalicious Boutique was the one place I could let it all go. The anger at the cops for not finding Vera. The impatience with the doctors for not curing Sydney. The sadness over missing Marin's friendship. The regret of secrets that my family kept from each other. The frustration with Oliver for not fixing everything. But most of all, the fear that terrorized me. Physically my body still hurt from the hit-and-run. Mentally my brain was fried from wondering who was after me and why. Emotionally my heart was empty of hope. My dog-grooming business, my cute little store that I'd started from the ground up, was the one place I could rest my embattled soul.

I remembered the day Oliver and I came to see this location that would soon serve as my storefront. The town of Oakmont was quaint, classy, and affordable. On one side of Allegheny River Boulevard sat huge potted plants and wrought-iron benches that invited passersby to sit and enjoy the row of contiguous shops, each with a unique and inviting facade. Carved pumpkins sat in clusters in front of Annie's Antiques; a scarecrow stood sentry beside the door of a A Cut Above the Rest. Across the brick street was a narrow strip of grass where railroad tracks carried the occasional freight. Trees hung with plastic ghosts offered shade and colorful foliage for shoppers, hiding the view of the cliff face that plunged down to meet the river that had almost swallowed me and Cody. Oakmont was the perfect blend of vintage homeyness with a modern update. A perfect match for me.

Home was only a five-minute drive from town, a fifteen-minute stroll. With three kids at home, I had wanted something close enough to allow me to pop in on Debra and Joe when they watched the kids, in case they needed anything. After more than a decade of being a stay-at-home mom, I had wanted something for myself. With no real job experience, my choices were limited, until my passion for entrepreneurism and pets evolved into an idea. From that idea the boutique was born. I traded our minivan for a conversion van, transforming it into a traveling dog-grooming service where I drove into low-income areas every Wednesday to offer free pet grooming. Even amid a struggling economy, the pandemic, and our family hardships, thanks to my innate business acumen and Oliver's marketing expertise I had managed to keep my business afloat.

After the last employee left for the night, I flipped over the Open sign to Closed then locked the front door of my doggie boutique. I exhaled all of the anger and impatience and sadness as I finished my day of customer greeting, dog grooming, floor sweeping, and forgetting.

Animals were my preference to people most days. Dogs never argued or complained, and their biggest demands were for basic needs and petting. They were loyal, supplied endless love, and knew when to give you space. They understood the word *no*. When it came to showing love and compassion for helpless critters, though, that word wasn't in my vocabulary.

Take today for instance, when a strange woman rapped her knuckles on the entrance door almost thirty minutes past closing. On the sidewalk I saw a white husky puppy on a leash, its lolling tongue creating wet smudges on the glass.

I unlocked the door and opened it a crack. "Can I help you?" I asked.

The woman's eyes settled on the bandage taped to my forehead. I self-consciously covered it with my hand.

"Car accident," I said.

"Ouch." She winced with empathy. "I heard that you took in stray dogs?" Her voice rose with the question, frantic but hopeful. "I found this one running around the neighborhood and I wasn't sure what else to do with her."

Not again! This would make dog number four if I brought her home. The kids would be ecstatic, but Oliver would be livid. Somehow the kids always won, because even Oliver couldn't resist puppy-dog kisses.

"Technically we don't take strays, but if the animal shelter is full, sometimes we're able to place a stray with a home. Did you check with the shelter to see if she's got a microchip?"

"Yeah, I stopped by our local shelter and she wasn't chipped. They ran an online search to see if anyone had posted looking for a dog that matched her description but found no hits. Unfortunately, their kennels are full so they said right now they don't have room for her and told me to take her to another county shelter. That's when I posted on social media about her and someone told me to bring her here."

Oliver would kill me. Absolutely freak out. One by one, as each of our three dogs was brought home with the promise that I'd find homes for them, I gave up after a week (or a day, if I was being honest) and let the kids name them. Never name a pet you don't intend to keep. Thus the bond was formed, the kids got attached, and our fur family grew. What else could I do? Like I said, I didn't know the word *no* when it came to animals.

I swung the door open wide and took the leash. "Okay, I'll take her and try to find a home for her. She's beautiful. Certainly someone will fall in love with her."

The woman thanked me two, three times before rushing down the sidewalk before I could change my mind. After guiding the husky pup into the waiting area, I let her run loose around the store while I finished closing the register and wiping the counters. Bowing to my OCD, a trait Marin and I shared, I took a moment to straighten the pictures on the wall of some of Barkalicious Boutique's satisfied customers: a chow-chow modeling a lion's mane. A bow-bedecked Pomeranian. A shiny golden retriever wearing a classic red paisley bandana.

I grabbed the dog's leash and the keys to Oliver's car. Although my car had a shockingly minimal amount of damage, the vehicle was officially ruined for me as even sitting in the leather seats caused a PTSD-level panic. As I pulled the front door open, the landline phone rang. The machine picked up.

"Felicity Portman, I know what you did." The woman's voice was gruff and low, not a voice I recognized over the crackle of a bad connection. "You are the reason she's dead. You deserve what's coming to you."

My blood ran cold. The hairs on my neck prickled. The dog pulled at her leash. My fingers loosened. My knees wobbled as the door pushed back against me, holding me upright. Terror from the hit-and-run poured into my veins. One hard tug, and the dog took off out into the street just before the door slid closed. I demanded my legs work, carry me to the phone. I reached for the receiver, pressed it to my ear, screaming, "Hello? Hello?" into dead air. She had hung up.

I scrolled through the missed call log, but the number was unavailable. I didn't know if anyone still used *69 to trace a call, but I dialed it anyway. A maddening beep bounced off my eardrum.

Who was this stranger? Was it the same person who ran me

off the road? What did she mean? Was Vera dead?

I was certain my heart was about to explode from my chest. My vision swirled, and sweat popped up across my forehead. One arm felt numb, both legs barely held me upright. The phone receiver clattered beside me as I dropped to the floor. Everything hurt. I couldn't breathe. A heart attack? Panic attack? I didn't know how to tell the difference.

I closed my eyes, focused on each breath. For Vera. I needed to stay calm for Vera. I was reminded numerous times by Detective Montgomery not to overreact to every threatening call or misleading letter. I'd gotten hundreds of them when the news first broke that my daughter had gone missing. Angry recluses with nothing else to do wrote accusations of us hurting our own child. Fake sightings filled up my voicemail. Egg spatter and spray paint defaced my store windows. Our house had only been spared because of its distance from the road—and Oliver's "Trespassers Will Be Shot, Survivors Will Be Shot Again" sign, which discouraged most (but not all) wackos and curiosity-seekers. After a couple months, the threats and sightings and vandalism waned as Vera's disappearance was forgotten by the general public.

Except one person who apparently didn't get the memo.

Whoever left the message knew something, it would seem, but it was worded vague enough to cast doubt. Another prank call I could shrug off? Or intimidation from someone who knew what I was hiding? After the hit-and-run, everything felt like a threat.

Out in the street, a distant barking pumped my weakening body back to life. A car swerved past my door, leaving a long honk in its wake. The dog—I had forgotten all about her!

Whatever strength was left in me coursed through my veins and I ran into the street just as the dog darted in front of an oncoming car. Tail happily wagging, the husky dutifully locked me in her sight, trotting toward me in the middle of the road. I waved my arms frantically as I ran into the street, hoping to catch the driver's attention before it was too late.

The screaming tires melded with my screams. Another five feet and the dog would be crushed. I couldn't look. I turned away, eyes squeezed shut, waiting for that horrible thump any moment now...

My body was knocked back a couple steps as I felt a handful of fur, opened my eyes, and bent down to scoop up the dog in my arms. She rewarded my bravery—or insanity—with a lavish tongue bath as the driver of the car yelled obscenities at me.

"Keep your dog off the street, lady! I almost killed it!" He stuck his arm out the window and flipped me off.

"You're all class, you know that?" I yelled halfheartedly as he peeled away.

Well, at least one thing didn't die today.

The phone call—there it was, back fully formed and present. *"You are the reason she's dead. You deserve what's coming to you."* My first instinct was to call Oliver, the ever-present hero in my life story, the one who held me as I wept and chased away my fears with kisses. But he was no good to me now; I needed professional help. After stowing the dog in the backseat, I pulled out my phone and autodialed Detective Montgomery. Somewhere along the way I had memorized her direct line.

"This is Detective Courtney Montgomery," she answered.

Clearly she hadn't yet memorized mine.

"It's Felicity Portman. I got a phone call at my store today about Vera."

"What kind of phone call?"

"A threatening one, I think."

She paused, exhaled into the phone, then said, "I'll meet you at your store in a few minutes. I have some news for you too."

Chapter 20
Felicity

"We don't think the body we recovered from the river is Vera."

This was the only part of Detective Montgomery's long-winded scientific explanation about DNA and estimated time of death and victim age that I fully understood as she announced the good news at Barkalicious Boutique. While she still couldn't guarantee certainty, instantaneous relief washed over me that it was most likely not Vera. *Most likely not* didn't offer the fullest extent of comfort I wanted, but it was promising. The most reassuring words one mother could hope for, yet the biggest heartbreak for another. It almost felt wrong to celebrate the news as I hugged the detective in gratitude, while another mother out there crumbled to her knees. The possibility of me being that other mother someday was sobering, but for now I would be grateful and keep standing.

When I pulled up my driveway, the detective's unease about the voicemail followed me home. *"If that hit-and-run hadn't just happened,"* she admitted, *"I would consider this just another media junkie looking for attention. Especially with Halloween around the corner, which brings out the crazy in some people."*

Like Eliot and Sydney, who had put the finishing touches on their costumes after ransacking the boxes of vintage Halloween decorations dating to Vera's girlhood and plastering the house with them. They picked out the household's most capacious pillowcases to hold the pounds of goodies they anticipated getting when I took them trick-or-treating door to door in Oakmont. Cute little plastic pumpkin buckets, they informed me—besides being corny—were woefully inadequate.

"But I think we need to look into this further," Detective Montgomery had added. *"I'll see if my tech people can trace the call. For now, try not to worry about it."*

As if I could just turn the worry off. It was the only emotion living inside me anymore.

In the backseat the husky whined and whimpered, ready to run. I parked Oliver's car in his usual spot and led the dog around the front yard on her leash, letting her take in all the smells and mark the territory—first the rabbit bush, then a hibernating rose bush—as her own while I considered any possible way to hide her from Oliver. But he was already trotting down the front porch steps when I emerged from behind a dormant hydrangea.

"Tell me that dog wasn't just now getting hair all through my car." His words shot out in pellets. "And it better belong to someone."

"She does now!" I teased. "C'mon, Ollie, you're going to turn this sweet face away?" I bent down and let the dog lick my chin.

"Not another dog. Absolutely not. Take it to the shelter. We've got enough to deal with without adding another animal to care for."

"I bet Syd would adore her." Using the kids as pawns was usually off-limits, but ever since her diagnosis, Sydney got what Sydney wanted. When you didn't know if it was your child's last day on earth, you tended to overcompensate.

"I bet Syd would prefer quality time with her mother over a furry surrogate." When Oliver hit, he made sure it hurt.

"Now you're just being cruel."

"Felicity"—Oliver sucked in a breath, then continued—"wake the hell up! Your actions affect the rest of us."

"I'm not saying they don't, but I don't understand why you're all worked up right now."

"You almost died in that car accident. And now you're late getting home, not bothering to even answer your phone. I tried calling you a dozen times, and I would have driven around looking for you if Sydney wasn't napping. After you nearly got run off a freakin' cliff, you can't just go MIA. Don't you understand that I worry about you?"

"I...I don't know what to say, Ollie. I appreciate your concern, but you can't micromanage every minute of my day."

"It's more than that. You leave me to handle the kids while you self-medicate, or take secret late-night trips with Cody. And all that time you spend on social media and online support groups, or hiding in Vera's room searching for clues that aren't there. It's not fair to me, or the kids, to be gone ninety-five percent of the time, then come home with a puppy as if that will fill the hole in your kids' hearts while I'm forced to pick up all the pieces."

It wasn't true. None of this was true. I was there for my children. I was making snacks and cleaning up messes and tucking them in bed. How dare he say I wasn't present?

"You have no right! No right to tell me how to feel or act! You think I'm a mess? Well, I *should* be a mess! And why aren't you? Fifteen years we've dedicated every part of our lives to Vera, and you're just going to give up on her after six months? Forget her as if she never existed? No, you're the broken one, not me. I've lost one daughter, and I'm faced with the possibility of losing another, so I think I'm allowed to grieve in my own way, in my own time, Oliver."

Amid my screaming I didn't notice the tiny figure standing at the door. The watery eyes watching us, the young mind absorbing all of this, piecing it together like one of his 300-piece LEGO sets.

"Is Syd going to die?"

Oliver spun around. I rushed toward the porch.

"No, sweet boy, Syd's going to be fine," I said as I reached out to push a sprouting tuft of hair behind his ear.

Eliot backed away from me, pressing himself against Oliver's legs. "Don't touch me!"

"Hey, bud, your mom is right," Oliver said, scooping his son up. "Syd's going to be okay. You don't need to worry."

Eliot clung to his neck, glaring at me. I tenderly rubbed circles on his back, but he wiggled away. "Leave me alone!" Eliot yelled. "I want Daddy!"

Where was my sweet boy in this madness? Was Oliver right—had I created this gulf between mother and child? Had I pushed Vera away too?

I heard the crackle of a car pulling into the parking area, then turned to see Debra getting out of her car. Eliot was whimpering now with his face buried in his daddy's shoulder. Debra quickened her step.

"What's going on with Eliot?" she asked, full of concern. "Everything okay?"

Great. I *so* did not want to involve my mother-in-law in this argument. But here she was, arms folded, expecting an explanation.

"No, Mom, it's not okay. Your grandson overheard us talking about Sydney, and your son apparently thinks it's unhealthy for me to worry about my children."

She cast a disappointed look at Oliver. She was a mother too; we understood each other. "Ollie." It was all she needed to say to chasten him.

PAMELA CRANE

"That's hardly the issue, Felicity. You're oversimplifying it," he retorted.

"Enough fighting in front of Eliot," Debra said, kissing Eliot's ruddy cheek. "Your sister's going to be fine, sweetie. The doctors are working hard to fix her."

Eliot peeked out at her from Oliver's shoulder. "Pinkie swear?"

Debra latched her pinkie around his. "Pinkie swear." Then she kissed his tiny knuckles. "And who is this cute little thing?" She reached down and patted the dog's head.

"A stray someone brought into the shop. I'm not sure what to do with her yet."

"Let's name her Ploppy!" Eliot said with a giggle.

"Why Ploppy?" Debra asked.

"Because she just plopped a big poop on Dad's foot!"

"What?" Oliver looked down in dismay. "Ohmygod! My brand-new Air Maxes!" He sat Eliot down on the porch steps, then hopped on one foot into the grass to clean the soiled shoe.

"Daddy got a doody shoe, Daddy got a doody shoe!" Eliot chanted.

Debra and I shook with suppressed laughter. As much as we loved him, we shared the unspoken opinion that Oliver was the kind of guy who *needed* to have his shoe shat on every now and then.

"Cute *and* clever, aren't you?" Debra chuckled to the dog in baby talk, leaning down making kissing noises.

Oliver returned to the porch steps, dangling the befouled Nike by the laces. "Mom, what are you doing here?" he sighed.

"I came to see if Felicity wanted to go out for some girl time with me. Just us two. I was going to run down to the antique mall in town. Then maybe we could grab dinner out." Debra turned to me. "You up for it? Dinner on me?"

I shrugged, not really interested in shopping, but even less interested in sharing space with my husband right now.

"Sure. Let me take the dog to the backyard and get her situated, and I'll be right out."

"We're not keeping the dog!" Oliver hollered as I led the dog away.

"It's too late—Eliot already named him," I hollered back.

I walked around the side yard that led to a fenced-in area where the trampoline and playset took over one corner, and a stone outdoor patio jutted out from the back of the house. Opening the latch, I released Ploppy—name still undecided as far as I was concerned—into the yard and watched her run around, legs bounding, tail wagging, tongue lolling. I'd introduce her to the other dogs later this evening after she got acclimated—and after Oliver, as he always did, warmed to the idea of another fuzzy muzzle to feed.

After a wardrobe change out of my hair-covered scrubs and into a festive burnt orange sweater and high-waisted mom jeans—which I had once vowed never to wear and yet now lived in, thanks to Vera's fashion advice—I slid into Debra's car, debating whether to tell her about the strange phone call. When she started asking about Eliot and Oliver, I decided to keep it between myself and Detective Montgomery. The family clearly wanted me to move on, stop wallowing in anticipatory grief, forget my trauma. So I'd give them what they wanted and pretend everything was fine. I'm fine. You're fine. Everything's fine.

"Don't worry too much about Eliot," Debra was saying as we pulled into the parking lot, "kids are resilient. He'll probably forget all about this by bedtime."

"I hope so." A question I hadn't intended to ask aloud floated up and out. "Do you think Vera left because she overheard us talking about Sydney's kidney match and didn't want to donate to her?"

Debra parked and shut off the car before she answered. "I don't know, honey. Do you really think that's the kind of person she was—a girl who wouldn't be there for her own sister when she was most needed?"

Many nights I had lain awake pondering this same question. As the days passed, weeks slipped by, months eroded, I felt like I was stuck in a fever dream, reminiscing about a girl who never existed. A happy girl. The more memories I collected, the more a portrait emerged of a girl who resented quickly, begrudged fiercely, and whose anger was too big for her body. Had Debra asked me six months ago if Vera would do anything for family, I would have wholeheartedly said yes. But now…after finding out more and more of who Vera truly was outside of our four walls, I realized I didn't know anything about her.

"Was it too much to ask of her, to donate an organ to help her dying sister? Because if there was any other way, Mom, I would do it in a heartbeat. I would give up my own life to save Syd's…but I suppose it's unfair to expect Vera to do the same."

"There's no right or wrong here, Felicity. Whether or not that's why Vera left, you did nothing wrong. You weren't going to force her into anything, and she should have known that, not taken off."

Except Debra wasn't there the night I broached the subject with Oliver. Debra didn't hear our heated conversation, didn't know what I had said to Oliver in a weak, emotional moment. I had replayed the argument a million times since the night Vera left, memorized every word, wondering if there was any possible way Vera could have heard and how she might have interpreted it. Every time I came back to the same conclusion: it was enough to drive my daughter away.

My words echoed back at me: *The fact that Vera is a match*

is nearly impossible, Oliver, given her history. Clearly it's a sign that she has to do it! Right now Syd's life is more important, and if Vera can't understand that, then maybe she's not the daughter we thought she was."

If only I could rewind to that night, to that conversation and delete it...but life didn't have a rewind button.

We stepped into the cool October air and strolled along a covered walkway festooned with crisscrossing strings of LED ghosts flashing orange, green, and purple. Grinning jack-o'-lanterns, spooky in the gathering darkness, squatted atop artistic arrangements of hay bales, corn stalks, and friendly scarecrows. Paper bag luminaries adorned with witch and bat silhouettes lined the walkway. A ginormous inflatable archway in the form of a jolly Jack Skellington, natty in signature pinstripes, welcomed visitors at the mall entrance. It was about an hour before closing and only a few cars dotted the nearly empty parking lot.

I was walking a little ahead of Debra, admiring the Halloween extravaganza, when I heard her scream. I whipped around to see my genteel mother-in-law engaged in a fierce tug-of-war over her purse with a mugger wearing a cheap but creepy Pennywise mask (at least he had the holiday spirit) under his hoodie. Rather than let go like a sane person, Debra lunged at him, pulled the mask out by the elastic strap, and snapped it with a *zing*. The thug cursed and released the purse strap, but Debra was just getting started. In one fell swoop she poked him in the eye and kneed him in the crotch. He doubled over, hands on knees, moaning and rocking painfully on his heels. Before he could recover, she wound her arm up like a major league pitcher and *whack!*—the purse caught him square in the jaw. I knew that purse weighed a good ten pounds because Debra, like every good grandma, kept it overstocked with useful sundries and could produce from it, like a magician's hat, practically anything you needed on demand. She kept swinging her lethal weapon with the terrifying skill of a ninja flourishing a katana, until the hapless thug, walloped at least six times across the head, face, and back, skittered away on all fours like a scalded dog.

"Why don't you get a job!" Debra yelled after him. "Instead of picking on defenseless old ladies!"

Out of breath, she smoothed her hair and casually slung the purse strap over her shoulder as if she hadn't just kicked the ass of an attacker twice her size.

"Defenseless?" I said, after I'd picked my jaw up off the ground. "Mom, if you're defenseless, I guess Chuck Norris is defenseless too. I never knew you were so scrappy!"

"What do you mean? The jerk tried to mug me. And I didn't let him get away with it. Simple as that."

"No, Mom, you beat that thug up. How weren't you afraid?"

"It's not complicated. I took a class and learned how to defend myself."

"But...how?" I was incredulous. Who was this fearless woman before me?

"If you knew how I grew up, Felicity, you'd understand that self-defense is one of the most important gifts you can give yourself. I'll never be a victim again. And I'm not afraid to stand up for others."

I only knew bits and pieces of Debra's past, but I hadn't given it more than a passing thought until now. We never made it inside the mall, as I was too freaked out to head anywhere but home after that. But I saw something in Debra that I wanted. Strength to fight back. Courage to face my failures. And it started with the truth, no matter what it cost me, even if that meant jail.

I considered all the secrets that needed to come out, especially my own. And Marin's.

"Do you think that's what Marin was doing for Vera when

she kept her secrets for her, like the tattoo and the boyfriend? Was this Marin's way of standing up for Vera?"

Debra shook her head. "Standing up for her against what?"

"Against me. I know I sometimes…expected too much from Vera."

She scoffed. "No, dear, I don't think Marin was trying to protect Vera. But I do think Marin is the reason Vera's missing."

Chapter 21
Marin

I had been warned beforehand that Felicity was still upset with me. But I insisted on showing up to family dinner with an apology, because I didn't want to hide and my sister needed my support. Dad had raised me to confront problems, fix them, not to run from them because the chase only makes them grow. My mother had never learned this lesson as she buried her addiction, and in the end it buried her. I refused to follow in her footsteps. Besides, the more I hid, the more they'd dig. And I couldn't risk anyone digging.

Debra and Joe hadn't been able to make it tonight, which gave me the freedom to loosen up a bit. By the time dinner was served I was on my third glass of wine, which was two glasses beyond my limit. At least I wasn't the only one. Felicity was already plastered when I arrived, and I wasn't sure if I was more annoyed or relieved. She tended to either get argumentative or overly affectionate when she drank, and I waited to see which version of her would emerge.

We sat around the dinner table, Oliver at the head, me catty-corner on one side with Felicity across from me, all avoiding the topic of Vera, instead picking random topics. The new COVID variant going around, Eliot's science project (he was debating whether to feature bugs or wind—*breaking* wind, he added with a laugh, as they were studying weather right now), the Earth Day carnival coming up…and then Argumentative Felicity arrived.

"I'm taking a poll. Who thinks it's okay for Cool Aunt Marin to give a teenager pot?" Felicity looked around the table, eyes wobbly, words a slurry of vowels and consonants. "Or am I just an unhip, cringey mom who doesn't get it?"

Oliver, the only sober adult among us, bowed his head and rested his forehead on his palm. He thought *he* was embarrassed?

"Felicity, I wasn't trying—"

"Shush!" Felicity aimed her finger toward my face, missing my mouth altogether and instead landing on my cheek. "I'm speaking, Cool Aunt Marin."

"Mommy, you're as cool as Aunty Marin to me and Idiot," Sydney chimed in.

"Aw, thank you, babycakes. But apparently your daddy doesn't think so," Felicity slurred.

"I think you've had enough party time," Oliver interjected. He stood up, slid his hand under Felicity's elbow, and tried to lift her. But she resisted with a slap on his arm.

"No! Let me friggin' speak, Ollie! I wanna know how to be cool like Marin. I always gotta be the one who rains on the parade. I'm tired of it! I want Vera to like me again, like she did when she was a little girl. She idolized me, you know? Now she hates me so much she ran away from me. So"—she turned her glassy gaze on me—"Marin, tell me, how do I win my girl back?"

"I don't know what to say, Felicity." It was the first time I questioned my father's advice. This was one problem I didn't want to confront: Argumentative Felicity.

"You could try dessert," Eliot suggested. "That would win me back!"

"Me too!" Sydney chimed in.

"Good idea, Syd Squid. Do you mind if I give them a slice of that cake I brought? I added extra chocolate," I asked Oliver with a wink toward the kids. The less interaction I had with Felicity, the better.

"First you two need to go upstairs and get in your pajamas, then we'll have cake," Oliver agreed.

In a stampede of bare feet on hardwood, Oliver and the kids scampered up the stairs whooping while Felicity disappeared into the kitchen carrying her plate, Cody following her.

"What can I do to help?" Something about Cody's offer was strained. Pleading.

"Nothing. I've got it," Felicity spat back.

But Cody followed anyway, and as I stacked dishes and silverware, I watched the two disappear into the guts of the house. I had read something in his expression over dinner, an unease. Guilt. With everything piled into a tall stack of plates, I carried it down the hallway toward the kitchen. Intense voices echoed in stern whispers. I crept up to the swinging door that separated the kitchen from the hall, overhearing first Cody, then Felicity exchanging harsh words. An argument, but over what, I couldn't make out. Part of me wanted to interrupt them, see what excuse they'd come up with to explain the heat between them, but another part of me wanted to remain a silent, undetected observer.

I stood by the door and eavesdropped, hearing bits and pieces of the fight. Words like "lied" and "hurt" were tossed back and forth between them, and all I could wonder was who lied, about what, and who hurt who. I suspected that Oliver and I stood to hurt the most, though.

When I overheard Felicity sternly order Cody to "please just leave me alone, I'm dealing with enough already," followed by his approaching footsteps, I scurried down the hallway, searching for a place to hide. I don't know why I felt the need to hide; they were the ones who were clearly hiding something. But tucked safely in the corner where the hallway emptied into what had originally been a smoking room, I waited until Cody passed by before I slipped out and headed back toward the kitchen.

On the way I bumped into Felicity, almost causing her to drop the wine bottle she carried by the neck, and the plates swayed with me.

"Oh my gosh, sorry!" I yelped, jumping back.

In her other hand she held two wineglasses, her palm cupping the bottom of the glasses as the stems poked between her fingers.

"It's okay," she muttered.

"Do you want me to grab the other glasses?" I offered, trying to make peace, though I wasn't sure what we were warring over.

"No thanks. I'll get them." Raising her chin, she shifted to step around me, but I stepped in front of her.

"Are you still upset with me about giving Vera that baggie of pot?" I asked. "Because honestly, Felicity, I never meant to do anything behind your back. I was just trying to prevent Vera from going to someone else for it."

"Would you still be upset if I did that to your child?" Good ol' Felicity, so political, answering a question with a question.

"I'm not a mother, so I can't answer that. But I want to fix things between us, and I don't know how."

"Really? You're going to claim you don't know how to fix things? How about you bring my missing daughter home?" The accusation behind it bit me. She blamed me. Hell, I blamed me too, but for very different reasons.

"You know if I could I would."

Felicity pointed at me, her finger hovering an inch from my nose, the wine bottle bumping my chin. "You, Marin, are lucky you don't have to suffer the weight of motherhood. It's an awful beautiful burden. And it hurts so damn much."

Her arm tilted; her whole body tilted under the influence of the five glasses of wine and two fingers of whiskey. And that was only what I had witnessed her drinking.

"I'm lucky, huh?" Shoved in my face, dangling from her wrist, her gorgeous bracelet sparkled under the light. "If I was lucky, I'd have children who loved me like yours do, a home that wasn't falling apart, and I'd be wearing a bracelet like that. You're so spoiled on love and wealth and attention that you don't see what you have. But the rest of us commoners do, Felicity."

Felicity looked at the jewelry as if seeing it for the first time.

"You want jewelry? A fancy house? Here." She fumbled to unclasp the bracelet, dropping the bottle of wine in the process. A tongue of red licked the floor while glass shards sparkled like stars in a crimson sky. Felicity gazed at the mess she had made, then contorted as she began to cry.

"This bracelet means nothing without Vera," she muttered between sobs. "And I don't care about all of this stuff. I'd give everything up to get her back, even though I know I never deserved her."

I felt my cheeks flush with embarrassment at this intimate glimpse inside her heart.

"Don't say that—you've been a great mom. And she loves you more than anything, Felicity."

She sniffled, snatched a breath. "I hope so. I know you love her too. I'm trying so hard not to be angry at you, but it's...complicated. I wake up wanting to feel okay, but then all the worry heaves itself on me, and suddenly I can't breathe, can't think, just wait for news about whether Vera is alive or dead...and just keep waiting and waiting for answers that may never come. I've watched one child disappear and another slowly fade away...and I need someone to blame. Someone other than myself."

"Hey, it's not your fault," I said. My eyes watered with shared pain. I loved Vera like my own sister. "We all want to support you. I'm sorry I made this about me. I don't want to get swallowed up in drama that doesn't matter. All that matters is bringing Vera home, right?"

I thought this would be the end of the grudge over the baggie of pot. I was wrong.

I offered to clean up the broken glass and wine snaking its way into the cracks between the floorboards. By the time I finished, Oliver had set the kids up at the kitchen counter with their dessert and announced to Cody and Felicity, who had moved to the living room, that he was going to get some fresh air. I decided I needed some too.

"We're all out of Collins mix, so I'm gonna make a run to the store," I said with a grin, hoping to lighten the mood.

Only Oliver laughed, recognizing the line from *Meet the Parents*. Oliver understood me in ways no one else did. Cody and Felicity threw me questioning looks, shrinking my laugh down to silence.

"There's Cool Aunt Marin again, not a care in the world." Argumentative Felicity was back.

Lately Felicity had become Robert De Niro to my Ben Stiller, always scrutinizing me, finding fault with me as I struggled to fit into her family. No matter how much I won over everyone else, Felicity would make sure I lost in the end.

I followed Oliver to the back porch, taking my fourth glass of wine with me. Pinpricks of white decorated the sky. The chilly night air invigorated me, sobering me up just enough to realize how close Oliver stood next to me, our arms brushing. I could almost feel his body heat smothering the cold.

"You okay?" I asked.

He stared straight ahead into the darkness. "Nope. Not really."

"Anything I can do to help?"

He scoffed. "Unless you can perform miracles, I'm not sure anything would help."

"How about a hit?" I offered him the vape pen that I brought with me to Felicity's—her anxiety was contagious—and his lips curled up in a grin as he shook his head.

"Didn't you learn your lesson about this stuff? If Felicity sees that she's going to rip you to shreds."

"It's CBD oil, without THC, the stuff that gets you high. Perfectly legal. You can even buy it on Amazon."

"Still…" Oliver shrugged. "You know Felicity and her sanctimony."

"Eh, she's all bark and no bite. You're a big boy, aren't you?"

Our eyes locked, frozen for a long moment. A rustle of leaves across the garden, at the edge of the porch where a massive lilac took over the corner, broke the spell.

"Did you hear that?" I stepped toward the increasing crunch and snap of yard debris, searching the gaps in the bush for movement.

Oliver took the e-cig. "Probably just Meowzebub rustling through the leaves on another mouse murder spree." Taking a long drag, he exhaled and closed his eyes. "Wow, I haven't done pot since college. What are you doing to me? Turning this responsible dad into a pothead."

I chuckled. "Like I said, it's not pot, it's CBD, you old man. Besides, one hit won't make you a junkie. You've had a lot going on and this can help ease anxiety. God knows I need it to deal with my boss's racism and sexism."

"Still that bad, huh?" Mortimer Randolph was notorious among my family by now.

"It's getting worse. His sexual harassment is getting more blatant, and when it's not sexually suggestive, it's racist."

183

"Why don't you just quit?"

I rolled my eyes in shameful admission. "I need the money, Ollie."

"I'll give you money if you need money, Mare. You're family."

"Absolutely not. I don't take charity. I just wish I didn't have to debase myself to earn a buck."

"He's ancient, isn't he? Maybe he'll die and leave you all of his money."

I chuckled. "If only I was so lucky."

A click behind me startled us both. Turning around, we saw Felicity standing in the doorway, scorn writ large on her face. Oliver quickly passed the vape pen back to me, and walked to the door as if nothing had happened. I tucked it back into my pocket.

"You need me for something?" he asked.

Felicity observed me carefully, harshly.

"Your mom called and needs your help fixing her toilet. Something about the seal leaking. Can you run over there real quick?"

"Sure, honey." Oliver kissed her cheek on his way into the house.

Felicity remained standing in the doorway, hands propped on her hips.

"What were you just doing with my husband, Marin?"

"Can you relax a bit? I know things are hard for you, but you need to lay off Oliver."

"Don't tell me how to handle my own husband. Clearly you're not doing a bang-up job with your own marriage, Marin."

"What does that mean? I thought we had mended this schism between us." I had forgotten I was dealing with Argumentative Felicity.

Felicity stumbled back a step, then swiveled to head inside.

"Can you tell Cody I'll be out here if he needs me?"

"Yeah, sure."

Twenty minutes and an empty e-cig and wineglass later, I needed another drink. I slipped into the house, not wanting to draw attention to myself. I could overhear Cody and Felicity talking in the living room. No, not talking. *Arguing.* Again I found myself hiding in the shadow of the doorway, listening. Whatever was going on with them, it was hush-hush enough that they were hiding it from me and Oliver.

"I keep apologizing, but you keep refusing to forgive me. What else am I supposed to do?" It was the same tone Cody used with me when he knew he was wrong.

"Prove you actually care," Felicity argued back.

"I don't know how, Felicity."

"I think you do."

"Look, Felicity, that was a long time ago." Cody was speaking in a voice I'd never heard before. Low and husky and...needy. "We can't go back to that. Think of our families."

"I don't want to think," she replied with that same yearning.

I shifted enough to glance inside, my breath held and blood screaming in my ears, just in time to see Cody leaning forward to kiss Felicity. Their lips were hungry and eager as his arms pulled her in. I choked on that breath.

When Felicity broke the kiss—not my husband, but Felicity!—she cupped his hand and walked toward me. I found myself rushing down the hallway, my body working on autopilot as I slipped into the powder room beneath the stairs. The echo of their footsteps above me broke my heart step by step. On a stair just above my head they stopped, and Cody spoke first.

"I don't know, Felicity." His voice was muffled by the inches of wood between us. "Marin is just outside. What if she comes in?"

"She won't. I just watched her light up a joint." Not a joint, but no matter. "She's probably as high as a kite right now…or on her way to it."

Cody heaved a heavy sigh. Remorse? Hesitation? I silently begged him to stop. "I don't know if we should be doing this."

"I'm tired of the pain, Cody." Her voice was silky and full of longing. "I just want the pain to stop. Please, help me make it stop."

I could no longer breathe the pungent smell of lemon cleaner and despair. I couldn't stand here, lurking under the stairs, waiting to hear my husband take my sister-in-law to bed. My stomach clenched at the imagery. My heart dropped to the floor. I ran out the front door, into the yard beneath the wedge of moon, jumped into my car, and cranked the engine. It rumbled an attempt, then stalled. I sobbed and screamed into the steering wheel, angry and devastated that Felicity's grief was about to swallow the rest of us whole.

Chapter 22
Marin

Mortimer Randolph lived up to the expectations his hoity-toity name conjured. White. Uber-rich. Part cutthroat attorney, part asshole. I was Anne Hathaway to his Meryl Streep in *The Devil Wears Prada,* only he wore Brooks Brothers. I was unlucky enough to work for him as his personal assistant, a job description that included no end of humiliating chores. Such as fetching his socks along with his coffee. Or massaging his bony shoulders along with his inflated ego. Or ironing his KKK robe. Kidding, but I wouldn't be surprised if the sonofabitch had one tucked away somewhere. I stuck around long enough to discover that he had one good quality. The only quality that made him redeemable to me and gave me the motivation to put up with him rather than kill him:

He thought everything—and everyone—was for sale, and no price was too big.

Karen Delacroix, his long-suffering legal secretary, also experienced firsthand the old pinchpenny's many disgusting habits and sexism and prejudices, and despised him almost as much as I did. We often compared horror stories, a great tension-reliever, sitting in his expansive kitchen over coffee (of course, making sure Maleficent Morty, as we hatefully called him, wasn't skulking about) and trying to one-up each other with regard to who had suffered the worst from his latest humiliation. Sadly, I usually won. But I was grateful I had an empathetic confidante in Karen. I don't know how I would have survived without her.

I entered his home office with fear and loathing. The room was as big as my entire first floor, lined with rich cherrywood bookcases stuffed with legal books, several obscure Lawyer of the Year awards, and a lion head mounted on the wall behind his desk. Several times a year Mortimer went on exotic hunting expeditions with his stuffed shirt cronies from the bar association, always returning home with another grisly trophy for his collection. There wasn't a room in the house where I didn't feel the glass eyes of a caribou or a muskox or a grizzly bear staring down mournfully at me. Shooting defenseless beasts was Old Morty's way of compensating for the fact he probably hadn't gotten his wrinkly willy up in twenty years.

Although Mortimer worked from his multimillion-dollar Tudor home in the ritzy Squirrel Hill North neighborhood, he always wore a suit. As if he slept and showered in one. Never once, not even when he came down with COVID last year, did I ever see him in anything but a jacket, trousers, and shined shoes. Mortimer was as stiff as his starched shirt.

Sitting at his antique Kittinger desk, his wrinkled hands were focused on peeling an apple with the paring knife he demanded moments ago.

"What would it cost me to convince you to join me for a dinner with the partners on Friday night?" His icy blue eyes rose to ogle me—lingering on my legs—before returning to the apple peel that fell to the table, which I would later be expected to clean up. One white caterpillar eyebrow was raised in anticipation of a win. He always won.

"What's the dinner for?" I asked.

While he was still the managing partner of his law firm, he rarely showed his face at the office anymore. Most of my job entailed that of a trophy assistant, running personal errands with the occasional trip to his downtown Pittsburgh office to pick up files for the more demanding cases that required the input of *"the best lawyer east of the Mississippi."* His words, not mine.

"I need to impress some potential clients, but we have to show more diversity in our firm. Since you're Black, but not *too* Black, I thought it would look good to have you there."

Not too Black. I guess I was light enough to impress these pricks but not too dark to embarrass him.

I should have known not to be so bold to assume I had anything else to offer him but my skin color. Mortimer Randolph would have fit in perfectly during the days when selling people was as normal as selling cotton. But my leaky plumbing and rotting floorboards demanded I take advantage of the offer. Maybe if I could pretend it was an acting gig of sorts I could suffer through it...

I thought: *How much do de job pay, massa?* I said: "What's the pay?"

"How about an extra $50 per hour?"

A couple hundred dollars would hardly do anything for my home improvement. My pride was worth at least double that.

"Ehhh," I wavered. "I already have plans..."

"How about a flat $1,000? Plus I'll cover your meal, of course."

Now we were negotiating.

"Okay, I can cancel. But if you want me to dress up, you've got to purchase what you want me to wear."

He thought for only a moment, bushy eyebrows wagging.

"Deal. Just pick out a dress you like and charge it to my American Express. Don't come looking like a...what's the word you people use? A ho. This is a classy affair."

A ho.

"Oh, and make sure you do your hair to look extra Black. I want to make it clear we support colored folks."

Colored folks.

"I'll have my driver come pick you up at your house on Friday night at seven o'clock sharp. Although I dislike the idea of venturing into the ghetto at night. Only low-class people there. Barely human."

The ghetto. Low-class people. Barely human.

I inhaled a calming breath. I bit my bottom lip. I counted to ten. But something snapped inside me. I couldn't go on being a doormat for this demeaning prick. Job be damned. If I didn't speak up for myself now, I never would.

"Mr. Randolph," I began calmly, "I have something to say, and I would appreciate you not interrupting. First of all, I would never dream of showing up at the dinner wearing anything that might embarrass you, your prospective clients, or myself. Second, I suppose I should thank you for not using the N-word, but the term *colored folks* is just as offensive and ignorant. And third, yes, I live in Wilkinsburg in a modest house in a poor part of town, but it is far more of a home than this, this…shrine to your inflated ego!"

I felt a trickle of sweat running down my forehead and angrily flicked it off. Mortimer looked at me like I was a human oddity in a sideshow exhibit, more curious than angry at this point. I kept going.

"For years I've endured your ogling my goodies, making me feel less than human. And I've been your arm candy for more stodgy dinner parties than I care to remember, overhearing your pompous ass partners refer to me as 'Morty's brown sugar,' and worse. I'm supposed to be your personal assistant, but you treat me like a glorified maid. You like to see me steppin' and fetchin' like some simple-minded slave out of *Gone with the Wind*, don't you? Well, welcome to the twenty-first century, old man!"

Mortimer reared back in his chair and steepled his knobby fingers. He was smirking, enjoying the show, daring me to keep digging my own grave. I obliged the old bastard. There was no stopping me now.

"I'll have you know, Mr. Randolph, that I'm proud to be a Black woman, a Black woman with intelligence and talent. I'm a damn good actress too, did you know that? No, because you never once asked me a personal question, treated me like a real person. To you I'm just as much a trophy as those pathetic animal heads on your walls. I don't intend to stay a poor nobody, working for chump change, all my life. I'm going to start my own production company someday, once I get the funding. And as for looking extra Black, sure, I can do that. I'll get a huge Afro, so wide it won't fit through the door! Maybe I'll stick an Afro pick with a Black Power fist in it! But why stop there? I'll put a bone in my nose too. That should convince your white-bread clients I'm Black enough!"

Mortimer looked at me inscrutably. "Are you quite through, Miss Portman?"

"Almost. You know, Mr. Randolph, I could raise quite a stink with a sexual harassment suit against you and your firm. I could file a racial defamation suit too. Don't think I haven't thought about it. But it would be a waste of time. After all"—I flashed a sarcastic smile—"you are the best lawyer east of the Mississippi, aren't you?"

Mortimer rocked forward in his chair. "I am indeed. Now, Miss Portman, would you mind putting down the knife?"

"What?"

"The knife in your hand. You have made quite a mess of my desktop."

I looked down. The paring knife was indeed in my hand; I

must have picked it up at some point. The desktop was riddled with small punctures where I'd stabbed it during my tirade. I gently sat the knife down next to the spiraling apple peels.

"I'll get my things," I said, turning to leave. "I'd appreciate it if you would mail me my last check."

"One moment, Miss Portman. You're not fired. No one's ever had the—pardon the expression—balls to stand up to me like you just did. You've given me a lot to think about. I'll make you another deal. If you promise not to raise a stink, as you say, I'll let you keep your job—I rather think you need it, yes?—and I won't ruin your reputation in this town, which I promise you is well within my power to accomplish. And just to show you what kind of man I am, I'm giving you a raise. How does another dollar an hour sound?"

Skinflint. "That sounds fine, sir." I could feel my swallowed pride hitting my gut like an anvil.

"Very good. I'll see you at seven on Friday. Oh, and Miss Portman?"

"Yes?"

"I'll double your rate if you flirt a little with the new clients. Flash a little chocolaty thigh, make a few risqué comments. Get 'em a little hot and bothered."

Same old same old. "Yes, sir."

"Incidentally, Miss Portman, I will take the cost of repairing my desk out of your pay, of course. Now, before you leave"—he gestured at the apple peels—"do be a lamb and clear these away. Good night, Miss Portman."

"Good night, Mr. Randolph."

I grabbed the peels in my fist and was about to deposit them in the waste basket when Mortimer said, "No, no. The kitchen."

I should have stabbed him with that paring knife when I had the chance.

Heading down the hallway, a cleaning woman I'd never seen before scuttled into the kitchen.

"Nasty old bird, ain't he?" The gray-haired woman tossed the words behind her, pulling her mop and bucket, whistling tunelessly.

I couldn't put my finger on it, but for some reason she seemed strangely familiar.

**

I dropped my heels inside the doorway when I got home that night, aching for a foot rub that I knew Cody would be good for. He loved doting on me, even when it meant massaging my sweaty soles. In fact, the guilt of what he had done with Felicity might even motivate him to do a little extra, as if he could ever make up for it.

The debate on whether to say something to Cody plagued me all night, well into the morning as I slipped out the door on my way to work. It was a thin-ice decision. Say something and create a crack in our relationship that would eventually send us both falling to a frigid marital death. Or skirt the whole topic by staying safely on shore and pretend everything was fine.

I was an actress, so pretending was in my blood.

Cody called to me from the kitchen when he heard the door swing shut behind me. "How was work, honey?"

It smelled like tacos tonight. Spaghetti, tacos, and ribs were about the extent of Cody's culinary abilities.

"I'm seriously about to either quit my job or kill my boss," I grumbled as I set my purse down on the dining room table on my way through the house.

"What demeaning thing did Mortimer do today?" Cody was well aware of my racist boss and often begged me to change jobs.

I decided it would serve no purpose to tell him I'd told the old bastard off but had miraculously managed to keep my job. We had enough drama in our lives without him harping on that incident.

"He wants to pay me to basically prostitute myself to some clients and act as his diversity hire."

"Wow, seriously? You said no, of course." Cody stated it as if fact.

"No, I agreed to do it. We need the money."

"Marin, come on, we don't need it that badly."

"Our plumbing says otherwise. It's two grand, if I flirt." I could play Julia Roberts in *Pretty Woman* for a night.

Cody looked up from stirring the taco meat. "Your dignity is worth more than two grand, Marin."

Not when Cody hadn't made a car sale in over two weeks. With his commission-based income at a used car lot, most months we scraped to get by. This was especially troubling because the shortage of computer chips due to the pandemic had resulted in the sharp decline of new car production, which put used vehicles in high demand. Cody should have been making that cheese hand over fist, but he just didn't fit the fast-talking mold of the stereotypical used car salesman. His ethics were extremely high. He was apt to blow a sale by revealing some mechanical or cosmetic flaw, simply because it was the right thing to do. His manager kept him on because the customers liked his self-effacing personality and his honesty, which generated a great deal of repair and maintenance business. But that didn't put good grub on the table. Hence we ate a lot of spaghetti and tacos, but never ribs.

"Do you realize how hard it is to find a good-paying job that doesn't require me to get a degree? It doesn't exist." I moved down the despised orange countertop to where a head of lettuce and a tomato still needed to be chopped. I picked up the knife and imagined the tomato was Mortimer's heart, slicing the blade through the red skin with demented glee.

"How about starting your own company, like Felicity did? People are making a killing as entrepreneurs. You're smart enough and creative enough."

I found Cody's word choice—*make a killing*—ironic, given the urge I felt. "What exactly would I do? I don't have a business plan or any capital, and getting a business loan is too risky right now."

"You could revisit the acting goal. Maybe start your own community theatre?"

"There's no money in that. I'd still have to work full-time to support it until it took off." With the tomato fully mutilated, I switched to the lettuce. It was about the same size as Mortimer's head. The knife blade sunk in. "It'd be a passion project, which we just can't afford. Especially if we want to keep trying for a baby."

I was tired of nothing working out for me. Not a baby. Not the acting. Not even a job I thought I would love. Even my marriage and homeownership dreams were crumbling through my fingers.

"You mentioned getting new headshots. Why not at least try?"

I sighed. "I don't know. What kills me is that Felicity is wearing a bracelet—a piece of jewelry!—that costs enough to fix our house, and it's just not fair. You work as hard as Oliver, probably harder. And she runs a doggie boutique? I mean, how is there so much money in that?"

Cody stopped stirring, then sidled up to me. "Marin, I'll never have the income potential that Oliver has. I'm sorry, but I don't have the brains or charm that he has. I'm just...me. I thought that was enough when we got married. When did that change?"

"It changed when I watched our house fall apart and we can't afford to fix it. When my car breaks down and I can't afford a new one. When I have to take racist, sexist remarks from my boss and can't quit or else we'll go hungry."

"I'm trying my best. We both are. Give it time. We'll get there."

But Cody didn't even know where *there* was. Just yesterday he had been kissing Felicity; today he was telling me to pursue a pipe dream. I had no idea what was overtaking my husband, but I was petrified to confront him about it. The Portmans were the only family I had, and no matter how angry I was about whatever happened between him and Felicity, I had to forgive him. Because what I did was a million times worse. Cody may be a cheater, but I was a murderer.

"Well, until we *get there,* I've got to sell my soul for two thousand bucks." My grip tightened on the knife's hilt, the silver blade reflecting a hazy image of Cody.

"Hey, I meant to ask you. Last night after dinner you disappeared. What happened?"

I had already recited what I would say when he finally asked, which I hadn't expected to take him so long. "I needed a breather from Felicity. I know she's going through a lot, but sometimes she just gets so…dark…and I can't live in that space for long."

"Oh, okay. I just wanted to make sure you're okay."

Okay? I was as far from *okay* as Precious from the movie of the same name.

"Yeah, I'm fine. Though Felicity seemed awfully…I'm not sure how to describe it. Secretive?"

Cody froze. I had him where I wanted him. He deserved to be tormented a little.

"What do you mean?"

"Just her behavior was odd, that's all. Like she had something to say but was afraid to say it. Has Oliver mentioned anything to you?"

"I'm sure it's just her way of trying to cope with Vera's disappearance."

"Maybe." I stared at him, he glanced away. "But it seemed like something else to me."

"It's just in your head, Marin. You tend to think the worst of Felicity because they're the haves, while we're the have-nots. It's starting to get... irritating."

Wow. Was Cody really trying to gaslight me right now? Because *that* irritated me, especially considering he was a cheating bastard and I hadn't called him out on it...yet.

"This has nothing to do with their money."

"Whatever. It's obvious this is jealousy talking, Marin. And it doesn't look good on you." Cody passed me a know-it-all look. I passed it right back.

"You really want to say that to me right now?" The edge to my voice was sharp, ready to cut. The knife in my hand looked awfully inviting right now.

Cody apparently wanted to say nothing, so I turned and walked away. Out of the kitchen, through the dining room, across the entry where the scratchy blue carpet had been worn through in spots. I couldn't handle any more drama today. I needed something calming. Something reassuring.

I stomped upstairs, making sure Cody knew I was pissed, texting on my way up:

Can we talk?

Three little dots hung for less than a moment before a reply popped up:

Always here for you, babe. What about?

I didn't know what I was looking for until I found it on the tip of my fingers:

It's time to kill the husband.

Another row of dots, then:

You sure you're ready this time?

I wasn't ready, maybe never would be, but I had to do something. I couldn't be a victim my whole life.

As ready as I'll ever be.

The dots took longer this time before another reply surfaced:

What made you decide to finish what we started over two years ago? You know we've been working on this murder for that long, right?

How had two years passed in a blink?

I wasn't sure it was the right thing to do, but I need to do this before I lose my courage.

The reply was swift this time:

Let's get to it then. You free to meet in person tomorrow?

My finger hovered over the screen, itching to reply. I knew it was a mistake, a huge one, but I had reached the end of my rope. I needed to cut off the noose before it hung me.

The Pittsburg Press

Pittsburg, PA
Wednesday, October 19, 1910

SUFFRAGE GROUP GETS MESSAGE FROM MISSING WOMAN ALVERA FIELDS

Missing Wife and Mother Reported to Have Either Sent Message Herself or Through a Friend

It is stated that a message has been received by woman suffrage secretary Cecile Cianfarra, presumably from Alvera Fields, wife of importer Robert Fields. The message reached Miss Cianfarra at home early yesterday.

Detective Roger Levvy, who has been working on the Fields mystery for months, would not discuss it. Miss Cianfarra could not be reached, keeping herself imprisoned at home.

Where the message came from and what it conveyed to Miss Cianfarra could not be learned. When inquiry was made of her neighbors and fellow members of the suffrage auxiliary, it was admitted that no one had read the message in person. Miss Cianfarra was in communication last week either with Mrs. Fields or someone acquainted with the woman. This word came as the result of the personal advertisement Miss Cianfarra inserted in the Pittsburg newspaper.

The message Miss Cianfarra got is said to have told the

whereabouts of Mrs. Fields. If she did not actually send it herself, then the understanding here is it was sent by a close friend who has known the secret of Mrs. Fields' disappearance.

It is no longer doubted that Miss Cianfarra can solve the Alvera Fields mystery. It is fully expected that within a few days she will disappear to join the vanished wife and mother.

Chapter 23
Felicity

The restaurant Oliver dragged me to after Debra dropped me off at home was bustling with pandemic-weary customers desperate for a slice of normalcy, yet I felt so alone. Although my dinner was cooked to perfection, I pushed the prime rib across the ceramic dish, through its juices, while my stomach churned with nausea. At the table next to us a teenage boy, with a mop of blond hair and a face that matched Kurt Cobain's, strummed his air guitar to music pumping through his earbuds while his poodle-haired mother and shar-pei-faced father were glued to their cell phones. Oliver sat across from me expectantly, watching me with eyes that had dulled to a blue-gray that coordinated with the dying sky outside my window.

"Not hungry?" he asked.

I shrugged. I wasn't sure if I'd ever find my appetite again. The river roiled at the bottom of the hill that fell beneath the quaint eatery. Pennsylvania burned in the fall. Fiery trees lit the land ablaze, while a milky fog curled above the water in tendrils. I thought of Sydney and how the chill of autumn kissed her chubby cheeks with rosy lip-prints. Would those cheeks still be here for me to smother with kisses a month from now? A year? Ten years, when she would be too old to accept my smothering kisses?

"If we hurry," Oliver continued, and I realized I had missed a whole conversation somewhere in there, "there's a production of *Steel Magnolias* being staged at the theatre. I called earlier today and they still have a few open seats. What do you think? It's been forever since we've seen a play."

Steel Magnolias had long been one of my favorite sagas of female empowerment. Partly because the movie was timeless. Partly because seeing it in a local theatre production was our first real date. Young and broke, Oliver had wooed me with Chinese takeout and two tickets to the show. That date sealed the deal for me as he timidly grasped my hand ten minutes in, and let me wipe my tears on his sleeve during the part where Shelby died.

"I don't know. I'm kind of ready to just go home." I knew he was trying, trying to move forward, trying to live, trying to be *us* again. But I simply couldn't. I didn't want to. Not until life was whole.

"Please, Felicity? My dad's watching the kids, so we have the whole evening to ourselves. We need a night to forget everything and just have fun together."

"I don't want to have fun, Oliver." It was the truth. I wanted to brood, wonder, solve, figure everything out.

He slammed his fork down. "Why do you do this?"

"Do what?"

"Ruin every single moment we have together. Can't you at least *try* to have a nice dinner out?"

I knew he was tired of me. Tired of my silence. My anger. My pain. My guilt. Hell, I was tired of me too.

"I am trying. I don't know what else you want from me."

Oliver rested his hand on mine, bridging the gap between us. "I want you to acknowledge me. See me. Smile with me. Anything. We're all going through this together, but there comes a point where we have to hold it together for the kids, for each other. Are you just going to stay miserable forever?"

"How can I feel any other way until we find Vera?"

"And what if we never find her? What if she's gone forever?"

I gripped my fork and felt the muscles tense and tremble with an unfamiliar rage. "She's not gone forever."

"You don't know that."

"Yes I do. I feel it in my bones. And I have this awful feeling that Marin had something to do with her leaving. If only I could figure out what—"

"Stop!" Oliver's yell yanked the couple's attention from their phones, paused Kurt Cobain's doppelgänger's latest guitar set. All eyes pivoted to my raving husband. "Stop obsessing with Marin! Has it ever occurred to you that it's because of you—*us*—that Vera left? Have you ever considered that maybe she found out what we did and wants nothing to do with her messed-up fake family anymore?"

I silenced him with a stony stare, resuming the argument at a near-whisper. "People are listening, Oliver. How would Vera have found out about something that long ago, anyway? It doesn't make any sense. No one knows but us. Unless…do you think Cody would have told Marin?"

"No, we swore him to secrecy. He knew the risk of jail time. There's no way he would have said anything to anyone."

"Are you sure? I could see him telling Marin…and with how close she was to Vera, something could have easily slipped out."

Oliver leaned back against the faux black leather chair, folded his arms. "I would have known, Felicity. She would have said something to me about it first."

My eyebrow darted up. "And why's that? Because from where I'm sitting it looks like you're protecting Marin."

"Are you listening to yourself? If you drag Marin into this whole thing with Vera's disappearance, what do you think the cops will dig up about that night? How long do you think it will take to put the pieces together of what we did? We'll go to jail, Felicity. Or do you keep forgetting that?"

Of course I hadn't forgotten. I remembered it every day. It was the only reason I kept silent. But as desperation slithered into my veins, the vow of silence slithered out. Just one shot of courage was all I needed to come clean…one sip of faith.

"Maybe I need to take that risk if it could lead us to finding Vera."

"Absolutely not. Stop acting reckless and stupid. What we did back then has nothing to do with Vera's disappearance now. Or Marin."

And yet a specter living deep inside me told me there was a connection. Maybe only a loose one. But it was there. Marin had something to do with Vera's disappearance, but I had no way to prove it. *She's the key to bringing Vera home,* the specter hissed.

Oliver's phone beeped with a text. His eyes darted down at the table, where a green bubble popped up on the screen. He turned the phone over, face down.

"Who was that?" I asked.

"No one."

"Then why did you flip your phone over?"

"Because it's not important. This"—he gestured to me, then himself—"is more important right now than a text."

I noticed the way he glanced aside, then stared out the window at the now black sky. His fingers drummed on the table. He was lying.

"Can you be honest with me about one thing?" I prepared my bait.

He blinked slowly, then looked at me with a dead gaze. I took it as a yes. I needed to know his secrets, because I knew him well after twenty years. He was hiding something. And everything pointed to Marin.

"Was I right—was there something going on between you and Marin that you never told me about?"

Oliver shoved his seat back and rose to his feet as the chair tipped over behind him, the leather back hitting the floor with a *thud*. "I'm done."

"Wha—"

Grabbing his coat that had fallen to the floor with the chair, he pulled out his wallet and slapped a $100 bill on the table.

"Hey, where are you going?"

Instead of answering me, he turned and left. Frantically grabbing my purse, he was already halfway out of the restaurant before I shrugged into my wool jacket, chasing after him. I hadn't expected him to get up and leave. We always talked through things, but I had crossed an invisible line I didn't know existed until now.

"Oliver, please stop!" I begged.

"I told you, I'm done. I'm calling a taxi."

By now we were standing in the parking lot, the chill wind snapping the hem of my skirt around my calves. "Do you mean an Uber? I don't even know if they have taxis around here anymore."

"An Uber, whatever." He turned on me, eyes boring into me. "I'm so sick of everything being everyone else's fault when we all protected you. You could have gone to jail, Felicity, but we covered for you years ago. And I still cover for you today. And how do you repay me? By blaming Marin, me, Cody…everyone but yourself for what happened. I could handle what you did before, but this…the secrets and lies and obsessive behavior…I just can't. I'm done."

Oliver pulled out his phone and slammed his finger on the screen, I assumed looking up a nonexistent taxi service.

"Are you coming home tonight?"

"I don't know, Felicity. I can't be around you right now. And don't go looking for me. I'm not ready to be found." He circled back to the restaurant entrance as he placed the phone to his ear.

Through stinging tears I found the car, almost missing the ticket tucked under the windshield wiper. I pulled it out, wondering why on earth I would get ticketed in the parking lot. I swiped away the wetness dampening my eyes, noticing that one edge was torn, as if ripped from a notebook.

Or a journal.

"Oliver!"

He glanced up at me, then returned to his phone call.

"Oliver! You need to see this!"

By the tone in my voice, he knew this was serious. Pocketing the phone, he rushed across the pavement, fancy footwork saving him from getting hit by a car backing up.

"Look—read this."

I held out the paper, watched his eyes hop across the bubbly handwritten words like skipping stones:

I realized today I have to do something drastic. Austin thinks I'm crazy, but in the end he understands why. He grew up with a dysfunctional family too. I guess that's why he's willing to help me. Part of me wishes I could talk to Mom about this, but I have no reason whatsoever to believe her word after finding out she had been lying to me practically my entire life. It's not like there's anyone I can talk to who hasn't been a total fraud my whole life. The only way forward is on my own. But I'm afraid. Terrified. This whole thing...what am I supposed to make of it? Would it be safer just to ignore it? That is, if that's even possible. No, knowing myself, I can't just ignore it. I have to do something, but at the moment, I'm afraid to do what it takes to know the truth. God, why did I have to see that stupid picture?

It was from Vera's journal.

"Vera was here, Oliver." My daughter had been here while I was inside the restaurant. One hundred feet away, I was arguing with her daddy while she was placing a note on my car.

"Unless it's from the person who took her," Oliver replied. "A message of some sort."

I shook my head. "No, you're wrong. Why send a message now, six months after she disappeared? It has to be Vera. She's reaching out, wanting to come home but afraid to." Yes, that's what it was, I convinced myself.

"I don't know, Felicity..." Oliver wasn't buying it, but this was more than anything Detective Montgomery had uncovered in the past six months. This was hope.

"She might still be in the neighborhood, if she's on foot," I said. "You go that way."

"Felicity, it's a waste—"

"Just do it!"

Shaking his head, Oliver walked toward the other end of the parking lot where it dipped down into a hilly tree line.

Clutching the paper to my heart, I looked up the vacant street for any sign of life. Nobody, just a homeless man lying in the doorway of a closed bakery. Then I looked the opposite direction...

A young woman, a petite blonde, walked briskly along the sidewalk, her back to me. The swish of her hair, the confident stride, the way she hunched her shoulders up against the cold. And that purse. Vera had one just like it.

I took off after her, fast-walking, staying in the shadows, careful not to spook her. She turned her head quickly, too quickly for a good look, and noticeably quickened her pace. If it wasn't Vera, why was she running from me?

Please be Vera. I need it to be Vera!

"Vera! Please stop! I just want to talk to you!"

The girl glanced around again, broke into a fast trot. I matched her pace. In another few seconds she would round the corner where a throng of people waited at the bus stop, and lose me in the crowd.

Five feet away. Three. Lunging, I snagged her shoulder and spun her around.

"What the hell, lady? What you chasing me for, huh?"

This girl was so *not Vera.*

"I'm-I'm sorry, I th—"

"Weird psycho." She whipped out her smartphone and began snapping pictures of me. "These are going on my Instagram page."

"I don't think so." Oliver snatched the phone out of her hand and deleted the photos with a few deft taps, and handed it back. The girl stood there gobsmacked as Oliver grabbed my waist and led me back to the car.

"You don't have to explain," he said, pulling me closer. "I thought it was her too, for half a second. But Vera's a lot prettier."

I cracked a tiny smile. "That's for sure."

We arrived back at the car, adrenaline spent, optimism faded.

"Okay, so we're back to square one," Oliver said. "What do you think this means?"

"I don't know."

Skimming the torn edge with my fingertip, I wondered if I'd be able to match it to a missing page from the journal to get an idea of when it had been written. I reread it, interpreting every word. *A secret. Fraud. Austin. Do something drastic. A picture of some sort.* They were all clues to finding her. If I could piece them together just right...

"She obviously found out about what you did," Oliver speculated. "Do you think she was planning to out you?"

"Maybe. But she didn't."

A tiny thought crawled into my brain. Had Vera planned to turn me in until something—or someone—stopped her? But who? Only me, Oliver, my in-laws, and Cody knew about what I had done…and possibly Marin. She had always been a loyal sister to me until I found out she wasn't, but capable of hurting Vera…? No, she couldn't have. But then there was Austin Miller. What was his part in all of this? I grabbed Oliver's arm, tightening my grip as I imagined confronting the boy who hurt my daughter once. Got kicked out of school for it, even. Was destroying our family his way of getting revenge?

"All I know is Austin Miller hasn't been honest with us and I'm going to find out what he's hiding."

Chapter 24
Marin

I hadn't been to this house in ages. Now that I was here, I remembered why I had avoided it for so long.

Five total strangers shared the four-bedroom one-bathroom house on Roslyn Place, last I remembered. A scruffy fifty-something starving artist who made sculptures out of garbage he found while Dumpster diving. A one-armed vet with PTSD living in squalor because apparently his sacrifice and service to our country wasn't worth the price tag of consistent mental health services. A college dropout girl who slept on the couch and did everyone else's bidding. A wealthy hipster chick who wore pricey vintage but wanted to "experience life" by slumming it with four other strangers. And the person I came here to see. Though new faces were always coming and going, one consistent body waited for me inside. The one who made promises, promises.

Heading toward the house, I nervously fingered the delicate By Chari gold chain that rested on my collarbone, a Christmas gift from Debra after she discovered it was one of my favorite Black-owned businesses. I paused at the foot of the porch steps, second-guessing myself, wondering why I was even here.

Roslyn Place had the distinction of being one of the last remaining streets in the United States comprised entirely of wooden blocks. Installed in 1914, the creosote-soaked blocks were smoother and quieter than cobblestone, and served to muffle

211

the clickety-clack of the horse-drawn carriages prevalent then. I remember reading somewhere that 26,000 blocks were required to cover the 250-foot thoroughfare. Amazingly the wood had held up over a century later, surviving the advent of the automobile in remarkably good condition. I imagined the iceman driving his wagon down the street with kids stealing chunks when he wasn't looking, and a newsboy in knickers barking headlines on the corner.

I climbed several steps to the porch landing where Scruffy Artist sat on an Adirondack chair strumming a banjo, the bottom half of a Peeps marshmallow chick sticking out of his mouth, completely unaware of my presence. I knocked on the door. My nerves tingled. They always tingled when I showed up here. Fear of being seen. Fear of getting caught. Fear of the unknown. There were a lot of unknowns every time I came to Roslyn Place, because I only came here for one thing. And that one thing was make-it-or-break-it for me.

The door swung open.

"Mare Bear! Get your cute little ass in here for a hug!"

Brad Walters—I mean Brad *Spielberg*, as he insisted on calling himself in honor of his idol, the legendary director-producer-screenwriter—pulled me into his arms. At five-foot-two and a buck ten, he looked more hobbit than man. I imagined slipping him into my pocket for safekeeping, my little personal muse. When I lacked the courage to get a job done, the aspiring scenarist was there to remind me of the end goal. This time: murder.

I stepped into the living room where two people I'd never seen before were smoking dope while watching ESPN, casually arguing over player stats. I followed Brad up two flights of narrow, creaky stairs, my eyes fixed on the back of his red hair curling at the nape of his neck.

His bedroom—if you considered an air mattress on the floor a bed—took up the entire third-floor attic. A single window framed a flotilla of clouds, pink as wads of cotton candy in the westering sun. A guttering candle's citrusy scent fought bravely against the lingering stink of stale sweat and week-old pizza boxes and dirty clothes strewn about the floor. An episode from the *Asylum* season of *American Horror Story*—Brad was obsessive about that deliciously disturbing show—streamed on a wall-mounted flat-screen TV. In another nod to his penchant for the macabre, he had repurposed an antique coffin—God knows where he got it—as a combination dining table/computer table/everything table. His computer sat on it, along with a lamp and a dragon-shaped ashtray overflowing with marijuana roaches.

"Still got the grow room in the cellar?" I asked, sitting in a cowhide chair that smelled like it had just come from a pasture.

"Shhh! I don't want one of those lowlifes to snitch on me to the landlord. Yeah, still got it. Why, you need some weed again? I got a good crop of Purple Kush coming in."

"No, I'm good."

"Suit yourself. Now, about the screenplay. You're not going to leave me hanging again, right?" He raised a red eyebrow.

"No, I promise I'm for real this time."

"Great! Alright, we've got a murder to plot." He slipped into a rolling office chair behind the coffin desk and moved his mouse around to find the cursor. "So what made you decide to finally help me finish this screenplay, Mare Bear? Because I thought you had given up on the Hollywood aspirations."

"I had, but I can't take my boss anymore."

Brad groaned. "That guy's still alive?"

"Hopefully not for long. I told him off pretty good the other day. I had just had it. I either need to quit—which I can't afford to do, and he knows it—or kill him. But I need a backup plan first, and this is it. This screenplay is my ticket to freedom."

Brad swiveled his chair to face me with a deadpan expression. "You want me to take out your boss for you?"

If I hadn't known Brad since my theatre days, I would have believed him capable. A tiny nerd-man who plots murders for a living and sleeps on a blow-up mattress in an attic of a house full of assorted misfits, druggies, and ne'er-do-wells wasn't exactly the picture of good mental health. Considering he hadn't sold a screenplay yet, I often wondered where his income came from. Guess selling weed was pretty lucrative. The little weirdo was probably a grave robber on the side.

"I would do it myself if I wouldn't get caught. But he's so mean he'd probably haunt me from beyond the grave."

Brad rotated back to his computer. "You know it's going to be an uphill battle to sell this, right?"

"I know, but Cody mentioned something that I've been considering and wanted to discuss with you. I'm thinking about starting my own production company. Instead of proposing this as a movie, how about producing it as a play and starting our own theatre company together? Will you help me?"

Brad considered it for a long moment, bare foot tapping on a pair of boxers strewn under the desk. *Ew*, as Vera would say.

"You know what—why not? Let's do it! Let's make a killing killing."

I chuckled at his terrible play on words. "So I finally have an idea for how to murder the husband and get away with it." I envisioned Mortimer Randolph slicing his apple, carelessly dropping the peels for me to pick up. "And it involves a paring knife."

"You've piqued my attention."

As I gathered my ideas in my mouth, ready to tell my new partner all the ways I had imagined killing my boss, my cell phone rang. Speak of the devil, it was Mortimer's number. If I didn't need the *Pretty Woman* gig so badly, I would have ignored him. But two grand could be enough to get my new business venture started. I accepted the call.

"Miss Portman"—Mortimer sounded agitated and out of breath—"I need you to come down here *right away*."

I wondered why he would call his assistant rather than an ambulance. If I kept the old coot on the line long enough, maybe he'd die before help arrived. "What's the emergency?" I answered reluctantly, feigning concern.

"I can't find my lucky cufflinks."

All I could think as I agreed to rush over there *right away* was jabbing those lucky cufflinks into his two beady eyeballs.

**

The sun had sunk into the horizon, and the moon grinned high above me by the time I got home. I didn't want to face Cody right now, as we hadn't yet made up after our "disagreement"—a fight would have drawn blood—and I didn't feel like playing the dutifully apologetic wife. This was on him to fix. He was the cheater, not me.

I softly clicked the car door shut and headed down the brick road that led into the heart of Wilkinsburg, each red block a reminder of the hands worn raw a hundred years ago. Massive Victorian homes that once upon a time belonged to elite families had been transformed into triplex apartments where kids crowded the postage-stamp yards. I walked until I reached the newly constructed Abraham Lincoln statue, a dedicated effort by a passionate local historian to commemorate the Lincoln Highway that brought life to this small community a century ago. With over 3,000 miles of transcontinental road, one could potentially drive from New York City all the way to San Francisco. Realizing I had been walking for over an hour, I turned back home, hopping over jagged cracks where maple tree roots had effortlessly lifted the sidewalk.

Three houses down from my own I pulled out my cell phone from my back pocket. Two houses away I dialed and hoped—despite knowing that hope only led to disappointment—that someone would pick up. By the time I reached my next-door neighbor I got dropped into voicemail. Not a personalized voicemail, but the generic default one:

"The person you have called is not available right now. Please leave a message at the tone."

I hesitated before speaking. "Please call me back. I need to know if Vera is with you, if she's okay. Her family is in a panic looking for her, and the cops are involved." Talking while walking, I lowered my voice while I ambled up the driveway. The windows were two bright eyes against the inky abyss of night. "Please, I need to speak with you. Before it's too late."

I inhaled, uncertain what else to say, then whispered, "If you care at all what happens to you—to *us*—call me back." Then I hung up.

Upon passing my car, I realized I had left my purse on the passenger seat. I grabbed it and swung it over my shoulder, heading toward the walkway that passed under a bare crab apple tree limb. I'd need to prune it soon.

My cell phone rang as I was just about to step up onto my front stoop. It was Karen Delacroix, Mortimer's legal secretary. I had no idea why she'd be calling at this time of night, but I answered immediately.

"Hey, Karen. What's up?"

"Are you sitting down?"

"Huh? No, why?"

"Good, then you're in the perfect position to jump for joy. Get this, sister: Maleficent Morty's dead."

I wasn't sure if I'd heard her right. "Did you say...dead?"

"As the proverbial doornail. I'm at the mansion. Morty and I had a row over the phone. What else is new, right? So I came over to try to patch things up. When I got here the paramedics were getting ready to haul him away. Apparently the old bastard had a heart attack."

I was still in a state of shock but managed to ask, "How did the paramedics know to come?"

"Somebody called 9-1-1. They wouldn't say who. But that's unimportant. Now you really *will* want to sit down."

"Are you kidding, Karen?"

Karen giggled. "No. Sit, Mare."

I sat on the curb. "Okay, shoot."

"Okay. I shouldn't be telling you this, it's not my place—and remember, you didn't hear it from me—but the old boy left you everything. The whole kit and kaboodle."

I was glad I was sitting down, or else I might have fallen into the path of a speeding car.

"You're not shitting me, are you, Karen?"

"No way. I'm his legal secretary, right? I have access to all his personal legal papers, including but not limited to his advance directive and his last will and testament. There's no mistake, Marin Portman. You have just won the lottery."

I let the news wash over me. It made no sense, but Karen wouldn't lie to me.

"But why? Mortimer treated me like shit."

"Simple. He told me how you stood up to him. He admired that. I think you actually got to him, Mare. Morty may have been a sonofabitch, but he was old school. Beneath that racist and sexist exterior there was a chivalrous old fart chomping at the bit to get out. He had no family, no friends. He realized he only had a few good years left, if that. His naming you the beneficiary of his estate was his last chance to actually do something worthwhile in his miserable, misbegotten life. Not to mention, it was a great way to piss off his partners. They never saw eye to eye, you know."

It still seemed unreal to me. "Are you sure about all this?"

"Absolutely. Listen to this, straight from the horse's mouth. His will is extremely detailed and complicated, as you can expect, but it contains this simple but eloquent remark: *To Marin Portman, my personal assistant whom I should have treated with more respect and dignity, I leave everything in my estate. I have complete faith she will use my assets for greater good than I ever did.* There's a ton more legalese, but that's the gist of it. You are one rich bitch now, Mare."

I didn't know what to say. The man I loathed most in the world was dead. And irony of ironies, I had inherited his vast fortune. If the frozen air sending shivers through my skin and into my bones hadn't reminded me that this was real, I would have thought I was dreaming. A perfect, beautiful fantasy.

"Mare? You still there?"

"Yeah, I'm still here. Just trying to keep from floating away on a cloud of ecstasy."

Karen laughed. "I understand. I'm so happy for you! I hate to bring this up, but you know the partners aren't going to take this lying down. Even though Morty's will is pretty airtight as far as I can see, they're going to fight the will after it's probated. Count on it. And they're going to say nasty things about you. I have to warn you, Mare, it could get ugly. At the very least, they're probably going to accuse you of sleeping with Mortimer."

"Sleeping with him? Ewww! I'd rather die first."

"You and me both, sister. Even though the paramedics said it looked like a clear-cut heart attack, the partners are going to demand an autopsy. So don't be counting all that wonderful wampum just yet."

"I won't. Thanks, Karen. For being such a good friend. For everything."

"You can thank me properly later, Mare, when I hit you up for a great big loan. Bye."

"Bye."

I didn't have time to savor my windfall as the shadows shifted as I hung up. Movement where the driveway dropped down behind the house drew me closer. A rustle of branches startled me out of my euphoria.

I searched the dark. "Hello?" I called out.

Curiosity trumping fear—and good sense—I crept toward the sound rather than away from it, like the witless victim in a horror movie. Probably just a stray dog or cat, I rationalized. I tiptoed halfway down the walkway, armed with a broken branch from the crab apple tree. "Who's there?"

An outline lurched forward into the light.

"Mom?" I gasped, pressing a palm to my frantic heart.

"Hi, Marin. I was just parking behind the house."

"You almost gave me a friggin' heart attack!" I exclaimed.

I thought I was glad to see Debra, until I saw she wasn't glad to see me. She didn't speak, only shot me a withering Obama Frown. For a petite white woman, she had the expression down pat.

"Sorry to scare you, but I couldn't help overhear your conversation. What's this about someone being dead and you being the beneficiary?"

I could see how when heard out of context, it could raise some concern.

"It's my boss. Apparently he died tonight and left me his

money. What's crazy is that I was planning to quit...and then this happened. This money could change everything for me and Cody!"

Another judgmental silence. Another Obama Frown. Why didn't she share my joy?

"What's wrong, Mom?" I ventured. This was not the sweet mother-in-law I knew and adored.

"It's awfully suspicious timing, is all. And what makes you think Cody will even want that horrible man's money?"

"Why not? Do you think Cody loves being a used car salesman working for commission? And what about me? I've given up my pride, my self-esteem, my joy to bend over backwards for that man. I deserve payment for what I suffered. I can't believe you'd want me to turn down something that could help us."

Debra didn't seem convinced. The silence was brittle, until she splintered it.

"I also overheard your message about Vera. It seems like you've been keeping secrets too, Marin."

What was she suggesting? I tried to string together a lucid explanation for what she had heard, but the words kept dancing around me. Only one thought finally surfaced: *confess.*

Chapter 25
Felicity

Confess.

The word lagged behind me like an elderly dog. I had finally reached the last resort.

Austin hadn't been much help when Oliver and I stopped at his house on our way home from our dinner date disaster. Within a minute of Austin opening the door, I shoved the torn-out journal entry in his face. The way his trembling hand took it, the quickness of his gaze passing over the words, his lack of shock— this told me everything I needed to know. Austin had known why Vera disappeared all along, but he wasn't telling.

My only consolation? Vera hadn't just betrayed me, but she lied to her best friend Blythe too. It took the threat of calling the cops right then and there—my index finger tapping the 9, and the 1, then hovering over the 1—before Austin spit out the truth like it tasted sour.

The breakup was because of *me*. Not because of Sydney, which had been my first assumption, but because of a picture Vera had found in Marin's belongings that proved me a liar. Austin hadn't seen the picture, only knew that whatever it was erupted all over Vera's perfect life, destroying her. Austin used words like *outraged*, *heartbroken*, and *hypocrite.*

Vera had determined then and there that she would find out what else I had lied about. The only way to do that was to visit some long-lost relative—one we kept Vera far away from for her own protection—who could answer all her questions. Austin insisted, his conviction pure and pleading, that he didn't know anything more than that. She never told him where she was going or who she was going with, only that she'd be off the grid until she figured everything out.

I bought Austin's story, but Oliver remained skeptical. "The trust of the innocent is the liar's most useful tool," Oliver cautioned, using Stephen King's words as he stripped down to his boxers and T-shirt on his way to the master bathroom.

I had heard Debra say the same thing a time or two. I shouldn't trust Austin. I couldn't trust Marin. I couldn't trust Cody. I couldn't even trust my own husband who'd been keeping his phone hidden in his pocket since we got home. Who was left to trust?

I was tired of running in circles. Hence back to the word of the day: *confess.*

That was all there was left to do.

As a rush of water pounded against the shower glass, I glanced in to see Oliver hidden in the steamy modern all-glass stall adjacent to the original clawfoot tub. Washing off the filth of our fight, his hands ran up and down his lithe body, his mind clearly elsewhere. He was singing what sounded like Talking Heads' "Psycho Killer" so off-key that I could only be sure of the song based on the recognizable lyrics:

"I can't sleep, 'cause my bed's on fire.
Don't touch me, I'm a real live wire."

Based on the pace of his scrubbing, he'd be another ten minutes. I knew this from years of showers, two decades of living together, knowing each other's insides and habits as if I'd adopted them for myself. And in some ways I did.

Now was my chance to take a peek at his phone. I searched the pockets of his pants that he'd dropped beside the bed; empty. Checked his bedside table; not there. Opened his top dresser drawer; nada. I couldn't imagine where else he'd put his phone, so I snuck into the bathroom while he rinsed his sudsy head, soap running down his muscled back, and found it tucked under his boxers on the floor. I grabbed it and scooted into the hallway, through the bedroom, onto the bed. Golden lamplight draped over my shoulders. I slipped my finger across the glass screen, putting in his password.

Incorrect password. Try again.

That couldn't be right. I knew his passcode just like he knew mine. Did he change it? And if so, why? I tried again, same message.

So he'd indeed changed it. I tried another collection of digits, which didn't work. I only had a couple more tries before it'd lock me out, so I tapped an old one he had used for his very first smartphone. Oliver was one to recycle old passcodes rather than memorize a new one, and my knowledge of him paid off this time.

In I went, deep-diving into his online activities.

I went straight to his texts, my focal interest. The first screen full of messages were from Annoying Little Brother, Mom, and Don't-Answer Dickhead Daniel. Daniel was Oliver's nemesis, an arrogant colleague whom everyone loathed but was forced to deal with as the entitled son of one of the directors. When Daniel called, you didn't answer unless you had an hour or two to kill listening to him ramble on about himself. The only good thing about his random rambling—*say that three times fast*, I imagined

Eliot saying—was that I discovered he had contact information for a highly esteemed private investigator. When Vera had first gone missing, Daniel held that contact info out to Oliver like a carrot on a stick, if Oliver stroked his ego sufficiently. Oliver had refused, instead preferring bleeding ears to listening to Daniel. Hence the PI's identity remained a mystery.

I continued scrolling, until a name arrested my attention:

Vera

My heart squeezed into a tight fist with a sharp pain. A pulsating, monstrous anger surged through me. My hand trembled so hard I could barely press my finger to the screen. But when I did, there it was. Message after message between Oliver and *Vera*. For days, weeks, months. Up through today. I tapped the info button—it was indeed her cell phone number.

I flicked down, down, down to the bottom of the message train, following text after text like a twisted scavenger hunt. I skimmed countless conversations exchanged over the past three months, each one elbowing the previous one aside. Finally reaching the very first message, sent from Oliver in July, twelve weeks after Vera first disappeared, I saw the words in the green bubble, though they didn't quite set off the alarm bells in my addled brain:

Hey, honey. It's Daddy. I miss you so much. We're falling apart without you.

A bubble below it on the other side of the screen in gray: *Daddy? I miss you too. I would give anything to see you again.*

His reply: *Are you okay? Please tell me where you are.*

Vera: *I'm where I've always been. Waiting for you.*

Oliver: *Waiting for me? I'll come get you. I need to see you. How do I find you?*

Vera: *You know that's not possible. No matter how much I wish it was true.*

Oliver: *Everything is crashing down without you. Your mother isn't going to survive this. And your brother and sister…it's too hard with you gone.*

Vera: *I understand. I feel it too.*

Oliver: *Then why did you have to go?*

Vera: *I ask that question every day, Daddy.*

I didn't understand what I was reading. My body couldn't handle the overload. My husband knew Vera was alive and let me believe she could be dead since July. All that time watching me worry, observing my slow ruin. Saying nothing. For the past six months my darkness had tumbled out in wails. Now it ripped through me in fury. I clenched my jaw, holding in the screams that wanted out.

When Oliver walked into the bedroom, towel wrapped around his waist, he stutter-stepped back and stiffened, seeing his cell phone in my hand.

"I can explain, Felicity—"

"No!" I roared, so angry I bit my cheek, tasting blood. It was the coppery taste of betrayal.

The Pittsburg Press

Pittsburg, PA
Thursday, October 20, 1910

FAMILY SUSPICIONS GROW AS FAKE MESSAGES EXCHANGED IN MISSING WOMAN CASE

Several relatives of Mrs. Alvera Fields, the missing wife and mother, cast aside all hope of her return as news came early yesterday that the advertisements in the newspaper claimed to be for Mrs. Fields were indeed false.

Although letters were found from Miss Cecile Cianfarra in Alvera's writing desk, when questioned about them, Miss Cianfarra stated:

"Alvera and I were friends who supported the same cause. I have nothing to do with her disappearance, nor was I behind such advertisements. If you want a suspect, look at her husband Robert Fields, who staunchly rejected Alvera's involvement in our women's suffrage fundraising, so much so that he committed her to a sanitarium to prevent her work and hired ruffians to mug her."

Miss Cianfarra has since remained silent on the matter as detectives were put to work tracing Miss Cianfarra's movements throughout Pennsylvania. Although Miss Cianfarra denies knowing Mrs. Fields' whereabouts, the family has their suspicions and is quite outspoken about them. Robert Fields

227

denied Miss Cianfarra's accusation and said to authorities,

"Miss Cianfarra knows something about what happened to my wife, and she will be held liable for her involvement."

Chapter 26
Marin

Debra's glare reached me through the darkness. "It seems like you've been keeping secrets too, Marin."

I wondered how much Debra had overheard, what she suspected, what she knew. A confession was brewing in me, heavy in my gut, something I hadn't yet spoken aloud. *I'm the reason Vera is gone. I know who took her.* The admission crawled across my tongue…then I squashed it.

Instead I went on the defensive.

"I've been keeping secrets *too*? What's that supposed to mean?"

Debra took a step toward me. "I overheard you on the phone mentioning Vera's name, asking if she was with whoever was on the other end. Who were you talking to, Marin?"

"I was leaving a message." I was being evasive and she knew it. Debra had a special x-ray vision where she could see through people right into the heart. Up until now she had accepted the darkness that she had glimpsed inside mine, but now I saw a change in her. Judgment.

"So you're not going to tell me." Another step brought her up to where the driveway met the grass. "I've welcomed you into my family, loved you like a daughter, given you nothing but respect and kindness. And you still feel the need to lie to me? Especially when it pertains to bringing my granddaughter home safely?"

"I appreciate all you've done for me, Mom—"

"No, don't *Mom* me. Not now. Not when you're lying to me." One more step brought her into the yard.

"I swear to you, I don't know where Vera is. I had a possible guess, but it turns out I was wrong." I wanted to tell her, but I couldn't. Not if there was any other way.

Debra shrugged. "Alright. I'll let you have your lies." One last pace carried her face to face with me on the sidewalk, jagged tree branches stabbing me. In this space, beneath the awakened windows, her angry lines glowed like a campfire storyteller. "It's dirty business, digging up secrets, Marin. It's just as dirty burying them. I know this from experience."

I had no idea what secrets Debra could possibly have, with her perfect husband and perfect family and perfect life. Her past wasn't up for scrutiny, though; mine was. Her distrust burrowed into me like the wormlike creatures in *Tremors*. She wasn't here to tell her secrets, but rather to find out mine.

"Did you come here to eavesdrop and then tell me this?"

"No, I came to bring you and Cody dinner." She handed me a covered casserole, which I awkwardly held while my purse strap slipped down my shoulder. "And to ask if you're cheating on Cody."

"What? Why would you even think that?"

"I have eyes, Marin. We all know how flirtatious Oliver can be, and normally it's part of his charm, when it's kept in check. But I see how you and Oliver act toward one another."

I couldn't believe the hypocrisy. The gall of her to charge *me* with cheating when I watched *Felicity* make out with my husband!

"Before you start accusing me of this, you need to get your facts straight. It's actually the other way around, *Debra*." I emphasized her name with scorn. "You should ask Felicity about what happened between her and Cody."

"About what? What happened?" Debra perched her hands on her hips.

"I watched Felicity kiss Cody. She practically threw herself at him."

"Are you sure that's what you saw? Because that doesn't sound like either of them."

"But it sounds like me and Oliver to cheat?"

"You and Oliver are...different. You both command a room when you walk in. You strive for more. People just hand you their attention. And you're hungry to win. People with that hunger tend to get into compromising positions to get what they want."

"The only compromising position I've been in is the one I'm in now...with you. Because I feel like you're about to ask me for something...or threaten me with something. And the only thing I want is a solid marriage with Cody, despite what you think of me."

She huffed. "You're an actress, Marin. Your body is your instrument, able to adapt to whatever role you need to play. I've seen you kiss other men in a play; how much of a step further is it to kiss Oliver in real life?"

"It's a huge difference! On a set it's all acting, no emotion. Look, I'm not going to debate this with you. Oliver and I never crossed a line. As for Cody and Felicity, I saw it with my own eyes. Go reprimand them instead." The sting of his infidelity watered my eyes. A tear dripped down, and Debra reached across and wiped it dry.

"I...I didn't know. I'm sorry, honey." She patted my cheek. "I shouldn't have assumed...as they say, assuming only makes an ass out of you and me. But I'm sure it was just a one-time thing. Felicity is grieving, she's out of her mind. The whole family is right now. You can forgive them one mistake, can't you?"

Another tear fell. "Would you forgive Joe if he cheated on you?"

She sighed and touched the wedding band on her ring finger. "I've forgiven a lot worse."

"Like what?" It was hard to imagine anything dark ever touching this pure old woman.

She chuckled. "Let's just say that I've forgiven a host of sins, some of which lesser people would kill over, and I'm a better person for it. Forgiveness isn't for them, it's for you."

"Well, maybe I'm not as good a person as you."

"Yes you are, dear. In fact, you're better. Look, can we just keep it between us? For now, at least? Oliver has already been through so much with Vera going missing, and he doesn't need a cheating wife heaped on top of that. It would break him. Just think about it before you say anything."

But I had already thought about it. Over and over. My husband cheating on me with my sister-in-law. Part of me felt murderous rage; the other part felt a deep sadness, because it was all probably just their twisted grief trying to find a way out. It didn't make the adultery hurt any less, though.

The porch light flicked on. The front door opened. Cody called out, "Mare, is that you? And…Mom? What are you doing here?"

"We're just chatting. And I wanted to drop dinner off, dear. I thought you and Marin might like to try this recipe I found. It was one of your great-grandmother Alvera's favorites. Supposedly it was the last meal she made her family before she disappeared. With everything that's happened with Vera, it made me think of it."

It was eerie, the mystery that circled the Portman-Fields family. Cody's great-grandmother disappearing shortly after giving birth to her first—and only—child. No suspects ever identified. Her body never recovered. Vanished, as if she had never existed. All that remained of her was a recipe.

"That's so…thoughtful, I guess?" Cody's compliment lifted with awkward gratitude.

"It's just food. You've got to eat, right?"

"Thanks, Mom. Oh, I might as well tell you both that I just got promoted to manager of a second location."

Debra brightened. "So you won't have to sell used cars anymore?"

"Yeah, Mom, the boss knows I'm no great shakes as a salesman, but he likes my personality, my style, and my people skills. The customers seem to like me too. The boss thinks I'll make a better manager than a salesman."

"Well…I guess it's better than nothing. Will it be twice the money?"

"Not yet, but maybe eventually, if the other location does well," Cody explained.

I felt mortified for Cody, always trying to impress his mother and always failing. Cody could never compete with Oliver, and I understood why. While Cody worked hard, he didn't have the looks, or the drive, or the natural business sense that his older brother did. While Oliver pursued academia and went on to college earning his bachelor's in business and working his way up the ladder of a prestigious marketing firm, Cody scraped through high school and flipped burgers to earn cash that he'd blow at the bar. From burger flipping he eventually got nudged into management because his boss saw something in him that Cody didn't see—something worth more than minimum wage. When he got tired enough of coming home smelling like cooking grease every day, he switched to used cars.

My husband was the ongoing butt of every joke, unable to live down the stigma associated with used car salesmen. Sketchy.

Sleazy. He endured the taunts and epithets because he hated his job anyway.

I handed the casserole to Cody and invited Debra to join us.

"No, I already ate hours ago. Plus your father is waiting at home for me. I'll see you soon." She kissed Cody on the cheek, gently squeezed my arm, and left.

I followed Cody inside, shutting the darkness out behind me. A trail of cool air swept over my shoulders. It wasn't much warmer in the house than outside.

"Is the heat working?" I asked.

Cody pressed his fingers against his temple. "I'm working on it, Marin. The furnace broke again."

"You've got to be kidding me."

When would I catch a break? And then I remembered Mortimer's inheritance. I could handle a freezing cold house a little longer. I was tempted to tell Cody about it, but I needed to know for sure first. I didn't want to build him up, only to crush him.

Instead I skipped to the subject poking at my curiosity. "Your mom told me she's got some big, dark secret. Any idea what it might be?"

"My mom?" Cody chuckled. "No, that woman doesn't have a secretive bone in her body."

"It was such a strange thing for her to say. It makes me wonder about her past."

He picked at his cuticle. "She never talked much about it with us. I'm sure it's as plain old vanilla as it gets."

"I don't know. It's as if she's hiding something pretty shady. Though, I guess we're all hiding things, aren't we?"

I looked him dead in the eye as I said it, inviting the truth to come out. Here was his chance to right things. I needed to know he would always be honest with me. Hypocritical, I know, given I was hoarding dishonesties, but my lies were different. Mine were to protect everyone.

Cody must have gotten the hint, because he cupped my hand and led me to the living room. He tugged me down onto the sofa beside him, angling his knees toward mine. He hunched over like a question mark. I could feel the guilt unburdening itself as he first examined our hands, still clasped as one, then lifted his eyes to meet mine. I suddenly felt afraid.

"Marin, honey, I have something to tell you. And I'm terrified that it will ruin us, but I can't keep it from you anymore."

And I waited for my world to blow up.

Chapter 27
Felicity

Four is the number of bedtime stories I read to Sydney before she fell asleep. Three is the number of piles of dog poop Ploppy—the cringeworthy but apt name became permanent, over my protests—left on the floor when I got downstairs. Two is the number of times Eliot got out of bed whining that he was hungry, then thirsty. One is the number of looks Oliver gave me when I finally settled into bed next to him and told him there was something very very wrong with him.

I only needed that one look to know I had hurt him.

I didn't care. It needed to be said.

My husband was communicating with my daughter's ghost.

I touched the empty space on my finger where my engagement ring used to hug, the ring Oliver sold his 1957 Corvette graduation gift for, back when we were still practically kids and lived off ramen noodles. The ring now sat taunting me from the French country accent table I'd fallen in love with during our Parisian honeymoon. When a sudden downpour pelted the cobblestone streets of Le Marais, we escaped into the vintage boutique, soaked in rain and romance. When my gaze rested on that tiny, round table, Oliver insisted I have it, shipping costs be damned. We arrived home three weeks later to find the package outside our South Side apartment doorstep, and inside, a rat infestation from the Dumpster behind our building. By the time the landlord exterminated the rats, we were in escrow on our first real home together, starry-eyed with baby fever and passion.

When the baby didn't immediately happen and the passion faded, we had loyalty to hold us close.

Now that loyalty was gone.

"I read all the texts from *Vera*." I paused. "Well, from Vera's phone. You know that's sick, what you're doing, right?"

Shame pushed his face down in a frown.

"It's the only thing I have left of her, Felicity."

"But it's not *her*. It's her *phone*. And her phone could lead us to her. Whoever is texting you is messing with you. Clearly it's some deranged person playing with your emotions."

"No, it's a girl who misses her dead father, Felicity." Then Oliver proceeded to show me a succession of back-and-forth replies:

Oliver: *You're not my daughter Vera, are you?*

Fake Vera: *No. Just like you're not my dad. But it feels real, doesn't it?*

Oliver: *How did you get this cell phone number?*

Fake Vera: *I found the phone in the woods and kept it. When you texted me, you sounded so much like my dad. He died recently, but it just felt comforting to believe he's out there missing me too. I'm sorry. I should have said something sooner.*

Oliver: *No, don't apologize. It's helped me*

too. My daughter went missing and you remind me of her.

Fake Vera: *I hope she comes home. You seem like a great dad.*

Oliver: *I don't know. I wonder if I'm the reason she left.*

Fake Vera: *She's lucky to have you. I'd give anything to get my dad back.*

Oliver: *I'd give anything to get my daughter back too.*

Fake Vera: *You're probably the only person in the world who understands me.*

Oliver: *Losing someone you love is the heaviest burden one can bear. Hang in there, kid.*

Oliver had never gotten her name, just as he had never told her his. The texts continued on for weeks, sharing details about school, books, movies, favorite foods, favorite music…just like they had been father and daughter in another life on another plane. It would have been sweet had it not been so creepy.

"You think this is healthy?"

"I'm not saying it's normal, but it's clearly helping this poor girl. And me too. I don't know how else to explain it, Felicity."

"Why didn't you tell me you were communicating with Vera's phone all this time? And why didn't you tell the cops? They need to see these texts. She found Vera's phone—which means Vera was wherever this girl found it. That's helpful information for tracing her movements."

"First of all, she only found the phone three months ago. And if I ask her who she is and where she lives, it might freak her out. I don't want to spook her. She's a young girl."

How was Oliver so dense? "I don't give a crap about that girl. If it's a clue to finding Vera, we need to follow up on it!"

"You realize she found the phone months after Vera disappeared, right? Vera was probably long gone by then. And besides, the cops were already tracking the phone for the first three months and saw no activity, no location, nothing. I'm telling you, pinning down this girl isn't going to lead us to Vera."

He could be right, but he could also be wrong. Vera's phone usage had been a dead end back when she first left. No unfamiliar calls, no unusual texts. The police spent weeks tracing her cell phone, following up on all her past text and call history, but no leads came of it. Then no phone activity for three months. Which led them to believe it had been wiped and tossed, and that's when they stopped putting manpower hours into following up on it.

In fact, Vera didn't call or text her secret boyfriend or best friend. According to the police, she could have been communicating with them via a number of instant message apps, but without knowing all of her social profiles, there was no way to know. Her phone was the key, because her whole life was on it. Every app she used, her search history, everything. Unless this mystery girl knew how to completely wipe a phone, there could be something on there.

"I still don't understand how chatting with a strange man pretending to be her dead father helps."

Oliver shook his head. "You of all people should know that everyone grieves differently."

"That may be, but you still need to show the police all of this.

Right now it's the only lead we have. *She* could be lying and in fact be a *he* who abducted our daughter. Please, Oliver, for your daughter. For me."

There was no other way to put it plainly. Oliver wasn't thinking straight. He was mentally replacing this girl with Vera, and it was beginning to worry me. Not only because it wasn't Vera, but because the person on the other side might be responsible for what happened to Vera.

"What if I don't want to stop?" His voice was thick with sadness. "What if I stop and I never hear from Vera again? If the texts disappear, it's like Vera disappears with them. It's my only connection to her."

"Exactly, Oliver. It's our only connection to Vera, so we have to know who is on the other side. Don't you get it? Because of this, Vera could be dead! You've been hiding this from me, from the police, for weeks, and it could have cost our daughter her life! I'm going to the police with this, and you better tell the police everything, Oliver. We can't keep anything from them."

Except for the one big secret I was keeping from everyone. Oh yeah, make that two secrets.

Oliver snuffled, handed me his phone. "Fine. Do what you need to do."

It pained me to watch my strong, sturdy husband wilt. While he clung to some make-believe fantasy that this texter was a connection to Vera, I clung to the reality that our daughter was out there...and someone had her phone, her lifeline. Whoever was texting Oliver was toying with him, enjoying this sadistic game. But I'd had three kids and knew all about games.

Game over.

Chapter 28
Marin

"Marin, honey, I have something to tell you." I couldn't tell if it was me trembling or Cody's voice. "And I'm terrified that it will ruin us, but I can't keep it from you anymore."

His tiny gasping breaths filled the short silence as I waited. He was nervous. Terrified. Regretful. All the same feelings pouring over onto me.

I knew exactly what he was about to say. *That he cheated on me with Felicity.*

I knew exactly how I would reply. *A slap on the face and the classic one-two punch of how could you? And what were you thinking?*

I knew exactly how I would feel. *Heartbrokenly angry.*

I had played the scene in my head often enough. I was prepared for this moment. And then I realized…

I knew exactly *nothing* as I blurted out, "Whatever it is you have to tell me, I don't want to know."

I couldn't hear it. The moment it slipped from Cody's lips, I would have a decision to make. A punishment to execute. A marriage to abandon. A sin to announce to the whole family. I didn't want any of that. I wanted blissful ignorance and my deserved happily ever after with a husband who adored me, a family who enfolded me, and Mortimer's inheritance.

Please, Cody, don't take that all away from me.

"I can't keep this from you, Marin."

It was a no-win Sophie's choice. No matter what I picked, we all would suffer. Choose to live in a lie to keep the family together, or choose the freedom of truth that tears the family apart.

I decided to beat him to the punchline. "I forgive you for cheating on me with Felicity."

Cody sat there, mouth agape. "You already know about the kiss?"

"I don't just *know* about it, Cody. I saw it. I'm guessing there was a lot more than just a kiss?"

"No, I swear, nothing else happened. We kissed, Felicity tried to convince me to go upstairs with her, but then we just sat on the stairs while she cried. That's all. I promise you." I saw honesty in his unwavering gaze, felt it in his warm palm as he slipped his fingers through mine.

"You didn't sleep with her?"

"No, I could never do that to you. I love you more than everything. It was just a kiss and her sobbing on the stairs while I listened, the whole time feeling awful about it."

Then came the one-two punch: "How could you do this? What were you thinking?"

He ran his other hand through his hair, resting it on his forehead, shadowing his eyes. "I'm not going to make excuses for what I did, Marin. I wasn't thinking—that's just it. I could blame it on the alcohol, on Felicity's begging, on grief...but it was *not* about you. You've always been perfect, always been an incredible wife. I don't deserve you; I've known this from the moment I saw you that even if I did somehow miraculously win your heart, I wouldn't be good enough. Not because you make me feel less than good enough, but because you're just so...everything." He rambled on as he leaned into his plea. "I know I screwed up, and

I'm sorry, Marin. I'll leave if you want me to, or stay if you want me to. Whatever you want, I'm willing to do. I just hope I can earn back your trust."

I crossed my arms. "Why should I ever trust you again, Cody?"

"Honestly, you shouldn't. You should find a better man. But I'll spend my life trying to make up for this. I'll do anything to fix this. Even if it means never seeing Felicity again. You're my family, you're my future. I'd give everything else up for you."

I believed him. He'd been doing it since day one, putting me before everything else, even when I didn't want him to.

"I just want to understand…why? Why did it happen? Do you have feelings for her?"

He gave a short never-in-a-million-years laugh. "No, never. We had our shot years ago and I knew even back then it wasn't like that."

"What? You two were…together?" This was news I should have heard before now.

"Oh, God, no, not like that. Only one time, and it was just…empty. No chemistry."

"Alright, you're going to have to give more detail than that. What happened between you two?"

Then Cody told me a story. A story that shocked me.

It was the story of a college freshman girl at the University of Pittsburgh meeting a fry cook at an Oakland bar. Their chance meeting bloomed into an instant friendship as Felicity unburdened her woes on Cody, feeding his ears—and ego—with her disappointments in life. He saved her that night, because their meeting would months later lead her to his handsome Dean's List older brother Oliver. The man she would ditch Cody for and follow to the ends of the earth.

That night Cody introduced the two, a third wheel too blind

to recognize he was unwanted, while Felicity and Oliver drifted closer and closer together, eventually pushing him out. By the end of the night Cody was sitting on the curb outside watching his brother steal his almost-girlfriend.

It had been a sore spot at first, a sibling rivalry that had always been simmering and then came to a boil. But eventually all was forgiven, not quite forgotten, as Felicity and Oliver said their "I do's" with Cody standing in as the supportive Best Man.

But the Best Man wasn't always at his best.

"I was pissed for a long time. Not necessarily over Felicity, but because Oliver had the balls to swoop in and take my girl. But eventually I saw they were good for each other, a better match than I was with her, anyway. In the end, I got my revenge, or whatever you want to call it."

"Revenge?" That wasn't a word that fit Cody.

"Not like it was intended. It was a couple years after they got married, about a year before Vera came along, when Oliver was working nonstop, so consumed by his job and business trips that he'd leave Felicity home alone for days and weeks on end. She was constantly coming to me to vent or complain, y'know? She didn't want to tell Mom or Dad, because she was sure they'd side with Oliver, but she was lonely and depressed and needy. Eventually she had enough and wanted to separate. All this time she had been trying to get pregnant but it's kind of hard to do when your husband's never around."

I had a bad feeling I knew where this was going.

"That's when one night, after they had a huge blow-up fight, she showed up on my doorstep with wine and a sob story, begging for a listening ear. That was our thing back when we first met—I *listened*. She always told me that it made me different from all the other men, that I genuinely heard her, that I cared. I was the shoulder she could cry on. That's a death sentence for a guy, though. Guys don't want to be the shoulder; we want to be the arms carrying the girl to bed."

I nodded. I understood all about putting men in the Friend Zone a little too well. Though why couldn't men be happy being either?

"She loved Oliver, but he was killing their marriage. Well, anyway, a listening ear turned into a one-night fling, but we both knew the next morning that she needed to tell Oliver and see if they could fix things or if she should walk away."

And there it was. The bomb.

"In a way, that was the catalyst for Oliver to get his priorities straight. He cut back his work hours, put their house up for sale to start fresh, and Felicity had Vera. I'm not saying it wasn't rough working my ass off to get back in Oliver's good graces—I still am—but eventually we worked it out. My mom, however, never quite forgave me for what I did to my brother. I can still today hear whispers of her resentment."

I could see the regret, the guilt, the self-loathing all over him. He reeked of it. He also reeked of something else. Something he wasn't telling me.

"What do you mean by you're *still* working to stay in Oliver's good graces?"

His face flushed. Uh-oh. I had stumbled upon that *something*.

"Nothing really. I'm just always going to be indebted to him. But all of that is ancient history. I don't care about the past. All I care about is my future—with you."

Outside the living room window the morning sky bloomed in a riot of reds and pinks. We had talked all night, something we hadn't done since our early months of dating.

"I appreciate you telling me everything. I'm glad we have that kind of honesty in our marriage. And with everything Felicity has gone through, I'm giving her a pass this time. I'd prefer if we could keep all of this just between us." *And Debra*, I didn't add. "But Cody, if you ever do anything like this to me again, I'm out. Done. Do you understand?"

He leaned across the sofa to hug me, but I held my hand out to stop him. I pinned him with a glare.

"No. I'm not ready for that yet. I forgive you, but I don't want to be near you right now. You have a lot of making up to do first."

He nodded understanding.

"Does Oliver know?" he asked.

"I don't know. I don't think so."

"He should probably know the truth."

No, I was pretty certain this would be Oliver's tipping point. Missing teen, sick child, *and* cheating wife? There was only so much two shoulders could carry.

"That's between them, Cody. If Oliver finds this out right now, it's not just his marriage that you're messing with, but the whole family. Do you think he'll ever be able to trust you again? Even if he keeps his wife, he'll lose his brother. You need to stay out of it."

"Secrets aren't good, Marin. They're toxic. And I know you're hiding something from me too. I can feel the schism between us. It's been growing for the past couple weeks."

I knew I had been slipping. It was hard to wear a mask all the time.

"Whatever it is, you can tell me. I'm willing to put everything out there for you. Please do the same for me. I can handle whatever it is."

No, he really couldn't.

Hazy morning light crept along the windowsill, revealing the chips of paint that needed a touch-up. The house embodied my family, falling apart, dripping with secrets like that leaky kitchen plumbing, groaning for repairs to the rotting floorboards. But it was ours, and although a mess, I wasn't ready to give up on it.

"I've told you everything I was hiding, Cody. About seeing Vera the night she disappeared. There's nothing else to say."

That seemed to satisfy him…momentarily.

"So all of our secrets and lies and stuff are out in the open now, right?" He swallowed, tempering all those worrisome thoughts that boggled his brain any time he was afraid I was about to pull the rug out from under him. "Because now is the time to say whatever else needs to be said if we have any chance at moving forward."

Forward with Cody was the only direction I wanted to go.

I sighed, then said, "Well, there is one more thing you need to know…"

Chapter 29
Felicity

"I have good news and bad news." Detective Montgomery sat across from me in what the stained-glass couple would have called a parlor, but what I called a living room. A cup of coffee—no cream or sugar, thanks—steamed in front of her seat, while a cup of tea—more cream and sugar, thanks—was nearly empty in front of me. The empathy in her tone, the softness of her expression, the slight lean forward and pat on my arm—the combination told me everything I didn't want to know.

"We weren't able to trace the call made to your dog grooming store. It was likely made from a burner phone, so unfortunately we're at a dead end with that."

I had anticipated as much. "What about with the girl you found in the river? Any idea when we'll know for sure who she is?"

"Like I told you before, the pathologist is pretty sure it's not Vera. But it's our top priority to confirm the identity." *Pat pat.*

"I'm hoping that's all the bad news?" I wondered aloud.

"Yes." She picked up her coffee and sipped. "The good news—while we hadn't had success earlier in tracing Vera's phone while it was turned off, we did follow up on that after you and I spoke. This time we were able to locate the cell phone and the user that your husband has been texting with."

"And?" The creepy fifty-year-old orthodontist who lived in

248

his mother's basement and collected used retainers from his victims popped back into my head.

"And we paid a visit and spoke with her in person."

"It's a *her*?"

"Yes, a girl and her mother."

So Oliver was right.

"Do you think there's any connection between her and Vera?"

The detective set her mug down, and here came that not-as-comforting pat on the arm. In fact, it was downright infuriating. "The girl is exactly who the texts say they're from—a twelve-year-old who lost her father in a car accident. She had found the phone in the woods, and when Oliver first texted her, she took it as some kind of sign that her dad was contacting her from heaven."

Just like Oliver, the girl thought it was a connection beyond the grave. It would have been magical if it wasn't so tragic.

"I spoke to the girl and her mother, and I retrieved the phone, which unfortunately had been completely factory reset. So we couldn't pull anything, no app history or online searches that would help in finding Vera. But like I said, I'm pretty confident there's no connection between the girl and Vera."

"Where did you say she found the phone?" I asked.

Detective Montgomery checked her little black notepad that she had on her every time I saw her. "In the woods on Marigold Street."

Marigold Street. Why did that sound so familiar?

This couldn't be so simple that she just happened upon my daughter's phone. I didn't believe in coincidences. There was *always* a connection.

"Does that street name mean something to you, Felicity?" Detective Montgomery was reading me.

I nodded. "I can't think of why, but if it comes to me, I'll let you know."

"Hey, I get it. You want to think this is a clue linking to Vera, but in this case, there is nothing to lead us to believe the family knows of Vera's whereabouts. The girl doesn't go to Vera's school, they run in completely different circles, and this girl is clearly still a child. There's no connection, Felicity."

She was right. What would a twelve-year-old have to do with my fifteen-year-old? I was so furious and sad and disappointed in myself for ever believing that this could be it, the glimmer of light at the end of that endlessly dark tunnel. It was snuffed out and I was still stuck in the dark.

Detective Montgomery, clutching her black notepad, got up and headed for the door.

"Detective, would it be possible for me to get the girl's name and number? I think it would mean a lot to Oliver to at least say goodbye."

"Sure, I think she would appreciate that. Oliver comforted her and helped her through her loss, from what it sounded like. In fact, she had asked if she'd ever hear from him again, so I'm sure a text would mean a lot." The detective tore a paper from her pad and scribbled a name and number on it:

Tasha Briggs

I held myself together until after Detective Montgomery left. Then I let it all crush me. The defeat. The desperation. I alternated between screaming at the empty walls and sobbing into my sleeves until the kids got home from school. Then I held myself together again until after Oliver got home from work and the kids were in bed, alternating between pacing the bedroom floor and conjuring up a link between Tasha and Vera.

There was none. Just like there was no link between Vera and Marigold Street.

While Oliver brushed his teeth, I fell into bed, exhausted from too much thinking about Vera, Sydney, my marriage, the kiss, the dog crap all over the floor, the page from Vera's journal, the voicemail threat. Every hope swept over me like fresh air I could breathe. Every closed door sucked the air right back out. I stared at the vaulted bedroom ceiling, tracing the opulent moldings from corner to corner.

Oliver walked to the window, focused on something beyond the glass. "You know what we have to do, don't you?"

"I can't." I turned on my stomach, pressed my face into my pillow to shut out the conversation.

"Felicity, I'm not asking you to do anything. I'm going to turn myself in. I already made sure you're okay financially before I do so. I was thinking about doing it tomorrow. Get it over with."

Flipping over, I peeled my face off the pillowcase, sticky with salty tears, and looked up at him.

"No. Absolutely not. And you know why."

"Honey, I will take responsibility for everything. Nothing will fall on you. I'll do the jail time. I'll do whatever I need to in order to protect you. But we can't hide it anymore, Felicity. We're out of options. It's the only chance to bring Vera home…if she's still out there."

The question of *what if she wasn't still out there?* had been growing more each day. What if the detective was wrong and Vera was the body they'd found—and Oliver went to jail for nothing? I couldn't lose them both. There was no way I'd survive that kind of news without him.

"Not yet," I begged. "Not until we know for sure who they found in the river. Please."

"It's not Vera. Detective Montgomery already pretty much confirmed it."

"Why do you have to rush into a confession? Can't we think

about it first?"

"For how much longer, Felicity? We're out of time."

A flash of light passed over his face, a headlight as someone crested the hill that led up our driveway.

"Are you expecting someone?" Oliver asked.

I bolted upright. "No. Not at this hour," I said, flinging on my robe.

Bounding downstairs, I tripped on the runner, slid across the hardwood, knocked my hipbone against the banister, and smacked the door's edge with my forehead in my haste to see whose unfamiliar car had crawled up my driveway, now idling near the llama-shaped bush.

I flicked on the floodlights.

"Hey!"

Never announce your presence when you're trying to sneak up on someone. The lesson didn't hit me until a hoodie dashed across the driveway.

"Stop! Please!" I scream-begged.

My legs pumped faster than they'd ever moved before. I fancied myself an Olympian in the 100m hurdles, vaulting over those topiaries like I had wings on my feet, closing the gap on the fleeing intruder until I was close enough to tackle him and rip off the hood in a stunning *aha* moment.

I closed the gap alright, but when I reached out to snag the retreating hoodie, I tripped and staggered several feet, arms frantically windmilling, before taking a header. I felt the air explode from my lungs as I hit the ground chest-first, jaw next, and slid to a crumpled stop. I spat out the mouthful of gravel I'd inhaled like a bulldozer, then sat up and scraped the dirt off my scraped knees while I got my breath back.

I was examining my poor toes—every one of the bare piggies got stubbed on the rocks—when I saw a pair of no-name high-tops rushing toward me out of the gloom.

"Oliver! Help! There's a prowl—"

"Mrs. Portman! You okay?"

"Austin?" I looked up. The boy had thrown back his hoodie and stood over me, eyes bugged with concern.

Marigold Street! That's where Detective Montgomery said the little girl found Vera's phone. It all made sense now—Vera's phone had been found near Austin's house, the last place she'd been seen.

Austin held out his hand. I grabbed it and let him pull me to my feet. "That fall looked pretty bad," he said.

I was already banged up from the car accident, and now this indignity. But I smiled and said, "I'll live. But what are you doing here? And why did you run from me?"

"I came to drop something off, but when you came running out screaming, I freaked out. I didn't want to get caught."

"Get caught doing what?" Oliver's voice boomed from behind me. My tardy white knight ambled up to us nonchalantly, cinching his robe.

"I'm fine, by the way," I said. "Thanks for asking."

"I came to give you this." Austin handed me a scrap of paper. I instantly recognized it as another torn piece from Vera's journal.

"Was that *you* who left me the other page on my car?"

Austin nodded meekly. "Yeah, I'm sorry I didn't bring it to you directly. I was afraid you'd turn me in, so after school I parked down the street and waited until I saw your car pass when you were going to dinner. I figured for sure no one would notice me if I slipped it under your wiper at the restaurant."

"I guess you were right," I said.

"How long were you sitting there watching for us?" Oliver asked. "You know that's stalking, right? And do you even have a driver's license?"

"I've got a permit. I was only waiting, like, an hour. I didn't know how else to send it to you."

"Have you ever heard of mail?" Oliver grumbled.

"Cut him a break, Oliver. Teens do impulsive stuff." I lifted the page. "So why bring this one to the house now, Austin?"

"I couldn't wait any longer. I just wanted it off my hands."

Austin stepped around me, eyes wide with wonder at the monstrosity of our house on full display now that the lights lit it up. We got that a lot from new visitors.

"Vera had told me you lived in the Execution Estate, but I had no idea the house was so humongous! Can I see the room where the family got whacked?" Austin turned to Oliver with wild-eyed interest.

"No!" Oliver grumbled. "This is my—*our*—home, and you're already trespassing."

"Oh, come on." Austin's excitement picked up steam. "You know everyone still talks about what happened in this house. Do you ever see ghosts or hear strange noises?"

Yes, but I would never admit it out loud. It was hard enough keeping the rumors away from Sydney and Eliot's curious little ears. It took months to wean Eliot out of my bed the first time he came home from school crying over one of his classmates' Execution Estate ghost stories.

In the harsh floodlight, I skimmed Vera's words. "Are there more of these?"

Austin shook his head. "It's the last one I have."

"How did you get this?"

He tossed his head, shifting his hair out of his eyes. "A few days before Vera ran away, she was at my house and I started looking through the entries. By then she had already told me her plan to find some dying long-lost relative, and I was afraid that if someone found this journal mentioning details about me, they'd think I was behind it. So I ripped out any entry that mentioned my name."

Dying relative? Was that just another one of Vera's lies, or was someone baiting her with a sob story?

"Really looking out for *numero uno*, aren't you?" Oliver snapped.

"I had no choice! I'm the only protection my mom has from her psycho husband, and if something happened and I was taken away again, he'd end up killing her for sure. Besides, I told Vera not to go. We even had a huge fight about it the night she left because I told her that she hadn't thought it through and she should just talk to you guys first, but she could be pretty hardheaded. Guess I don't have to tell you guys that."

Yes, I knew exactly how stubborn Vera could be. She got that from me.

"You lied, Austin," I said bluntly. "You told me you weren't home the night Marin dropped her off in front of your house."

"Of course I lied. I promised Vera I would if anyone came asking. Snitches get stitches. All she wanted was to meet some relative before it was too late. I knew where she was coming from. My real dad died in prison and I never got to say goodbye."

"Why didn't you tell us sooner? You've held on to this for six months, Austin."

"I…I was in a group home up until recently. No phone, no internet, no outside communication, so I had no way to get in touch with anyone. By the time I got out of there, I was dealing with my mom and psycho-stepdad, trying to get in touch with Vera, and when I didn't hear from Vera through our usual messaging apps, that's when I started to worry. That's why I'm here now."

His tragic story aligned with what Blythe had told us. I had to trust his word…because it was all I had. And it seemed like it was all he had too. He knew what it was like to be a victim with only your word to save you.

"Were you the one who ran her car off the road?" Oliver glared at Austin and pointed at me.

Austin's hands flew up in defense. "No, sir! You can even check my car. I would never do something like that. I only want to help bring Vera home."

It was getting late, and all I wanted was to sit down with Vera's words and absorb them. Find the message within them. Austin left with an awkward goodbye, and I spent the rest of the night reading and rereading the entry, picking it apart, searching between the lines, interpreting it every which way. My answer was in here somewhere, right in front of my eyes.

No matter what Austin thinks, morals are one of the few things I actually value in life. Personally, I believe in "always telling the truth" no matter the situation. Like Alvera did when she stood up to her husband for what was right. I wish other people valued that moral as much as I do. Like Mom and Dad, who lied to me about my past. Anyways, I guess I'm writing this as a release of my guilt. Honestly, I'm more ashamed of myself for breaking my morals than ashamed of what I plan to do. Running away isn't as bad as lying to everyone. Maybe it's justified, maybe it's necessary to protect them. That doesn't make me a bad person, right? I'll worry about that later I guess, but right now, I have bigger things to worry about. Like meeting the family my parents kept from me.

The Pittsburg Press

Pittsburg, PA
Friday, October 21, 1910

MISSING WOMAN'S FRIEND TALKS

Miss Cecile Cianfarra, friend of Mrs. Alvera Fields, who has been missing since April 16, came forward this evening sharing news of Mrs. Fields' recent stay in a sanitorium in Pittsburg. Letters were produced between Miss Cianfarra and Mrs. Fields where Mrs. Fields requested Miss Cianfarra's help in excusing her from her stay.

Detectives were sent to the sanitarium in question and demanded to speak with the doctor in charge, who confirmed the rumor that Mrs. Fields had been admitted for a short time:

"Mrs. Fields had a brief stay at the bequest of her husband, Mr. Robert Fields. Mrs. Fields was suffering from hysteria and needed treatment immediately."

Following a successful treatment, Mrs. Fields was sent home. But according to Miss Cianfarra, threats were made by husband Robert Fields, should Mrs. Fields' hysteria return.

"Her passion for the women's right to vote should not be misinterpreted as hysteria," Miss Cianfarra spoke out when interviewed by detectives. "Her husband is behind her disappearance, I tell you. I blame him, and him alone."

Fields denies any involvement in his wife's disappearance,

but detectives assured the public that they would investigate all leads and any suspect, be it friend, family, or foe.

Chapter 30
Marin

All that glitters isn't always gold. Sometimes it's a diamond-encrusted turquoise bracelet.

It looked gorgeous in the case. Even more so on my wrist. As the lady behind the counter handed me the black velvet box that it came in, I wanted her to snap it shut like Richard Gere did with Julia Roberts in *Pretty Woman* when he gave her the necklace. When Cody did it upon my request, it wasn't nearly as comical, as my reflexes weren't quick enough and I broke a fingernail in the process.

Cody always talked about how you should dress for the job you want, look the part you want to get. Except it only seemed to apply to him. As I watched him play rounds of golf that cost more than our car payment (sometimes on his dad's dime, sometimes not), or buy athletic shirts that were finer than anything on my side of the closet, I couldn't help but feel that it wasn't equal. He always had to look great, while I was "pretty enough that I didn't need to wear fancy things."

Double-standard much, Cody?

Today it was all about me. For once. Thank you very much, upcoming Mortimer inheritance.

This morning, on the living room sofa, as dawn rose along with all our buried secrets—well, *most* of them—I had told Cody about the inheritance from Mortimer Randolph, who rested peacefully among the corpses at the Allegheny County Morgue. To celebrate Mortimer's life—who am I kidding? we were celebrating his death—Cody insisted we go shopping. The first place we landed? The same jewelry store that sold Vera and Felicity's bracelets.

The one I'd chosen looked similar to theirs, minus the numerous multiple-karat diamonds. This one was a more modest version, more *me,* but still in the several-hundred-dollar price range that made me queasy. But I deserved it, damn it! I had worked my butt off for a boss who objectified me, took care of a husband who had cheated on me, and grew up in a family that neglected me. When my mother died, she left me a tangled pile of cheap costume jewelry and a plastic jewelry case from the dollar store. For once in my pathetic life I wanted something shiny and sparkly and beautiful and flashy.

Plus, it was part of the deal. I'd keep my mouth shut about Cody and Felicity's kiss, and this was my reward. Looking between the bracelet and the credit card in my hand, I inhaled a shuddery breath. I had worked hard to get us out of debt, and this would be a setback until the inheritance came through. But setbacks were okay once in a while, right? Especially when we needed something shiny and sparkly and beautiful and flashy to pull us out of a depressive slump.

I glanced back at Cody, who had wandered across the mall, lingering at the mouth of a men's athletic wear store fingering a designer polo shirt. He was wearing the Heath Miller Steelers jersey I had bought him as a surprise gift just because. He looked up. Our eyes met. He nodded—*get the jewelry*, the gesture said.

And yet…

And yet that was one of the things I hated about him. Always having to have the best clothes while our house fell apart. Always looking like a million bucks while our bank account shrank down to pennies. Always about appearance, but never true depth. He dressed up his shallow personality with beautiful things…and yet he was the same narcissist underneath it all. A self-loathing man who doused himself in Ralph Lauren cologne and charm to get people to like him, to buy his used cars, then he insulted these same people the moment they were out of earshot. These were people he looked down on because they were never good enough or smart enough. People like me. People like him.

I refused to be like him.

I refused to allow *stuff* to define me.

I set the bracelet back down in its black velvet home and thanked the associate for her time, saying, "Maybe later." There would be no later. I had a dream that needed this investment more than my wrist.

I was going to finish writing that thriller screenplay with Brad, start my theatre venture, and work my butt off to lift my production company dream off the ground. Hollywood wasn't *it*; I was *it*. I had something way better in mind for me than LA could ever offer. Something I could control, something I could nurture, something all mine.

As I met Cody in the middle of the aisle between a hair station and a row of massage chairs, he pointed to my empty hand.

"Decide not to get the bracelet?"

I shook my head. "Not worth it."

He pulled me to his chest, and I rested my cheek on his shoulder as he hugged me tightly. "You're incredible, you know that?"

My nod was blocked by his neck. "You remind me every day," I murmured.

"I mean it every day, Mare." He parted slightly from me, looking at me, adoring me. "Now that you have all that money coming, do you even want to be with me anymore?"

I wasn't sure how to answer that. Not so much because of his kiss of betrayal, which did hurt me but oddly didn't break my heart like I had expected it to. I wasn't sure I liked who my husband was anymore, certainly not the head-over-heels-in-love guy who once upon a time wanted to rescue me. Maybe that was the whole problem. I used to be someone he needed to rescue. He lived to be my savior, but now that I didn't need to be saved, I served him no purpose. I had become expendable.

We were already walking out of the mall entrance before I finally answered his question.

"I need time to figure things out," I said honestly. "So much has changed, Cody. Felicity hates me, Debra doesn't trust me, you've hurt me...there are so many lies and secrets and resentments. It's all suffocating me, and I haven't even had a minute to process everything."

Cody's pace slowed, then stopped in the middle of the sidewalk as the tide of shoppers flowed around us. I saw curiosity in his expression. He wanted to know what lies and secrets I was referring to.

"Then let's start by being honest with each other—about everything."

I had been too honest with him already. About killing my mother. About being the last one to see Vera alive. But there were some things I could never tell him. Some sins I had to take with me to the grave.

"I *have* been honest with you, Cody."

I sprinted for the car with Cody clinging to my heels like a stray mutt.

"Have you, though? Because there are a lot of holes in your past that were never quite filled in. I never asked for details about what happened with your mom, because you're entitled to your privacy, but what else haven't you told me? You're saying secrets are killing our marriage. So let's get rid of the secrets and keep the marriage."

It took the entire drive home before I found the words that had been lodged in my throat. I didn't want to lose Cody. Or my family. He had accepted me after my confession about my mother. And again after withholding details about seeing Vera that night. Maybe he'd forgive everything else I never told him.

I was afraid to ask, but I did it anyway: "What do you want to know?"

We slid into our driveway and got out of the car a moment before a sheriff's department cruiser pulled up behind us, hemming us in. A deputy stepped out of the vehicle, hands on hips, and walked straight toward me.

"Are you Marin Portman?" he asked.

I was hesitant to answer, but he obviously knew I was. "Yes."

"I'm Deputy Levine, ma'am. I need to bring you down to the sheriff's department."

"Whoa, what's this all about?" said Cody, getting in his face. "You got a warrant? If not, you can get the hell off my property."

The deputy put his fingertips on Cody's chest and lightly pushed him back. "Mrs. Portman is not under arrest," he said, "but you will be, sir, if you don't calm down."

Cody swallowed his pride and shut up.

"If I'm not under arrest," I said, "why are you here?"

"We need to question you about the murder of Mortimer Randolph."

Chapter 31
Felicity

Today was the day, Oliver decided.

"I will take full responsibility for everything. I'll do jail time, whatever it takes to protect you and the kids, but we can't hide the truth anymore, Felicity. We're out of options. It's the only chance to bring Vera home...if she's still out there." Oliver had finished round one of his argument. I sat at the kitchen counter feeling like I'd been knocked out, waiting for a boxing bell to ding.

"What if she isn't? What if she's..." The question died on my lips, because it was unspeakable. Any suggestion of Vera being...gone...was as unfathomable today as it was six months ago. "I still feel like we should wait until we hear about the body they found."

"What if it takes as long as last time? That took weeks, Felicity! I don't want to wait any longer. I just want to come forward and take my chances with the justice system."

"But if you tell the police what we did, and Vera's not coming back, you'll go to jail for nothing, Ollie. Sydney needs us both." Round two goes to the challenger, *ding*.

"At this point I don't care what happens to me. Insurance will still cover everything with Syd, and you can live off of savings until I get out of jail. Mom and Dad will help with the kids until I'm out. It'll be fine."

My husband going to jail for my crime was absolutely not fine. I didn't understand how telling the cops that we found a baby on the side of the road, and decided to keep that baby, would then help find that baby who grew up to be a fifteen-year-old runaway named Vera. We had no name for her biological parents, no original birth certificate, nothing but a verbal confession that we picked up a nameless orphaned newborn girl swaddled in a car seat and took her home and fell in love.

At first it didn't sound so bad, certainly not criminal, to rescue an abandoned child. But over the years I'd read countless news reports on women who stole babies and went to prison for twenty-years-plus. I scoured the internet for the worst-case criminal implications of taking an abandoned child. In one situation, a mother was charged with infant abduction and sentenced to twenty-two years for rescuing a child she found in an abandoned car in a parking lot. Another woman was charged with kidnapping and sentenced to twenty years for not reporting the baby she found in a Dumpster to the authorities. Twenty years in the pokey seemed to be the average penalty. Two decades of missing out on Eliot's middle school science projects, high school graduation, college campus tours, meeting his girlfriend, maybe even missing his wedding. If I was lucky and got out early on good behavior, I might get to be there when he had his first baby.

Then there was Sydney. What three-year-old could survive without her mama? Especially a child with kidney failure? Not being there to remind her when she needed to rest, monitoring her diet, taking her to doctor appointments, mommy kisses to distract her from the many shots, fighting her way up the organ transplant list…not being there for Syd scared me more than anything.

"How are the cops going to be able to find something out of nothing?" I argued. "We literally have no idea where Vera came from, so without a past to trace her back to, what good will

265

involving the police do?"

"How did Vera find out? If a teen can do it, certainly the cops can too."

"I wish I had your faith. It sounds like we're just setting ourselves up for disappointment."

"Listen, Felicity, we have to at least try. We won't know what the cops can find out until we tell them everything. What if they're able to find something out through a DNA match? If she's got a relative who's in the criminal system, they might be able to use that."

"And then what, Ollie? *If* that's where Vera went—to find her long-lost relative—then what? They find Vera, great. But they'll take her from us because she's not legally ours! Even though she was abandoned, a biological relation might want her back. Even if no one stepped forward to claim her, there's no way they'd give her back to us after we *kidnapped* her. You're not even considering the fact that one, possibly both, of us ends up in jail while some other family gets Vera. According to the law, regardless of which one of us confesses, we're both complicit! Do you really want to risk losing her for good?"

"We've already lost her, Felicity! Don't you see that? She's gone! It's been six months. I'd rather find her and give her up than never find her at all."

Fifteen years ago, Oliver and I had made a pact. We had decided never to tell Vera the truth about her past, which quickly spiraled into *our* past. Back then it seemed like the only option, keep the baby and keep it hush-hush, because it was the only way we kept Vera with us and kept us out of jail. But now we were backed into a corner, down to one option: coming clean.

I had considered the DNA match possibility many times, weighed the pros and cons. But if a match was discovered through the criminal database, did I really want to surrender my daughter to a family with a criminal history? Present company excluded, of course.

I even wondered if perhaps Vera had obtained her own ancestry DNA report—they were easy enough to order online. I even dared to mention it to Detective Montgomery, asking if there was a chance Vera might have found some long-lost relative through a DNA database. When they scrubbed her computer and found no internet history or purchase transaction that would suggest a DNA search, I breathed a sigh of relief.

"The decision's made," Oliver stated bluntly.

It was a decision we had debated numerous times, and every time we circled back to the conclusion that one had nothing to do with the other. Vera's biological past had nothing to do with her disappearance. Period. Because there were no dots to connect. No names to look up. Without facts, no good would come from telling the cops I had stolen a baby and never bothered to report it.

But now suddenly Oliver disagreed. And he demanded to take the fall for me. Oliver was a survivor; it's what he did best. Let's say Vera went looking for her biological family, who knew what danger she was in? I knew nothing about the family, other than that they left a days-old newborn baby on the side of the road. If Oliver was going to do this, he couldn't go in blind. There was something I had never told him, and it was time he knew.

I stood up from the kitchen bar stool.

"Come with me. I need to show you something."

Then I headed for the stairwell.

"What do you need to show me?"

And I started to climb.

"If you're going to go the police and confess, you need to know everything that happened that night."

I led Oliver up one flight of stairs, past the watchful eyes of the stained-glass couple, up a second flight, to the door I seldom opened. The creepy library. It groaned as I pushed it, releasing a waft of musty air. It wasn't late at night, but it was black as tar inside the room. Through the darkness I saw movement, felt a presence, heard a whisper, and I clutched Oliver's arm. My hand searched the wall for the light switch, found it, and scattered the ghosts with a *click*. Eddies of dust motes swirled in the dim light, and I coughed to clear my lungs.

Still holding on to Oliver's arm, I walked him along the bookshelves stacked with rare, priceless volumes, past the fireplace hearth where the family had been brutally murdered. In the corner sat an old chest covered in over a decade's worth of dust. The lock had long ago rusted apart. I opened it, and inside it was filled with mementos belonging to Oliver's ancestors. Photographs of his grandmother Olivia holding a teenage Debra's hand. Newspaper articles about his great-grandmother Alvera's work in the women's rights movement, her marriage announcement, Olivia's birth certificate, a century-old missing persons report.

I picked up a golden-brown leather journal, oddly shiny against the dust-covered items surrounding it. I had examined it recently and suspected Vera had also, before her disappearance.

"Check this out," I said. "It's your great-grandmother's journal. I wonder if Vera found this when she was looking into Alvera for her suffrage movement project."

The first entry, written in Alvera's beautiful copperplate script, dated back to February 1898. Oliver looked over my shoulder as I read aloud:

One must never flee from one's calling. I learned this only when it was taken from me. I visited Washington DC with dear Miss Cianfarra, a lady I have come to cherish and adore. The guilt of lying to Robert haunts me at this hour, but the calling is worth the contrition. Today I heard the inspiring words of a fellow suffragette of color, Miss Mary Church Terrell. Her message at the National American Woman Suffrage Association pierced me, gutted me, and drove a new hope within me that all women of all skin colors could fight for this cause together. Miss Terrell won me over with her words and passion. May she win over our broken world as well. A woman's voice. A woman's right to vote. A woman's value. It is much more than gender or skin hue. It is about humanity and fairness.

My life has been less than fair. As one of great wealth none would empathize with this statement of mine. But my enforced marriage has brought me nothing but grief, and I fear Robert is desperate to make me with child to tighten his grip upon me.

A woman bears the right to be heard and seen. Yet how do we achieve the fullness of this birthright when we must remain silent and hidden? I must do the hard work of preparing a place for women's voices of the future. I must plan. I must fight. And if necessary, I must flee in the pursuit of justice and truth, no matter the sacrifice. Even at the cost of my very own lifeblood.

"Pretty corny stuff," Oliver snorted with his usual cynicism.

"Spoken like a male chauvinist pig."

"Hey, I'm not knocking her. I admire my great-grandma; she was a fearless woman, way ahead of her time. But her writing is kinda flowery, you gotta admit."

"Whatever. You just don't recognize passionate writing when you hear it."

I sat the journal down and continued my search. Countless mysteries filled this chest, but only one concerned me. I rifled through the artifacts until I located the tiny wooden Russian nesting doll tucked into the back corner. I handed it to Oliver.

"What's this?" he asked. He opened it. "There's nothing in here but shit."

"What do you mean?" I grabbed it from him, shocked to see it full of mouse droppings. "There used to be a piece of paper in this. The only link I had to Vera's past." The edge of the doll was chewed. "I think mice got to it."

"What do you mean, a link to her past? I don't understand."

An anxious pulse swept up my spine. "There's something I never told you about that day..."

Rolling my mind back, like a mental flip-book, I spanned days, months, years faster and faster until I stopped on the night I found newborn Vera.

Chapter 32
Felicity

Responsible drivers use their blinkers. Everyone knew it was the law, but not everyone followed it. I was a good little law-abiding citizen. The car whose fender I just hit, however, was not.

The street was fairly empty for this time of day, early evening, and the sky deepened into a shade of blue-gray. The radio DJs were discussing the *American Idol* final four contestants this season, with sound bites from Paula Abdul, Simon Cowell, and Randy Jackson interspersed. Hard rocker Chris Daughtry was heavily favored to win the competition, a notion the DJs hotly debated. I had voted for him, so I tended to be biased. Oliver, maybe just to irritate me, was rooting for gray-haired soul-meister Taylor Hicks. I loftily informed him that buffoon didn't have a chance in hell of winning the fifth season of *Idol*. Famous last words.

I wasn't in the mood for radio chat, so I reached down to change the station. Settled on Rihanna's "SOS" before returning my focus to the road. I only glanced down for a moment, but that single moment was all it took for a car to swing out from the berm, right in front of me.

I swerved onto the open shoulder to avoid a collision, but not quickly enough, as I heard the crunch of metal scraping our bumpers together. I winced as I pumped the brakes, careening to a stop.

The car I hit pulled over in front of me, both of our vehicles idling while my brain attempted to work out what to do. I was shaken. A little scared. The sky was growing darker and the road emptier by the minute. The only car accident I'd ever been in involved me bumping an orange traffic cone during driver's ed class, but I knew enough to assess the extent of the damage and go from there. Was it always the fault of whoever rear-ended the other car? Or did it matter that he pulled out in front of me? Visibility wasn't ideal, so maybe it could have been both our faults—mine for not turning my headlights on, him for pulling out without checking for oncoming traffic. Or maybe it didn't matter. Was all this for the cops to sort out?

I grabbed my Motorola RAZR cell phone and flipped it open. Oliver had wanted to buy me the new sliding keyboard version, but why trade in a perfectly good cell phone when this one worked fine? Even if it did take forever to type a text by going first through each number, then each letter one at a time. God forbid you type past your intended letter and have to start over. It didn't matter much, though. With limited texts and minutes, I avoided using my cell phone like the plague after my last $300 bill.

I pressed the 9...and the screen blinked black. I held down the power button. Nothing. Why did I always forget to charge the darn thing? I was certain my charger was packed somewhere among the moving boxes and I had yet to find it.

By now the other driver had stepped out of his car, a dark-colored beater maybe ten, fifteen years old with one busted taillight. I turned on my overhead light and rummaged through my center console, found a pen and scrap of paper, then jotted down his license plate number. In my dashboard compartment I found my insurance card, readying myself to hash out the details with this strange man.

Walking around his car, investigating the damage, he eventually ambled toward my car with a crooked gait. His clothes were nondescript—greasy jeans, button-up shirt hanging loose, T-shirt underneath. He reached up and made a token effort to neaten his flattened crop of hat hair. Just a working stiff, I figured, dog-tired from a long day on the job. Pissed to be involved in a fender-bender. But I wasn't taking any chances as I instinctively locked all the doors with the master button.

I checked the time. I really hoped I made it home in time for the *Gilmore Girls* season finale. Oliver hadn't shut off our cable or loaded the television onto the moving truck yet because of it. The show represented the dream mother-daughter relationship that I hoped one day would be my own, but until then I'd binge on Rory and Lorelai.

The driver was at my window now and bent down to my level. Bathed in the intermittent glow of his hazard lights, his face sported a three-day scruff—out of laziness, I figured, not trendiness. His dull eyes couldn't seem to find a focus, darting from his car to me, to the road and back to me. When he suddenly rapped a dirty knuckle on my window, I gave a start, then nervously rolled it down only a sliver. We were completely alone, no cars, no witnesses, in the middle of a deserted road, and the sky was black as pitch.

I would have done just about anything for Rihanna's SOS about now.

"Ya hit me," he said so matter-of-fact that I was actually a bit terrified.

"I'm sorry, but you pulled out in front of me, sir." I added the *sir* to hopefully cool any rising tension.

"Did ya call the cops?" he asked. "'Cause if we can settle this without involving the cops, I'd be mighty appreciative..." His eyes traveled down to the phone in my hand, then detoured to my insurance card in the other. "Felicity Portman."

Now the stranger was gathering information about me. I shouldn't have been afraid, right? That's what people did after a car accident—exchanged personal information. But something about him hovering there, sticking his grimy fingers in the gap of my window, shook my bones. I would have given him my bank account number just to get away from this man.

"Whatever is easiest," I agreed.

"Damage looks minimal. Just a few scratches a good buffering can take care of. You wanna come look?"

Stranger danger! My mother's deeply ingrained childhood motto reverberated inside me.

"I'm perfectly fine just settling this here. I have"—I pulled out my wallet stuffed with cash Oliver had handed me when he told me to buy more moving boxes and bins and anything I could find to pack stuff in—"$500 cash that should cover your repairs. Would that work?"

Why the heck did I just tell this stranger I had five hundred bucks in cash? Worse, why did I flash the wad? *Okay, brace yourself, stupid—he's going to smash the window and then bash your brains out with a hidden tire iron any second now.*

But he didn't.

"That's mighty generous of you. I'll be honest with you 'cause ya seem nice. I don't have insurance right now. My wife just died—that's why I wasn't really paying much mind when I cut you off just now. And I'm raising my kid on my own, and I fell into tough times. I was hoping to avoid the whole insurance thing, if that's alright by you."

He wiped a brown tear that rolled down his cheek, streaking his filthy face. Either he was a seasoned scam artist, or he was telling the truth. By the looks of his beater car, clearly he was barely scraping by. I felt terrible for this man who lost his wife and was thrown into single parenthood. I'd never suffered—not really—and I couldn't imagine what it would be like to lose Oliver.

"You know what? Here's the $500, and I have an extra $300 I can give you too. It's all I have, but clearly you need it more than I do. I'm really sorry about your wife."

"Shit happens." He looked down at his feet. "Just seems to always happen to me."

I didn't know what to say, how to console him through the metal and glass between us. Had it been a friend, I would have offered a hug. But I didn't trust this stranger enough to step out of my safe haven. I turned my back and fished into the secret compartment of my purse for my emergency money—three hundred bucks—and added it to the five hundred. Eight hundred total—a tidy sum. I handed him the thick stack of bills through the gap in the window.

"Thank ya for the cash. You seem like a real nice lady." His grin betrayed a missing premolar, tobacco stains, and something else—relief, satisfaction; I couldn't read the expression.

"We've all been in tough spots."

"Well, you saved my life today. I better be on my way. Got a kid waiting at home for me."

"I hope things get better for you!" I called out to his fast retreating back. A hand shot up, waving the wad of cash.

His brake lights blinked on and off, and spraying gravel his car sped down the road and disappeared into the gloom. I wasn't ready to drive, my nerves weak from emotional overload. As I turned off my overhead light, I flicked on my high beams, the headlights snagging on a large object on the side of the road next to where the stranger had just been parked. It looked like a...baby carrier?

I stepped out of the car and approached it cautiously, as if I expected it to contain something other than what was inside: a tiny infant—couldn't have been more than a day or two old—snuggled sleepily up to a tattered stuffed toy. A velveteen rabbit, just like in the book.

It could only be the strange man's child, and I wondered what kind of human would abandon a baby on the road. There was no way I was returning this newborn to a monster.

Glancing around, still no cars. Still no witnesses. I picked up the car seat by the handle and hefted it back to my car. It was heavier than I thought, and I wondered if hauling this around was what created mom strength. After clipping it into the seat belt as best I could without the base, I sat in the driver's seat deliberating. I had never found a baby before—well, duh! The situation was surreal, like something that happened only in the movies. Should I take it to the police station and turn it in? Should I bring it home and feed it and change it first, just to make sure it was cared for? A lot of shoulds ran through my mind, but just because I should didn't mean I would.

I pocketed the scrap of paper with the license plate number, half tempted to tear it up as if it never existed. Then I put my blinker on like a good little law-abiding citizen as I headed home with my new stolen baby.

Chapter 33
Felicity

The FOR SALE sign jutting out from my front yard glowed against the dark as I drove up the street way too slowly. The whole trip home I was petrified of getting into an accident with my precious cargo. The housing market was a mess, but not as big of a mess as what I'd just made of my life as I pulled into my driveaway with my newborn baby girl. Yes, it was a she! I had checked, of course.

Outside in the yard, Oliver, Cody, Debra, and Joe were loading boxes into the moving truck. I hadn't planned to share my kidnapping escapade with the whole family, but they'd all find out sooner than later. It wasn't exactly easy to hide a living, breathing baby from in-laws you saw weekly.

Pulling up the driveway, my brain raced with a million scenarios:

Take the baby to the police.

The baby will end up in foster care anyway.

What if there's no other family?

What if there *is* other family?

I had answers to every possible question, every possible challenge, as if I'd been preparing for this debate my entire life. I wanted this baby. Needed this baby like I needed air. Oliver and I had been trying for years, every month making pregnancy test manufacturers rich when I was barely a day late. And every month I kept tissue manufacturers in business with the tears when it displayed that mocking negative symbol.

Oliver's dream was to become CEO of the marketing agency he worked for. Mine was to become a mother. It's why I quit college and got married so young, because a career paled beside the joys and, yes, the sorrows of being a mom. And here that dream was, wrapped in swaddling clothes and lying in a car seat waiting for me.

We had the means to support a family. And if the strange man had someone else to care for the baby, he would have certainly passed her off to them, not left her on the side of the road. The answer was as clear as the star-spangled night sky. This was my destiny, to become this girl's mother.

I stepped out of the car, then opened the back door. I unclipped the car seat and hefted it out, resting the handle on my forearm. It felt so good to be lugging this exquisite burden around, using muscles I hadn't known existed before. I carried her past the scratches on my fender and up the walkway with a proud motherly stride.

Across the lawn Oliver was calling it a night, inviting everyone inside for drinks before heading home, thanking them for all their help. As I approached, a questioning silence settled over everyone as all heads turned. Oliver broke the spell.

"Felicity, what are you carrying?"

"It's a car seat."

"Please tell me there's not a baby in there."

I turned the car seat toward him, showing off the pink-faced and chubby infant, sleeping peacefully. I smiled at her perfection. Oliver didn't.

"We'll talk about this inside," he said, his voice verging on frantic.

I stepped into our naked house, the family following me, and in the dim living room light, Oliver looked at me with so many questions I couldn't read them all. I set down the car seat and touched my pocket where the scrap of paper with the license plate number crinkled beneath the denim. I had two choices—to tell the truth, or to lie.

The only real choice was to lie. Because Oliver could never handle the burden of truth. The truth would have required I turn the baby over to children's services or suffer the guilt of keeping her illegally. Oliver, like I used to be before tonight, was a law-abiding blinker-using citizen. So I took the burden upon myself. Lie, it was.

"Before you panic, I found her on the side of the road."

"You know you can't keep her, right?" Joe rarely chimed in with unsolicited advice, which caught me off-guard.

"Hear me out," I pleaded. "I have no idea where she came from, but here's the thing. If we turn her in to the police, they'll likely find her parents and she'll end up right back in the horrible situation she was already in. But if we keep her, she'll lack nothing! She'll get endless love. We're her second chance at a great life."

"There's proper channels for this." Joe again. "She needs to be in the custody of the state where they'll place her in foster care. Maybe you could then arrange to be her foster parent and adopt her."

"Do you know how long of a process is involved? There's no guarantee I'll get her."

"I'm pretty sure you'd go to jail if anyone ever found out, Felicity," Cody added. "I'm pretty sure it's considered kidnapping, even if you technically didn't steal her."

I couldn't help but notice Oliver's silence. What was he

thinking? I needed to appeal to his shared desire for a family.

"We've been waiting for a baby, Oliver. What if this was what we were waiting for? We're her miracle just as much as she's our miracle."

Still Oliver contemplated, or perhaps he was in shock. I'd never known him not to have a strong opinion, about everything from what color to paint the bathroom to who played the best James Bond (his pick: Daniel Craig, though Sean Connery still did it for me). No one spoke, just stared. At me. At the baby. Her eyes peeled open and she cooed, pursing her lips and rolling her head, searching for a nipple.

"No foster care. You should keep her." Everyone turned to look over at Debra, the most law-abiding blinker-using one of us all.

"Mom, what are you saying?" Cody replied.

She shrugged, reached down and unclipped the car seat, lifting the baby into her arms. Her gaze fixed lovingly on her new granddaughter. "I don't know if Cody will ever give me grandkids, and you two have been trying for a while with no luck, so what if this is my only chance to be a grandma?"

"Mom, you're talking crazy. They shouldn't steal a baby just to fulfill your dream of being a grandmother," Cody grumbled.

"It's not like I'm the only one who wants this," Debra said pointedly. "Felicity was created to be a mom. She'd be amazing at it."

"And how do you propose they get away with it?" Joe asked.

"It won't be hard." Debra turned to me. "Sweetheart, all you have to do is go to the hospital tomorrow pretending you've given birth at home, and ask how to file for a birth certificate. They'll help file one for you. I'll go with you. Considering she looks to only be a day or two old, she probably doesn't even have a birth certificate yet. Once they issue that, we just...raise our beautiful little addition to the family as our own. And never speak of what happened tonight—ever. She must never know. If we can all do that, everything will be fine. It'll be more than fine. She'll have a wonderful home, you'll have the most loved baby in the world, and no one will ever know the difference."

"Are you kidding?" Joe yelled. "Oliver could go to jail over this. How could you endorse this madness?"

"You know why, Joe." Debra shot him a silencing glare, her word stern and final.

"Is this about you? Because it shouldn't be. It should be about the baby. And about our kids staying out of jail."

"What's he talking about, Mom?" Cody asked.

"Nothing," Joe interjected, holding his hand out to end the conversation.

"Mom?" Cody pleaded.

"No, it's not nothing. They deserve to know," Debra said. "When I was little, my biological parents abused me. Tortured me, actually. It was a horrific life, if you even want to call it a life. They tried to hide the abuse from everyone by pulling me out of school, never letting me leave the house. Eventually I slipped outside one day and I just kept running and running until I had no idea where I was, but I was more afraid of being in that house than I was being lost out on the streets."

Tears welled in her eyes as she sniffled, adjusted the baby in her arms, and sucked in a breath.

"Well, a really sweet lady, Miss Frances, I called her, saw me and asked me where I came from, and I was petrified to tell her, because I didn't want to be taken home. Despite my tight lips, I think she knew it was somewhere bad, because she ended up taking me in that night. We spent the next couple days together baking, gardening, watching movies…she even took me shopping and made up a bedroom for me. A beautiful pink princess room.

She gave me the best days of my life up until then."

The baby's coos intensified, and Debra shifted naturally into mama mode as she silenced the baby with a rocking motion.

"A couple days later Miss Frances told me she hated to do it, but she needed to go through the proper channels, but her intention was to foster me. This was back in the day where the foster system didn't have many checks and balances, and hardly any good families wanted any part in it, only people who wanted the paycheck. So Miss Frances called social services and asked if she could have temporary custody of me until the paperwork was completed. They denied her, came to pick me up, and tried to reunite me with my biological family. Of course I ran away again, but I had no idea where to find Miss Frances. I was very young, you know? Again I got picked up, and this time they put me in a new foster home. I never saw my parents—or sweet Miss Frances—again after that."

Debra paused to kiss the sleeping baby on her forehead.

"I don't know if my parents simply never tried to see me, or what, but it was a relief. Until I got put into foster care with a family who was only in it for the money. She fostered several of us—they didn't have all the rules that prevented overcrowding back then—and we were all treated like garbage. Again, I ran away. Again, I was found. This happened about a dozen times before I finally fit into the right family. A single woman, no less, which was highly uncommon back in those days. That woman I called my *real* mom—Olivia Fields." Debra turned to Oliver. "Your grandmother, Ollie. The woman you were named after."

Debra handed me the baby.

"She fostered me, loved me, ended up adopting me, and it was the most beautiful, purest love in the world. I don't want this baby to suffer like I did. I don't want her to be passed around, to end up broken and unloved. The chances of you getting to keep her are slim, just like with Miss Frances. We never found each other again, and I don't know what happened to her or if maybe she decided against it, but whatever the case, right now you have a chance to save this child. I think it's the right thing to do, screw the law!"

Oliver bent down to pick up the worn velveteen rabbit. Then he took the baby from me, gently placed the plush toy under her arm, and snuggled her up to his chest. "It's settled then. Welcome home, sweet angel." He swung her gently around to view her new family. "Meet your Nana and Pappy Joe and Uncle Cody. And most importantly, your mommy."

As I watched my husband fall in love with his first child, I felt the crinkle of that paper in my pocket. The only evidence of my lie. I had indeed spoken to the father. We could have helped him get on his feet instead of pretending he didn't exist. Some might call me selfish, some might call me selfless. But in that moment I didn't care about anything but that baby. So I decided then and there that no one could ever find out the truth.

Eventually it would hunt me down.

Chapter 34
Felicity

The library lights flickered, and Oliver choked on a cloud of dust that hung over us like an apparition. The air in the room was stifling tonight. I set the Russian nesting doll back in its corner of the trunk and sighed resignation. This whole search for answers was hopeless.

"So you knew all along who her biological father was? And you've been lying about it ever since?"

I was the kid whose hand was caught in the cookie jar, mouth smeared with chocolate, and yet I still proclaimed innocence.

"I wouldn't call it lying exactly. I had his license plate number, so if I really wanted to dig, I could have found out who he was probably. But we had all decided to keep her. We all agreed that it was best not to give her back to someone who would leave her on the side of the road."

"Why didn't you just tell the truth about meeting the father? We probably would have all still said the same thing—to keep her."

Could have, would have, should have. It got you nowhere.

"I didn't think that at the time. I assumed everyone would tell me to help her find her family. Who knows if the dad had a brother or a cousin who could take care of her? But I didn't want to consider that option. I'm sorry for lying. It was selfish of me to want to give a little girl a better life."

Oliver rolled his eyes, because he knew a pity party when he was invited to one.

"So the license plate number is gone?"

"I don't know. I thought I had put it in this nesting doll in case I ever needed it, but it was so long ago. I remember coming up here with Vera a time or two to dig through ancestry records for her school project, but I don't remember checking for it. Last I saw it was fifteen years ago, when we were moving. God knows where I might have misplaced it over the years."

Oliver scratched his chin, smearing dirt into his day-old stubble. "Do you think maybe Vera found it?"

"Even if she did, it was just letters and numbers. I highly doubt she could have made any sense of them, or knew what they meant."

My gaze skimmed across the gaping mouth of the chest, glancing at the relics from Alvera's past. A flawed hero. In her own way, a dark horse of a woman who had done so much for women's suffrage, and likely died for it. I picked up the stack of newspaper clippings chronicling her life.

"What's that?" Oliver asked.

"Alvera's life and death, summed up in a few pieces of paper."

"Oh, wow, look at this." Oliver lifted a loose article from the trunk and read it. "Her work in the women's rights movement. This one is talking about her fundraising work." Oliver gently handled it, set it down, and picked up another. "And here's her marriage announcement in the newspaper. Can you imagine being forced to marry a man twice your age and having to produce his heir?"

I examined a picture of Alvera and Robert, noticing their stiff postures, and the misery etched across both of their faces. "Just because something's the norm doesn't make it right."

"My mom told me that supposedly her personality changed after the baby was born."

"Isn't that when she disappeared?"

He nodded solemnly.

Debra had told me about the family mystery, regurgitating the macabre details as if she had lived them herself. A couple months after giving birth to Olivia, on a cool April evening, Alvera disappeared, never to be heard from again. No one knew exactly what had happened to her, though many suspicions arose. Olivia had been told by her father, Robert, that her mother was kidnapped and murdered by someone seeking revenge on the family over their wealth and prestige. Others speculated that, in order to send a strong message, she had been killed by a faction trying to squash the women's suffrage movement. But a few rumors circulated that she went on to fight the battle under a new identity. That the mystery went unsolved, and we would never know the truth, was heartbreaking.

Another leather journal rested in the pile of memorabilia. I opened it up and scrolled through the pages, coming near the end where I saw a drawing of a symbol, followed by Alvera's explanation for its significance:

This Celtic sign of courage depicts the shared struggle that we as women must face and conquer together. Only through courage can we fight for our voice and win.

It was Vera's tattoo.

Vera had seen this.

"Oh my God," I whispered.

"What?" Oliver echoed.

"I think I know how to find Vera!"

It was the first warm thought in a heart that had been frozen for months.

Carrying Alvera's journal with me, I ran downstairs and into our bedroom, Oliver's loud footsteps storming behind mine. I pulled open my bedside drawer and flipped open Vera's journal. I had memorized its contents page by page, finding the image within a moment. The same exact drawing—mimicking the symbol from Alvera's journal.

"Look, Oliver. It's like she's following the path of her great-great-grandmother. Down to the very same day she disappeared."

April 16 was the day Alvera had found the courage to leave her husband, her child, and rediscover herself. One hundred and eleven years later, my daughter had done the same.

"Well, obviously she didn't run off to join the women's suffrage movement, Felicity. So what does this mean? And what does this have to do with where she is?"

I flipped page by page through her journal, searching for anything that stood out to me. All of Vera's secrets were contained in this book, every clue we needed in order to find her. Of this I was certain. From cover to cover I searched, finding nothing, until I closed it with a heavy heart. Holding it, that's when I felt the minutest difference. At the very back of the book, against the cover, I felt it more than saw it. A small, telltale lump where something protruded from under a page that had been glued to the back cover. I gently tugged the page free, letting loose a tiny scrap of paper that fluttered to the floor. I picked it up, recognizing the shape of it, the scrawl of numbers and letters.

Seven, to be exact. The license plate number.

"She's with him! Her biological father!" I screamed, nearly jolting Oliver out of his skin. It was a wonder I didn't wake the kids. "She must have found a way to trace his license plate number to his name. We can find her, Oliver!"

I was so happy, I broke into a herky-jerky dance to celebrate.

I heard Oliver snickering and stopped. "What's so funny?"

"You dance like Elaine Benes on *Seinfeld*."

"Ha ha. You're no Justin Timberlake yourself. Why the gloomy face? You should be celebrating too."

"This number is from fifteen years ago. What are the chances it's still going to belong to the right name and address?"

"There are records, Ollie. We'll figure it out. Obviously Vera did. At least we have something now! We don't have to tell the cops what we did. We can bring our girl home!"

"Got any ideas how?" Oliver Naysayer asked.

"How about we call our car insurance company and tell them we had a hit-and-run with a car using this license plate number. Maybe they'll give us the information?"

"It's worth a try."

We headed into the den, where Oliver located our insurance agent's contact information. I picked up the phone and dialed. I had rehearsed with Oliver all the questions I needed to ask, and exactly how to word it, then crossed my fingers that it would work.

The agent answered on the fifth ring.

"I'm calling because I was involved in a hit-and-run and the other driver took off. But I have their license plate number. Are you able to give me the contact information for the person who hit me?"

The agent wavered. "I'm sorry, ma'am, but we can't give out that information. If you'll give me the license plate number, we can pull it ourselves and find out if they have insurance and handle it for you."

"There's no way I can contact them myself to deal with it?"

"I'm afraid not. It's private information."

"Okay, thanks anyway."

Dead end. I hung up and shook my head. "No luck. It's

confidential."

Turning on the computer, I Googled license plate websites that claimed free access to vehicle owner information. After the third scam, I realized it was a lost cause. There went that unfettered hope.

"Any other brilliant ideas for how to trace this back to a vehicle owner from over a decade ago?"

I wanted to shove Oliver Naysayer's snide words right back down his throat.

"If you'd stop being such a jerk about this, I have an idea, but you're not going to like it."

"Have I liked any of this so far?" he retorted.

He had no idea how bad it could get, because it was going to require him to do something he hated more than anything. In fact, Oliver probably would have preferred jail to what I was about to ask him to do.

Chapter 35
Felicity

Dickhead Daniel was the only person in the world who Oliver hated. Truly loathed. Daniel was a one-upper. A name-dropper. The kind of person who would ask how you're doing, then talk over you about how he spent the weekend picking up college chicks on his new yacht.

He always cajoled his way to the front of the buffet line at company picnics and then complained about the subpar food, insisted he was best qualified to umpire the traditional softball game (so he could ogle and rate the female batters' "juiciest asses"), and once got so stinking drunk he peed into the lake in full view of a horrified Brownie troupe. Around the office his gossipmongering and brown-nosing and goldbricking were legendary. And a talker—he was one of those guys in love with the sound of his voice, and while he had absolutely nothing worthwhile to say, he could ramble on for hours about politics (don't get him started on conspiracy theories), his sexual prowess (a highly inflated view), or how much money he made (too much). If you wanted to keep your job, and Oliver did, you tolerated Dickhead Daniel's boorish behavior. You see, he was related to one of the directors.

But Dickhead Daniel had one thing I needed, and thus I begged Oliver to suffer the fool…for me. For Vera.

It was at an after-work get-together when Dickhead Daniel's

name-dropping came in handy as he held court at a neighborhood bar. Three sheets to the wind, he bragged that he'd worked undercover with the private investigator who worked a huge national child trafficking case and put the ringleader behind bars. Everybody knew this was pure bull, and several challenged him on it, but he really knew the woman and flashed a business card from his wallet to prove it. At the time, pre-Vera's disappearance, Daniel's spurious claim to fame didn't mean much to me. But now it meant everything.

I knew enough about private investigators from my research and countless calls and interviews after Vera disappeared to know that most couldn't help me. Without a single viable lead, their hands were tied. They could interview all the same friends, question all the same people, follow all the same leads as the police, and land back at the starting line. One PI called our case "an untouchable"—the cases of runaway teens who didn't want to be found. With virtually no traceability—no electronic bank transactions, cash only, house-hopping, no phone—they were the ones no PI wanted to touch. Except Dickhead Daniel, after a grueling two-hour lunch entertaining him with surf-and-turf and the most expensive wine we had in the cellar, was certain that Private Investigator Ari Wilburn could help us. How could someone in Durham, North Carolina—a solid eight-hour drive—help me from two states away?

"That's tech for ya," Daniel slurred as we shoved him out onto the porch. "Hey, stay in touch, man! And you"—he pointed a wobbly finger at me—"stay gorgeous."

I offered him a polite smile, urged him to call an Uber, then slammed the door shut.

I was glad to be proven wrong.

Ari, as she told me to call her, didn't need to meet in person. Apparently she was a seasoned pro at locating missing people with a blank canvas past. One was her best friend's little girl who was stolen by a child trafficking ring. If this woman could face hardened criminals and find a child with no past, I was willing to put my trust in her to find out who a license plate from over a decade ago was registered to.

I had given her the only details I had—a license plate number and state. I couldn't recall the make or model of car. Then she told me she'd call me back when she had something. When the phone rang barely an hour later showing her number on my screen, my heart raced. From the kitchen where I diced vegetables for dinner, I called out to Oliver over the sound of the kids playing the board game *Guess Who?* in the living room.

"Does your person have green eyes, Idiot?" Sydney yelled.

"Nope!" Eliot yelled back.

They tended to shout everything these days, one always talking louder over the other, when all I wanted was silence.

I answered the phone on my way up the stairs toward the den, where I hid and hoped the kids wouldn't find me, as they did any time I dared answer my phone. They had a special radar for when a call was extra important, and thus their own petty squabbles became extra urgent. Like Sydney sticking her tongue out at Eliot. Or Eliot taking her game piece. Well, this time they'd have to settle their differences themselves.

"Hi, Ari. I hope you have good news for me," I answered.

"Actually, I do. I found out who that license plate was registered to," she replied. "A man by the name of Bennett Hunter."

Bennett Hunter. Bennett Hunter. Why did that sound so familiar?

I gasped.

Ari continued, though my thoughts were stuck on that name. "I was able to locate a current address for him, but no updated phone number. I'd need to do more digging to find that out."

"Is the address local to Pittsburgh?" I asked.

"Yes, about twenty minutes or so from your home. But Felicity"—her voice lowered in a warning—"I know what you're planning on doing. Please do not go to his house. I'd suggest letting the police handle it from here."

I couldn't do that. The whole point was to prevent the police from discovering I had kidnapped my daughter.

"I understand."

She must have dealt with my type before, because after giving me the address, she followed up by saying, "If you do decide to go without the police, at least bring your husband with you. Absolutely do not go alone. You never know what kind of danger you could be putting yourself in."

"Okay."

"Do you want me to follow up on getting an updated phone number?"

I didn't need her digging for more. Contacting Bennett herself and finding out what I had done. I had no idea if she was required by law to turn me in if she discovered I had committed a crime. The fewer people who knew, the safer.

"No, that's okay. Not right now, at least. I'll see where this takes me first, and if I end up needing more, I'll let you know."

"Sounds good." She paused, then said, "Hey, take care of yourself, Felicity. And be safe, whatever you do."

I hung up, and for the first time since Vera disappeared I sensed we were nearing the end of this very long, harrowing search.

"Ollie!" I screamed, searching for him room to room. I finally found him outside in the backyard raking leaves—lately, a favorite tension-reliever. Against the brilliant blue sky random speckles of orange and red clung stubbornly to the skeletal branches, falling with feathery elegance when a breeze at last dislodged them.

Oliver passed one look over me, dropped the rake, and ran toward me. "Hey, are you okay?"

I shook my head, nodded, I didn't know what I was doing. "I know where Vera is. And it's bad. Real bad."

"Where?"

"She's with Bennett Hunter."

He looked at me quizzically, the pieces not quite fitting.

"Bennett *Hunter,* Ollie. Marin's maiden name is Hunter. Vera is with Marin's father!"

Chapter 36
Marin

"Mortimer Randolph's law partners must really have it in for you." Deputy Levine, who had hauled me to the police station in the back of his cruiser, opened the metal door of the interrogation room, releasing me to the myriad suspects and criminals waiting in the lobby for their turn.

"I've never seen an autopsy turned around so quickly," he continued.

It took two hours for me to plead my case, that no, I did *not* put a lethal dose of ibuprofen in Mortimer Randolph's coffee. And no, I had no idea over-the-counter NSAIDs could cause a heart attack, which was exactly what dear Mortimer died from in the middle of chastising Karen, his legal secretary, over the phone. Yes, Mortimer and I had had our differences, and yes, I had told him off rather royally on one occasion—the partners had clearly done their homework. And yes, Mortimer took a heap of pills each day that I never administered—it wasn't part of my job, I was only his assistant, not his home nurse—so it's possible he mixed up his meds himself. And of course it was unexpected when I discovered I was his sole beneficiary—I admitted this news came from Karen, but I didn't disclose the circumstances— because it sure looked a lot like a murder motive to Levine.

Motive was not a word that should have applied to me; it was a word used in *Law & Order: Special Victims Unit,* an episode of which I happened to have a small speaking part in.

I was lucky enough that my alibi held water, and Mortimer's time of death didn't coincide with when I was at his house. Though it did beg the question: who spiked his coffee, and what did they have to gain? Because it certainly wasn't me, even though I had the most to gain.

I was surprised to see the remnant of daylight outside the police station when I exited through the double doors; it felt like I'd been in there throughout the night. It was early evening, yet my eyelids felt heavy, my heart exhausted from overworking itself, even my jaw ached from clenching so long. It was stressful being interrogated for homicide! As I spotted Cody sullenly waiting in his red truck, I realized the night was just getting started.

"You're saying secrets are killing our marriage. So let's get rid of the secrets and keep the marriage." Those were the last words Cody had left me with before Deputy Levine had showed up at our house. And Cody still wanted an answer.

I was afraid. Not of Cody. But of the bomb I was about to detonate.

We drove home in an uneasy silence that I wasn't used to with him. I could smell the faint odor of alcohol on him, and I could sense confrontation flowing in his blood. Fifteen minutes and a million thoughts later, we walked into the kitchen together. Cody tossed a stack of mail and a small brown package on the counter, addressed to me. Normally I loved getting packages, but right now I was too stressed to give it another thought. In the middle of the counter was a bottle of Absolut Vanilia vodka. It'd be empty before the night was over.

Wedging the ugly orange counter between us, he glared at me, his gaze intense, almost terrifying. Jack Nicholson in *The Shining* terrifying. And I felt every ounce of anxiety all at once as

I prepared to tell him my darkest secret ever. The secret that brought me into his life and took Vera away.

"You ready to talk?" he asked me.

"Are you ready to listen?" I snapped back.

I was no shrinking violet, even when I was in the wrong. Because he was in the wrong too. We stood on equal footing. Him a cheater, me a liar. At least I had an excuse. I knew he'd never be ready for the truth. Beneath the superior exterior, he was just a scared little boy afraid of things that went bump in the night. The things he couldn't see or didn't understand. I breathed in, breathed out, then dove in:

"I know where Vera is."

Cody's jaw dropped. "What? And you haven't told Felicity or Oliver yet?"

"Well, I don't know *exactly* where she is. I don't have an address, but I know *who* she's with."

Never mind. I wanted to stop right now. I couldn't tell him. This was a huge mistake I wanted to reverse. But it was too late, and I knew it was the right thing to do. I winced at the sickening wave of nausea roiling in my belly. I was taking too long to speak.

"Tell me!" Cody yelled.

"She's with my stepfather, Bennett Hunter," I blurted out. "I don't know if she sought him out or he kidnapped her or what. All I know is Vera found out about him and connected with him. I checked the only place he's ever lived—the house I grew up in—and he's not there. The place was vacant. I have no idea where they could be, and I tried calling him, left a million messages begging him to speak to me, to let me know if Vera was okay, but he wouldn't call me back and now his phone is disconnected. I don't know what to do or how to reach him."

"I don't understand. What does your stepdad have to do with

Vera? Why would *Oliver's* kid be with *your* family, Marin?"

I realized none of this made sense without context. Okay, we were about to go down the rabbit hole, and it was gonna get messy. I grabbed the bottle of vodka and took a full-mouthed swig, then slid the bottle across the table at him. "You'll need this."

He lifted the bottle and gulped.

"It's a long, complicated story…and I hope you'll forgive me after you hear the whole thing. I promise you Bennett is not a threat to Vera. But if he isn't already dead, he will be soon."

Chapter 37
Marin

I had scrubbed and scoured, ruining my Mary J. Blige T-shirt with bleach stains trying to wash the blood residue out of the bathtub. Chunks of afterbirth and placenta collected near the drain, almost making me vomit as I scooped them up in a paper towel and flushed them. Only after the fact did I pray I didn't clog the pipes. A faint ring of red still circled the ceramic basin, but my muscles were too tired to keep cleaning.

A lingering excitement mixed with relief still pulsed through my body after a long afternoon helping Mom deliver the baby at home in this very tub. Mom didn't trust doctors, and Dad didn't like hospital bills. After hours of labor, all that mattered were those final moments—a body-shuddering animalistic scream as Mom stood under the running shower, Dad circling his arms around her while water coursed over them, me like a major-league catcher with arms and hands splayed, ready for my new sibling to fall into them. I relived the slippery baby dropping into my arms, the full-throated wail, my big exhale, Mom crumbling into the corner of the tub with exhaustion...I would never forget this moment. A little sister. So perfect. I had high hopes for her. She'd get Mom clean. Repair our family. Our love for her would fix all wounds.

A SLOW RUIN

It was halfway through the season finale of *Gilmore Girls* when I noticed the time. Mom and Dad should have been home by now. They were only supposed to take Mom and the baby—they hadn't named her yet, but I liked the name Jasmine—to the hospital to get checked out, but it had been over two hours and still they weren't home.

A normal kid in a normal family wouldn't have worried. Parents two hours late? No big deal. But I wasn't a normal kid and I didn't have a normal family. I spent my life being conditioned into a state of perpetual fear. And it all circled around Mom.

It wasn't Mom I was afraid of. She'd never laid a hand on me. It was being alone—particularly being alone *with her*—that terrified me. Not like there was much of a difference between the two.

It was shortly after my real dad—*Devin and Josie forever*—died in battle in Afghanistan when the fear started. I was ten, and the day was crystal clear in my memory. Mom's new boyfriend Ray stopping by, bringing candy for me and coke for Mom. He left her passed out on the floor, and hours later, as lunchtime turned into dinnertime, my tiny tummy rumbled for something of more substance than the empty orange box of Reece's Pieces. I shook her arm, trying to wake her. I screamed and cried until the neighbor, Mr. Bennett, overheard me and came running over. Ten minutes later an EMT revived her, finger poised to dial social services to come take me. But Mr. Bennett came to my rescue that day, came to Mom's rescue too, as he assured the EMT he was family and would take care of me until Mom was better. Soon after that, Mr. Bennett became Bennett, then Bennett became Dad. And Dad became the buffer between me and the constant pain and humiliation of having a druggie mother.

That wasn't the only time life with Mom left me scarred and

scared. Like when she took me out grocery shopping, only we never made it into the store. We got as far as the parking lot when she did a hit of something that knocked her out, and as the summer temperatures climbed, I yelled from the backseat for her to wake up. A kindly store associate saved me when she called Dad to come get us. A week later Dad sent Mom to rehab, but it wasn't enough to change her. I had a feeling nothing would ever change her. By this point I was tired of being saved from my own mother.

Her own selfish feelings were her drug. Whatever made her *feel*, regardless of how it damaged her daughter. Now plural daughters.

When I had found the positive pregnancy test in the bathroom garbage can, I was elated. My Pollyannaish thirteen-year-old imagination conjured a magical bond between mother and embryo, one even addiction couldn't break. But pregnancy didn't stop Mom until near the end, when the guilt of her crimes against her unborn finally set in. It was three of the best months of my life post-real-dad, packed with endless hours of classic tearjerkers like *Love and Basketball* and *Beaches,* and every chick flick in between. Just me and Mom and her huge quivering belly, movie-sized candy and overflowing popcorn, snuggled on the couch giggling like the girls we wanted to be.

Then today happened. The baby came and broke her.

"I just needed something for the pain, Bennett," Mom cried out. She wasn't asking. She was explaining away what she had already done, drugged out so bad Dad couldn't reason with her.

"Josie, what did ya take?" Except it was too late. She was already nodding off while the baby wailed in the background. As he carried the baby and then Mom to the car—we had been down this route many times before—he assured me she'd be okay.

He meant Mom, but I didn't want her to be okay.

I hated her for abandoning us every day as she lolled into her high, leaving me and Dad and now a baby to fight for her life when she so carelessly threw it away. I should have been sad for her, not angry. And yet I couldn't cry anymore. I had tasted happiness for those perfect months, and now it was…gone. And now I just wanted her gone too. So I told her as much.

"Why do you keeping doing this to us? Why won't you just die already and let us live?" I shot the words at her like bullets intended to kill.

"Marin Hunter! Don't say that. She's your mother!" Bennett to Mom's rescue again.

I scoffed. "My mother? What kind of mother abandons her child day after day like this? Because that's what I still am—a kid. No matter how much it seems the other way around!"

Mom was just cognizant enough to shout back, "I'm not too high to whup your ass, girl!"

"Whup my ass, huh? You can't even see straight! We'd all be better off if you died and went to hell, where you deserve to go." I stormed away to my bedroom.

Before Dad left, he found me sobbing into my pillow. He thought I was wracked with regret over my outburst, but I was sobbing a prayer to God that He just take Mom away once and for all.

Dad rubbed circles on my back. "Your mom just needs a doctor's check-up, Mare. Birthing a baby is a mighty big strain on the body. She'll be back home in no time."

I believed him. I shouldn't have.

That was now two and a half hours ago. It was dark outside now, and the credits for *Gilmore Girls* rolled down the television screen. I channel surfed to a rerun of *Fresh Prince of Bel-Air* to distract me, wondering if the clock-checking would ever go away, the fear of a parent leaving and never coming back, especially now that a baby relied on us, on *me*. I was thirteen years old, but most days I imagined this was what thirty felt like. Old. Exhausted. Burdened. Ready to give up.

On the stove I was stirring Hamburger Helper, the only edible thing we had in the pantry. As I heard a single set of footsteps, I glanced over my shoulder. Dad ambled through the door, his limp more exaggerated than yesterday.

"Where's Mom and the baby?"

He shook his head. He wouldn't speak.

"Dad?"

He sat in his recliner, the one no one else was allowed to sit in. "They're gone, kiddo."

Gone? That made no sense. They had just been here, Mom high as a kite, me screaming at her that I wished she would just die and go to hell, Dad yelling at me not to talk to my mother that way, Mom screaming that she was going to whup my ass, the baby's hungry cries the backdrop of our screaming fits until one of us finally gave up and walked away. It was always me. But this time it was Dad…taking the baby with him. Now he was home, minus the baby and Mom.

"I don't understand. Where are they?"

Tears pooled in his eyes, his shoulders slumped defeatedly, and suddenly I felt panic. Something had happened while he was gone.

He patted his lap for me to sit, like I'd done countless times as a girl.

I slowly walked to him and sat. He hugged me and wept.

"I'm scared, Dad." I didn't know what to think. Only a dark brooding feeling that my wish had come true. That my parting words to my mother—*we'd all be better off if you died and went to hell*—had come to pass.

"It's gonna be okay."

"Daddy, what happened? Please tell me."

"Your mom…died, kiddo. We made it to the hospital but she OD'd. Nothing they could do. The drugs she had taken…it was too much. But when you use like she does, the stuff eventually kills ya. I'm so sorry, sweetie."

I didn't have any shock left in me. Only relief. "What about Mom's…body?" I asked, dreading the answer.

"Oh, uh…the hospital's going to take care of her cremation. I can't afford a real funeral, honey. The hospital said they'd give me the ashes in an urn at some point."

"But what happened to the baby?"

He wiped his face dry. "I gave her away. A really nice lady has her now. From the looks of her car, mighty rich, too." He took his wallet out from his back pocket and opened it for me to see several bills, bills I'd never seen in real life, all fifties and hundreds.

"She'll give her the life she deserves so that I can give you the life you deserve. I can't raise a newborn. But with just you and me, we'll be okay. You can understand that, can't ya, kiddo?"

The emotions swirling inside me were so convoluted I didn't know what I was feeling. Sadness. Anger. Grief. Relief. Pain.

Lots and lots of pain.

I wrapped my arms around my second dad, weeping all the sorrow out together. I had never seen him cry before then, and I would never see him cry again. Though he wore his sadness every day. I saw through the fake smiles and awful dad jokes he tried to mask it with. This was the first time he was real with me. And maybe even a little hopeful.

"Did you at least make sure the baby had her velveteen rabbit with her?"

"Of course. She'll have it to always remember you by."

I kissed his rough cheek. "We'll be okay."

"Because we're built tough." He smiled. "What do you call an alligator in a vest?"

I grinned weakly. "What?"

"An investigator."

I chuckled, not because it was funny but because Dad needed it.

"How about you take a $100 and get yourself a new wardrobe?" He handed me his wallet as he got up and walked to the kitchen, stirring the Hamburger Helper and smelling it with a satisfying *mmm*.

I laughed for real this time that Dad thought I could buy a decent wardrobe for $100. But I learned how to stretch a dollar. I pulled out the bill and noticed a name written across the top:

Felicity Portman

In my dad's neat block handwriting.

Never before had we had this kind of cash. I wondered if this money was a payment from the nice lady who adopted my sister. Pocketing the bill, I memorized that name, *Felicity Portman,* because I had a feeling one day I would need it.

Chapter 38
Marin

For my twentieth birthday I decided to treat myself to freedom. I didn't have enough cash from waitressing and doing community theatre to treat myself to a spa day like I would have preferred, but freedom was the next best thing.

Tiptoeing to where my father sprawled out on the couch, asleep while watching archeologists uncover the mysteries of ancient Egypt on the History Channel, I kissed his forehead. He stirred, eyelids fluttered open, gazed hazily up at me.

"Hey, kiddo." I loved how he still called me *kiddo,* when ironically I felt like I'd never been a kid. "Ya need something?" His breath reeked of whiskey, assaulting my nose. He shifted to sit up, but I rested my hand on his shoulder.

"No need to get up, Dad. I'm just heading out for a bit. Go back to sleep."

"Mmkay, honey. Could you pick me up a six-pack on your way home?"

"Sure thing, Dad."

I turned to leave, but his hand touched mine, stopping me. "The past, present, and future walk into a bar..." I grinned, already knowing the punchline. He'd told me this one before.

"It was tense," I said with a light chuckle.

"Aw, I musta told you that one already."

"Nah, I'm just that clever, Dad."

"Ya really are, kiddo. Ya really are."

I would miss his riddles, his lame jokes, the humor he always tried to infuse into our family even during the most difficult times. One last kiss on his head, then I headed out the front door, where I had already dropped off two duffel bags. I loved Bennett, but I didn't love how much he had become like my mother over the years. I guess death and depression did that to a person. Changed them. Emptied them. Destroyed them.

I couldn't watch Bennett's demise anymore, so on my twentieth birthday, I packed everything I owned, which wasn't much beyond what I could fit in two large Army duffel bags I'd swiped from Mom's closet after my real dad died. Then I bought a one-way ticket heading out West, to Hollywood, where dreams either went to bloom or die. Community theatre wasn't paying the bills—nor was waitressing at a dive bar where I was sick of being groped by drunk guys—and I had nothing else to lose. As I hopped in the cab I had called earlier, I watched the home on Mount Washington that I had grown up in, with its yellow brick green with moss and startling front yard view of a sparkling city skyline, disappear behind me.

The bus station was nearly empty at this late hour, but it was the cheapest ticket they sold, so a red-eye it was. Everyone in my ACA—Adult Children of Alcoholics—group agreed that leaving might be the best decision. Trust my Higher Power. Find something else, somewhere else. Break the chains. Crumble the bondage. Free myself from the past. All those empty mantras that felt meaningless…until now. For once I understood just how powerful they were as each step further away from the brick house that held me hostage crumbled away in the background of my life.

A SLOW RUIN

I sat down on a plastic bench, waiting for the bus as red taillights flickered along distant streets that wound through and around the Steel City. I set my bags at my feet and unzipped one. My finger felt around inside, between folds of clothes, until I contacted the hard ridges. Pulling the item out, it was wrapped in my real dad's gray Army T-shirt. I had never washed it after he passed, and sometimes I held it to my nose and imagined his scent on it. I unfolded the soft cloth and came face to face with the only memory I brought with me to LA.

A small framed picture of Mom, Bennett, my newborn baby sister, and me. In the picture I held out the stuffed velveteen rabbit that my dad had given me when I was first born, now out there somewhere in the world keeping my little sister company. She would be seven years old now. I wondered if she still had the rabbit, or if it had ended up in a landfill somewhere. I wondered if Bennett wondered about her every day like I did, or if Mom guarded her from heaven.

Thoughts of reconnecting with my sibling, of finding Felicity Portman, flittered in and out of my head often. Just to see my sister. Just to make sure she was okay. Every day I resisted it. Every day I shut off the voice. Every day the voice reminded me that it would only cause more devastation than good if I sought her out.

Sometimes I wasn't so good at listening to that voice.

Chapter 39
Marin

Los Angeles, California, chewed me up and spit me out like a wad of tasteless gum. It was mortifying, going on endless dehumanizing casting calls and being treated like a piece of meat, getting rejected over and over because I wasn't the right type—too young, too old; too cute, not cute enough; and yeah, even too Black, not Black enough. One callback for a speaking part as a police dispatcher wouldn't pay the bills, but that two-line role at least earned me a lone credit on IMDb. Even the competition for background actors was fierce. After getting a handful of jobs as an extra—and pay bumps for providing my own clothes and, a time or two, miscellaneous props—I couldn't pay my astronomical rent. Reality set in. The dream popped.

I hadn't expected instant fame, though maybe deep down I had. Every wannabe actress clung desperately to the fantasy of being discovered, of basking in the limelight. We expected the unexpected. I fantasized about seeing my face thirty feet tall on the silver screen. My name above the title—that's how you know you've really made it. The press referring to me as the next Kerry Washington. *Entertainment Weekly* calling me for an interview and photo shoot—talk to my people, ha ha! Except I never got discovered. I never got my limelight. I had wanted it hard, but not hard enough.

I returned home to Pennsylvania with my tail between my legs and only one person on my mind. The baby who was no longer a baby. My sister.

The house on Grandview Avenue hadn't changed since I last walked away. The yellow brick still needed power washing. The railing still left a rusty residue on my hands. As I rang the doorbell, I looked behind me at my gorgeous hometown Pittsburgh landscape, colored in hues of ripe sunset oranges and pinks while deep blue rivers snaked their way through the skyscrapers and mountains. The city held an aloof cinematic splendor that I suddenly realized I had missed.

When Dad answered the door, I hardly recognized him. Had it been that long?

"Marin!" He hardly finished my name before he pulled me into a hug that I feared would break every bone in his body. I hated how skeletal he felt in my arms. When he finally released me, I looked him over.

"Daddy, you look thin. Aren't you eating?"

"Eh, your old man is getting too old, kiddo. And I stopped drinking. Totally sober now. Been going to AA and everything. Once I lost my beer gut there wasn't much left of me."

"That's great! I'm proud of you. Did you get a sobriety chip?"

"It's somewhere in the house. My memory isn't as sharp as it used to be."

"When was your memory ever sharp, Dad?"

He wagged a gnarled finger at me. "True, true."

He ushered me into the living room and urged me to sit down. "Let me get ya something to drink."

"I can get it."

He held his hands out to stop me. "No, no, you sit. You want a pop?"

I thought back to the time I used that word to describe a soda in LA. It was the last time I would say *pop* after the ridicule I received.

I stepped around him. "Dad, I've been sitting for fourteen hours straight. I need to stretch my legs anyway, and I'm capable of grabbing myself a drink. What'll you have?"

"Same as you're having," he called from the living room. His recliner squealed as he dropped into it.

As I opened the fridge, on the bottom shelf was a six-pack of beer. Sober, huh? Last I heard, if you were trying to stay sober you shouldn't keep alcohol in the house. And certainly not in the fridge nice and cold and ready to crack open. As I grabbed two orange *pops*—I was in a safe place to use it again—I decided now wasn't the time to ask about the beer in the fridge, or the half-empty bottle of whiskey sitting out on the counter. I was too tired to entertain excuses.

I carried our drinks in, handed Dad his, and sat across from him.

"Cheers to my prodigal daughter returning home," he said, lifting his can.

"Hardly prodigal, Dad. I didn't have time to be reckless, but cheers anyway." I leaned forward and clinked mine against his.

"I've been working on some new material," he said.

I grinned. Of course our reunion would start off with a riddle. "Give me your best one."

"In the morning I have four legs. In the afternoon I have two legs. In the evening I have three legs. What am I?"

I pretended to think about it, then finally gave up. "I have no idea. What?"

"A baby, an adult, and an old person with a cane."

I chuckled. *Oh, Dad.*

"At least the jokes never get *old*." Ha.

"What's new with you, kiddo?" he asked.

"LA was a bust."

"I'm sorry it didn't work out, Mare. Did you know they filmed that *Fences* movie with Denzel Washington and Viola Davis here? In the Hill District, I think. Maybe you could find acting work here in the 'Burg?"

"Yeah, maybe." Except I had already given up on the dream. It was too demeaning. "In any case, I'm home for good now. Do you mind if I stay with you until I can find work and a place to live?"

"You don't need to ask. Your bedroom hasn't changed since ya left."

"You even left up my Will Smith and Snoop posters?"

"Even Will and Snoopy are still there."

I rolled my eyes. Years of correcting him and he still called the rapper *Snoopy.*

"I appreciate it, Dad. I promise it won't be for long. I already have some stuff planned."

I wasn't going to tell him that the plans involved something illegal. Probably even jail-worthy. He didn't need to know I had a whole sister-stalking-reunion planned. Better I kept it to myself.

"You ever think about retiring?"

His job as a truck driver had been tough on his body. Catching forty winks in the cramped sleeper cab of his rig before hitting the road again, eating at greasy spoons. A body could only take so much abuse.

"I've still got a few more good years left in me. As they say, idle hands are the devil's tools."

From where I was sitting, he didn't look like he had many good years left. His pallor and jutting cheekbones said there was something severely wrong. Something he wasn't telling me.

"You look so much like your mother, Marin. God, I miss Josie so much. Even the crazy parts of her."

"C'mon, Dad. It's been years. Why haven't you gotten out and tried dating? I could help you find someone. Even if it's just someone to keep you company."

"Nah, there's no point trying to fill the hole your mom left. I'm too wounded an animal."

"Stop being so dramatic. You're not wounded. You deserve to be happy. Mom would have wanted that for you."

He chuckled, then coughed. "Not if it meant me being with someone else! You know your mom woulda wanted me miserable without her."

I laughed with him. It was true.

"Hey, mind if I use the bathroom?" I stood up.

"It's right where you left it," Dad said.

I slipped into the bathroom and peed eight hours' worth of gas station coffee mixed with orange soda. As I washed my hands, I noticed a pill bottle on the sink. Picking it up, I read the very long drug name that stretched across the label:

Leuprolide Acetate

I grabbed my phone from my pocket and Googled the term. The very first result pulled up the National Cancer Institute website, along with a complex description of what the drug did. All I saw were the words *prostate* and *cancer,* and my heart sank. It was the same thing that killed his dad. Hereditary.

Carrying the bottle out of the bathroom with me, I held it up to Bennett.

"Care to explain this?"

He jumped up, the recliner wildly rocking behind him, and grabbed the bottle from me.

"There's nothing to explain. I was sick, but I'm getting treatment and will be fine."

"Do you have cancer? The same kind your dad had?"

Dad looked at the floor and shook his head…but it wasn't a no. It was an apology. When he looked back up at me, his eyes were wet, but he refused to cry.

"I'm sorry, I should have told you, kiddo. But yeah. Prostate cancer. I didn't want to worry you, being so far away. I'll be fine. I'm seeing a good doctor. And they caught it early. I'm tough. I know I'll beat it."

Except our family never beat anything. My mother never beat her drug addiction. My dad couldn't beat the waste of war. Bennett wasn't beating his alcohol abuse. And I couldn't beat my demons.

Chapter 40
Marin

FIVE YEARS AGO...

The little girl swinging on the playground looked nothing like me. It was hard to believe we were biological sisters. She looked just like her father, while I looked like mine. My skin was hazelnut, hers cream. My inky black hair was wild and curly, hers dirty blonde and poker-straight. But our eyes, full of life and light, were the same. I saw our mother in them.

Even though my life and light had long ago faded.

Luckily for me, there weren't many Felicity Portmans in the Pittsburgh area. Or anywhere, for that matter. A little online digging and social media stalking gave me the home address—if you could even call the mansion they lived in a home. A quick property records search showed a house so steeped in opulence and notoriety that it had its own name, the Execution Estate. Not the most welcome-home designation, but who cared when you had three stories of classical-meets-modern splendor?

The challenging part was figuring out a way to randomly run into Vera Portman—my sister's name, I came to learn—without drawing attention to myself. I wasn't even sure why I needed to meet her, or what I would say. I didn't want to completely upend her world...or did I? I wasn't sure what I wanted anymore. Just a connection.

A SLOW RUIN

The little girl had constant activities: school, gymnastics class, soccer. I couldn't just sit in front of their house, spying, and get hauled off by the cops. Lucky for me the house was in a remote, rustic area, and there was a dilapidated barn down the road, reachable by an overgrown cow path from bygone days when the woods were surrounded by farmland. The path was rough on my car, but I was able to park behind the barn and spy on the Portmans with compact binoculars with an excellent zoom—thank you, Amazon! And the few instances where they went out to dinner or to get ice cream—a family favorite, I quickly realized—Vera doted on her little brother, who was always in tow. But my persistence eventually paid off. One random outing to a nearby park, and the golden opportunity presented itself.

Only a handful of kids scrambled all over the playground on this warm sunny day. I scanned the perimeter for parents and found a group of moms huddled under the pavilion, and a man sitting beneath a tree. The distance blurred his features, but it looked to be her father absorbed in his phone.

I approached the little girl on the swing and offered to push her.

"Need any help getting super high in the sky?" I asked in a playful voice as I walked up behind her.

She scrunched her face at me. "I'm able to push myself, thanks. But you can swing next to me if you want."

Ah, now I understood the face scrunching. I had talked down to her. Ten-year-olds were more articulate than I thought.

"You're not around many kids my age, are you?" She smiled to soften the blow. At this age she would want to prove her maturity.

"Not really, no. How old are you?" I asked, though I already knew the answer.

"Ten. But I'm small for my age. People always think I'm younger."

"Nothing wrong with being small. You can hide easier."

"Why would I want to hide?"

"Oh, I don't know. I guess if you're playing hide-and-seek."

"I don't like that game."

"Why? I thought all kids loved hide-and-seek."

"I don't like being chased. It scares me."

"Me too, kid. Me too."

"I like your shirt," she said. "It matches your eyes."

I leaned forward, meeting her gaze. "Hey, it matches your eyes too. We have the same eye color. Green."

"Yeah, I'm the only one in my family with this color. Everyone else has blue."

"What if we were long-lost sisters? Wouldn't that be cool?" I instantly regretted it the moment I said it. It was too much too soon.

Thankfully she giggled. "You're too old to be my sister! Though it'd be nice to have an older sister. All I have is a younger brother, and he's exhausting. I guess that's why Mom calls it the terrible twos, though he's already three. He's constantly messing up my room."

I chuckled. "That's what siblings are for—to wear us out and keep us on our toes." Not that I knew this from experience. My only sibling had been taken away from me the day she was born. "So what's your name?" I already knew this answer too.

"Vera."

She didn't look like a *Vera* to me. "Oh, that's a unique name." *Unique* was the best adjective I could find for a name like that.

"I'm named after my great-great-grandmother Alvera Fields. She was a women's rights activist and disappeared one day. No one ever found her."

"Well, that's morbid. Why would your parents name you after a missing ancestor?"

"Because she was pretty heroic, I guess. She was well-known around Pittsburgh for her women's suffrage work. She raised tons of money for the cause by throwing huge fundraiser parties. I guess her husband knew a lot of rich people."

Rich. Well-connected. Sounded a lot like the Portman family alright. The difference was that Felicity took advantage of a grieving father's terrible situation by basically stealing his newborn baby from him. A few hundred dollars could never make what Felicity Portman did right, no matter how much she needed to sleep soundly at night. It was black market child trafficking.

"Wow, you're very articulate. Do you know what that means?"

She nibbled on her lower lip in thought. "Knowing a lot of words?"

"Yeah, that's right. Plus you seem pretty smart and know so much about history. Most kids your age don't even know what women's suffrage is. I learned everything I know about it from watching *Suffragette.*"

"Most adults don't know much either, especially if they're getting their history lesson from a fiction movie."

I chuckled. This one was clever, alright. Just like her father— the biological one. "That's probably true. How'd you get so smart?"

"I read a lot. And I take after my mom, I guess." *No, honey, those brains definitely didn't come from your mother.* "She's really smart and loves books. We have a library so big that it has a rolling ladder to reach the top shelves. Though my dad's pretty smart too. He's teaching me how to build stuff and draw."

"It sounds like you have a good dad. Is that him over there?"

I pointed to a swing under a tree where a man intently watched us.

"No, that's Uncle Cody. My dad's at work."

I flipped a wave at Uncle Cody, and he waved back and stood up. Uh-oh. I hadn't intended to meet the family. But it was too late to leave now.

"Hi there. I'm Marin." I extended my hand as he approached. "I'm having a nice chat with your niece."

"Cody." He cupped my hand in his. It felt soft, nice, warm…like a home should. "You make it a habit to talk with random little girls at parks?" He smiled. It was a joke laced with accusation.

"No, this is a first for me. You make it a habit to interrogate all your niece's new friends?"

"Only ones as pretty as you."

"Ew, Uncle Cody!" Vera squealed.

There she was—the child beneath the big-girl façade.

Cody wasn't my normal type—only a couple inches taller than me, pudge rounding out his clean-shaven features, decked in athletic wear, early signs of hair loss. He was the whitest white boy I'd ever seen—pasty white, like the love child of Robert Pattinson and Kristen Stewart of *Twilight*. I preferred the musclemen with tight torn jeans, lots of scruff, and a fedora. But his smile was genuine and his laugh easy. I could envision myself cuddled on the couch with this one. After all, where had all the hipster men gotten me? Still living in my old bedroom with my father because they wouldn't commit. Cody looked like a guy ready to commit. And I needed to get as close to Vera as possible if there was any way to save her.

Because I knew the truth. She needed saving before this entitled family dragged her into their web of lies even more. I doubted they'd ever told her who her real family was, or how they bought her life off the street. Maybe that's why I was here—to give this girl a *real* education.

As Cody hopped on the swing next to me, Vera's joy swelled. I watched her adoration glow for this man who called her niece. Maybe it wasn't my place to deflate it. For what purpose? Uncle Cody had somehow managed to get me all mixed up.

All three of us swung in unison while Cody dared Vera to swing higher, higher, higher while I laughed louder, louder, louder. For the next several hours we talked, we laughed, we flirted, we teased. Cody on my left, Vera on my right. And that's exactly how everything felt for the first time in so long—*right*.

Chapter 41
Felicity

I was exhausted and agitated and starving by the time Oliver parked the car on the narrow street. Tiny ant legs skittered over my feet from sitting in the car too long driving all over Pittsburgh, under a low autumn sun that lit the leaves on fire while we searched for the Grandview Avenue address Ari Wilburn gave me. We found the house, but no Bennett Hunter. The place had long been dark and empty. Cobwebs hung over the door, and a peek through several dusty windows revealed not a scrap of furniture. Completely vacant. Abandoned.

Driving around, talking in hypotheticals around how Marin was involved, Oliver and I didn't know what else to do, so we went to the one person who could answer our questions. We went to the source.

Side by side, one after the other, the lean row houses ignited to life beneath the bedazzled sky, while Cody's remained in brooding darkness. Oliver stepped out of the car first, but I couldn't seem to move across the leather seat. Every interaction with Cody was a strategic game of Risk. Tactical. Dangerous.

I hadn't told Oliver about the kiss yet, and I wasn't sure I ever would. He had forgiven me once before for cheating, but a second time? No. But there the secret hung on the tip of my tongue, waiting to slip out. When the three of us—me, Cody, Oliver—were together, and lately Cody had been drinking more and more, the secret became more slippery. One innuendo, one side-look, it would only take one tug to unravel the whole damn ball.

My phone buzzed. A text from Debra that the kids ate grilled cheese and soup for dinner, and they were in jammies watching a movie before bed. I imagined Sydney in her Cookie Monster slippers and Strawberry Shortcake nightgown, curled up next to Nana asking a million and one questions throughout the entire film while Eliot, the serious one, shushed her so he could hear. For six months I missed out on these simple joys, and I needed them back.

Oliver was already slamming his fist against the wooden front door by the time I got out of the car. Across the yard I could hear the pounding echo through the home's innards. By the time Cody yanked the door open with a groan, Ollie was worked up. Clipping Cody's shoulders on his way inside, Oliver cut through the house to the living room, grumbling, ranting, raving.

"We know Bennett Hunter has Vera. Tell us the truth about what's going on, Cody!"

Cody barely had a moment to catch up before he closed the door behind me, then trailed us with a wobbly shuffle.

"Whoa, rewind a minute. I'm not following. What's going on?" Cody's voice was groggy with sleep. At dinnertime? His downhill slide into depression was unmistakable.

"Bennett Hunter—you know, Marin's father? We know about him."

Cody squinted as if my words were hurting his head. "You mean her stepdad? What about him?"

"Do you remember the day I brought Vera home?" I asked, trying to ease the tension.

"Of course."

I chose my words carefully. "I wasn't exactly…forthcoming

about the details. I had actually met Vera's biological father that day. He was the one who left her on the side of the road. I never got his name at the time, but I got his license plate number. Anyway, with the help of a private investigator, we were able to get his name. Bennett Hunter. Marin's father—well, apparently stepfather."

Cody said nothing. Not even a glimpse of surprise on his placid face. He...knew all along?

"You knew." Oliver had noticed it too and wasn't afraid to call his brother out on it.

And he kept it from me? Sound bites of his consolations whispered in my ear. All of the empathetic words. All of the reassurances he had offered. All lies. All fake. My little puddle of disbelief swelled into an ocean of anger.

"How long?" I jabbed my finger at him.

Cody stood there dumbfounded.

"How long did you know Marin was Vera's sister, Cody?" This time my finger struck his chest. Hard.

"Since a few days after Vera disappeared."

"You've been sitting on this information for *six months*? Why the hell wouldn't you tell me?" I was screaming now, the words pouring out of me rushed and furious. "I've been grieving and searching and dying inside every day for the last six months—189 days since she went missing, Cody! 189 days I couldn't sleep, barely tolerated food, worried if Sydney would ever find a kidney donor, all while you *knew* that Vera was with Marin's father! I can't believe you would do this to me. We're *family,* Cody!"

Cody leaned away from me, giving me a clearer look at the disheveled mess that he was. Glassy eyes, streaked with red veins. His face gaunt and pale. He'd developed a potbelly from sloth and perpetual drunkenness, yet his grimy sweatpants hung off his bony hips like a sagging tent. Only now did the state of the living room come into focus. Empty beer bottles scattered everything. Forties of malt liquor drained to the last drop. Shot glasses and food scraps and dirty tumblers. If I wasn't so livid I would have pitied him.

"I wasn't trying to hurt you, Felicity. I was trying to protect you. Protect everyone."

"Bull! How was allowing my daughter to stay missing protecting her?" My voice had never reached this octave before.

"Will you stop yelling at me for a minute? I can't think." Cody pinched his temples, wincing in pain. "Marin couldn't tell you or go to the police because she was trying to keep you out of jail. What was I supposed to do? It's not like Marin knew where he was, only that Vera was with him and that she was safe. That's all I know, and Marin made me promise not to tell you."

Oliver stormed to the wall and smashed a fist-sized imprint into the plaster. "Are you friggin' kidding me? You *promised* not to tell, and that's why you withheld information? This isn't a grade school pinky swear. This is a missing child—*your* missing niece."

Cody dropped onto a chair and ran his palms down his face.

"I'm sorry, I know. I wasn't thinking clearly." Tears filled the gaps between the veins in Cody's eyes, making them even redder. "But Bennett is terminally ill; how dangerous could he be? He assured Marin right after Vera left that she was safe with him and that he wanted to spend time with her before he died, that's all. But he threatened that if Marin told anyone or came looking for her, he'd tell the police that you kidnapped Vera."

Cody leaned back into the chair, eyes closing us out, tears streaming down, breaths strained.

"When Marin tried to get in touch with him again, his phone was shut off and he wasn't at his house."

I should have trusted my gut that Marin was involved

somehow. "So it was Marin who told Vera about everything?"

"Not exactly, no. Vera found out on her own. She was doing some kind of ancestry project for school and asked me about Alvera Fields, what I thought happened to her. I told her there might be some stuff in our spare bedroom, old documents and articles she could look through. Apparently she found a picture in Marin's things that convinced her she was adopted. When she confronted Marin about it, Marin told her the truth—that they were sisters and that their father was dying, in case she wanted to meet him before he was gone. Marin thought they would just talk on the phone, maybe have a visit together. She never expected Vera to run away...and certainly not for this long."

Oliver had been quietly absorbing all of this from the window while nursing his knuckles. "Be honest with me, brother. Do you think Bennett did something…"

"No, Marin swore to me that her father was a good man and would never hurt Vera. He loved her."

"A man who leaves a baby on the side of the road does not love her. He didn't care enough to raise her. She's *my* child. He has no right to her. He sold her for a few hundred bucks. That's the kind of man he was. A man who left his child for dead."

Cody's eyelids flew open.

"Felicity, she was *never* yours to begin with. Legally, you stole her! Don't you realize you're no better? You could have gone through proper channels. You could have helped his family. Instead you took her, lied to her, and played mom all this time. Bennett was her biological father. She had a right to know the truth. That's all Bennett wanted to give her."

"Are you serious right now? You're going to side with a total stranger over your family?" Oliver stepped in, physically and verbally closing in on Cody.

I angled myself between them. We weren't getting anywhere

325

with this. "Guys, I don't want to fight. I just want to find Vera. Did Marin mention where else they could be? With another relative?"

"No, Marin's mom died and there were no other relatives that she knew of." Another dead end.

"What now? How do we find out where Vera's hiding?" Oliver stomped to the window. "We could have brought her home months ago…" Then he pivoted back around, his hands balled and eyes filled with fury. "And it's your fault that my daughter is still out there with a man none of us can find!"

It all happened so fast. One moment Oliver was standing by the window, the next he lunged at Cody, tipping the chair over and tossing Cody to the floor. Oliver fell atop Cody's chest and pinned his upper arms with his knees. He whaled on his brother in a blind rage, landing savage hooks to his cheeks and jaw with alternating fists. Cody squirmed fruitlessly under Oliver's weight, forearms flailing, groaning as the punches rocked his head back and forth. I screamed to drown out the sickeningly moist thud of bone smacking flesh.

"Stop! Please, Oliver, you're going to kill him!"

But Oliver only heard whatever voice in his head urged him on. I leapt on his back, pushing and pulling at him, but he flung me off as if I were a feather. The beatdown went on.

With sudden superhuman strength, I grabbed Oliver's shoulders and yanked him off. Cody lay deathly still; he looked like he'd gone three rounds with Mike Tyson. Oliver sprawled against the overturned chair, panting and absently massaging one bruised hand with the other as light and reason slowly returned to his smoldering eyes.

"I can't take this anymore. I'm turning myself in!"

Oliver's heavy breaths stopped. He pushed himself to his feet. Blustered to the door. And never looked back.

The Pittsburg Press

Pittsburg, PA
Saturday, October 22, 1910

ALVERA FIELDS CASE MAY BE SOLVED BY RAID

The mystery of Mrs. Alvera Fields, the beautiful Pennsylvania wife and mother, whose disappearance earlier this year became an international sensation, will finally be cleared and her vanishing explained, the district attorney believes, as the result of a raid made yesterday afternoon by county detectives on the Fields Estate.

Although no arrests were made in connection with the case, the district attorney believes they are close to solving it.

Women Detective at Work

Shortly before 1 p.m. yesterday afternoon, the entire county detective force was stationed in separate groups at the Fields Estate. A woman detective in the employ of the County Detective Bureau, who posed as Mrs. Fields' distant second cousin, was granted entrance into the home by Robert Fields' maid, whereupon the detective set about examining the residence for evidence.

Upon searching Mr. Fields' office, she discovered several letters neatly hidden in a hole in the hollow leg of a desk. The letters suggest Mr. Fields is behind Mrs. Fields' disappearance. One such letter was an exchange between a doctor at the sanitarium insisting he could no longer in good conscience keep Alvera hostage against her will, for she is otherwise healthy and sane. The details of the other letters are still being investigated as detectives continue to search the estate.

The house, which is a large three-story building, is on the edge of a steep hill, its rear overlooking the Ohio River and the Bellevue Station of the Pennsylvania lines west. On one side of the house is a deep ravine, while on the other side steps lead to the station. In front of the large yard before the house the street becomes a muddy road and turns to the right.

At the turn in the road the machine containing the detectives stopped. The driver alighted and pretended to be tinkering with the engine, when the taxicab containing Robert Fields came down the street also. As the car containing the detectives had a large limousine body, Fields entertained no suspicions. He jumped from the taxi, aided his fellow passengers to alight, and pointed to the house. The next minute he found himself handcuffed.

Mr. Fields is being contained at the county jail on a charge of murder. He persists in claiming his innocence while his attorneys assure the public he is not in any way guilty.

Chapter 42
Felicity

As ambivalent as I felt about Cody, I couldn't leave him in that condition. Neither of us said a word as I helped him to the sofa and doctored and bandaged his wounds. He was so liquored up I doubted he felt much of anything. The pain would hit him tomorrow. *Good.*

Ever the compulsive neatnik, I started tidying up the place and stopped myself. I wasn't Cody's maid. When I left, he had fallen over on his side and was lightly snoring.

Oliver and I had arrived home to a hundred distressed questions from Debra about Oliver's injuries, but she never got the answers she was looking for as he ushered her out the door without barely a thanks for watching the kids. She wasn't the only one stuck with unanswered questions. I sorted through them while Oliver nursed his hands. Had Marin targeted our family to get to Vera? If Vera was truly safe with Bennett, was the threatening voicemail about Vera being dead just a twisted newsmonger trying to scare me? Who ran me off the road? And the biggest one of all: how many of us had been keeping secrets, and how deep did they go?

Vaults full of mysteries stretched deep in Oliver's family line, all starting with Alvera Fields, the loose end that seemed to tie everything together. She was the reason Vera dug into the past. She was the reason Vera discovered the truth. She was the catalyst for Vera running away. Even a dead woman, long gone as ashes in the wind, could scorch the earth. Something deep inside me knew she was the key to finding Vera. But I didn't know how. I couldn't see the connection clear enough.

There was only one path on which to move forward. The treacherous one I had dreaded and avoided all this time, but it was the inevitable one.

Oliver was stretched across the sofa with his feet in my lap. Pressing frozen peas to his bloody knuckles, he showed not an ounce of remorse for what he had done to his brother. I hardly recognized any of my family anymore. Six months had chipped away who we were and replaced us with monsters.

"I'm going to tell the police everything and turn myself in." I looked at Oliver's socked feet as I said it, unable to meet his gaze.

"No, there has to be another way."

"What other way? We have no idea if Bennett is still alive, or where he took Vera. She could be stranded somewhere with his dead corpse. I can't wait for answers anymore. I'm all out of hope. Look at us!" I threw my arms wide in exasperation. "You beat the crap out of your own brother, not that he didn't deserve it. Cody's becoming a drunk. Meanwhile I'm so zoned out I'm forgetting my kids at karate class. Only the police can help us now. We know who she's with. Maybe they'll be able to find them now that we have a name that they can trace."

Marin had never spoken much of her mother or father—or her stepfather, for that matter—out of shame or something else, I never knew why. They were ghosts in the shadows, nonexistent for all we knew. Her father was a military hero, she had once told me. I never questioned that no family on her side showed up to Marin and Cody's wedding; I never even saw a photo of Bennett. If I had, would I have connected him to that stranger with the limp on the fateful night of the fender-bender when Vera had come into our lives?

"How will they trace him, Felicity?" Oliver persisted. "Bennett has no listed phone number, isn't at his last known address. The PI already investigated him for us and came up with bupkes. We can figure it out without the cops. Eventually Vera will contact us."

"We've waited six months! I'm done waiting, Ollie. My freedom isn't worth losing my daughter. My time is up."

"You think the cops will be able to find Bennett when Marin couldn't?" Oliver's voice dropped to a soft beg. "Please don't do this. Twenty years, Felicity. That's how long you'd be in jail. You'd miss everything."

"I'm already missing everything. I have no other choice."

I lifted his legs off of my lap, stood, and grabbed my keys. I couldn't sleep on this or I'd change my mind. I needed to do it while I still had the courage. I headed outside, walked to the car, tears rolling down my face. Oliver scrambled to step into his loafers while chasing me to the driveway, knowing he was broken and beaten. Vera and I shared the same stubborn streak.

I paused at the car door, kissed Oliver long and deep and lovingly, as if it was the last kiss we'd share for the next two decades. Our lips were full of a lifetime's worth of love and memories and baby births and house hunting and family vacations and job changes and business startups and preschool graduations. Our whole life together was in that single kiss.

"I can't see the kids like this. I'll never be able to follow through if I have to say goodbye to them. Just tell them I love them, and Mommy will see them soon."

He grabbed my hand, pulled me away from the vehicle. "Felicity, you don't have to do this. I promised you I'd protect you. Let me do this for you."

I shook my head. "No, this is on me. It started with me, it

ends with me."

"That's not how marriage works, Felicity. We both have been in this together since the beginning. I'm not asking. I'm telling you—I'm taking this from you. I'll lie to the police and say whatever I have to in order to protect you."

"Oliver, no—" But he wouldn't let me speak as he slid past me, sank into the driver's seat, and closed the car door. He pressed his palm to the window, and I pressed mine against his on the other side. We were one, separated by glass. Ironically symbolic of what was to come.

As his car faded from view down the road, I imagined Oliver walking into the police station, straight to Detective Montgomery's cubicle. Her looking up from her computer, expectation on her face. I could hear the chatter and phones ringing and someone yelling in the background, all draining away as Oliver fixed his attention on the woman who would seal his fate. I envisioned my sweet husband exhaling all that fear bubbling up inside him, uncertain how to push the words out. My brain rumbled a million possible outcomes, all ending with visions of Oliver being hauled away in handcuffs.

A maternal yearning drew me upstairs. I needed to be close to my children; I had been a confession away from losing them. As I passed Vera's open door, I recalled the day six months ago when Marin had found the pot stashed in Vera's desk. I had been so angry at her, unable to understand the relationship between her and Vera. I knew even back then she was hiding something...now I wished I could speak with her. Pick her brain to understand everything...but it was too late for that now.

I blinked and found myself crouched under her desk, looking for whatever secret enclosure Marin had found that day. Running my hands up and down every square inch of surface, it seemed like a typical antique writing desk. The drawer, the pull-out slides, the pigeon-hole shelves, the folding writing lid, the tambour door, everything appeared normal. Something special about this desk had drawn Vera to it. She had mentioned it to me when I first showed her the articles in the creepy library, pointed her finger at the words in the article. What were those words?

Something about a woman detective…and a hollow leg. I focused on each tapered leg, tracing each husk inlay with my fingers, until a piece of wood on the back leg wobbled against my pressure. I slid the wood out and reached inside. Further, deeper until my hand couldn't fit anymore. My fingers curled around a slick, glossy tube. When I pulled the rolled-up photo out and straightened it, I realized why Vera had known instantly she was adopted. The faces, unfamiliar at first, congealed into recognizable forms. In the picture was a teenage version of Marin, newborn Vera, Bennett from how I remembered him that night, and a woman, haggard and hollow-cheeked—presumably Marin's mother. Held beside baby Vera was the velveteen rabbit that Sydney had left on Vera's bed next to a curled-up Meowzebub, for once not up to any mischief.

So this was how Vera figured it out. I had never given her enough credit for her cleverness. The girl was far smarter than I ever was. I was following Vera's trail of crumbs, but it wasn't enough. I was missing a big piece. The piece that would show me where she had holed up. I sat at her desk, hands flat against the desk's top, imagining myself as a brilliant, curious, budding genealogist. Wherever Vera went, it was somewhere familiar to her. Somewhere special.

Ding! If a realization had a sound, that would be it.

I knew exactly where Vera was. I jumped up, eager to tell Oliver… Crap, he was on his way to the police station to turn himself in! Where had I put my phone? I had to stop him before it was too late.

Running downstairs, I found my cell beside the sofa and my fingertips danced across the screen as I typed his cell phone number. *Riiing*—and then straight to voicemail. I couldn't leave a message in case the cops listened to it later. I pulled up a new text and frantically typed as ALLCAPS words dashed across the bubble:

URGENT! SAY NOTHING!

I waited for the three dots to pass across the screen, showing that he'd read the message. Nothing. Deducting how long it would take me to get the kids out of bed to drive down to the station, I wondered if I'd have enough time. No, there was no way I'd make it there soon enough. I punched more letters in:

I KNOW WHERE VERA IS!

There was nothing to do but pray my message reached him in time. Somewhere along the way my faith had returned, and I hoped God was listening.

Chapter 43
Felicity

One arm held Sydney in her Strawberry Shortcake nightgown firmly against my hip, and the other pulled Eliot in his Marvel footie pajamas close to my side as we entered the police station. Sydney rested her head on my shoulder, her little finger sucks squeaking in my ear. Eliot yawned and shuffled sleepily behind me as I tried to keep him close. At this late hour the station was fairly empty, with only a few officers sitting at desks and a couple people loitering in the waiting area. I stretched up onto my toes to see if I could spot Oliver somewhere within.

"Can I help you, ma'am?" the receptionist asked, drilling me with her eyes.

My brain was stuck on pause. I wanted nothing more than to get my husband and my kids out of here.

"I'm here to speak with Detective Montgomery. My husband, Oliver, came in a little earlier and I'm trying to find him."

The receptionist glanced down at her clipboard. "Was that"— her finger ran down a list of sign-in names—"Oliver Portman?"

"Yes! That's him. Is he still here?"

"One second." She picked up the phone and punched in a number, asked if Oliver Portman was still there, then hung up. "I'm sorry, ma'am, he left."

"He left?" I could have sworn I saw his car still parked outside. Unless...oh God, had he been formally arrested? How did I even ask such a thing with the kids listening?

"Yes, right before you came in, actually."

I had been too late. I shouldn't have brought the kids, I shouldn't have come. I felt sick. I turned to leave, rushing for the exit doors, for the fresh air to wash over me. Oliver was going to jail and I was going to be a single mother and technically I was the one who committed the crime and what if the police figured that out and put me in jail too and Sydney didn't get her kidney transplant and…

"Felicity!"

I stopped mid-step, spun around looking for the man who matched the voice. Coming out of the bathroom was Oliver, jogging to meet me in the middle of the tile floor.

"You're not in jail," I whispered excitedly.

"I couldn't do it, honey. And then I saw your text."

"So you didn't—"

"I didn't say anything." As he hugged me, Sydney reached for him and slid into his arms. "What's going on? What did you find out?"

I grabbed his hand and led him outside into the parking lot.

"We're dropping the kids off at your mom's, then picking up Cody and heading to the Fields Estate."

"The Fields Estate? What makes you think Vera's there?"

"In her Vera-esque way, she practically told me."

**

Cody had sobered up when we arrived at his house, but his face was badly bruised and swollen. He and Oliver regarded each other silently for a few tense moments before Cody forced a grin and joked, "You should see the other guy."

"I *am* the other guy," Oliver reminded him, and pointed at his own face. "Not a mark. Still pretty."

Cody snorted. "Right. Well, you hit like a girl."

Oliver tried not to smile, then laughter burbled up in his throat and came out in a cleansing rush.

Cody laughed too and grabbed him in a bro hug.

"You know," said Oliver, "you kinda deserved that ass whupping."

"Yeah, I guess I did."

Vera was nothing if not methodical. Had I been listening, I would have heard her calling me to her. Her murmurs were in the ancient newspaper articles she framed that mentioned the hollow-legged desk, in the drawings she rendered of the Fields Estate, in the thoughts she chronicled about her ancestor's life there. All of it led back to that house. The realization came as a whisper, but it hit me like a hurricane.

The house we pulled up to had become overgrown with knee-high weeds since the last time we were here, like something out of *The Haunting of Hill House* where I imagined the ghosts of families past wandering the hallways chained to their sins. Darkness shrouded the massive Edwardian dwelling perched atop a hill that dropped into a ravine, leaving only a spooky skull-like glare as two windows glowed against the night. The gate in the security fence around the historic structure, erected to deter vandals and trespassers, had either been jimmied, or someone with a key—namely Vera—had entered the grounds freely.

The huge front door was likewise unlocked so we entered quietly, first Oliver, then me, then Cody, hoping not to alert anyone inside as to our arrival. Exploring the first floor, the rooms were empty and black. Desolate and dusty. I couldn't imagine my daughter living in this nightmare, alone with a man she didn't know, for six long months. Assuming she was indeed here and still alive.

I slunk into the kitchen, my weary gaze transfixed by the black-and-white checkered tile floor. Filling a shelf in the butler's pantry were stacked cans of soup, crackers, a short supply of easy-to-prepare meals. Crusty pots and pans filled the ceramic standalone sink. Indeed, someone had been living here. And for quite some time, it seemed.

My hope soared.

I headed toward the center staircase, each step creaking my arrival. When I reached the top, light poured out from an open door at the end of the hallway. I followed the century-old Persian Malayer runner, where a fine trellis of faded red and mint flowers sprawled across the woven fabric, chewed by mice and frayed by time.

At the entry to the door I stood, listened, then peeked inside. In a four-poster bed lay a man. In a cushioned chair next to him sat Vera, head down. As the floorboard creaked under another step, she glanced up. My daughter, healthy and alive!

"Vera!" I called out and ran to her.

Her chin tilted upward, her eyes widened with shock. "Mom!"

I was still Mom! I was already smothering her in hugs and kisses before she had a chance to rise from her seat. My arms circled her protectively, as if they'd never again let her go. I knelt down on the floor at her knees, holding her hands, searching for an explanation.

"Why? Why didn't you come home? Or at least tell me where you were."

Vera released my hands, gently nudged me away, and I felt a strange detachment. "You really don't know?"

"No, honey, please help me understand." I just wanted to close the gap between us.

"I was angry at you for so long, Mom. You and Dad lied to

me. All my life, you kept this whole other family from me. It's why I left, and why I didn't tell you."

"You wanted to punish us? We had the entire Allegheny County Police Department searching for you. All your friends and family. Austin. Blythe." I lifted an eyebrow—*I know all your secrets*.

"I'm sorry I never told you about them, but I knew you wouldn't approve."

"You don't give me much credit, do you?"

The man in the bed coughed, smiled wanly. "You remember me?"

I stood up, straightened my back. "Of course I remember you, Bennett. You're the man who abandoned his newborn daughter on the side of the road. Then took her away from me for six months, allowing me to think she was dead." I wasn't going to play polite at this reunion. This man threatened to send me to jail while he abducted my child.

"Mom, stop." Vera stepped in front of me, forcing me to look at her. "I'm the one who pursued Bennett and asked to meet him when I found out he was dying. I'm the one who suggested coming here. I wanted a chance to know my biological father before it was too late. He didn't do anything wrong."

Except for abandon his baby on the side of the road, I didn't say. I wasn't letting that tidbit go.

I studied the sick man, so clearly close to death. His body was emaciated, his face and eyes badly jaundiced. His pale skin was mottled with swollen blood vessels radiating outward like spider webs. The palms of his hands were unnaturally red. He itched himself absently, his arms covered with scratch marks. His breath came in ragged gusts. A trash can by his bedside reeked of vomit.

I noticed how Vera called him Bennett, not Dad.

"You've raised a beautiful kid. Compassionate too," Bennett said.

"Yes, I know. She's amazing." I wanted to kiss her forehead, tell her how amazing she was. Instead I gave her space. "Six months, though, Vera? That's a long time to make me worry about you."

"It wasn't about you, Mom. It was about me. And my own closure."

I nodded. She was right—only about that, though.

"I'm sorry I kept her from you for this long," Bennett wheezed. "But she insisted on staying with me until the end. I didn't expect it to take so long."

"Cancer?" I asked.

Bennett chuckled. "Not this time. Believe it or not, I beat prostate cancer. This time it's liver damage. The drink finally caught up to me."

"I'm sorry to hear that." Though I didn't know this man, it was heartbreaking to watch anyone—even the man who abducted my daughter—die like this.

"We can get you proper medical care. This isn't where you should be, in an old abandoned house. Which is freezing, by the way." I shivered under the harsh chill. "You should be in a hospital getting medical attention."

Bennett waved me off with a brittle hand. "Nah. I've spent the last several years in and out of hospitals. This time I was ready to go. I got to spend time with my daughter—*your* daughter—and that's all I wanted before I died. But before I go, kiddo, I've got one last joke for ya."

Vera ambled to his side, held his hand. Her love inspired me as I watched her care tenderly for a man who had fifteen years ago cast her aside to die.

"In a classroom, a professor asks his brightest student, 'What would a peaceful death be like?' 'The same way my grandfather died,' the student replies. 'And how did your grandfather die?' the professor asks. 'He fell asleep,' the student answered. 'And what would be a terrible death?' the professor asks. 'The way that my grandfather's friend died,' the student replies. 'And how did your grandfather's friend die?' the professor asks. 'He was in the car with my grandfather when he fell asleep,' the student says." Bennett chuckle-coughed and I could see his charm.

"Did you know that people often see a light at the end of a tunnel in many near-death experiences?" Vera asked solemnly.

Bennett cocked his head.

"They should really get off of the road," Vera added with a shaky smile that released her tears.

"Oh, you're my best student yet, kiddo! Even better than Marin."

"I learned from the best. Speaking of Aunt Marin, where is she?" Vera asked, her voice unsteady. "She should be here to say goodbye to her stepdad."

"I'm afraid…I'm afraid she's gone," I replied. The words weighed too much. It only occurred to me now that Vera was losing a father *and* a half-sister today.

"Gone? What do you mean?" Her voice was full of fear.

"I mean she had an accident and…didn't make it."

"What kind of accident?" Vera's voice trembled, rose a pitch. From fifteen years raising her, I knew the sobs would come next.

I didn't know what to say. How to explain it. But I didn't need to.

"It's my fault Marin is dead." Cody's words hung like lead weights in the sick room's stifling air.

"How?" Bennett asked. The single word seemed to sap what spark of vitality he had left.

No one spoke. Then Cody opened his lips, and I could hear

the grief oppressing him as he began. "It was six months ago," he turned to Vera, "shortly after you left, Vera. Marin and I had been fighting when she first told me that you were with Bennett. I stormed out in anger, and that was the last time I saw her alive...I'll never forgive myself for leaving like that, or that Marin had to die alone."

Bennett broke through Cody's memory, tugging Vera's hand upward, pointing. Veins bulged beneath paper-thin skin, his grip tightening.

"It's Marin! She's here!" His eyes widened as he stared at the empty space beside me. A cool rush of air fluttered my hair, and for a moment I sensed her. The laughter, the fights, the joy, the betrayal, all of it slid over me like a breeze. Although Marin's ashes were scattered to the wind, she had scorched my earth. And yet my love for her rose from those flames.

"And Marin didn't die alone," Bennett rasped, then he muttered something in Vera's ear before he exhaled his last breath.

Chapter 44
Marin

A breeze carrying the spring chill swept through the kitchen.

It indeed had been a long, complicated story as I poured all the details out into Cody's ears. I fed him every sour detail, every bitter blow. While Vera had only been missing for six days now, it felt like six months. Sipping vodka between confessions, I told Cody everything, starting with the day my father dropped my mother off at the hospital to OD and die. *Sip.* How I found the huge sum of money in his wallet when he got back and my baby sister gone, and the name *Felicity Portman* scribbled on a $100 bill, then stamped on my brain. *Sip.* My father's cancer. *Sip.* The day I met Vera in the park. Our matching eyes. *Sip.* The instant connection I'd felt with Cody. The velveteen rabbit and the missing photograph I had freaked out about. Vera's questions. My answers. My father's last text message. It was my confession. My secrets unfurled. My last hope at coming clean and reconciling everything, fixing everything, bringing Vera home. *Sip, sip, sip.*

Cody stood in the exact same spot while I doled it all out, elbow propped on the orange counter with the metal trim while I recounted every sordid moment. Then I begged for his forgiveness, for his understanding. But Cody wanted none of it. He accepted none of it. Forgave none of it.

He slammed his fist on the counter, rattling the forty. "You lied. You deceived me. You betrayed all of us. Was our marriage also a sham?" Vodka spittle sprayed from his lips.

"No, it wasn't a sham, Cody. I didn't marry you to get to Vera. I married you because I fell in love with you, and with your family. I wanted to be a part of this beautiful life with you. I never meant for Vera to find out we were sisters. But she's smart, she's clever, and that's how I know she's okay. She's with our father, and he would never hurt her."

Cody paced back and forth on the scratched linoleum floor, shoulders hunched like he was carrying the heavy information on his back. "You know I have to tell Felicity and Oliver everything you told me, right?"

"No!" I grabbed his arm, pulling him to a stop. "They can't ever find out. If they do, not only will my dad probably go to jail and die there, but he'll tell the police about what Felicity did too. Technically she took a baby and never reported it. He just wants to spend his last days with his daughter. Please, Cody. However angry you are at me, don't punish my dying father or Felicity. Because they are the ones who will pay for the lies. They're the ones whose lives will be ruined."

"I don't know, Marin. I feel like all this time you've had a secret identity, and not telling anyone you were the last person to see Vera alive...or that you're her sister... I don't know the real you from the person you pretend to be anymore."

I couldn't believe he was pinning everything that had desecrated our life all on me.

"What about *your* lies, Cody? You owe me this! You cheated with your brother's wife, my best friend. You betrayed both me and Ollie. My past may have hurt you, but your present hurt me. I can't change what I did before I met you, but you hurt me while you were married to me. Don't forget that."

I had him there, and he knew it. He ran a hand through his tar-black hair, slick and stringy with sweat. The tract of bare scalp stretched further back. He pinned me with a watery gaze.

"How long do you think Vera will be gone? Felicity's crumbling, Marin. Every time the police show up at the house, any time a body is found—it's destroying her."

"A man is dying—my father! I can't predict how long until he passes, Cody. But we have to wait as long as it takes. Please, for me." I choked on the emotions. I couldn't think of anything other than my dying dad, and me not being by his side right now. "I'm trying my best to find him. Don't you think I want to be with him right now? I abandoned him during his time of need, and this is the only way I can make amends. I know it's hard to have faith through this, but Vera will come home soon." It broke my heart that there was only one *home* my father was going to…and it wouldn't be with me.

When Cody fumbled with his car keys, the conversation was over.

"Where are you going?"

"I need a drink." Except he was already drunk. "And I'm not able to look at you right now, Marin. I need time to think about this. I'm going out tonight and won't be home. We'll talk about it later." Cody tottered into the cool spring night.

I didn't chase my husband down. I didn't beg him to stop, although he was probably unfit to drive. As much as he needed space, I needed it too. On the counter, sitting on top of today's newspaper, was the small brown mystery package. No postage or return address. I picked it up, glancing at the *Pittsburgh Post-Gazette* headline under today's date, April 22: "Prominent Attorney Murdered and Inheritance Disputed."

It was a little shocking to see Mortimer's death had made the front page. Skimming the article, I wasn't surprised to see that the law partners were disputing my inheritance tooth and nail, just as Karen predicted, and dragging my name through the mud. I wouldn't fight it, though. I didn't have the battle left inside me. As Vera would have said, *FML*. Eff my life.

I returned my attention to the package and the bottle of vodka Cody had been nursing while I was at the police station, based on the state of him. Ripping the packaging open, I saw a note that I recognized as Felicity's handwriting:

I know I haven't shown it this past week, especially with Vera suddenly gone, but I appreciate how you were always there for her and how you're trying to be there for me right now. You were more than an aunt to her. You were like a sister, and I'll always cherish you as my sister too. I'm sorry for all the stuff coming between us right now. I'm not coping well, but I'm trying to stay as optimistic as I can. Maybe I should be trying that CBD to "chill" a bit, as Vera would say, huh? I hope this gift adds some sparkle in your life.

Inside was a small black velvet box. *No she didn't.* I flipped it open and gasped. The turquoise bracelet. A perfect match to the one Felicity had worn and the one given to Vera for her fifteenth birthday. I imagined the day the three of us girls could wear them together…soon…if I hadn't already irreparably ruined my relationship with my family. Unless Cody was right. Maybe the lies were just too much to overcome.

Grabbing the bottle of liquor, I turned off the kitchen light and headed upstairs. I didn't need a glass. I'd be emptying the rest of the bottle tonight, enough to wipe out the memory of today. It was ironic that in the depths of my own personal darkness I did the one thing I had judged my parents for—turning to a destructive high. Maybe the apple didn't fall far from the tree. In my bedroom a breeze wafted through the open window. A clatter two stories below provoked a dog to bark. A chill dove down my spine. I never fully felt alone here, as if eyes were always watching, skimming across my skin. Nothing was ever there, but their presence was always felt.

The rest of the forty-ounce and two episodes of *This Is Us* later, I could barely stand up when I heard the back door scrape open.

Cody. He'd come home after all. Maybe we could have drunk sex and wake up hung over together, forgetting all the stuff in between. A *crack* shortly followed as something fell and broke, and I headed down the dark stairwell, barely making out the edge of each step as I gripped the handrail on my descent.

"Cody?" I called out. My voice shook.

As I rounded the corner to the kitchen, an unfamiliar shadow passed across the room, reaching for me.

I screamed, my fingers fumbling for a weapon. Then suddenly everything went Clark Griswold Christmas lights bright.

Chapter 45
Marin

Murder, much like love, required the right person in the right place at the right moment. And also like love, it was a blurred line where passion ended and fury began. I had been lost in that fury for so long that it filled the hollow of my heart and poured into my veins. The problem was that I wasn't the only one fueled on fury.

As the overhead fluorescent light doused the kitchen, I saw a very different version of myself standing before me.

"Mom?"

It couldn't be. She was dead. OD'd the day we fought, when my last scathing words—*"we'd all be better off if you died and went to hell, where you deserve to go"*—sent her to her drugs, and the drugs sent her to the hospital where she died that night. The last thing I'd watched was *Gilmore Girls,* the mom-and-daughter duo we would never become. We had made plans to binge on junk food along with the season finale of *American Idol,* which I couldn't stomach watching without her. It was supposed to be *ours,* our Gilmore Girl moment together, until she simply *ceased.*

And now Mom was back from the dead.

"Hello, Marin."

The shock hadn't settled yet, but I found a handful of words.

"How are you alive?"

"I know this must be hard for you to understand, Marin, but I didn't die. Your father told me to leave and never come back. It was what was best for you and your sister. It took a long time before I was ready to face you again. I needed to be clean before you saw me. But it finally happened. I'm sober!"

Was she expecting my congratulations? She'd left me to raise the baby that ended up sold on the side of the road for a wallet full of hundreds. And now, a decade and a half later I was supposed to throw a party for the neglectful bitch.

"You dare come back into my life after what you did to me? I was traumatized! Bennett and I had a damn memorial for you at Dad's gravestone, to which no one came, by the way. That's how beloved you were—no one even cared that you were fake dead."

"Honey, I'm sorry for that. But at the time, I was as good as dead if I didn't get space."

"*Space*? Space is doing a few months in rehab. It's not disappearing and pretending to be dead for, oh, I dunno, a decade and a half. Do you know I blamed myself for killing you? I blamed myself that my sister was taken away, that our family was broken apart. All because of you. Get out of my house! Get out of my life!" My screams pulsed through me, buzzing from deep in my gut, up through my lungs.

And yet Mom just stood there, arms open as if a hug could make everything better like when I was three years old.

"Can we at least talk?" she asked, stepping toward me.

"Stay away from me!" I swung my arms out, vodka and rage pumping through me as my hand made contact with her face, then her chest.

The abrupt impact of bone on bone jolted my body backward and I felt the earth shift and slip under me. My arms circled like a cartoon character as I fell, then a sharp *thwack* crushed my skull. I blinked, but it wasn't a blink. It was nothingness.

**

I couldn't remember how I ended up on the dingy linoleum floor where flakes of dried food collected hairballs along the baseboard, or whose blood blossomed beside my head. Although it was bright—too bright—I could vaguely make out the details of the kitchen through the blur. The scene slowly focused, one piece at a time. The metal-rimmed counter with the dented corner. The fridge humming like an angry bee.

Touching the place on my skull where it hurt the most—though everything hurt—my palm sank into a matted mess of wet hair. My fingers traced a gash a pinkie-length long. Trying to push myself upright, my hands slipped across the floor. A crown of discomfort pinched my head. I looked up. A shadow looked back.

"Don't move!" a voice ordered me from above.

Cody? No, it was a woman caught in a fog.

"Do you have a phone?" The voice was frantic and distant now.

Pain swept across my temples. I fell limply back. My body thrummed with the pulse of blood seeping out. I closed my eyes, but they wouldn't reopen. I felt utterly alone. Then footsteps. No, I wasn't alone. I sensed more than saw a presence somewhere in the closed-eye murk surrounding me.

Darkness had a way of hiding things. Like the dirt crusted in the corner where the peeling linoleum met the pine wood cabinet. Or the blood seeping out of my head into a puddle on the floor. Every bit of our poverty showed in the details of the house. It wasn't until I heard the voice that I realized who knelt down beside me. I peeled my eyelids open. A streak of light crossed my resurrected mother's face. A groan escaped from my lips as I tried to turn toward her, my headache worsening with the movement.

It frightened me that I couldn't remember what exactly happened.

It frightened me more that I would die here, in the same wet spot by the broken sink that I had just yelled at Cody to fix, before saying what I needed to say to the woman who killed my soul fifteen years ago.

"Where's your cell phone? I need to call 9-1-1." She was begging now. "Do you know what happened?" she asked me.

I couldn't answer. None of my body parts seemed to be working. Then I pushed every bit of willpower into opening my mouth just barely enough to let a word escape. "No."

"Don't close your eyes. Stay awake until an ambulance arrives. Where's your phone?"

I felt weaker by the minute. I felt my life seeping out on the floor. But I wouldn't give her the absolution she came for. Not yet.

"Not until I get answers," I replied.

She gave a motherly cluck, as if she had ever played the role of mother. "What do you want to know?"

I had to push the words out. My eyelids grew heavier by the moment. I felt like I was nodding off, but not into a peaceful slumber. More like an eternal one. "I want to know why. Why you lied. Why you did what you did."

It was the question I knew she couldn't answer: *Why did you give up your family for drugs? Why did you choose being high over being my mom? Why did you let my sister go? Why weren't we enough?*

"Tell me where your phone is first. You're not looking good, honey. I need to call for help. Now, please!"

"No!" I yelled with a grunt. "First tell me the truth!"

"Will an answer take it all back? Will it make everything better?"

I tried to shake my head but couldn't. "No," I said, "but maybe I'll understand." I would never understand.

She held an envelope near my face, letting it hover between us. "Here. This explains everything," was all she said.

Willing my leaden arm to rise, I grudgingly accepted her offering, knowing it would never be enough. No words could replace the empty years without her. A tickle ran down my nose, dripped to the floor beside my face, dark…like blood? I wanted to wipe it away, get the blood off of me, but my arm was a dead weight now and lay limply at my side.

Mom left my side, returning a moment later to shove her hands along my pockets before she jumped up and grabbed the landline phone, a seventies relic from a previous tenant Cody had insisted we keep for its kitsch value. She scowled, discovering it was dead. I could have told her that.

"Your cell phone—where is it?" she screamed.

"Living room…table," I finally gave in.

When she returned, she was nothing but a hazy silhouette.

"I need your passcode."

"0509." I wondered if she would catch the significance, and it was the last thought I had.

It was everything and yet nothing. A lie that I had believed for fifteen years. It was the day my mother had left us. The anniversary of her fake death: May 9. The day the *Gilmore Girls* died.

"Don't leave me!" Mom's words echoed down the long dark chamber that my consciousness numbly drifted toward.

Rushing to my side, Mom scooped me into her arms. For the first time in my life I felt like I had a mother after all. Inside myself, I shut out her fearful stare and shut in something more beautiful. All the panic, the pain, the sadness lifted as I glided further and further away, toward memories of evenings when we shared a blanket on the couch while binging on chocolate chip cookie dough ice cream, snuggling through chick flicks and the occasional classic Hitchcock film. Or when we held each other and cried the day we buried the stray dog I named Antonne—after the first boy who broke my heart—on that gray misty afternoon. Or when we laughed until I peed myself after I tripped over that same dog who always slept at my feet. And the day Mom told me she was pregnant with my new baby sister, and her vow to sobriety. The nostalgia tasted good. Or were those figments of my imagination floating on the surface of memories that didn't actually exist?

No, they were real, just like she was really kneeling next to me, waiting for me to come back to her. Her hands roughly grabbed me—I could feel her frantic touch—and shook me hard, but I couldn't respond. I couldn't do anything but feel her shaking, calling me from the end of the tunnel. Her hair tickled my cheek as I felt her body heat warm my chin, her ear pressed against my chest. "Ohmygod ohmygod ohmygod," she repeated.

For an instant, time froze in a breathless moment like when you're sailing off the cliff, into the gorge. I was Thelma to Mom's Louise. Then she was gone.

I wanted to call her back, tell her that yes, now I was okay. Maybe for the first time in my life I was okay. I wanted to remind her of everything we had been through together, how much I loved her, but the words wouldn't come. My mouth wouldn't obey. I heard her voice echoing from the other distant end. I wasn't scared anymore, though. I felt safe and warm and loved, ready to be with my birth dad on the other side. With that last breath I made peace with the woman who birthed me, who chose drugs over me, who abandoned me, but who came back for me. If only she could have saved me.

Chapter 46
Josie

"Go reconcile with your daughter before it's too late, Josie." Those were Bennett's last words to me when I found him slowly deteriorating alone in the yellow brick house perched atop Grandview Avenue—and what a grand view it was—that we had once called home together. Although we had been estranged for fifteen years, he had never filed for divorce because he loved me. I never filed because I hated him.

To be fair, I hated everyone who stood in the way of my high. That all-consuming hit of euphoria that chased the demons away was my only friend back then. Little did I recognize the face of the devil. As if stealing my past wasn't enough, now that same devil came back to pilfer my future.

"Which daughter?" I had wondered aloud, me sitting on the same ratty sofa we bought off Craigslist, Bennett lying in his favorite recliner.

I hadn't known when I showed up that random spring afternoon that my husband had given away my youngest child. Just like I hadn't known that reconciling with Marin would cost me her life.

"I'm talking about Marin," Bennett replied. "I don't think she's ever gotten over losing you, Josie. I'd hate to die with a lie stuck between all of us."

So I took his advice and watched Marin from afar, waiting for the perfect time to reveal myself. The plan had never been to say my sorries and disappear. *Reconcile*, Bennett had said. And there was only one way to do that—by reuniting the *Gilmore Girls*. All three of us.

I never saw Bennett after that first and last time, but I had gotten what I came for. Everything I needed to know—about Marin, my other daughter, where they both ended up. While Marin had distanced herself from Bennett over the years, they'd kept in touch just enough to share the basics. I could work with the basics.

When I had returned to see him again, he had disappeared...taking with him my second-born child. Which complicated my plans to tell *Vera,* they called her, who I was and where she really came from. I had figured it all out—exposing the baby thief Felicity Portman to the police, reuniting with my girls, and *living our best life*, as the PTA moms who sipped wine out of long-stemmed glasses would say.

I admit I was furious when I discovered Vera was missing. Initially I suspected the parents had something to do with her disappearance. What else could I assume but murder from a couple that steals a baby, which turns up missing fifteen years later? Felicity Portman was the reason I had lost both my girls, and she deserved to suffer as much as I had. I thought the message I'd left on her work voicemail about Marin was pretty clear, proving that I could reach her if I wanted to:

"Felicity Portman, I know what you did. You are the reason she's dead. You deserve what's coming to you."

After I found out Vera was alive—and hidden away with Bennett, no less—I felt mildly guilty for running Felicity off the road, but not enough to lose sleep over it. She did buy my child for a few hundred bucks, after all.

Mortimer Randolph's demise was the icing on the cake. I'm not a killer, in case you're wondering. I was *reconciling*, that's all. It had been child's play convincing the old fool that I was on the staff of his cleaning service; he didn't question my arrival at irregular times, separate from his regular cleaning lady, the better to spy on Marin and see how my baby girl was getting on. I almost blew it when she nearly saw my face in the hallway. I was afraid she'd recognize me, but I'd changed a lot in fifteen years, and thanks to a cheap wig and glasses, she didn't see through my gray-headed charwoman disguise. When I overheard how the bastard talked to her, I was livid—but at least she stood up him. Good for her! But no one treated my daughter like trash and got away with it. Not even me. So I spiked his coffee with an extra dose of all the meds he was already taking…and then some. It was merely serendipitous that he happened to die from a heart attack and left his inheritance to Marin. She deserved every penny of it. And it was my fault she never got to enjoy it.

In a way, I was that knife in the first act, the harmless prop that turns out to be the linchpin of the whole damn play. I was there when it all began, and I was there in the end when it all was split wide open and gutted. After watching Marin die, I followed the news for the next six months, reading details of how Marin's husband Cody—I would never understand what she saw in him— arrived back at their house to a kitchen full of paramedics and cops who had responded to my 9-1-1 call. I had been too shocked to speak, too panicked to stick around as the operator spoke to the empty air, eventually tracking the address and dispatching help. I couldn't explain why I ran instead of waiting around for the EMTs to announce what I already knew—her time of death. Maybe it was fear of the police connecting me to Mortimer's untimely—well past due, if you ask me—passing, or paranoia that they'd call it *murder* instead of an accident. I was a drug user, after all, with a rap sheet, forever stereotyped as all class of criminal. Most of all, I couldn't risk losing my chance to reconnect with Vera. Being the only witness to a suspicious accidental death was the last thing I needed.

Whatever pushed me out the back door, whatever prompted me to flee into the night, I would never forgive myself for what happened in that kitchen. The image of my daughter's body being hauled out of the house, rolling by on a stretcher and cloaked in a body bag, would forever burn in my mind as I waited to be discovered. And it'd keep burning, burning, burning.

For days, weeks, months I waited and waited. For a DNA sample to out me as Mortimer's killer, even though I'd been extremely careful and worn gloves. For a fingerprint to emerge and tie me to Marin's death. Month after month, nothing. Cases closed. Funerals were held. Mourners wept. All that mattered was that I was with her when she died, and that I had found my other child in the process. Now that Vera knew I existed, I imagined her wondering who I was, thinking me dead. Had Bennett told her I was alive? It didn't matter, because I would resurrect the truth. I had learned from watching that eventually Vera would come to me if I left the right breadcrumbs. She was clever, just like her older sister. And just like her mom.

Maybe I wasn't the first act knife after all. My intention had never been to harm anyone, only to reconcile. I'd given up my family, my two perfect girls and my husband, to get clean. All of it, the disappearing, the endless rehab, the months of self-improvement, the sobriety, it all was for them. A fifteen-year-long journey that cost me everything. But here I was, recovering, sober, and empty-handed. My eldest was dead, and my youngest thought I was dead. No, I wasn't the knife; I was the happy ending that the hero deserved before the final curtain fell.

Epilogue
Vera

The trees surrounding the Execution Estate were barren, brittle arms reaching for the gray sky. Vera Portman had sat in this same wingback chair in this same parlor countless times before, reading a book or playing a game with her siblings, Eliot and Sydney. But on this particularly cold November day, she sat here for an entirely different reason.

To say goodbye.

In one hand was the picture of her, Marin, Josie, and Bennett that she'd kept from Marin's belongings before they were donated to Goodwill. In the other was a bloodstained envelope she had found on her bed this afternoon, shortly after the memorial for Bennett started, a simple affair hosted by her parents in their home. They had decided against a funeral home at Vera's request; more than once she had described in vivid detail the picturesque mansion to Bennett, who was equally intrigued by its infamy and its grandiosity, and pleased that his daughter, far from being spoiled by such opulence, remained delightfully down-to-earth. It seemed only fitting to Vera that her father, a beautifully humble man who had endured with grace a lifetime of privations, should go out in stylish surroundings.

For all that, the family decided to keep the ceremony itself—

like the man—simple. Vera had sketched a portrait of Bennett in Contè crayon, depicting him as a young, vibrant man before the ravages of illness and sorrow and guilt took their toll. The picture, in a barnwood frame, sat upon an easel in the sitting room where the ceremony was held. It had been Bennett's wish to be cremated; at Vera's insistence, his urn sat upon the antique writing desk, the beloved heirloom of her great-great grandmother Alvera Fields, she and her father had restored.

Vera recognized most of the callers—relatives, classmates, friends of the family, her parents' colleagues—who dropped off condolences and flowers. Some were opportunistic looky-loos, taking advantage of the circumstances to infiltrate the fabled Execution Estate; tipped off by their blatant snooping into private areas, the security guards Oliver hired discreetly escorted them off the premises. Austin and Blythe, on the other hand, were given the grand tour of the mansion by Vera herself, with especial attention to the library, which they pronounced way-cool.

A precious few acquaintances came to pay their respects to Bennett. He had long ago lost touch with most people, especially after Josie—aka *bio mom*—disappeared and he sank into a slow ruin. But this letter meant that not everything had been lost. Her biological mother was still out there. Possibly even here in this very room. And just like her great-great-grandmother Alvera, the mystery of who she was tugged at Vera. Yanked at her. Heaved and hauled her into its grip.

The envelope dotted with her sister's blood was addressed to Marin but left behind for Vera's eyes only:

My sweet, sweet Marin. You're angry at me, I know. You'll be even angrier as you find out I'm alive and well. As well as one can be after I gave up my children because I had to, not because I wanted to. I never meant to abandon you, and I certainly never expected Bennett to tell you I had died. But what other choice did he have, if it prevented you and your sister from following down my dark path after me? The fear of death can be mighty persuasive.

If there's any way I could explain it, to make you understand why I had to murder my old self in order to become my new self, I would use every word to do so. But there aren't enough words, are there? So I hope that my simple I'm sorry is enough. I hope that my love is enough. I hope that the years I spent missing you, giving up my family in order to give up my addiction, is enough.

This letter is more than an apology for all the wrong I've committed against you. It's my amends, my attempt at reconciliation—Bennett's favorite word—with you and your sister. I hope it's not too late. I hope that me getting help to be a better person didn't ruin the only good things left in my life—my girls. Rehab kicked my butt, but it was the butt-kicking I needed to rescue me from the constant treading water as addiction sucked me under. I finally rose to the top, still treading water, but I'm getting used to it now.

If there's a chance we can reconnect, a chance you'll forgive me, a chance I can be your mom again, I hope you'll take it. I may not be worth a second chance, but you are. Anyone who doesn't see that isn't worth your time. You and your sister will forever own my heart, no matter what you decide.

Love, Mom

Slipping the letter back into the envelope, Vera tucked it under her leg along with the picture, desperately missing the woman she never knew but hoped to one day meet. She had been here, after all, but somehow got washed away amid the ebb and flow of bodies. At the front of the sitting room Uncle Cody stood, eyes skimming across the room of faces. He cleared his throat into his fist, then spoke.

"I want to thank everyone for coming to celebrate the life of Bennett Hunter, my wife's father. As you know, Marin passed away about six months ago, and after a frustrating legal situation, an estate was left in her name from her former boss. To commemorate Marin's passion, and the life of her father, I've decided to use the inheritance to fund a theatre scholarship for aspiring creative artists who are interested in theater and acting—The Marin Bennett Drama Scholarship. I think this is the legacy Marin would have wanted to leave behind. Thank you again for being here for our family after such a difficult year."

Sitting beside Vera was Tasha Briggs, the young girl Oliver had innocently befriended during his daughter's disappearance. Tasha glanced over at Vera and smiled sympathetically. Like Vera, she knew the loss of a father. And like Vera, she had stumbled onto a path toward healing. A friendship with Vera, a father figure in Oliver, and the camaraderie shared exclusively among those who have felt death's harsh touch. On the other side of Vera sat Nana, dab-dabbing at her eyes like she'd known Bennett her whole life. Pappy Joe wrapped his arm around her, running his hand up and down her arm, as if rubbing the sadness away.

Nana leaned over to whisper in Vera's ear. "I'm proud of you, you know. For your willingness to help Sydney by donating a kidney. It's a brave thing to do."

But Vera didn't consider it brave; to her, it was what sisters did for each other.

"You know I'd do anything for my family."

"Yes, that I do know. Even if it meant disappearing for six months to help a dying man you barely met," Nana said with a chuckle. "Oh, did I tell you how Miss Frances, the sweet woman who tried to foster me back when I was child, contacted me recently?"

The cloak-and-dagger way Nana said it piqued Vera's curiosity. "No, how did she find you, Nana?"

After Vera's return home, her bond with her grandmother gelled as Nana shared a delicious taste of her life with Vera, drawing her into a time with Elvis Presley on the jukebox, Marilyn Monroe on the silver screen, and Dwight Eisenhower in the White House. More than that, Nana was once an orphan, just like her. And Nana had found her forever family, just like her.

"Miss Frances connected with me on Facebook. She's probably in her nineties now, but I've got to hand it to her for her sleuthing skills and tech-savviness."

"What'd she say?"

Nana glanced at the front of the room, where the last visitors mingled about, then returned her gaze to Vera. "Like I told you, she had tried to find a way to adopt me back when I was a child, but in the 1950s it wasn't easy for a single woman to adopt without the support of a man. When she finally did get through the red tape, I had already been moved around a lot. She eventually lost track of me, but never forgot me. She ended up adopting five other kids over the years—one of which is the one who introduced her to Facebook." Another *dab-dab* at the tears. "She just wanted to tell me that she never gave up searching for me."

Never give up. The cliché was a lifestyle for Vera, words she breathed in and lived out. It helped uncover her past, introduced her to Bennett, revealed her *sister* Marin, and exposed another mother somewhere out there.

"Which brings me to something else I thought you should see." Nana handed Vera a newspaper clipping, one Vera hadn't seen before. "I found this in an old hat box my mother had given me before she died. I had never really looked through everything inside it until just recently."

At the top of the article was a grainy picture of a woman who resembled the countless images of Alvera Fields that had imprinted on Vera's memory. The headline sat large and bold in the center:

**

The Pittsburg Press

Pittsburg, PA
Tuesday, November 22, 1910

MISSING WOMAN MAY BE DISGUISED

RIVERFRONT MERCHANT CERTAIN MILLIONAIRE'S WIFE TRIED TO BUY MAN'S CLOTHES AND WAS AFRAID OF IDENTIFICATION.

Many false clues telephoned by persons who located Alvera Fields at various places are run down vainly by her distracted husband, Robert Fields.

Except for one clue, which may or may not be worth anything. Since the first day of the public search for wife to millionaire Robert Fields, and mother to newborn daughter Olivia Fields, who disappeared so completely the evening of April 16, no further productive results have been made. Until now.

Through the medium of police, detectives and lawyers who have been conducting a search under cover for over six months, a possible lead has surfaced. This single clue centers about the identity of a mysterious woman of apparent refinement who tried to buy an outfit of male apparel, avowedly for the purposes of disguise in a masquerade, and who wanted to pledge expensive jewelry in a waterfront pawnbroker's warehouse yesterday afternoon. The jewelry was identified by Robert Fields as belonging to his wife Alvera. Hours later police were notified of the suspicious activity. The woman was later spotted at a suffragette meeting, but fled before authorities could identify her.

Here was a young mother, aristocratic, refined and ideally happy in her home, devoted to her husband and child, balanced in her thoughts and life, according to her husband, who, taking with her only such funds as one might carry for casual purchases, stepped out of the house door on a cool spring evening, seemingly intent on plans to attend an event. From that moment she was gone from the ken of her whole circle of acquaintances as completely as if she had never existed. Yet friends of the missing woman have accused husband Robert of forcing his wife to take residence in a sanitarium or flee due to her zeal for the women's suffrage cause.

Did Mrs. Alvera Fields abandon her family to fight for the women's suffrage cause under a new identity? Or is something more sinister afoot in the Fields family? The public may never know.

**

But Vera knew. *Never give up*. While the public details of what happened to Alvera Fields were shrouded in the unknown, Vera saw the passion in her ancestor's journal that could drive a woman to give up everything for something bigger than her. Justice. Freedom. Empowerment. It was the root of her great-great-grandmother's sacrifice, to pursue rights for women across the globe, even at the cost of her child. Had that been what her own biological mother did for her? Sacrifice her family by running away in order to free them from her demons?

This thought hung around Vera as she felt the prickle of eyes watching. She had felt it often lately, the steady gaze of someone lurking in the background. Turning around in her seat, she caught a glimpse of a woman, tucked halfway behind a massive suit of armor, hazel eyes glistening. The same color as Marin's. As her own.

In that moment Vera realized her discoveries into her family's past had only just begun.

Acknowledgments

This is the part of writing I like the least. I won't dare say I hate it, because I've taught my kids that *hate* is a strong word and to use it sparingly, so that would make me a hypocrite. But how does an author remember to give credit to everyone who has inspired or supported the book? I'm a mom of four, with limited sleep hours, so my memory cannot be trusted to keep track of what we're eating for dinner, let alone who deserves acknowledgment.

But I'm going to try.

My husband Craig always gets first billing. He's the one that turned my daughter's portrait into my most prized cover because her beautiful face is on it. He's the one who takes kid duty and sends me off alone to write so I can meet my deadlines. Without his support, I'd still be on the first draft of this book.

My children—Talia, Kainen, Kiara, and Ariana—come second as my biggest littlest fans. They love having a murder-writing mom when most kids would be ashamed…or scared.

To Kevin Cook, my miracle-working editor at Proofed to Perfection Editing Services. The man is not only brilliant but long-suffering as he worked tirelessly wading through and refining my writing weaknesses and teaching me so much along the way. Any lingering issues or errors are on me for tinkering with it after he finished.

To my mom who shared tons of historical information with me about my suffragette ancestor. Thank you for being so tech-savvy and scanning it all for me. Keep your eyes peeled in the book for your cameo, Mom!

Thank you, Mary Kaja, for helping with Vera's journal entries. You have more talent in your pinkie toe than I have in my whole body. Your name will be among the literary greats someday.

To everyone at Bloodhound Books who believed in this book enough to invest in it. This was a unique publication deal, so thank you for working with me on it!

To the book clubs who have picked my books. For the Zoom meets and tech glitches you've endured just to chat with me. I love you all so much—that includes your whole group, Jilia, and the fabulous LT Book Club, among several others whose book club names I can't remember at the moment (I think I told you I'm a sleep-deprived mom, right?).

My Mental Mommy Readers Group, you all are incredible. Elaine, Melissa, Kris, Ruth, Cheang, Linda, Emily, Jess—among others—have been my biggest cheerleaders. Your book reviews and social media posts and word-of-mouth mean the world to me. You are why I keep challenging myself to put out better, twistier stories.

My biggest hug of gratitude goes to all of you who have bought the book, every one-click purchase is more precious to me than sleep. Your support feeds my family (and horses and dogs and cats and ducks...and any other animals I end up rescuing by the time you read this). I love you all.

Thank you for supporting this most incredible writing adventure.

About the Author

PAMELA CRANE is a *USA Today* bestselling author and professional juggler of four kids, a writing addiction, and a horse rescuer. She lives on the edge and writes on the edge...where her sanity resides. Her thrillers unravel flawed women with a villainous side, which makes them interesting...and perfect for doing crazy things worth writing about. When she's not cleaning horse stalls or cleaning up after her kids, she's plotting her next murder.

Join her newsletter to get a FREE book and updates about her new releases and deals at www.pamelacrane.com.

Enjoy what you read?

Then check out LITTLE DOES SHE KNOW, an "addictive psychological thriller!"

A missing boy. A dead body. Four decades apart, but connected by a mysterious link.

It's 1986, the height of big hair, power suits, and "Material Girl." Ginger Mallowan is the epitome of all of these things, until her son disappears during a beach walk one night. That's the moment girls don't want to have fun anymore, and the moment she starts hunting for answers.

It's 2022, and Ginger's hair is a bit flatter, she's retired her power suits, but she still dances to "Material Girl." She hasn't found—or forgotten—her missing son, but she has managed to survive the grief…thanks to her neighbor Tara Christie.

Tara is the friend who keeps Ginger's secrets. But that vow is tested one night when Tara is jarred awake by a scream coming from next-door, where she finds Ginger standing over a dead body. As the investigation shakes the town to its core, and Tara's husband is charged with the murder, Tara must choose between proving her husband's innocence or protecting Ginger's past.

Little does she know she's about to stumble down a twisty path that could destroy them all.